THE PATTERN OF HER HEART

Books by Tracie Peterson

www.traciepeterson.com

The Long-Awaited Child • Silent Star
A Slender Thread • Tidings of Peace
What She Left for Me

BELLS OF LOWELL*
Daughter of the Loom • A Fragile Design
These Tangled Threads

LIGHTS OF LOWELL*
A Tapestry of Hope • A Love Woven True
The Pattern of Her Heart

DESERT ROSES
Shadows of the Canyon • Across the Years
Beneath a Harvest Sky

HEIRS OF MONTANA
Land of My Heart • The Coming Storm
To Dream Anew • The Hope Within

WESTWARD CHRONICLES
A Shelter of Hope • Hidden in a Whisper
A Veiled Reflection

RIBBONS OF STEEL†
Distant Dreams • A Promise for Tomorrow

RIBBONS WEST†
Westward the Dream • Ties That Bind

SHANNON SAGA‡
City of Angels • Angels Flight • Angel of Mercy

YUKON QUEST
Treasures of the North • Ashes and Ice
Rivers of Gold

Books by Judith Miller

www.judithmccoymiller.com

FREEDOM'S PATH
First Dawn

*with Judith Miller   †with Judith Pella   ‡with James Scott Bell

TRACIE PETERSON
AND
JUDITH MILLER

THE PATTERN
OF HER HEART

BETHANYHOUSE
PUBLISHERS
MINNEAPOLIS, MINNESOTA

The Pattern of Her Heart
Copyright © 2005
Tracie Peterson and Judith Miller

Cover design by Dan Thornberg, DesignSource

Scripture quotations are from the King James Version of the Bible.

Published by Bethany House Publishers
11400 Hampshire Avenue South
Bloomington, Minnesota 55438

Bethany House Publishers is a division of
Baker Publishing Group, Grand Rapids, Michigan.

Printed in the United States of America

ISBN 0-7642-2896-X (Paperback)
ISBN 0-7642-0118-2 (Large Print)

Library of Congress Cataloging-in-Publication Data

Peterson, Tracie.
    The pattern of her heart / Tracie Peterson and Judith Miller.
        p. cm. —(Lights of Lowell ; bk. 3)
        Summary: "When tragedy strikes, Jasmine Houston must uproot her family
from the Northern mill town of Lowell and take over her family's Southern
plantation. Tensions are high, and the lives of the slaves they've promised to protect
hang in the balance"—Provided by publisher.
        ISBN 0-7642-2896-X (pbk.) — ISBN 0-7642-0118-2 (lg. print :pbk.) 1.
Women plantation owners—Fiction. 2. Southern States—Fiction. 3. Plantation
life—Fiction. 4. Slavery—Fiction. I. McCoy-Miller, Judith. II. Title III. Series:
Peterson, Tracie. Lights of Lowell ; bk. 3.

    PS3566.E7717P38 2005
    813'.54—dc22
                                                                    2005018442

Dedicated to Lana Nicol
A friend who brings joy to my heart.

Special thanks to
Martha Mayo
University of Massachusetts Lowell
Center for Lowell History

TRACIE PETERSON is a popular speaker and bestselling author who has written over fifty books, both historical and contemporary fiction. Tracie and her family make their home in Montana.

Visit Tracie's Web site at: *www.traciepeterson.com*.

JUDITH MILLER is an award-winning author whose avid research and love for history are reflected in her novels, many of which have appeared on the CBA bestseller lists. Judy and her husband make their home in Topeka, Kansas.

Visit Judy's Web site at: *www.judithmccoymiller.com*.

CHAPTER · 1

THE PRIMROSE-YELLOW skirt of Jasmine Houston's gown fluttered in the early afternoon breeze, the satin-banded hem settling like a field of daisies across the thick green grass as she stooped in front of her five-year-old daughter. Gently cupping the child's small dimpled chin in her palm, she issued a silent prayer of thanksgiving for Alice Ann's return to health before making eye contact with the child. "We must go upstairs and prepare for your birthday celebration before our guests arrive."

The little girl hopped from foot to foot while pointing at one of the distant barns, where the Houstons stabled their ever-increasing herd of Arabian horses. Her cornflower-blue eyes glimmered with anticipation as she turned back to her mother. "Am I going to get my pony today?" she quizzed.

Jasmine nibbled at her lower lip, for she didn't want to shed tears. This was, after all, a day for rejoicing, not a time of despair. The entire family had been waiting for over three months to celebrate Alice Ann's birthday, waiting and praying the child would live through the debilitating illness that had ravaged her frail body. *Scarlatina maligna,* Dr. Hartzfeld

7

had told them—a fancy name for a highly dangerous form of scarlet fever. A disease that could leave Alice Ann with lifelong medical problems . . . if she lived. The doctor had whispered his final assessment, fearing the pronouncement of a death sentence upon the child would send Jasmine into a depression.

Instead, his words had propelled her into bustling activity. With a mother's fear and determination, she enlisted the aid of attendants to assist with Alice Ann's care. Hopeful the disease would not spread to other members of their family or the community, Jasmine had immediately quarantined the household and ordered small doses of belladonna for all who came in contact with the child. She had diligently researched every piece of medical advice that came her way, and most importantly, she had requested that every person in the community pray for Alice Ann.

Now, looking into her daughter's bright blue eyes, she knew all those months of diligent care had been worth it. Dr. Hartzfeld's predictions had been wrong. Alice Ann's health had been restored, and she was now the same precocious little girl she'd always been. Amazingly, there was no evidence she'd ever suffered the debilitating illness. However, healthy or not, Jasmine believed the child still too young for her own pony.

So how could she best answer the child's question? "We never promised you a pony as a birthday present. What about the toys we looked at in Whidden's Mercantile?" Jasmine inquired as she took hold of Alice's hand and led her into the house.

"The doll was pretty, but I want my very own pony. Spencer has *his* own horse," she said, her pink lips forming a tiny pout.

"But you must remember that horses require a great deal of work. They aren't like a toy that you can play with for a short time and then put aside. They must be cared for every day."

"Spencer could take me with him when he goes to take care of Lockspur."

Jasmine smiled at the child's pronunciation. "*Lark*spur," she gently corrected. "And though it's true you could go with your brother to the barns, he might not enjoy having you in tow all the time. He and Moses like to spend time with the horses by themselves. They might feel as if you're intruding. Besides, Spencer didn't receive his pony until he was seven years old."

"But I can ride better than Spencer," she argued, her pout once again returning.

"What's this I hear? Our birthday girl isn't unhappy, is she?" Nolan called out as mother and daughter walked down the hallway, approaching his library door.

Jasmine stopped and met her husband's warm gaze. "We're discussing birthday gifts."

Nolan balanced his chin between his thumb and index finger and looked down at his daughter. "This sounds like a particularly interesting topic. Did you make a special request for your birthday?"

Alice tilted her head and looked up to meet her father's sparkling eyes. "You *know* I want a pony, but Mama said Spencer was seven when he got his pony. I'm a much better rider than Spencer was when he turned five, don't you think? And I'm almost five and a half," she hastened to add.

Jasmine wondered if the girl's remark was meant to evoke sympathy from him. After all, it was Nolan who had promised Alice Ann that she would have a superb birthday party once her health permitted the celebration. He had spent hours going over the details with her, planning a picnic on the back lawn, where everyone would come to celebrate the fact that she was now a big girl—a whole five years old. At the time, Alice had been too sick to care about any of it, but as her health began to return, she'd joined in with her father, planning the grandest of all birthday parties. Jasmine credited Nolan with giving Alice Ann a reason to fight the illness.

Nolan smiled adoringly at the child. "It's true that you're well on the way to six years of age, and you're certainly much more grown up than Spencer was at your age. I believe he was still playing with his toy soldiers and riding a pretend stick horse when he was five."

Jasmine gave her husband a warning look.

"The fact remains, however, that you're still very young. It seems that being around Spencer and Moses has caused you to believe you're able to do everything they can do. However, you must remember they are nearly ten years old, and that makes them a good deal older than you. They are also young men, and as such they may play in a much rougher fashion."

"But I'm a good rider, aren't I, Poppa?"

"Indeed you are. But your mother is correct; five is *very* young for a horse of your own. Come sit down with me for just a minute."

Alice Ann wriggled into place on the divan and then looked expectantly at her father.

"I want to tell you a story about a little prince who lived in a faraway land. His father, the king, loved his little boy very much and wanted his child to be happy. So every time the prince mentioned there was something he desired, the king gave him the item. The little prince quickly learned that all he needed to do was state his desire and the king would hasten to purchase it. So the little prince continued this ritual, making more and more lavish requests of his father. Each day the gifts would arrive and be given to the little prince."

Alice Ann's eyes danced with delight, her soft brown

curls bobbing up and down as she nodded her acceptance of the little prince's good fortune. "And did he want a pony?"

"Oh, that was one of his very first requests," Nolan replied. "But the prince received so many gifts that he didn't appreciate or take care of any of them. He soon grew bored and nothing made him happy."

Alice Ann gave her father a questioning look. "But his pony made him happy, didn't it." Her words were stated with absolute authority.

He shook his head. "Only for a very brief time. As I said, the prince quickly tired of each gift he received. But then one day the prince was at the market with a servant, and he saw a man with the most wonderful puppy he had ever seen. It was a happy little pup with a wagging tail and lots of soft fur. He told the servant to get him the dog, but the owner refused. The puppy was not for sale." Nolan glanced at Jasmine.

"And *then* what happened?" Alice Ann asked.

Nolan settled back against the arm of the divan and rubbed his chin. "Well, the king sent word to the man and told him to bring his puppy and come to the castle. The king offered to purchase the puppy with several gold pieces, but the man still wouldn't give him the puppy. And no matter how many gold pieces the king offered, the man continued to refuse. Finally, the king asked what he needed to do in order to buy the puppy for his son."

Alice Ann straightened and gave her father her undivided attention. "What did the man say?"

"He said the prince would need to prove himself."

With her chin resting in one hand and her eyes shining with wonder, she asked, "How was the prince supposed to do that?"

"He would be required to care for the animal. So, in order to test the prince, the puppy remained at the castle.

Each day the man checked to make sure the prince had fed and played with the dog. Within only a few days, the prince thought the man should be willing to give him the puppy, but the man still said no. Each week the prince asked for the puppy, and each week the man said no. So the prince continued caring for the puppy, and the man kept coming to the castle to ensure that the puppy was cared for. At the end of the year, the prince asked if he could have the puppy."

"And what did the man say?" Alice Ann asked in a hushed tone.

"The man said to the prince, 'The puppy is already yours. Because you have cared for him and loved him, you've made him your own. Through your actions, you've shown the puppy he can trust you and you are his master.'"

Jasmine gave Nolan a warm smile and then patted her daughter's plump hand. "Come along, Alice Ann, we must go upstairs and get ready now."

The child grasped her mother's hand tightly. "Thank you for the story, Poppa. I've already picked out a name for my pony."

"Did you *listen* to the story?" he called after his daughter as she bounded down the hallway.

"Yes. And it was very good," she responded emphatically.

Jasmine glanced back at Nolan and shrugged as their daughter ran up the steps. "I'm not sure she completely understood. Unfortunately, I fear she's going to be terribly disappointed when she opens her package."

"We'll see," he replied absently.

Jasmine climbed the stairs and met Martha in the upper hallway. "I'll see to Miss Alice Ann if you have other matters that need your attention," the maid offered as she stacked sheets in the linen chest. "Being around Miss Alice Ann reminds me of being with your grandmother. This child was certainly named after the proper person—she's got the same bubbly enthusiasm."

Jasmine smiled at the comparison as Alice Ann scampered into her bedroom. Jasmine knew her grandmother's former maid missed the old woman very much. The two had been more than employee and employer; they had been the best of friends. "She reminds me of Grandmother in many ways also. I truly wish Grandmother had lived long enough to actually hold Alice Ann in her arms."

"But she died knowing that if you gave birth to a little girl, her name would be Alice. I know the thought that she would have a namesake made her very happy. And Alice Ann flits about this house with the same authority as her great-grandmother—just like she's in charge of the whole wide world."

"You're right on that account, Martha," Jasmine replied with a laugh. "If you're positive you don't mind helping Alice Ann dress, it would be truly helpful. I can fix her hair once she's dressed. I'd like to check on Spencer and then see to baby Clara. You can send Alice Ann to the baby's room when you've finished."

Martha nodded and whispered, "Alice Ann doesn't suspect she's getting a new doll, does she?"

"No, although I fear she may be disappointed. She's talked of nothing but a pony lately, and I believe she's positive her father won't fail her."

"Don't you worry. She's just like her great-grandmother Wainwright. She'll be happy as can be with whatever she receives."

"I hope you're correct." Jasmine was not nearly so confident of her daughter's reaction to the gift.

"You can always tell her that if she isn't pleased with the doll, you know several little girls who would be delighted to have it. She'll soon change her mind," the older woman said

13

with a wink. " 'Course, we can't go giving it away—I spent too many hours on that dress and cape for her dolly," she added with a chuckle.

When Jasmine brought the doll home from Whidden's several weeks ago, she had drawn Martha into her confidence and shown her the gift. It had taken only a moment for Martha to decide the doll needed additional clothes and that she would immediately begin the task. It would be her birthday gift to Alice Ann, she'd insisted. During the past weeks, Martha had used her free time to stitch a cream wool doll's dress and matching hooded cloak. With loving care, the older woman had embroidered tiny pink and blue flowers and green leaves around the hem of the dress and then attached a small pink tassel to the hooded cape.

"The dress and cape are beautiful, Martha. If Alice Ann isn't overly disappointed with the doll, I know she'll be delighted with the clothes you made."

"Mama, are you coming?" Alice Ann called from her bedroom.

The two women exchanged a knowing look and rushed down the hallway in opposite directions. If they didn't soon get the children dressed, their guests would arrive with no one at the door to properly greet them.

———

"Elinor!" Jasmine greeted. "I am so pleased you've come."

"I wouldn't have missed it," Elinor said, extending a package.

"You didn't need to bring a present. Having you join us is gift enough," Jasmine admonished as she took the ribbon-bedecked offering.

"I hope Alice Ann will like it. I saw Martha in Whidden's two weeks ago, and she mentioned the doll you had purchased. Mrs. Whidden gave me the doll's measurements. I fashioned a matching bonnet for Alice and her doll, but you must set it aside until after she has opened *your* present, or she'll wonder why I've chosen to make her such a gift."

"What a wonderful idea, Elinor. She will absolutely love it."

"I trust her health has continued to improve."

"Indeed! You would think she'd never suffered a sick day in her life. When I watch her running about, I'm truly amazed by her recovery. Now, do come out to the rose garden with me. I believe most of the guests have arrived, and we've gathered on the lawn to visit and allow the children to play some games before we have our refreshments. How have you been?"

"I've been just fine. It's so good to see you."

"Since you began attending church on Kirk Street, I don't see you often enough. It's been at least several weeks since we've seen one another, and Martha didn't mention seeing you at Whidden's. I was beginning to worry *you'd* taken ill," Jasmine said as she looped arms with Elinor and walked her to the backyard.

"It's difficult to get away from the boardinghouse. As you know, mill work is hard and the girls put in long hours. And of course they expect to find hot meals and a clean house upon their return. When I do have free time, it seems it's filled by attending one meeting or another and helping with various church functions. There's precious little time left to go calling, but be assured that I've missed our visits also."

"Speaking of helping with church functions, I met your new pastor and his daughter two weeks ago. In fact, Spencer insisted we invite them to the party today. He and Moses have become fast friends with young Reggie."

Elinor grinned. "I don't doubt that statement for a minute.

I believe Reggie is quite the tomboy, but she seems a very sweet girl."

"She can straddle and ride a horse better than both of the boys, though I doubt her father realizes she does so," Jasmine confided.

"I imagine someone will be quick to advise him. The ladies of the church are keeping both Pastor Chamberlain *and* Reggie in their sights."

"No doubt! After all, the women do outnumber the men in Lowell. I do believe every single woman in town views Justin Chamberlain as an excellent prospect."

"Not *every* single woman," Elinor said. "The last thing *I* want is another husband."

Jasmine tilted her head and arched her perfectly shaped eyebrows. "I stand corrected—*almost* every woman." Elinor had been widowed twice and was not yet thirty and three years of age. Jasmine eyed her friend cautiously. "Still, it always seems to be those who protest something that end up wading deep in its cause."

"I've seen the time when I was forced to wade deep in horse droppings," Elinor protested, "but it didn't mean I desired to be there."

The two women laughed and waved in return as Alice Ann and several young friends sprinted past them, waving wildly.

"It certainly does appear she has returned to full health. I understand there was a case of scarlatina maligna in Billerica, and the child now has dropsy. A terribly sad consequence," Elinor stated.

"I, too, heard that distressing news. Dr. Hartzfeld warned us early on to be very careful during Alice Ann's period of convalescence. It seems to be a surprisingly dangerous time."

"How so?"

"If the patient chills or takes a cold, the entire system can be affected, leaving the person with a chronic illness, such as dropsy or even permanent deafness," Jasmine explained.

An involuntary shudder seized her after she uttered the words, and Elinor patted her arm. "I know you've been through a horrible ordeal, but the child is living evidence of answered prayers. I believe a good number of Lowell's residents were on their knees for Alice Ann. And it looks as though you've invited most of them today," Elinor said with a smile as she looked about at the crowd gathered for the party.

Jasmine laughed and shook her head back and forth. "Not quite. However, Alice Ann would have been delighted had we extended an invitation to the *entire* community. Do come and greet Nolan before Taylor and Bella whisk you off to themselves. Bella frequently tells me they don't see you often enough."

"If my brother and his wife had their way, I'd quit my position as a keeper at the boardinghouse and move in with them. I know it would help them if I would do so. With that houseful of children, Bella needs all the assistance she can receive. However, I don't think such a move would be to my liking. I much prefer my life at the boardinghouse. Even with my long hours, I have more freedom than would ever be possible as a live-in nanny."

"I believe you're correct—but I do understand that both Bella and Taylor would love to have you with them," she said as they approached Nolan, who was standing among a group of men, holding their younger daughter on his hip.

"I'll take Clara," Jasmine said as she lightly touched her husband's arm. She took the child in her arms, but Clara wanted no part of it. She struggled until Jasmine relented and put her on the ground, then immediately grabbed her father's leg.

"Sorsey," she demanded.

Jasmine laughed. "Seems everyone wants a horse." She met Nolan's twinkling eyes and got the feeling she was missing something as he laughed. "Look who's come to Alice Ann's party," she said as she turned to Elinor.

"Elinor! We'd given up on you when you didn't arrive with Bella and Taylor," he said.

"I've taken to going places on my own rather than relying upon Taylor and Bella as escorts," she quietly replied as she bent to brush a curl from Clara's forehead. "I can't believe how big she's grown."

"Nor I—she turned two last month, and it seems she was born only yesterday."

Nolan grunted softly as a small towheaded child plunged against him and captured the leg not yet possessed by Clara. "And this is Zachary—McKinley and Violet's little boy, who will be four years old next month. It seems we're celebrating birthdays all the time," he said, tousling Zachary's hair.

"You said we could see the horses," Zachary demanded.

"Indeed I did, nephew. Why don't you wait for me by the stable door."

Zachary eyed him for a moment. "You won't forget?"

"I promise to be there straightaway." The boy hurried to the stables as if racing some imaginary friend.

Nolan turned back to Elinor while Clara gave up her hold and toddled toward a crowd of well-wishers. "We are delighted you've seen fit to join us for Alice Ann's joyous gathering. Perhaps you could convince my wife that it's high time we were favored with some refreshments. How much longer must we wait, my dear? We're all nearly famished. Isn't that correct, gentlemen?" he asked, raising his voice loud enough to be heard by the nearby collection of men.

The group nodded in unison, reminding Jasmine of little boys playing follow-the-leader. "I'm certain none of you would tell a fib since you're in the company of Pastor Chamberlain," she said, casting the pastor a glance. He was tall and well muscled, built more like her stable hands than a man of the cloth. At least he didn't look like any man of the cloth she'd ever met.

The preacher scrutinized the group with a stern look upon his face. "Please speak up immediately if you told an untruth by saying you're hungry. Believe me when I say that the rest of us are hoping there are several of you, because we'd feel it was our duty to eat your portion—and we'd do so with great delight."

The men broke into laughter at the preacher's remark, but none admitted he was willing to give up his portion of food.

"Well, it appears we had best serve our picnic, and Alice Ann can open her gifts afterward. We'll have cake and lemonade after she's finished with her presents. How does that sound, gentlemen?"

"Tell me where the line will form and you'll not hear another word out of me," Matthew Cheever replied. "My biggest fear is that some tragic event will strike one of the mills and they will call me away."

"That is what you get for being so important to the mills and the Boston Associates," Jasmine teased.

"Just follow me," Nolan said, waving the men forward. "I'll see to it that they never find you, Matthew."

Jasmine raised her eyebrows as she watched the men march off. "They do act like young boys at times, don't they?"

"Indeed. I'd say you'd best give the order to laden the tables with food," Elinor said with a giggle.

"If you'll excuse me, I'll see to matters in the kitchen and put Clara down for her nap," Jasmine said. "Promise you'll stay long enough that we can have a good visit before you leave."

"I promise. Now don't let me keep you from your responsibilities."

Elinor filled her plate and surveyed the small groups gathered at the tables arranged on the lawn. There wasn't a place for her at the long table where Bella and Taylor were seated with their children. Several other families had joined the Mannings, and it appeared as if two or three other individuals were still vying to find a seat. Accordingly, Elinor turned and headed off in the other direction, finally detecting a pair of available chairs.

"May I join you?" she asked.

Three youthful faces peered up at her. "If you don't mind listening to talk of horses and fishing," Spencer Houston replied with a wide grin. Moses and Reggie Chamberlain nodded.

"I enjoy both of those topics and many others," Elinor said while juggling her plate and attempting to be seated.

Moses jumped to his feet and hurried around the table. "Let me help you, Miz Brighton," he offered while pulling the chair out for her.

"Thank you, Moses. You'd think I could manage on my own, wouldn't you?"

"These chairs don' move very easy on da grass," he said. " 'Sides, it's proper manners for men to help ladies be seated."

"Men? You and Spencer aren't men—you're just little boys," Reggie teased.

"Big enough to know more than little *girls*," Spencer retorted.

"Perhaps I should look for another seat. It appears I've already started an argument," Elinor said.

"Nah, we's jest playing," Moses said. "We tease each other all da time."

"Right—it's 'cause Moses and me, we like each other," Spencer agreed, leaving Reggie out of the thought altogether.

Elinor took a sip of water, pondering the boy's statement. Spencer indeed saw himself and Moses as equal in every way; the only problem was, the rest of the world definitely didn't see it that way. Moses was part Negro, and in the eyes of the world he was not at all like Spencer Houston. It seemed a pity that such beliefs kept people from the kind of friendship enjoyed by Spencer and Moses. Seeing that the children had stopped to watch her, she leaned forward as though ready to plot a scheme. "If that is what teasing is all about, then I hope you'll soon be teasing me. Elsewise, I'll think you don't like me," she said with a grin.

The trio giggled with a hearty enthusiasm that drew the attention of guests at nearby tables, and Elinor placed a finger to her lips. "Shh—they'll all want to join us since we're having such fun."

"Do you like to fish, Mrs. Brighton?" Reggie inquired.

"Indeed. You know, portions of my early years were spent in Portsmouth, England, and Portsmouth is on the ocean's edge. Later I lived in London, and we had a marvelous river, the Thames. I've always loved the water, although I confess I'm not always a successful fisherman. Perhaps one day before school begins you'll invite me along on one of your fishing expeditions."

"Reggie always catches the mos' fish, but we all pretty good," Moses said.

"And I'd much rather go fishing than attend school. Let's don't even talk about that," Reggie hastened to add.

Elinor took a bite of fresh fruit salad before turning her attention back to the group. "*None* of you like school?"

"I do," Moses quickly replied, bobbing his head up and down.

"I'd rather ride horses, but I suppose school's all right," Spencer agreed.

"Not me—I don't like it. Not now and not ever," Reggie stated with an emphatic nod.

"Is that because you're going to be attending a new school, Reggie?" Elinor asked.

She shrugged her shoulders. "That too, but school is the same everywhere. It's tiresome."

A long shadow fell across the table as the girl spoke. Elinor looked up to see Justin Chamberlain standing nearby and nodded in recognition. She doubted, however, that the pastor would remember her name. Even though Elinor was a member of his church and attended services every Sunday, she had chosen to remain somewhat anonymous. After all, Pastor Chamberlain was new to Lowell and there were many names and faces to learn—especially those of the church ladies determined to seek his undivided attention.

Elinor turned her attention back to Reggie. "But you *are* going to give school your very best effort this year, aren't you?"

The girl squirmed in her chair for a moment before answering. "I suppose," she replied with lackluster enthusiasm.

Justin settled his plate and cup on the table and seated himself between Reggie and Elinor. "You must remember that doing the things you enjoy will be directly related to how well you perform in school," her father said before taking a bite of fried chicken.

"Well, I personally believe it is much too pretty a day to be worried about the next school term," Elinor said. "What have you found enjoyable here in Lowell that you've not found elsewhere?"

"Two friends who like to do the same things I like," Reggie answered quickly.

Moses giggled, his eyes wide with delight. "She's da first girl I ever knew who'd put a worm on her fishing hook."

"I'm awed by your fearless nature, Reggie," Elinor said, placing one hand upon her ruffled bodice. "No doubt one day you are going to lead an adventuresome life, and your father will be very proud of you."

Elinor could feel Justin Chamberlain's gaze upon her, but she refused to look up. Her words were meant to encourage Reggie, and she feared the pastor might not take kindly to them. Possibly he would think she was encouraging the child's daring behavior.

Nolan watched closely as Alice Ann opened her gifts, pleased by the child's enthusiastic thanks as she untied the beribboned presents and tore open the paper. Jasmine grasped his hand as Alice lifted the lid from the box containing her doll. With a squeal of delight, the child pulled the doll from the paper-lined box.

Nolan leaned down and whispered into Jasmine's ear, "You see? I told you there was no need to worry."

She nodded, her eyes fixed upon Alice Ann as the child hugged the doll tightly to her chest.

"She's pretty, isn't she?" Alice Ann asked, looking directly at her parents.

"Not as pretty as you, but she is a lovely doll," her father replied.

The clothing Martha had sewn and the ribbon-festooned hat Elinor had made both met with hearty approval from the guest of honor, who immediately began the process of changing the doll's clothing.

"Why don't you wait awhile longer before you begin

changing the doll's clothes and come along with me?" Nolan suggested, extending his hand. "There's something I want to show you while your guests are waiting for their lemonade and cake."

She carefully tucked the doll back inside the box, taking pains to place it atop one of the tables—out of reach of the younger children.

"Where are we going?" she asked as she took her father's hand.

"It's a surprise," he said while leading her across the lawn and toward the distant barns.

They trod along silently until Nolan stopped and waved his arm high in the air. At his signal, Paddy rode out of the fenced corral. He was sitting tall and proud atop one of the Arabians and leading a black, white-stockinged pony alongside. Nolan watched Alice's reaction as Paddy approached.

She looked up and met his intense gaze. "Is the pony mine?" Her voice was no more than a whisper and difficult to hear above the thumping hooves.

Nolan knelt on one knee and wrapped an arm around his daughter's waist. "Do you remember the story I told you earlier today?"

"Yes, about the prince wanting a puppy."

"And do you remember the rest?"

She gave several quick nods. "The prince took care of the puppy and became his master."

"But not right away," Nolan added.

"After a year."

"Yes. And a year is a long time to take care of an animal. So I think we should give you a year and see how well you're able to take care of this pony. What do you think, Allie?" he asked, using the pet name he'd dubbed her with shortly after birth.

"I think that's fair. But only if someone will lift me up

when I need to reach things," she added thoughtfully.

Nolan tilted his head and laughed at her serious reply. "I would agree. Why don't you say hello to the pony, and then we must return."

She gave him an impish grin. "Can I ride her for a short time?"

"In your party dress? Your mother wouldn't soon forgive me for such an offense. I think we had best wait until tomorrow for a ride."

Paddy jumped down from the giant Arabian and walked the pony closer. "I do na think anyone would be carin' if ya gave the pony a wee pat on the nose," he said with a wink. "And I promise to have 'er ready for a ride on the morrow."

"Thank you," she said.

"So what is it ya'll be callin' the animal?" Paddy asked as the two men watched Alice Ann stroke the animal.

"Winnie," she stated quickly. "All my life I've wanted to name a horse Winnie."

"All your life? Well, that's an extremely long time," Nolan said with a laugh. "Winnie it is." Then noting her serious expression, he said, "And a mighty fine name, I might add."

"I best be takin' Winnie back to the barn now," Paddy said, "but she'll be there waitin' for ya tomorrow."

Alice Ann fixed a childishly admiring gaze upon Paddy. "You're coming back for cake and lemonade, aren't you?"

"I would na miss it. Be sure and tell Kiara to save me a piece of cake," he said. "After all, it's na every day a lass turns five years old."

"I'm almost six. And today isn't really my birthday," she corrected in a hushed tone as though entrusting him with a weighty secret.

"Aye—right ya are, lassie. I'd nearly forgotten."

"Thank you for going to pick up the pony," Nolan said

while taking hold of Alice Ann's hand.

"Fer sure an' it was my pleasure," he said while swinging upward and settling into the saddle on the larger horse. He tipped his hat and rode off, the pony dwarfed in the shadow of the huge white Arabian.

"I like Winnie, and I'm going to take very good care of her," Alice Ann announced as they began to walk back to the house. "Can I go and tell Spencer?"

"Exactly what do you plan to tell him?" Nolan inquired, his curiosity piqued.

She stopped and stared up at him. "That I have a year to take care of Winnie and make her mine."

"Close enough. Yes, you can go and tell Spencer. But walk—don't run," he hastily added. He knew Jasmine wouldn't be pleased if Alice Ann appeared back at the party with grass stains on her new dress.

Nolan strolled across the open field, enjoying the unexpected respite from the earlier heat of the day. A cool breeze ruffled the tall grass that covered the acreage beyond the house, and he glanced at the sky. In the west, a narrow bank of gray clouds was beginning to form. A thunderstorm might be heading in their direction. They needed rain, but he selfishly hoped any impending downpour would wait until after his daughter's birthday festivities. Attempting to accommodate all of their guests inside the house could prove a challenge to even the best hostess. Entertaining the children alone would be a brutal test of skill.

Jasmine was hurrying toward Nolan as he drew nearer. He smiled broadly and waved, surprised by her frantic gesture for him to hurry.

"Are you ready to serve the cake?" he asked, panting to catch his breath.

Her face was ashen. "No, not now. I've received a telegraph. I must talk to you—*alone,*" she said, her voice choked with emotion.

Leaning against his side, Jasmine allowed Nolan's strong arm to uphold her as they walked into the library. "Read this." She handed him the message.

"After you sit down," he said, leading her to a chair. She acquiesced and then waited in silence as he read the telegraph.

"Something terrible has happened," she whispered. "I can feel it in my bones."

Sitting down opposite her, Nolan enveloped Jasmine's hands in his own. "Jarrod is likely traveling to simply attend to some business matters," Nolan said.

"Jarrod Forbes is my father's lawyer, Nolan. I can't believe he would journey to Massachusetts unless he's come to convey bad news. I wonder if he's telegraphed McKinley. Surely McKinley would have said something when he and Violet arrived at the party. His telegraph will likely be waiting for him when he arrives home. Do you think we should tell him?"

"Yes, of course. But let's not assume the worst."

Jasmine grasped his hands tightly. "Nolan, he says he will be arriving in a few days with news from The Willows! If the news were good, Father would have written or telegraphed himself. Something has happened to Father."

"Your brother David and his wife are with your father. If he had taken ill, they would have immediately notified you."

She clutched the bodice of her dress, her eyes frantic. "Nolan, I can't explain it, but I can't help but fear that something is terribly wrong. Please . . . go and tell McKinley that we must talk with him."

CHAPTER · 2

JUSTIN CHAMBERLAIN seated himself and smoothed a sheet of paper in front of him. Sunday was quickly approaching, but he'd not yet prepared his sermon. If nothing else, he wanted to begin his ministry by challenging his parishioners to use their imaginations and reach out to others. Not that Lowell wasn't one of the most forward-thinking communities in the nation—but even Lowell could do better. He was testing the waters with his new congregation and evaluating their response. He dipped the nib of his pen into the glass bottle of ink and had barely touched pen to paper when Reggie raced through the front door and slammed it with a mighty thrust.

Startled, Justin jerked his arm and grimaced as a blob of ink dropped from the tip of his pen and spattered upon the pristine sheet of paper. "Regina! Why are you running, and why did you bang the front door as though Satan himself were on your heels?" he called out before turning in her direction.

"Maybe not Satan, but close enough!" she panted while hurrying to his side.

Her hair was a shambles, with the braid that had been so neat that morning now flying wildly in every direction. A smudge of dirt covered her right cheek, and she was wearing a pair of trousers! He'd learned long ago that he ought not be surprised by his daughter's behavior, but *trousers*. He'd not overlook this particular offense.

"What are you doing in that unspeakable attire?" Thoughts for his Sunday sermon were evaporating as quickly as the ink on the nib of his pen.

"They're coming!" she said, pointing frantically at the front door. "Hide—unless you want to consume your afternoon entertaining them."

"Explain yourself, Regina. Who are *they*?"

"Church ladies—*hundreds* of them," she hissed through her teeth while still pointing at the door.

"Hundreds? I don't think we have that many church members. Even if every member were a woman, we wouldn't number in the hundreds."

"This is no time to discuss the number of church members, Father. They're coming down the street with cakes and pies and wearing their fancy feathered hats. I'm going upstairs to hide, and you should do the same. There will be no ridding them from the house once they get inside," she cautioned, running out of the parlor and upstairs to the attic bedroom, which she had claimed as her own the day they moved into the house.

Justin knew Reggie was correct. He'd not be successful in holding a large number of intrepid women at arm's length. Since the day of their arrival in Lowell, the good ladies of St. Paul's had been anxious to ingrain themselves into every aspect of his home life. Thus far, he'd been partially successful in holding them at bay, yet he doubted whether he could mollify a large group. He walked to the large front window and stood to one side before carefully moving the drape with one finger—just far enough to see the front street. Five women were marching toward the house with an undisputable determination.

"There aren't hundreds—only five," he called up the stairway.

"Five will seem like hundreds once they get inside the house!" she shouted. "Don't open the door!"

A sharp rap brought an immediate halt to their conversation, and Justin heard the creak of rusty hinges as Reggie closed the door of her attic bedroom. Rocking back and forth on the balls of his feet, he contemplated his decision. He needed to work on his sermon, yet he couldn't ignore the kindness these women were attempting to bestow upon his household. Perhaps if he explained his plight, they would understand and hasten off to help some soul truly in need of their assistance.

Another sharp knock brought him to action. He hastened to the hallway and opened the front door—but only wide enough to accommodate his slim body. "Good day, ladies."

"Good day, Pastor Chamberlain," Martha Emory greeted. "We've come bearing gifts," she said, motioning toward two other women carrying desserts.

"And daughters," he said under his breath.

"Excuse me?" Mrs. Emory said.

"And how very kind you are to do so," Justin said with a feeble smile. "I'll take them to the kitchen."

"No need. We can do that." Mrs. Emory gave the door a hefty shove that nearly landed Justin on his backside.

In the blink of an eye, they were inside, soaring about the house like a swarm of bees to honey.

"What have I done?" he muttered. Of course, no one heard or answered his question. The women were much too busy hurrying from room to room, taking inventory of his household. He stood transfixed as the women surveyed the rooms, discussing his lack of furnishings and how best to arrange what little had been left in the house.

"Ladies, please!" he said, raising his voice to be heard above their chatter. "I do not want any assistance. I have household goods I'll be bringing at a later date, and there's certainly no need to worry about the few items that are here. Besides, I must attend to my sermon. So if you'll excuse me," he said while walking toward the hallway. He earnestly hoped they would follow so that he could escort them out the front door without further discussion.

"You go along and write your sermon, Pastor. The others can unpack, and Caroline and I will rearrange the furniture in the parlor. You *have* met my daughter, Caroline, haven't you?" Mrs. Emory inquired, pulling her daughter forward.

"Yes, of course. We met on Sunday."

"And *my* daughters, Rachel and Sarah," Mrs. Sanders said, clutching her daughters to her side. "Rachel has a vast knowledge of the Scriptures, and Sarah is an excellent cook. Just wait until you taste the cake she baked for you."

"Thank you, Sarah," he said, giving the gangly girl a forced smile.

"Caroline baked the apple pie," Mrs. Emory hastened to add. "I doubt whether you'll taste any better."

"I don't doubt your word," Justin said. "Truly, ladies, I do not wish to have any assistance with the household, but I thank you very much for the pies and cakes. Right now what I need is peace and quiet in order to prepare my sermon."

"We'll be quiet as church mice," Mrs. Emory said with a loud chortle, obviously finding her play on words humorous. The fact that no one else was laughing didn't seem to bother her in the least.

Justin stood holding the doorknob of the open front door. "Ladies?" he encouraged, his eyes moving between the group of women and the door.

"I'll not leave until I've accomplished what I set out to do, so you might as well get busy on your sermon, Pastor. I'm going to clean this house. I can't imagine why it wasn't completed before your arrival," Martha Emory said, yanking a crocheted table runner off an old table and giving it a robust shake.

Reggie had been correct—it did seem as though a hundred women now inhabited their home. With a disgusted grunt, he gathered up his paper, pen, ink, and Bible and hurried off to retrieve a chair from the kitchen before heading to his bedroom. Once inside, he quickly arranged a makeshift desk by using one of the trunks for his writing area. There was little doubt he'd be suffering with an aching back come morning.

"I told you! You shouldn't have let them in."

"Reggie! How did you get in here?"

His daughter wriggled out from beneath his bed in the same unladylike attire she'd been wearing earlier. "There's a hole in the floor of the upstairs closet. I tied a rope and dropped down through it—I found the opening the day we moved in," she explained.

"An opening in the floor? And where did you land?"

"In the pantry. And I didn't knock over any of the food or utensils," she said smugly. "When the ladies weren't looking, I tiptoed out of the pantry and into your room."

"I think you would have been more satisfied upstairs. After all, there's nothing for you to do here in my bedroom. I'm going to be writing my sermon, and you'll need to sit and be quiet."

"As soon as they're all in the parlor, I'm going to sneak

out the back door and go play. We're taking Mrs. Brighton fishing today," she added.

"Who is 'we'?" Justin inquired.

Reggie heaved a sigh and furrowed her eyebrows. "Me, Spencer, and Moses. I told you after Alice Ann's birthday party that we were going to teach Mrs. Brighton how to fish," she explained.

She *had* told him, but he'd immediately dismissed the remark without giving it further thought. "And where do you plan to go fishing?"

"At the river. We found a nice spot, and Mrs. Brighton said she'd bring a picnic. It's going to be great fun. Did you know Mrs. Brighton is from England? She grew up in Portsmouth and London. I think I'd like to visit London one day. Mrs. Brighton said some of the people speak with an odd accent, but she talks just fine, don't you think?"

What would Louise think of their child, he contemplated. She'd likely be appalled at the girl's behavior. Or perhaps she would find Reggie's tomboyish antics acceptable. He wondered, yet he would never know.

How he had missed Louise throughout these past ten years as he'd struggled to rear Reggie. Managing a daughter had been more of a challenge than he'd ever imagined. Although Louise's parents had offered to raise Reggie as their own, Justin had refused. Reggie deserved better than losing both of her parents at birth, and truth be told, he needed Regina. Having the child all these years had given him a purpose—and kept a little piece of Louise alive too.

Reggie jostled his arm. "Don't you think, Father?"

"What? Oh, yes, I think Mrs. Brighton speaks quite eloquently."

He tapped his index finger against his pursed lips and waited for a moment. "It's very quiet out there," he whispered. "Do you suppose they've gone?"

"Take a peek and see," she suggested. "But open the door just a crack," she cautioned.

He nodded his head and tiptoed to the door, carefully turning the knob in a clockwise direction before slowly opening the door. After listening for a moment, he whispered, "I don't hear anything."

Reggie removed her shoes and walked over to him, her bare feet silently gliding across the wooden floor until she reached his side. "You go first, just in case. I don't want them to see me if they're still somewhere in the house."

Justin opened the door a bit farther, but still it remained silent. Careful to close the bedroom door after himself, he ventured onward, into the kitchen, his library, and then the parlor. With the exception of his bedroom, the sparse furnishings had been rearranged throughout the house, and the ladies had departed.

"They're gone! They've left their pies and cakes and rearranged the few sticks of furniture, but at least I can complete my sermon."

"And I can go fishing," Reggie said with a delighted smile.

"So long as you're home in time for supper."

"We're having a picnic, remember?"

He hesitated and gave it some thought. "I'm sorry—you *did* mention a picnic. Then please be home shortly thereafter. And, by all means, don't forget your fishing pole."

———

Elinor finished packing the picnic basket and then carefully tucked a checkered cloth atop the contents. "That should be enough food for *several* days," she muttered as she lifted the container from the table.

Careful to watch her step while approaching the Merrimack River, she failed to see Reggie near the water's edge until the child called out to her.

"Hello, Reggie. Have you been here long?"

The girl positioned her fishing pole on the grassy bank and came running toward Elinor. "No. I thought I would be the last one to arrive, but I'm first," she said. "There's a verse like that in the Bible, I think." She furrowed her brows for a moment.

"I believe you're talking about the verse where Jesus says that many who are first will be last, and many who are last will be first."

"Yes, that's it. I guess it has nothing to do with fishing, though," Reggie said with a cheerful giggle. "I told my father you're from Portsmouth and London and that we're going to teach you how to fish. I thought I would never get out of the house, though; that's why I'm surprised I'm the first one here. Another group of proper church ladies—that's what my father calls them—came to visit. They keep coming to our house bringing cakes and pies and more cakes and more pies," she said, waving her arms like an exasperated old woman.

It was impossible not to smile. The child was so expressive that she used her whole body to tell a story. "I would think you and your father would be pleased to have the pies and cakes," Elinor said.

"Not *that* many—there are only two of us," she said. "Oh, look! Here come Spencer and Moses. Come on, you two, before we've caught all the fish," she called.

The boys rushed down the bank and plopped down alongside Reggie and Elinor, each one holding a fishing pole.

"You find us some worms or grubs?" Spencer asked.

"Nope, you go find your own. I got enough for me and Mrs. Brighton to get started."

The boys appeared surprised when Elinor took a worm

and threaded it onto her hook, but Reggie withheld any reaction.

"She sure doesn't act like my mama." Spencer whispered, staring at Elinor in awe. "She'd *never* put a worm on a hook."

"You did a real fine job—now let me see you get a fish," Reggie said, obviously not so easily impressed.

Elinor adjusted her straw bonnet, then tossed her line into the river. "I'll do my best, but don't go too far away. I may need your help."

"I'll do my best," Reggie said, giggling as she repeated Elinor's words.

Moses and Spencer rushed off to find some bait and were soon back and settled on the bank beside Reggie and Elinor, all of them determined to catch the first fish of the day. Had any passersby come upon them, Elinor was certain they would consider their little group quite a sight: Spencer in his crisp, clean clothing and his hair freshly combed; Moses in his neat yet less expensive breeches, his complexion nearly as white as Spencer's; Elinor in her pale green day dress and straw bonnet. And then there was Reggie. Obviously, the girl was determined she'd rather dress and act the part of a boy, which was exactly the same way Elinor had felt at Reggie's young age.

"You understand this isn't the best time of day to fish," Reggie said with the authority of an expert fisherman.

"Ever'one knows dat, Reggie," Moses said, leaning forward to give her a disgusted look.

"Does not!" Reggie shouted

"Do too!" Spencer argued.

"Did *you* know it, Mrs. Brighton?" Reggie asked.

Elinor was unsure what to say, but she didn't want the children's arguing to continue. "I believe I may have heard something to that effect, but had you asked me when to schedule the best time to come fishing, I would certainly have been at a loss."

Spencer and Reggie looked at each other, obviously unclear about who had gained Elinor's agreement. Spencer shrugged his shoulders and turned his attention back to his fishing line. Her words had deflated their argument—at least for now.

"How come you and Moses were late?" Reggie asked as she wiggled to find a more comfortable position.

"My mama's been *disturbed* ever since Alice Ann's birthday party—at least that's what my father calls it—disturbed."

Reggie's interest was piqued, and she once again changed her position in order to gain a better view of Spencer. "How come? I thought the party was very nice—except that I had to wear a dress. And I really liked Alice Ann's pony. Were you jealous she got a pony, Spencer?"

"Naw. Besides, it's not really hers yet. She has to prove she can take care of it, and I'm thinking she'll lose interest in a few weeks. Alice Ann's not like us—she doesn't know what's important and what's not. She'll be off playing with her dolly and forget about Winnie. *Winnie!* Did you ever hear such a silly name for a horse?"

"Winnie," Moses mimicked in a girlish voice.

The two boys began giggling and didn't stop until tears rolled down their cheeks.

Reggie waited until they quieted and then said quite demurely, "I think Winnie is a perfectly suitable name for a horse. It's every bit as good a name as Larkspur. And you still haven't told me why your mother is disturbed," she added, suddenly sounding quite grown up.

Spencer peeked around Moses with a startled look etched upon his young face—almost as though he expected to see someone other than Reggie sitting on the riverbank. "She's disturbed because she got a telegram from Grandpa

Wainwright's lawyer down in Mississippi. He's coming to see Mama and Uncle McKinley. Papa says he should arrive later today or tomorrow. Mama thinks something bad has happened to Grandpa."

Reggie's eyes opened wide, and her eyebrows shot up like two miniature mountain peaks. "Like he's *dead* or something?"

"Reggie!" Elinor cautioned.

Spencer's head bobbed up and down in agreement. "Yep! That's what she thinks and so does my uncle McKinley—but not me. Me and Poppa think Grandpa's probably just sending the lawyer to take care of business for him."

"You're likely correct, Spencer," Elinor hastened to agree, not wanting Reggie to question the boy any further. "What do you think about eating our picnic lunch since the fish don't seem to be biting?" she suggested.

A chorus of agreement sounded and the children immediately jumped up and began to help. They spread the lunch of fried chicken, pickled beets, hard-boiled eggs, watermelon pickles, and thick slices of buttered bread on the checkered cotton cloth and then filled their plates, again and again and again—particularly Reggie, who couldn't seem to eat enough to fill her stomach.

"And I thought I had packed enough food to last us several days," Elinor told the children as she began repacking the basket. "There's one last piece of chicken if anyone wants it," she said while holding the drumstick between her fingers.

"I'll take it," Reggie said, quickly relieving Elinor of the crispy chicken leg and taking a bite. "This is gooood chicken," she complimented, waving the drumstick like a fat wand.

"Thank you, Reggie."

"Me and Moses can't stay much longer," Spencer said as

he once again dipped his line into the water.

"How come? You were late and now you're gonna leave early?"

"Don't get all mad at us, Reggie. We don't want to, but it was the only way I could even get permission to come at all. Mama wants us at home when that lawyer comes. She says she doesn't want to be worrying about where I am when she has to be focused on other important matters."

The response didn't assuage Reggie's irritation. "Didn't you tell her you'd be at our usual fishing spot?"

"*Yes*. But it didn't matter what I said. She told me I had to promise to be home early."

Elinor patted Reggie's arm. "It is obviously very important to Mrs. Houston that Spencer return home on time. We can stay for a while longer if you like, but I think Spencer and Moses should do as they've been instructed."

"I know. I guess we might as well all leave," Reggie replied dejectedly. "Want to walk me home?" she asked, her features beginning to brighten a bit.

"Of course. I'd be pleased to walk with you," Elinor said.

A short time later, Elinor and Reggie bid the boys farewell and headed for the parsonage.

"Don't forget to tell me what happens with the lawyer," Reggie shouted to Spencer as he and Moses climbed the bank and walked toward the bridge.

"I will."

Both boys waved, and Elinor noted the forlorn look on Reggie's face as the boys sauntered out of sight. "Do you wish you had a brother or sister—someone to keep you company, like Spencer and Moses?"

"They aren't brothers; they're friends."

"Yes, I know. But they live nearby one another, and they can be together almost as if they were brothers. I merely wondered if you would like that same companionship," Elinor said.

"I guess I'd like a friend that lived close by—but not a brother or sister. That would mean having a baby around, and babies aren't any fun. I want someone my own age."

"I see. Well it appears you've made two good friends even if they don't live in town where you can see them every day."

"Uh-huh. But it's not good to get too close to friends," Reggie said as she skipped along beside Elinor.

"Why is that?"

"Because every time I make a friend, we move to another town, and then I have to start all over again. Boys are easier to make friends with, though. Girls act snooty, don't you think?"

Elinor laughed. "Sometimes they do. But there are girls who are welcoming and kind too. Perhaps you've not tried as hard because you prefer doing the things boys like rather than girls' activities."

"Maybe. But you'd think more girls would like to fish and ride horses, wouldn't you?"

"You'd think," Elinor agreed. "I thought it was difficult growing up without having my mother around when I was a little girl."

Reggie swung around to face Elinor and began walking backwards. "Did she die like my mama?"

"She died when I was born, so I never knew her."

"Just like me," Reggie said.

"But I had brothers and sisters. We remained in Portsmouth for a short time, but then my father located a position in London and we all moved there and our grandmother lived with us. She helped raise me," Elinor explained.

"Father said my grandmother offered to take me too, but

he said no. He wanted to keep me with him. That was good, don't you think?"

"Absolutely! You're a very fortunate girl to have a father willing to rear a little girl all by himself."

"We've managed pretty well—except for the moving around. I don't like that part, but Father says maybe we'll be able to stay in Lowell until I'm all grown. Wouldn't that be wonderful?"

"Indeed, it would. We'll have to begin praying that God keeps your father as pastor at St. Paul's for a very long time," Elinor said as they approached the parsonage. "Thank you for the fine day, Reggie. I had a very nice time."

"Please come in and see my room," she pleaded while tugging on Elinor's hand. "It's in the attic, and I've found a secret hole in the floor."

"Yes, do come in," Justin Chamberlain offered as he stood up and stepped from behind a rose-covered trellis on the front porch. "I finally completed my sermon notes and came outdoors for a breath of fresh air."

"I really must be getting back to the boardinghouse," Elinor replied. She wasn't sure why, but the pastor's offer suddenly made her feel self-conscious.

"Pleeeease," Reggie begged. "I do want you to see my room."

"I'll come in, but only long enough to see your room. Then I must be on my way."

Justin reached for the picnic basket. "I doubt you'll want to carry this upstairs for your grand tour."

"Thank you," Elinor said and followed along behind Reggie, viewing the large attic room where the side walls sloped at a severe angle, making the room somewhat difficult to navigate without bending over. "You may need to do a bit of furniture rearranging as you grow taller. If not, you're apt to bump your head at night should you sit up too quickly," Elinor said with a grin.

"Father said the very same thing. Come see my special trapdoor."

Elinor viewed the opening that dropped into the kitchen pantry. "I wonder who made this opening. I bet there are lots of stories we could tell about why and who crawled down through that hole," she said in a hushed voice.

Reggie's delight was obvious. "It *is* exciting, isn't it?"

"Yes. In fact, it almost makes me long to be a little girl again," Elinor said as the two of them walked down the stairs.

"I didn't notice you two carrying any fish," Justin noted as they reached the bottom step.

"Actually, I did manage to hook one, but it was so tiny we let it go," Elinor said. "The children tell me that mid-afternoon is not a good time of day for catching fish, so I felt fortunate I caught even the little one."

"And she put her own worm on the hook and even took the fish off," Reggie informed her father.

"It appears my daughter is impressed with your abilities even if you didn't catch a lot of fish. And compliments from my daughter are not easy to come by," he added.

"Then I'll consider myself fortunate," Elinor said.

"Please stay and have a piece of pie or cake with us," Pastor Chamberlain offered.

Elinor glanced at Reggie, and the two of them giggled. "I'm sorry. I shouldn't laugh at your kind offer. However, Reggie confided that the good ladies of St. Paul's brought several cakes and pies earlier today."

He gave a firm nod. "Earlier today, later today, yesterday, and the day before that—and not merely the ladies from St. Paul's, but from all around town. I have more cakes and pies than we can ever hope to eat. I'd need to purchase a new preaching suit if I ate all of those sweets," he said with a grin.

"I don't think the ladies realize that man does not live by sweets alone. Come and see."

Elinor's eyes widened at the spectacle. All horizontal space in the kitchen and dining room, with the exception of Pastor Chamberlain's writing desk, had been covered by every imaginable dessert. The sight took her breath away. "Oh my! This is astonishing. You must begin turning them away."

"I have attempted to do so from the very beginning. None will take no for an answer. Even when they see the laden tables, they refuse to take their offerings home."

"Perhaps Reggie should begin selling some of these delicacies," Elinor teased.

Moments later Elinor left for home, completely unaware of the inspiration she had planted in a young girl's heart.

CHAPTER · 3

JASMINE HEARD the sounds of an approaching horse and buggy from her upstairs room and quickly walked to the window overlooking the small circular driveway that fronted their home. Jarrod Forbes stepped down from the carriage, and she watched as he slowly surveyed his surroundings. Mr. Forbes had aged since she'd last seen him and now wore spectacles and carried a silver-tipped walking cane. His hair appeared more gray than black, and there was a surprising stoop to his shoulders. The lawyer had always held his head high and his shoulders squared. At least that's what her father had said about him. Jasmine had long thought Jarrod Forbes aloof and proud, though she didn't get that impression at the current time.

She heard the front door open and then Nolan's and McKinley's voices as they greeted their guest. Mr. Forbes had sent word of his arrival at the Merrimack House yesterday and asked to meet with them this morning. She knew McKinley would prefer the early morning meeting—he disliked being pulled away from his work at the Corporation during business hours.

Bracing herself for what she was convinced would be bad news, Jasmine took a deep breath, pursed her lips, and slowly exhaled before descending the staircase. "Mr. Forbes," she greeted as she joined the gentlemen in Nolan's library. "I trust you had a pleasant journey."

She feared the lawyer's inability to meet her eyes didn't bode well for the discussion that would later ensue.

"My voyage was uneventful, thank you."

"Has my husband offered you refreshments?" she inquired.

Nolan nodded. "Yes. Martha will bring a tray shortly."

"Then I suppose we should all be seated," she said, suddenly feeling ill at ease standing in front of Nolan's oversized mahogany desk.

Mr. Forbes tugged on the hem of his vest and sat down opposite McKinley, his focus upon the wool carpet. He cleared his throat several times and repositioned his cane in varying stances until Jasmine finally jumped to her feet and removed it from his hand.

"I'll place this in the umbrella stand so you won't have to worry with it," she said without giving him opportunity to protest. "Now, why don't you tell us what brings you to Massachusetts."

Apparently her tone bore enough impatience to prod the man into action, since he immediately reached into his small leather case and withdrew a sheaf of papers.

"Perhaps I should sit near the desk so that I may arrange these documents," he said, finally looking at Jasmine.

"Of course. Let me assist you," she offered graciously.

Once the official-looking paper work was spread out on Nolan's desk, Forbes pulled a handkerchief from his pocket and wiped his perspiring forehead. "Your father entrusted me with the task of personally coming to meet with you. Unfortunately, I must begin by advising you that your father and my beloved friend went to be with the Lord on the six-teenth of June."

A loud roar filled Jasmine's ears, and she heard a scream. Was it her voice or had someone else shrieked? The room swirled. Nolan's face was above her, fading in and out, his voice calling her name. She willed her lips to move, yet they failed her.

Her eyelids fluttered open, and she could feel the damp-ness of a cool compress upon her forehead. She forced herself to focus upon Nolan's face.

"My dear! You gave me a fright," Nolan said as he con-tinued to dab her forehead with the moist cloth.

"I do apologize, Mrs. Houston," Mr. Forbes said. "For-give me for my lack of sensitivity. I should have better prepared you for the news."

The lawyer's words brought his earlier announcement rushing back to mind. Her father, dead for more than two months—and she hadn't even known. All that time she had overlooked his lack of communication by thinking him busy with the plantation.

Nolan assisted her as she struggled to sit up on the floor and then move slowly to a chair.

"What happened to my father?" she asked.

The lawyer looked at Nolan, obviously seeking affirma-tion that he should speak. "You must tell her," Nolan said.

"Yellow fever."

Jasmine gripped the chair arm. "Did he suffer terribly?"

"No more than the others," Forbes hedged.

"*Others?* Then there's been an epidemic?"

Nolan furrowed his brow and took her hand in his own. "There's no need to hear all the details at once, my dear. You're already in a weakened state of mind."

"I'm not in a weakened state of mind, Nolan. I'm sad

and frightened, and I need to know what has happened at The Willows."

"My wife has returned to her full capacity, Mr. Forbes. You may speak freely."

"Are you certain?" he inquired in a quivering voice.

"Yes!" Jasmine sat up straight to emphasize her forceful reply.

"The illness struck with a vengeance. It wasn't widespread, but where it did hit, the misery was tragic. Unfortunately, the area around your home was struck particularly hard."

Jasmine's eyes widened with sudden realization. "Our brother David and his wife?"

The old lawyer slowly moved his head back and forth. "Gone. Your brother Samuel as well."

"No!" she screamed. "Not our entire family."

Distress lined Mr. Forbes's face as he retrieved his handkerchief from his jacket pocket and began to once again daub his forehead. "I fear the news only gets more dreadful."

"I shall do my utmost to remain calm," Jasmine said.

"Your uncles and cousins . . . there are few remaining and—"

She motioned for him to halt while she grappled for the fan she'd placed on a nearby table. Snapping open the hand-painted object, she began to wave it back and forth with a fervor that stirred the air for all of them. "Continue," she said, as though her behavior were quite normal.

"None of them survived, except for your distant cousin Levi Wainwright," he said in a nearly inaudible voice. "Oh yes, and Lydia, Franklin's daughter."

"That few? How could that be?" This time it was McKinley who interrupted.

"The plague hit hard in the area. How a small number can endure while others perish is a mystery to all of us—

always is. I believe a few others survived—relatives by marriage. Lydia's husband, Rupert, and one or two others. Rupert advised me Lydia is traveling abroad and not yet expected home. Of course, your distant cousin Levi always was a strange individual—never did live on the plantation with his family. Had aspirations of becoming an artist and still travels a great deal—usually only comes back south during the winter months. As I said, the area was hit particularly hard, and with most of the family congregated on adjoining plantations . . ." His voice trailed off as though he'd lost the energy to continue.

Jasmine laid the fan on a marble-topped table and turned her full attention upon the lawyer. "I don't mean to appear unappreciative, especially since you've traveled all this distance, but why didn't you immediately send word back when we could have been of assistance to our father?"

"I was following his direction, Mrs. Houston. He forbade me from notifying either you or your brother. He feared you would contract the fever if you came to The Willows. He watched both Samuel and David die and said he wouldn't lose another child.

"He required me to give my word that I would not notify you until the outbreak had ended. In any event, you could not have come, for the entire area was under quarantine. I set sail as soon as I was notified that the quarantine would be lifted. Your father wanted me to personally deliver these papers and go over the details with you and McKinley."

McKinley pulled his chair closer to the desk. He seemed unnaturally calm. "What are these papers?"

"Your father's last will and testament and handwritten letters to each of you. Obviously, you must make decisions regarding the plantation and your slaves."

"*Our* slaves? Neither of us believes in slavery, Mr. Forbes.

You may turn the survivors free as far as I'm concerned," Jasmine said.

"Don't speak so hastily, Mrs. Houston. There are many considerations that must be addressed before you determine exactly what is to be done with them."

"Go on, Mr. Forbes," McKinley said. "We're listening."

"There's a cotton crop that must be harvested. Someone needs to go to The Willows and take charge—get the crop in first and then decide if you'll move back and take over the plantation." His final words were a near whisper.

McKinley appeared more stunned by Mr. Forbes's announcement about the crops than the death of their family members. "You want one of us to return and oversee the harvest? Why, that's preposterous! I can't leave Lowell or my position with the Corporation. My wife is due to have a child in a few months, and we're in the process of building a new home. Besides, I know nothing of harvesting a crop. Can't the overseer tend to the cotton?"

Mr. Forbes leaned back in his chair, the import of his task obviously weighing heavily upon him. He rubbed his temples and gazed at McKinley as though he were a child with an inadequate ability to understand the profundity of their circumstance.

"The overseer?" Jasmine inquired. But Mr. Forbes didn't need to answer. His expression revealed the answer.

"The overseer and two-thirds of the slaves are dead. I hired a man to act as overseer, but he can't possibly handle this situation. The plantation requires immediate attention by someone with more authority than a newly hired overseer. Under normal circumstances, that would be you, McKinley. However, your father drew his will giving his property to you and Jasmine in equal shares. He states in article three of his will that the two of you must come to an agreement as to how the plantation will be managed."

McKinley reached for the document. "Does he prohibit the sale?"

"No, there's no such prohibition. Upon the deaths of David and Samuel, your father rewrote his will. He knew neither of you would have any desire to operate the plantation, nor did he wish to force you into such a situation. However, in his letter he does ask that the crop be harvested if at all possible. Surely you must admit that permitting the crop to sit in the fields and rot would be improvident. Your father would abhor such inaction. On his behalf, I would plead for one of you to come back to The Willows and attend to matters immediately. The cotton will not wait indefinitely."

Nolan brushed a lock of hair off his forehead and shook his head. "There is no easy answer to this dilemma. Even if Jasmine or McKinley agreed to go and oversee the harvest, how could it be accomplished with so few workers?"

Jasmine gave him a tender smile. *Workers.* He couldn't even bring himself to say they'd be using slaves if they brought in the crop.

"Unaffected plantations in Louisiana are willing to hire out some of their slaves, and several plantations are planning to take advantage of the offer. The plantations nearby that suffered a large number of deaths have discussed the possibility of sharing their slaves. They would work one week at one plantation and the next week at another. Of course, you have to hope you don't get the week when it rains," he said with a halfhearted smile.

Jasmine fidgeted with her hands, overwhelmed by all she'd been told. It was impossible to imagine that most of her family had perished. But it was equally hard to make a choice about what should be done. "It's obvious we can't come to an immediate decision, Mr. Forbes. We need time to discuss the matter more fully before coming to a conclusion."

"Of course, of course. I didn't expect you to give me your answer today. I know there is much to digest, but you must remember the crop will be ready for harvest by the time you make the journey. You dare not tarry for too long."

"I presume arrangements were made . . . properly made . . . for my family," Jasmine said, suddenly changing the subject.

"Of course. Your father saw to those who went before him and left instructions with me for the remaining deaths, including his."

"That sounds very much like Father." Jasmine knew her father would have thought of everyone else, even if it took his last ounce of strength.

I'll leave these papers with you to peruse, and if you have questions, you know where to reach me. Otherwise, I'll await your decision." Mr. Forbes used the arms of the chair to steady himself as he began to stand.

"A moment, Mr. Forbes," McKinley said, waving for the man to remain seated. "Has any of this information been reported to the Boston Associates? Undoubtedly they need to know the state of affairs among those men with whom they have contracts. The mills are dependent upon receiving the anticipated cotton shipments."

Forbes nodded in agreement. "I understand. I talked with no one prior to coming here. My first obligation was to your father and the promise I made him. However, I am prepared to speak with the Associates prior to my departure, or you may report on my behalf if you desire."

"I believe they would appreciate hearing from you directly," McKinley replied. "I'll talk with Matthew Cheever, and we'll arrange a meeting as quickly as possible."

"Since I plan to depart for Boston once you've made a

decision regarding The Willows, could we possibly meet in Boston? My ship sails for Mississippi in ten days and I had planned to spend the remainder of my time in the city. I promised to bring my wife some finery, and it may take me a few days to complete my shopping," he added with an exhausted smile.

"I'm confident we can accommodate you. We can send a telegraph, and once we receive word regarding the time and date, I'll notify you."

"Good enough," Mr. Forbes said, once again struggling to stand.

"Let me retrieve your cane, Mr. Forbes, and I'll see you to the door," Jasmine offered.

"No. You remain seated, Mrs. Houston. You've had more to contend with this day than I."

"Indeed, my dear. You remain seated," Nolan said as he took the older man by one arm. "I'll accompany Mr. Forbes."

Mr. Forbes leaned heavily upon his cane as Nolan escorted him across the thick wool carpet. Jasmine waited until she heard the tapping of his cane upon the wooden floor in the hallway before turning her attention to McKinley.

"Do you want to return home and discuss this matter with Violet—or perhaps fetch her and we can all take our noonday meal together?" Jasmine asked.

He shook his head. "No. I can tell you, sister, that I'll not even entertain the notion of returning to The Willows and bringing in a cotton crop. If you want to do so, then that is all well and good, but I say we should immediately sell the place."

"That may prove more difficult than you think," Nolan said as he strode back into the room.

"How so? The Willows turns a handsome profit. There

ought to be any number of investors willing to purchase such a plantation."

"That's not what Forbes tells me. He just said there are two plantations that have been on the market for over a year now and still have no buyers. Additionally, he tells me that because the fever devastated the area around Lorman, it will prove more difficult to find a purchaser until the fear of a repeat epidemic dies down."

McKinley stood up and began pacing back and forth between the settee and Nolan's oversized desk, his shuffling feet brushing the carpet nap first in one direction and then the other. "This is indeed a fine predicament," he said while raking his fingers through his thick hair. "We can't even properly mourn the loss of our family because of a cotton crop. I say we let it rot in the fields. What difference does harvesting the cotton make if we're going to sell the plantation anyway?"

"Not a very fitting tribute to our father or our brothers, do you think? We should at least honor Father's final request, McKinley."

"Surely he realized what he was asking would be impossible for either of us to accomplish," her brother argued.

Leaning slightly forward, Jasmine watched as her brother paced in front of her. McKinley had always been the sensitive male member in their family, yet suddenly he appeared cold and indifferent. She'd never seen him so detached and aloof. His behavior was as disturbing as the decision they must make. Surely he didn't truly believe they should sit back and permit the crop to lay waste.

"Nothing is impossible if we trust in the Lord and maintain a proper perspective. Perhaps Violet would be willing to remain in Lowell with her parents while you traveled with Nolan and me to The Willows. With three of us, we could conduct the necessary business more rapidly. You or Nolan

54

could oversee the crop, and I could attend to putting the house in order to place it for sale and help with the bookwork," she suggested hopefully.

"Did you not hear me? There is no way I can travel to Mississippi. I'll not leave Violet with her parents when our child is due to be born in December. You know she's frightened something will go wrong again."

Jasmine nodded. Violet had suffered the loss of a stillborn child early in her marriage, and it had nearly incapacitated her throughout this pregnancy. Even though she'd subsequently given birth to one healthy child, the thought of another stillborn baby loomed in her mind, and she was convinced she would have difficulty once again.

"I thought Violet appeared happy and relaxed at Alice Ann's party. Only two months ago, she wouldn't have considered such an outing. You could at least ask her, McKinley. She likely relies upon her mother more than you for consolation at this juncture, don't you think?"

"How would you feel if Nolan left you in such a circumstance, Jasmine? Would *you* think it his duty to hurry off to harvest a cotton crop, or would you believe he should remain at home with you? I'd venture to say you would not bid him farewell without an argument. Violet's condition aside, I must see to my position with the Corporation. I cannot merely walk in and say I'll be back once I've harvested the cotton and sold my father's plantation. No, Jasmine. If one of us is to go to the South, it will be you, for I'll not be bullied or shamed into going."

"Is that what you think? That I'm trying to bully or shame you? Go home to your wife and your position at the Corporation, McKinley. Your primary concern appears to rest with the Corporation rather than the plantation," she said in a soft yet resigned voice. "I'll manage things in Mississippi without your assistance. However, I'll not seek your permission for the decisions I make. If you plan to wash your hands of this matter, then I expect you to sign over your right of authority so I may transact business without your signature. Otherwise, I'll be hampered at every turn as I wait upon the paper work being shuffled back and forth between Mississippi and Massachusetts."

McKinley leaned against Nolan's desk in a half sitting, half standing position. "You want me to sign over my portion of the inheritance? Is that what you're asking? Because I won't do that—I won't."

Her eyes filled with sadness as she met his piercing eyes. "I don't want your inheritance, McKinley—I want your help. But please understand that although you've refused your assistance, I would never consider taking your inheritance. Father intended it for you, and you shall have half of whatever remains when all is said and done. All I've asked is that you sign over your authority so that I can conduct business without the necessity of your signature."

"I'll ask Mr. Forbes to draw up a paper in the morning." His voice was cold.

"Until today, I hadn't realized how much you've changed, McKinley. I fear your position with the Corporation has begun to harden you. Please don't lose your kind heart and generous spirit. We've lost the rest of our family— we mustn't lose each other."

"You're right, of course." His voice cracked with emotion as she embraced him. "I'm sorry, but I just cannot accompany you. Please forgive me."

"There's nothing to forgive," she whispered.

———

Later that night Jasmine sat alone brushing out her long brown hair. She looked at herself in the mirror with each stroke. She couldn't comprehend that her father had died.

She couldn't make it real in her mind.

"I suppose I won't fully believe it until I see The Willows and his grave," she murmured.

"Did you say something?" Nolan asked as he came into the room.

She sighed and put down the brush. "I can't believe they are gone."

He came to her and put his hands upon her shoulders. Bending low, he kissed her cheek. "I cannot imagine a more difficult day for you, and yet you bore it with such grace. It is hard to even imagine one's entire family wiped out in a matter of weeks."

"I've seen epidemics like that before. There was one when I was a little girl," Jasmine remembered. "I think I was nearly six. I remember many of the older people dying, yet no one on our plantation seemed to get sick. At least I don't remember there being sickness." She turned and stood. "There is always something to worry about. I think of how close we came to losing Alice Ann. I worry every time one of the children starts sniffling."

"But you cannot live in fear."

Tears welled in her eyes. "No. I know the truth of that. Still . . . I'm afraid."

He pulled her into his arms. "Cast your cares upon the Lord."

"I'm trying to," she whispered, allowing his embrace to reassure and comfort her. "I'm trying."

———————

Reverend Chamberlain snapped open his pocket watch and glanced down at the time. The Ladies' Aid Society would be in the midst of their meeting, but if he entered the church quietly, he could be in and out without being observed. At least that was his plan. He silently chastised himself for leaving his sermon notes at the church when he'd attended last night's meeting. If he hadn't had to go searching for Reggie at the last minute, he wouldn't have laid them down.

No sense blaming the child for her inquisitive nature, he decided. At her age, he, too, would have been off exploring the nooks and crannies of the church. However, he had become concerned when, after a good ten minutes of searching, he'd not located his daughter and been required to enlist the aid of several church members. After another period of searching, Mr. Emory had located Reggie in a narrow crawl space off one end of the sanctuary. Of course, Reggie hadn't understood all the excitement. After all, she had followed her father's instructions and had remained inside the church. On their way home, Justin attempted to explain his concerns but had finally given up.

Reggie was correct; she hadn't disobeyed. Next time he would have to issue more explicit instructions, he decided as he carefully opened the church door and tiptoed across the wooden floor of the vestibule.

He could hear the muffled voices of the women drifting from inside the sanctuary. From the sound of the animated voices, he doubted their meeting would soon be over, and he exhaled a sigh of relief. He took another step toward his small office but stopped short. Had he heard someone utter his daughter's name?

As surreptitiously as a cat stalking its prey, Justin padded back to the sanctuary doors and placed one ear against the cool, hard wood.

"Well, I can't tell you the depth of my irritation when Rachel came home from town and told me she'd seen the preacher's daughter going door to door selling cakes and pies," Nancy Sanders proclaimed.

"*Our* cakes and pies?" another woman asked in a sharp voice.

"Well, of course, *our* cakes and pies. Do you think the preacher or that wretched child can bake?"

"She's not *wretched,* Nancy. Unkempt, perhaps, but I believe she's surely a sweet little girl underneath it all. You need to remember that she hasn't had the advantages of your Rachel. Growing up without a mother's influence and training has surely been difficult for the girl—and her father."

Justin couldn't determine who made the comment, but his lips curved slightly upward. At least not all of them considered Reggie to be wretched.

"Well, he certainly doesn't appear interested in doing anything to help the girl. He brushes off every attempt that Rachel and I, as well as these other ladies, have made to assist him," Mrs. Sanders responded. "And now he's permitting the child to venture about town selling the pastries we baked for them."

"She even attempted to sell some of them to Mrs. Whidden at the mercantile. When Mrs. Whidden questioned her, the child stated Elinor Brighton had made the suggestion."

"Do you suppose she's set her cap for the preacher and fears that her baked goods can't compare to ours?" Nancy Sanders inquired.

"Elinor? She's no more interested in finding a husband than I am," another woman replied.

"You're already married, Nettie," someone said.

"Exactly my point. I'm not looking for a husband, and neither is Elinor Brighton. She's been twice widowed and has hardened her heart against such matters."

"I say the entire situation is pitiable and a poor reflection upon the church," one of the women commented.

"Indeed! My husband tells me they had to drag the girl

out of a crawl space she was hiding in last night during the deacons' meeting."

Was that Martha Emory speaking? It sounded like her shrill voice, and Harry Emory had been the one to locate Reggie the preceding night.

"There's little doubt the child needs a woman's hand. She has come to a point in her life when she needs to be turned down the proper path. I'm sure she has no idea how to properly fashion her hair or put needle to cloth. What's to become of her when the time comes for her to find a suitable spouse? There isn't a man alive who desires a wife who can't keep a proper house."

"Absolutely! Can you imagine a girl such as Reggie attempting to act as hostess for her father a few years from now? Why, the girl will have absolutely no idea how to handle herself in proper society. Watching her these past few weeks has been a painful experience," another woman commented.

Justin's jaw tightened as he listened to the women discussing his only child—the daughter he dearly loved and cherished beyond his wildest expectations. Their words cut like a knife, and a part of him longed to rush through the doors and tell them all that he cared little what they thought—that their scathing words were of no consequence to him or his daughter. Perhaps a good sermon on gossip and maligning others would be in order.

Yet, as Justin crept back to his office, he knew at least a portion of what he'd heard was correct. Reggie *did* need a woman's guidance in her life. He should have realized his failure to provide someone to teach Reggie social graces would lead to disastrous results. Without a sound, he closed the door behind him and settled into the oak spindle-backed chair.

"What do I do, Lord? I don't want a wife, but the child

needs a woman's hand in her life. Who among these women could help my Reggie?" he whispered into the silent room.

He stared out the office window at the grassy side yard, where the parishioners occasionally gathered for summertime picnics and festivities, and hoped he'd be given a divine answer to his query. This was one problem Justin didn't want to solve on his own, for if he knew nothing else, he knew his daughter. She *would* resist.

The sound of clattering footsteps and Reggie's voice startled Justin from his silent reverie.

"Guess what happened!" she shouted, her arms flapping up and down like an agitated chicken as she skidded to a halt in front of his desk.

Justin surveyed his young daughter. Her hair was unkempt, her clothing was soiled, and dirt smudged her forehead and both cheeks. He assessed the child as though she were a stranger and knew he needed an answer to his prayer—immediately.

"Did you hear me, Father? Guess what happened?"

"What?" he asked, forcing himself back to the present.

Reggie plopped down in the one remaining chair and folded her arms across her chest. "Spencer is leaving. His grandpa and uncles died, and now his family has to go somewhere down south to pick and hoe cotton. Isn't that terrible? I wouldn't want to hoe cotton. Do you think Spencer could come and live with us? I don't want him to leave. He and Moses are the only friends I have in Lowell." She sat up straighter. "I told him we'd come and talk to his mother and see if she'd let him stay with us. What do you think? He wouldn't eat too much, and he doesn't get into trouble very often. Do you think we could?" she asked, her questions tumbling out in rapid succession.

"No, Reggie, we couldn't do such a thing. First of all, Spencer's parents are not going to leave him in Lowell if they're moving down south; second, I don't think Spencer or any other member of their family will be hoeing cotton; and third, we aren't going to go and talk to Mr. and Mrs. Houston. I am truly sorry your friend must leave, but this is none of our business."

"But, Father, I promised."

"You should have come and talked to me prior to making such promises," he admonished quietly.

She tucked one leg beneath her and wrinkled her nose. "Won't you at least talk to his mother?"

"Put your leg down, Reggie. That's a very unladylike position," he instructed. "If Mrs. Houston wishes to discuss Spencer's future with me, I'm quite sure she'll stop by the house."

"Why does it matter if I sit like a lady? You never cared before."

"Well, I should have. I've gone far too long without correcting your behavior."

She frowned and jumped up from the chair. "I'm going home," she announced, darting from the room and headlong into Mrs. Sanders, who was standing directly outside Justin's office with the other members of the Ladies' Aid Society.

"Why, Regina, how pleasant to see you. Have you been enjoying the cake Rachel baked for you and your father?"

Reggie hesitated for only a moment. "We didn't eat it. I sold it instead."

Mrs. Sanders gasped, obviously taken aback by the girl's forthright reply.

"I got twenty-five cents," she proudly announced. "Mr. Parker was going to give me only ten cents until I told him it was for the church benevolence fund, so he decided to give me an extra fifteen cents."

"You *lied* to him?" Mrs. Sanders directed a condemnatory glare into the preacher's office.

"No, Mrs. Sanders, she did not lie. She has donated all of the money toward the benevolence fund. Quite frankly, I thought it a better idea than letting the desserts go uneaten," Justin said. "After all, we are only two people and you all had been so very generous with your gifts."

With a downward glance, Mrs. Sanders sputtered an apology to the preacher and then busied herself searching her reticule for some unknown object.

"I thank you for your words of regret, Mrs. Sanders, but I believe it's Regina, not I, that you've affronted," Justin said as he took hold of his daughter and gently moved her until she was standing directly in front of him. With his hands resting upon Reggie's shoulders, Justin met Mrs. Sanders's embarrassed gaze. "I'm certain you'd like to offer Reggie your apology."

CHAPTER · 4

MCKINLEY WAINWRIGHT paced back and forth in front of the Lowell railroad depot, straining to his full height as he peered down Merrimack Street before turning his attention to Dutton Street.

His lips curved into an unconvincing smile as he stopped beside Mr. Forbes. "Mr. Cheever should be arriving at any moment."

Jarrod Forbes removed his spectacles and wiped them with his handkerchief. "So you've told me—twice now. The sun is much too bright for my liking. I'll wait for you and Mr. Cheever inside the depot," he said before glancing toward the sound of a shrill whistle in the distance. "Sounds as though the train should be arriving soon also."

Mr. Forbes leaned heavily upon his cane and hobbled off to the doorway of the depot. Matthew was seldom late, and McKinley began to worry that an emergency had occurred at one of the mills. He hesitated, attempting to decide if he should send one of the boys running to the mills. The train shrieked an earsplitting whistle, and McKinley motioned to a young lad. He'd just completed his instructions to the boy when he saw Matthew's carriage round the corner.

"I won't need your assistance after all. Mr. Cheever is approaching," he said, tossing the boy a coin.

"Thank you, sir," the boy said as he caught the coin and then tucked it into his pocket.

"I was growing concerned," McKinley said as his father-in-law stepped down from the carriage with his case in hand.

Matthew waved his driver on and then strode alongside McKinley. "I thought I had all of the contracts assembled, but after reviewing them this morning, I realized several were missing. I was required to stop at the mill on my way. Finding the remaining documents proved more time-consuming than I had anticipated. Where's Forbes?"

"He's waiting inside the depot. He was determined to be on the train, even if neither of us accompanied him," McKinley replied.

Matthew laughed. "Likely he's concerned about all that shopping he must accomplish in Boston before his departure."

"How wonderful it must be to have nothing more pressing than the purchase of a few trinkets weighing upon one's mind," McKinley said as they entered the depot.

"Pleased to see you made it in time for our departure," Mr. Forbes said as Matthew stepped forward and grasped the older man's hand. "I began to fear you wouldn't make it."

"I wouldn't miss an important meeting with the Association. As I told McKinley, I was delayed by a few misplaced contracts but have managed to set everything right."

"Then let us board," Forbes declared, suddenly seeming to have gained new momentum.

The three men boarded the train and settled into their seats. The train had barely pulled away from the station when Jarrod Forbes nodded off to sleep.

"Doesn't appear as though we'll be having much discussion with Mr. Forbes on the way to Boston," Matthew commented while giving the older man a sidelong glance.

McKinley grinned and nodded in agreement.

"How has my daughter reacted to all this news regarding the plantation?" Matthew asked. "Her mother tells me Violet appeared somewhat withdrawn when they visited yesterday. Yet when Lilly questioned her, she wasn't forthcoming."

"She's distraught. I've attempted to reassure Violet that I will not go to Mississippi, but I think she fears I'll relent if Jasmine becomes more forceful."

Matthew leaned back against the seat and closed his eyes for a moment. "Quite frankly, I don't believe this entire ordeal should rest upon Jasmine's shoulders, especially if you want to share in the proceeds of your father's estate," he said rather sternly.

"What? You think I should leave Violet—in her condition and after her difficulty? I question whether your daughter would ever fully recover if she lost another child. And there's my position with the Corporation to consider. Besides, I know nothing about harvesting a cotton crop."

Matthew rubbed his fingertips across the deep creases that lined his forehead. "It's entirely your decision. I'm pleased that you've put your love for Violet and the unborn child first. However, Violet mentioned the fact that you expect to receive your full share from your father's estate. Jasmine and Nolan have much at stake in this matter also, and I'm surprised they would agree to take on full responsibility. Leaving their horses and business to the care of others could prove very risky for them—and you can be sure they question their own ability to harvest a crop."

"Then you think I should go?"

"I find more fault with your ultimatum regarding the inheritance than in your decision to remain in Lowell. You might find spending some time in prayer to be beneficial . . . and you might want to say a word of thanks for your sister while you're at it."

McKinley stared out the train window and contemplated Matthew's words. Perhaps his decision had been hastily made. Yet the thought of going to Mississippi was out of the question. Instead, he would offer to assist Paddy and the other folks whom Nolan would leave in charge of his holdings. To make this issue a matter of prayer, however, would be impossible. Though he knew his stance regarding the inheritance was selfish, he would not accept less than the share allotted him in the terms of his father's will. After all, as the only remaining son, he could have contested Jasmine's inheritance. Besides, he *needed* the additional funds! The downward turn in the economy during the past few years had taken a heavy toll on his investments, which was a fact he did not wish to discuss with his father-in-law.

McKinley tried not to linger long on the topic. Thinking about the plantation made him remember his father and the conflicts they'd had over his own decision to remain in the North. He knew his father never fully agreed with his decision. Nor could Malcolm Wainwright ever fully understand McKinley's hatred of slavery. He could almost hear his father's protests, even now.

"But you benefited every day of your life from the work of our slaves," his father had once argued. *"How can you turn away from all that I offer? How can you turn away from your home?"*

And indeed McKinley had struggled at times with that decision. There were moments when he remembered the sweet smell of honeysuckle as it drifted on the evening air. He remembered the parties and family gatherings. He had, when young, imagined himself quite happily settled with his own plantation and slaves.

I'm sorry, Father. How could I explain to you what I never quite fully understood myself?

The train came to a jerking halt at the Boston railroad station and ended his musings, at least for the moment. Nathan Appleton's carriage awaited them outside the depot, and within a short time, the three men were delivered to the front door of the Appleton home, where Nathan personally greeted them.

"A pleasure to meet you, Mr. Forbes. I do wish it were under different circumstances," Nathan said as he led them into his library. "Many of the Associates are traveling abroad for the summer, but most of them will return to America in the next two weeks. Let me introduce you to the members who are able to be in attendance."

Nathan quickly made the introductions and invited the men to be seated. "I trust you've heard the latest financial news," he said with a worried look in his eyes.

"I've heard nothing of interest. Is something amiss with the Corporation?" Matthew inquired.

"We received word yesterday that the New York branch of the Ohio Life Insurance and Trust Company has failed. It appears the insolvency was caused by a massive embezzlement of railroad bonds, which will, of course, leave enormous debts," Nathan explained.

Wilson Harper mopped the perspiration from his forehead. "New York bankers restricted all routine transactions immediately. We've heard that investors who held stock and commercial paper immediately rushed to make deals with their brokers. The telegraph we received this morning says that stocks fell ten percent in one day. Fortunes are being lost overnight. Terrible! Terrible!" Harper said, shaking his head back and forth.

"The banks wouldn't honor routine transactions? Why?" McKinley asked, his fear mounting at this turn of events.

"All their depositors wanted payment in gold; however, the bankers knew they couldn't meet the demand until the expected gold shipment arrived from San Francisco. They announced their gold shipment is due by mid-September. I believe they gave the anticipated date in order to allay the fears of their depositors, but I'm not certain it's been successful. I'm hoping panic doesn't spread to Boston, yet we likely need to withdraw some of the Corporation's funds in the event there's a nationwide collapse."

"I doubt that's going to occur. This country is economically sound, don't you think?" McKinley inquired in a hopeful voice.

Josiah Baines glanced around the room. "You were but a child when the economic crisis hit in 1839, but those of us who struggled through that time haven't forgotten. I learned many a lesson then, which is the *only* good thing I can say about that period in my life."

"True! I think the most important thing I discovered was to diversify my holdings and always retain a fair sum of gold," Thomas Clayborn commented.

"So long as you don't put your gold in the bank," Wilson said with a hearty laugh.

Josiah and the other men nodded in agreement before Nathan once again took control of the group. "Mr. Forbes, why don't you tell us some *good* news? I think we would all appreciate an encouraging word."

Jarrod Forbes glanced toward McKinley and Matthew before addressing the men. "I doubt you'll consider what I have to say good news. However, it could be much worse," he began.

The Associates listened attentively. However, McKinley noted that each of them had paled a bit by the time Mr. Forbes finished his report.

"We are truly sorry for your loss, McKinley. I know this

must be a terrible blow for you," Nathan said. "Please be assured that if you are needed in Mississippi, we will make every attempt to accommodate you. We would be willing to secure your position on an unpaid basis for as long as necessary to close the estate."

"Thank you, but arrangements have already been made. My sister and her husband will soon depart in order to oversee the cotton harvest and sell the plantation," McKinley replied, careful to avoid eye contact with his father-in-law.

"I don't want to appear insensitive to your loss, McKinley, but I'm wondering if the plantation can be sold with an assignation of the contract we had with Malcolm?" Wilson Harper inquired.

Jarrod Forbes cleared his throat. "I believe I can answer that question. Malcolm placed a proviso in his will that if his heirs made a decision to sell the plantation—and he was confident they would—they were instructed to use due diligence in seeking a buyer who would enthusiastically embrace the fulfillment of his contractual obligation with the Boston Associates."

"I might add that any buyer would be foolish to look elsewhere," McKinley said. "The Associates have always been generous in dealing with the cotton growers."

Wilson nodded. "However, some may view the purchase as an opportunity to renegotiate. Such a possibility could eventually lead to a breakdown with the other growers. I'm not attempting to create problems, merely hoping we won't be blindsided by a sale."

"Of course, you understand that Mr. and Mrs. Houston are going to The Willows at great hardship to themselves and their young family," Matthew Cheever said. "I don't think anyone can expect them to be overly concerned about the ongoing contracts. They are, after all, in the horse business. The sale of cotton to the Associates in no way affects their future, and I don't believe we can have any expectation in that regard."

"Yes, of course," Josiah agreed. "However, if Malcolm made mention in his will, I believe his daughter will want to respect her father's dying wishes. Coupled with the news regarding the embezzlement scandal, this turn of events comes as a double blow. Do we know how many of our contracts were affected by the epidemic?"

Jarrod Forbes raised his eyebrows. "To some extent, all of them. However, the Louisiana plantations didn't suffer much damage. Most of them lost only a few slaves or possibly a family member, while the Mississippi plantations lost entire families and large numbers of their slaves." He leaned forward. "As you know, the cotton harvest will soon begin in earnest. Once I return home, I'll be able to supply you with a better estimate of what you may expect."

"In the meantime, since we already have a meeting scheduled for the third week in September, I believe there's little we can accomplish at the moment," Nathan said. "Matthew, if you would spend some time reviewing the contracts and prepare a report as to the amount of cotton we have on hand, I believe it would be helpful. And Mr. Forbes, once you return home, any additional information you can supply will be appreciated. Please assure the plantation owners we are aware of their circumstances and will make adjustments as necessary. We can always look to foreign markets if necessary."

"Please don't move in that direction too quickly," Forbes said. "After all, with the news I've heard today, it appears that if we're to keep this country from another depression, we must conduct business within our own borders."

Nathan shifted in his chair. "I agree—whenever possible."

"And profitable," Wilson muttered.

McKinley watched Jarrod Forbes for a reaction. It didn't appear as if he'd heard Wilson Harper's rejoinder, yet McKinley knew that the remark was the mantra of the Associates. As long as the ledger was showing a marked profit, they would continue doing business with the Southern growers. But if the foreign markets could compete by producing cotton at a lower price and of equal quality, the Associates would have no loyalty to their Southern brothers. And that argument would be McKinley's defense should his father-in-law attempt to convince him he should go to the South to assist in protecting the cotton contract with the sale of The Willows.

———

Jasmine opened the top center drawer of Nolan's desk and retrieved the letter Jarrod Forbes had given her on the day of his arrival in Lowell. The edging of her lilac print day dress caught on the drawer and snagged a small hole in the fine lace. She would mend it this evening. But for now she wanted once again to read the missive. Although she had already examined the contents of the letter many times, reading her father's message soothed her. The neatly scripted words connected her to those last days before his death, providing her with a window into his final thoughts and concerns.

After carefully unfolding the letter and pressing the creases flat, Jasmine permitted herself to focus upon the final words from her father.

> My dear daughter Jasmine,
>   It is with a sad heart that I commit to paper my final thoughts. You have been my heart's delight—a daughter any man would be proud to call his own. I don't discount that we've had our disagreements from time to time, but such is to be expected in the course of rearing a child.

Now my life on this earth is drawing to an end, and I find it difficult to say the many things I wish I had said to you throughout the years. Please know that I am proud of the woman you have become and the strength you have exhibited in difficult times. It grieves me that I must now place yet another burden upon you, but you will have Nolan and McKinley at your side as you accomplish the task of settling my estate.

I trust you will be judicious in handling the bequest you will receive upon my death. It has taken our family a lifetime to amass these holdings. Therefore, I pray you and your brother will be good stewards of this bounty. Obviously, it will be imperative that you and McKinley come to The Willows and oversee the final harvest. I am not disillusioned by any thoughts that you or McKinley will return and make your home within these walls, but I trust you will both make every effort to secure a good price for the cotton and exercise due diligence in locating a purchaser who will cherish this land as I have.

Jasmine refolded the page. There was no need to read further—she'd nearly committed the letter to memory. Had her father truly believed McKinley would leave his position with the Corporation and travel to The Willows?

"So here you are, my dear," Nolan said as he took three giant strides across the expanse from the doorway to her chair and kissed the top of her head. "I thought perhaps you'd gone off to town without telling anyone."

She laughed at his comment. "I think Alice Ann or Clara would fuss loudly enough to alert the entire household if I attempted to leave."

He glanced at the folded letter. "Rereading your father's missive again?"

She nodded and gave him a feeble smile. "I read his words and feel compelled to do as he's requested, yet my anger toward McKinley won't subside. I understand his concerns over Violet and his position at the Corporation, but he acts as though none of this poses any imposition upon our family."

Nolan sat down, giving her his undivided attention. "Your brother may project that attitude, but he knows how difficult leaving Lowell will be for us. He realizes the responsibilities we have."

"If so, he hasn't indicated as much to me."

"I imagine he's dealing with a hefty portion of guilt. After all, I'm certain your father's words to McKinley were very explicit—just as they were to you. We must accept his choice."

"I've accepted his decision, but I don't respect it."

Nolan reached forward and with one finger tipped Jasmine's chin upward until he was looking into her eyes. "As long as you continue to respect your brother, you need not like his decision. Don't judge him too harshly, my love, for if I were forced to decide between my wife and my father's estate, I'd most definitely choose you. Remember, I did not always have anything to do with my family business. I disappointed my father at every turn. My brother was the one he depended on."

"And Bradley could see nothing but business," she murmured. "There ought to be a balance. Must a man choose only one or the other?"

Before he could respond, Spencer walked into the room. His lips were tightened into an angry pout, and there was a stubborn look in his eyes. "What if I live with Reggie and her father?" he asked.

A moment passed before Jasmine could completely digest what her son was requesting. "You want your father and me to leave you in the care of Pastor Chamberlain while we travel to Mississippi?"

Apparently Spencer interpreted her calm response to

mean she might actually acquiesce, for the sullen look in his eyes was now replaced by a hopeful glimmer.

"Your father and I could list a host of reasons why such an idea is completely out of the question. However, suffice it to say that you may not remain in the care of Pastor Chamberlain. You, Alice Ann, and Clara will accompany us to The Willows."

The sparkle disappeared from his eyes. "If I can't stay with them, then let me stay here at the house. The servants can look after me," he countered.

"I've already told you we will not leave you here. Besides, the only servants who don't go to their own homes every night are Martha and Henrietta, and they'll be traveling with us. Please don't make any other suggestions, Spencer—you'll only be further disappointed by our answer."

"Poppa," he said, turning his pleading face to his father.

Jasmine could see the wavering look in Nolan's eyes. They had discussed this matter at length. She knew Nolan wanted to concede—tell the boy he could remain in Simon and Maisie's care, where he and Moses could begin the school year as scheduled. But he had finally agreed they ought not divide their family. Spencer belonged with them. If need be, she argued, they could hire a tutor or Spencer could attend school in Lorman. They both knew he'd be unhappy, but they were family and Jasmine was determined they remain together.

"I'm afraid we can't grant your request this time, son," Nolan said. "Try to view this as a grand adventure. You'll have opportunities to see new things and meet new people. Moreover, this may be the final time you'll have an opportunity to visit The Willows."

Spencer turned and marched from the room without another word.

"You see!" she said, jumping up from her chair and slapping the letter onto her husband's desk. "This situation is going to destroy our family while McKinley will continue with life as usual. Yesterday Spencer hid in the woods behind the barns and sent Moses to tell me he'd run away; today he's plotting to live with Pastor Chamberlain and his daughter at the Congregational parsonage! Who can guess what tomorrow will bring."

Nolan raked his fingers through his thick hair. "I believe if we're to survive this, it's going to take a lot of prayer and a sense of humor. I'm planning to spend time with Paddy regarding the contracts that must be fulfilled while we're gone."

Jasmine sighed. "We have much to lose if anything goes amiss with our West Point contracts."

"And the new ones with the Virginia Institute. I'm thankful I insisted Paddy be involved throughout the negotiations with both schools. He knows many of the details, and although he's young, he's become an astute businessman. I don't believe anyone will take advantage of him," he added before moving to the far side of his desk.

"You remain convinced that we must travel by train?" she inquired while watching her husband unlock the bottom drawer of his desk.

Nolan pulled a thick folder from the drawer and dropped it with a gentle thud. "If we're going to arrive in time to oversee the harvest, traveling by train will be the most expeditious. Of course, we'll be required to travel the portion into Lorman by boat," he explained.

"I was thinking it would be much more comfortable for the children if we traveled by ship rather than train, but you're correct—time must control our decisions."

Nolan's fingers rippled through the pages, his attention on the folder of papers, and Jasmine knew his thoughts were now fixed upon the vital contracts they must fulfill during the next year.

———————

Paddy ran his skilled hands down the leg of one of the Houston farm's finest Arabians. The animal was one of their best, and Paddy thought he had noticed a faint limp as one of the stable hands had led the animal to the barn a short time ago. The last thing they wanted was one of their top studs developing any problems. The horse farm prided itself upon the stellar care and the resulting excellent stock bred and raised on their premises. And even though large fees had been offered from time to time, Nolan refused to have their horses used for breeding purposes at any other farm.

"I'll not have others diminish the value or beauty of our horses by breeding them with animals of a lesser quality. The money offered pales in comparison to the damage that would result from poor breeding," Nolan had maintained when Paddy had asked why he would turn down such a large amount of money.

Paddy's respect for his employer had continued to grow through the years. His childhood of hardship and suffering in Ireland seemed to diminish a little more every day. Sometimes when he talked with his sister, Kiara, he would remember bits and pieces of the past, but for the most part, he kept those thoughts tucked away where they couldn't hurt him. Life was good here in America. Paddy knew that. He heard the stories of oppression that came with each new Irishman to Lowell. Times hadn't changed in his homeland. The famine might have passed, but landlords were still cruel and the government was neglectful. Paddy wondered in all honesty if anything good could ever come to Ireland.

He shook off the thought. His life was in America—not Ireland. With the passing of time, Nolan had increased

Paddy's duties and drawn him into every aspect of the business. Nolan had given Paddy opportunities to observe negotiations and discussions to purchase and sell the horses, acquire ancillary land, and help plan the new facilities being constructed for the additional horses. Yes, Nolan Houston was a man of honor and intelligence, and Paddy counted himself fortunate to be in his employ.

"Is there a problem with Glory's Pride?"

Paddy started at the sound of Nolan's voice. "I did na hear you come in the barn, Mr. Houston. I thought I saw him limpin' a wee bit this mornin', but it appears my worries are unfounded."

Nolan frowned and moved into the stall. "I'm not doubting your assessment, but let's move him out of the stall and take a look."

"Right ya are," Paddy said as he led the horse out of the enclosure and walked him out the barn doors.

Nolan remained at a distance, watching the horse as Paddy led him in a wide circle. "I can saddle and mount him if ya like," Paddy called.

"No. I believe he looks fine. Probably only a rock in his shoe that's worked itself loose, but you might keep an eye on him. If you notice he's having problems after we're gone, have the blacksmith take a look at him."

"Don't ya be worryin'. I'll take good care of this big boy," Paddy said proudly as he patted the horse.

Nolan nodded. "If it weren't for you, I'd be hard-pressed to leave the farm, but I put great faith in you and your ability, Paddy. I'm leaving you with a great deal of responsibility, but you know we'll see that you're properly rewarded."

"Go on with ya, Mr. Houston. You and the missus already pay me more than a fair wage. Truth is, I should be paying *you* for the privilege of workin' with these fine animals."

"You'll be required to do even more while we're gone, Paddy, and if you have some time, I'd like to go over these contracts with you. Once we've discussed all of your additional duties, I doubt you'll turn down the additional wages."

"I'll be with ya as soon as I get Glory's Pride back in his stall," Paddy said as he led the horse back into the barn.

The day was warm, and the smells of hay and silage mixed with the pungent odor of the celebrated Arabians stabled inside the barn. In early spring, the farmhands had erected a crude table from old boards and sawhorses and placed it under a large elm not far from the barn. Then on days when the weather permitted, they would join together for their noonday meal around the table, sharing stories and laughing as they ate their thick slices of soda or rye bread with cheese and drank cool water from the nearby spring.

Nolan had settled himself on one of the makeshift benches and was spreading out papers across the table as Paddy drew near.

"Ya best be hopin' a breeze does na come whistlin' through the trees and send those papers flyin' about the countryside," he said with a twinkle in his dark brown eyes.

Nolan laughed but heeded the remark, placing a smooth gray rock atop one stack of papers and his hand upon the other. "I've arranged the paper work into what I hope is an intelligible order. The contracts and other documents regarding the horses that are being sold to both West Point and the Virginia Institute are in this group. I've also included the authentication papers for each of the horses. Everything is set up exactly as I've handled it in the past, so there should be no problem. You will receive a bank draft from each of the institutions as set out in their individual contracts—I've prepared a separate sheet in the ledger for you to make the accounting, and I've talked with Mr. Cameron at the bank."

Paddy ran a finger down the list of instructions and

pulled the ledger book closer. "I understand. And all I need ta do is give the draft to Mr. Cameron? Will he na be givin' me a statement of receipt for the funds?"

"Indeed he will," Nolan said, pleased by Paddy's astute question.

"And what do the gentlemen sign showing they've received their horses?"

Nolan shuffled through the papers. "This paper is what they're to sign. And if you feel uncomfortable for any reason, you can ask the men to accompany you to the bank, and Mr. Cameron will assist you in completing the paper work. In fact, if you have any financial needs, you can rely upon Albert Cameron. However, I have great faith in you, Paddy, and don't think you'll have any problem at all. I'll leave these papers in the bottom drawer of my desk, and before we depart, I'll give you the key."

Paddy pushed the dark mass of curls off his forehead and stared at Nolan. Had the man gone completely daft?

"Ya're gonna give *me* the key to your desk?"

Nolan laughed and pushed away from the wobbly table. "I trust you with the horseflesh in that barn. Those Arabian Shagyas are far more valuable than anything in my desk, Paddy. There are other matters we'll need to discuss before my departure, and you'll likely think of additional questions for me, but I wanted you to know that I have every confidence that you can handle the business in my absence."

"Thank ya, Mr. Houston. I'm honored to be helpin' ya."

Paddy swiped his hand down the leg of his breeches before shaking hands with his employer, then hastened into the barn as Nolan strode off toward the house. Grabbing a brush, he walked into a stall and began grooming Fiona's Fancy, an exceptional sorrel Shagya that he'd always considered one of their finest animals. With a smile on his face, he ran the brush through the horse's thick coat and began

TRACIE PETERSON / JUDITH MILLER

singing the old Irish lullaby Kiara had sung to him when he was a young ailing boy back in Ireland. It was the one piece of Ireland he couldn't seem to shake.

Kiara stood with her hands on her hips in a mock display of anger. "Will ya look who's finally able to darken me doorway? I do ya the honor of offering ya a good home-cooked meal, and ya can na even show up on time," she scolded.

Rogan pointed a thumb at his wife while directing his attention at his brother-in-law. "I think yar sister is a wee bit upset with ya," Rogan said with a wide grin.

"It's been quite the day, what with the Houstons planning to depart within the week. I had to have me a chat with Mr. Houston, and then I got busy with the horses," Paddy explained.

"Don't be tryin' to soften me up with yar excuses, Paddy O'Neill. Sit yarself down while I tell Nevan and Katherine to wash up for supper. We're nearly starvin' to death waitin' on ya," Kiara said as she removed her apron.

Paddy embraced his sister and laughed. "Ya do na look to me like ya're starving to death."

Kiara laughed and slapped his arm with the apron. "Do na forget, I'm eating for two." She pulled loose and marched out of the room.

"Do ya think she's truly upset that I'm late?" Paddy asked as he and Rogan sat down at the table.

Rogan shook his head back and forth. "She's thinkin' Bridgett will be comin' and she won't have the dishes washed before she arrives. I told her to quit her frettin', that she could have little Katherine or Nevan wash the dishes. Somehow she did na think havin' our four-year-old daughter or seven-year-old son washin' her best dishes was a good idea."

"Then it may be up to me since I'm the one who was late. Of course, I do na think she'll entrust her dishes to me either," Paddy said with a laugh.

"Oh, but I will," Kiara said as she walked into the room. "Ya best be hopin' Bridgett is tardy also!"

"Uncle Paddy!" the children hollered in unison.

Paddy stood to hug his niece and nephew and then quickly directed them to their chairs. "We must eat with the greatest of speed tonight," he told them. "Perhaps we should have a contest to see who can eat the fastest."

"Stop that nonsense or they'll be choking down their food, thinkin' it's the proper thing to do," Kiara warned. "Just remember, ya're still my *little* brother—I'm sure I can find a proper punishment if ya're gonna misbehave."

Nevan and Katherine peeked at him from beneath their thick dark lashes, a smile dancing upon Nevan's lips.

"Ya're pleased it's me instead of yarself that yar mother's givin' a tongue lashin', aren't ya?" Paddy asked with an exaggerated wink.

"Aye and ya best be careful or she'll yank yar ear if ya do not mind yar manners," Nevan replied. Although he spoke with the same Irish brogue of his ancestors, Nevan's American birth toned the drawl down quite a bit. Paddy thought he almost sounded comical, but would never have told the boy such a thing.

Katherine bobbed her head. "And Nevan should know best about that. Ma says he has the manners of the pigs sloppin' at the trough."

Paddy's and Rogan's merry laughs and the smell of Kiara's tantalizing meat pie filled the room. "I fixed the special butter sauce ya like on yar meat pie," Kiara said to Paddy.

His nose tilted heavenward, and he inhaled deeply like a dog sniffing its prey. "And is that yar special sweet peas with mint?" He eyed the covered serving dish as she placed it in front of him.

"Aye—and mushrooms in cream sauce," she added, nodding toward another bowl.

He rubbed his hands together. "I can hardly wait to begin."

"Not until we give thanks," Kiara warned as she sat down.

The five of them joined hands and Rogan led them in prayer—less eloquent and briefer than Kiara would probably have liked but nonetheless duly thankful for the food that God had provided and Kiara had superbly prepared. Paddy added a hasty amen to the prayer and immediately spooned a generous serving of mushrooms onto his plate.

"So when do ya think the Houstons will be returnin'?" Rogan inquired.

"Hard tellin'," Paddy replied after swallowing a forkful of the meat pie. "This is mighty good," he said, using his fork to point at the dish.

Kiara smiled and nodded. "So Mr. Houston's plannin' to leave you in charge of the horses while he's gone?"

Paddy's chest swelled with pride. "Aye. And he told Mr. Cameron at the bank that he's to deal directly with me. And he gave me the key to his desk."

"It's proud I am of ya, Paddy," she said. "But I'm *still* not excusin' ya for being late to supper."

The children giggled at their mother's retort, and Paddy winked at them. The two of them were a delight—with dark lashes that matched their tawny brown curls and eyes the soft brown shade of a hazelnut. Katherine possessed her mother's lovely face and kind disposition, while Nevan was brave and puckish like his father.

Katherine leaned close to Paddy, her chubby cheeks made even fuller by her wide smile. "We're havin' nut cake for dessert," she whispered to her uncle with a gleam in her eyes.

"And were ya thinkin' ya might want to have yar uncle Paddy eat yar piece?" Paddy asked in a hushed voice.

Katherine rubbed her tummy while wagging her head back and forth. "I have enough room for me cake."

Rogan laughed and ruffled Katherine's hair. "Ya'll have yar share of trouble gettin' sweets away from this one, Paddy."

They finished their supper, and while Kiara cleared and washed the dishes, the men settled on the front porch and watched as Nevan and Katherine attempted to capture fireflies in the front yard.

"Looks like that's me cousin Bridgett headin' this direction," Rogan said, using his pipe as a pointer, a curl of smoke rising from it.

"And who's that with her?" Paddy asked.

Rogan shook his head and squinted. "I do na think I know the lass," he replied as Kiara stepped out the door and joined them on the porch.

"Bridgett said she might be bringin' along one of the girls from work," Kiara informed her husband and brother.

"Does she attend St. Patrick's?" Rogan asked.

"I do na know. She's new to Lowell and to the mills. I think Bridgett has taken a likin' to her."

Paddy watched from the porch as the twosome drew closer. Bridgett was gesturing wildly, and her lips were moving as rapidly as water pouring over the falls. Except for aging a bit, Bridgett hadn't changed much since Paddy and Kiara had first met her aboard the ship on their voyage to America. Bridgett, with her auburn hair and fiery temper, had been delighted when she learned Paddy and Kiara were traveling to the same town in Massachusetts. The three of them had been shipmates and then journeyed on to Lowell, where Bridgett moved into the Acre with Rogan and her granna Murphy, and Kiara and Paddy headed off in another direction to become indentured servants.

"It seems a lifetime ago since we first met Bridgett . . . and yet only yesterday," Paddy said to his sister.

"Aye, yet I'm happy to be livin' in the present and not the past."

Paddy nodded knowingly. "I hear Bridgett has finally got herself engaged."

"I'm makin' her weddin' veil and the lace for her gown," Kiara said. "She's wantin' to take a wee look at what I've got finished."

"A wee look? The last time me cousin came for a wee look, she was here for three hours," Rogan said with a hearty laugh. "So if there's any talkin' ya're wantin' to do with yar sister, ya best be speakin' up in a hurry."

Bridgett waved as she and her friend turned onto the flower-lined path leading to the front steps. "Sounds as though ya're havin' a merry time. We could hear ya laughin' a half-mile away."

"Do na be telling a fib afore ya ever reach the front door, Bridgett Farrell," Rogan called out to his cousin.

" 'Tis the truth I'm speakin' and ya know it fer certain," Bridgett said as she reached the front porch. "This is me friend, Mary Margaret O'Flannery. She's na yet been given her own looms, but she's training with me at the mill. Mr. Dempsey's been watchin' her, and he said she'd likely be on her own in another week," Bridgett announced, beaming at her new friend. "Mary Margaret, this is me cousin Rogan Sheehan and his wife, Kiara. This fine-lookin' lad is Kiara's brother, Padraig O'Neill. And the two lovelies out there catchin' fireflies are Nevan and Katherine."

"Pleased to make yar acquaintance," Kiara said while the others echoed. "Perhaps we can sit out here where it's a wee bit cooler than in the house."

Paddy watched as Mary Margaret sat down beside Bridgett on the carved wooden bench. She was a pretty lass, with long, slender fingers as creamy and white as a piece of ivory and thick auburn hair that had been fashioned into a braid and coiled atop her head.

"Do ya find the mills to be to yar likin', Mary Margaret?" Rogan asked.

"Aye. 'Tis true it's hot and humid inside the mills, but the pay is good, and if I get me own looms, I won't be complainin' about conditions. Bridgett tells me ya're a stone carver."

"Aye. Liam Donohue taught me the trade, and he's a far better carver. But together we're managin' a fine business."

"I took her through the cemetery on our way here," Bridgett put in, "and showed her the headstones you and Liam have carved with the shamrocks."

Rogan laughed. "And did ya show her the ones carved by the Yankees? They tried to carve shamrocks, but their shamrocks turned out lookin' more like trees. Back then, the Yanks had na seen what a shamrock looked like—but at least they tried to engrave somethin' that resembled one."

"And what do ya think of Lowell?" Kiara inquired. "Are ya findin' it altogether fine?"

"'Tis nice enough, I suppose."

At least ten questions popped into Paddy's head that he wanted to ask Miss Mary Margaret O'Flannery, but before he'd had a chance to ask even one, Bridgett called a halt to the visiting and insisted that the ladies go inside.

"I'm thinkin' it might be cool enough to step inside for a few minutes," she said. "It's anxious I am to be seein' what ya've accomplished on my veil and the lace for my dress."

"It's anxious ya are to be *married*," Rogan retorted with a broad grin. "I think Granna Murphy was beginnin' to think she'd never see ya put yar bottom drawer of linens and finery to use."

"Stop with yar teasin'—I'm na yet thirty, and a good single man is na easy to find in these parts. And ya need na be worryin' yarself over my bottom drawer. Every last piece of my finery will be put to *good* use."

"Ya best keep that information in mind, Mary Margaret. It pays for a lass to keep a sharp eye for a good lad," Rogan said. He slapped a palm to his forehead. "In fact—ya might want to remember that Paddy is an upstanding lad who's still not found him a lass to call his own. Isn't that right, Paddy?"

Paddy felt the blood rush to his cheeks and shot a quick look at Mary Margaret, who had visibly blanched to the shade of pale parchment. Fearing the lass might faint, Paddy moved to her side and supported her with one arm.

"Ya need na pay Rogan any heed. The man enjoys causin' others discomfort. Let me help ya to a chair inside, and once ya sit down, I'll fetch ya a glass of cool water," Paddy said, leading her into the house.

Paddy glanced over his shoulder at Rogan as he escorted Mary Margaret inside. Rogan gave him an exaggerated wink. "Ya can thank me later," Rogan whispered loudly enough for all of them to hear. "If yar na havin' that weddin' too soon, Bridgett, maybe Paddy and Mary Margaret could join you and Cullen at the altar and have ya a double weddin'," he added with a loud guffaw.

Paddy gazed heavenward and wondered if the meat pie and nut cake he'd eaten only a short time ago were worth the embarrassment of the moment. And poor Mary Margaret—she'd not even had the pleasure of Kiara's cooking before being subjected to Rogan's torment!

CHAPTER · 5

THE WHITE COTTON curtains fluttered at the window as a breeze drifted into the kitchen of Elinor's boardinghouse. Although she'd mixed and set the bread dough to rise before the girls departed for the mills, the kitchen had already become uncomfortably warm when she finally placed the loaves in the oven. After wiping her hands on a linen towel, she removed her stained apron and tossed it atop the wooden worktable. If she hurried, she would have time to take a cool, damp cloth to her face and properly fashion her hair before the girls arrived for the noonday meal.

Unbraiding her hair as she walked down the hallway, she stopped short as a knock sounded at the door. Holding her unbridled tresses in one hand, she stared at the door. "Who could that be?" she muttered.

For a brief moment, she contemplated ignoring the unwelcome interruption but finally yielded. A new boarder might be standing on the other side of the door, and she could certainly use the additional funds. Still holding tightly to her loosened hair, she yanked the door open with her free hand. Her mouth went dry. Oh, why hadn't she ignored the knock?

Justin Chamberlain stood across the threshold, staring at her. His lips were moving, but the only sound that she heard was the roaring noise in her head. After his lips stopped moving, he smiled and waited.

Utterly embarrassed by her unkempt appearance, Elinor stood rooted to the floor, unable to speak. After all, what respectable woman would answer the door in such disarray? It wasn't until the pastor had turned and stepped down off the small stoop that she finally found her voice.

"Please! Wait! I apologize. I didn't expect to see you when I opened the door. I thought perhaps it was a boarder that had come looking for a room. I was going to my rooms to brush my hair. I don't usually wait until so late in the morning to prepare myself for the day," she hastily explained.

Her words flowed forth like a babbling brook, and Justin grinned as he returned. "I'm the one who should apologize. It was rude of me to appear on your doorstep without first inquiring when it would be convenient to come calling. However, I find myself in a dilemma. I've been praying for an answer to my problem and you came to mind. Not that you should . . . well, that is . . . consider yourself a-a . . . divine answer to my prayer and feel . . . well . . . compelled to fulfill my request," he hastened to add.

He was stammering and tripping over his words, and now Elinor smiled at him. "Come in, Pastor Chamberlain." She stepped back to allow him entry. "I promise I won't feel duty bound to carry out your request if you'll promise to overlook my untidy appearance,"

"You don't look untidy in the least."

The pastor was stretching the truth with his kind remark, but at least his words helped ease her self-consciousness. She directed him to the parlor and then said, "If you'll excuse me for one moment, I'll find a ribbon to tie back my hair; then I'll join you. Do be seated."

Moments later, Elinor rejoined the pastor, who, instead of sitting, was pacing back and forth in front of the faded settee. "You could quickly wear out a carpet with your pacing," she said lightheartedly. "How may I help you?"

Justin immediately ceased his pacing and sat down opposite her, hunching forward and resting his arms atop his thighs. Beads of perspiration dotted his forehead. The poor man appeared to be at a complete loss as to how he should begin speaking to her.

"Is there a committee at the church you need me to assist with?" she asked, hoping to aid him.

"No. In truth, this has nothing to do with the church. Things are going as well as can be expected. It's generally difficult when a congregation must adjust to a new preacher—and his daughter," he added.

"And even more difficult for the preacher and his daughter to adjust to a new community, I would guess."

"Not so difficult for me. I was ready for a change. But the move has been more challenging for Reggie."

"Most people say that children easily adapt to change, and I suppose to some extent that is true. But for some it proves a difficult task. Reggie is a charming young lady, and eventually she will find her niche here in Lowell. You must give her time."

Justin appeared to relax and settled his weight against the back of the cushioned chair. "Reggie is the reason I've come to speak with you." His voice cracked.

"There is some problem? Has she taken ill?"

"No, nothing so easily solved as a visit to the doctor," he replied. "This matter is a bit more complex. When you visited the parsonage with Reggie, you may have noticed the house was rather sparsely furnished."

"Well, yes, but Reggie told me the remainder of your household goods were in Maine and that you would be going back to retrieve them before summer's end."

"Exactly—and therein lies my problem. I should have returned to Maine before now, but the timing never seemed proper. And now school will soon begin. I must go after our belongings before winter sets in, yet I don't want Reggie to miss school, especially the beginning of the school year. I fear that being gone when school begins will only make her adjustment more difficult."

Elinor tucked an errant strand of hair behind one ear. "I agree."

They stared at each other for a moment, and Elinor suddenly realized the preacher's dilemma. "You want Reggie to live here at the boardinghouse while you go to Maine?"

"I know it's a great deal to ask, what with all your other responsibilities here at the boardinghouse and throughout the community. Preparing a little girl for school each morning when you're already busy cooking three substantial meals for your boarders and . . ." His voice trailed off.

She tapped her finger across her lips and thought for a moment. "Do you think it might be more suitable to have Reggie live with someone who has children—perhaps a girl her own age?"

"I truly understand your reluctance to take on such a responsibility," he said.

"I'm not averse to the arrangement; I was merely wondering if your daughter would be happier and adjust more easily if she were with other children."

Justin folded his hands and met her gaze. "You went fishing with Reggie, and she tells me she's stopped by on a couple of occasions to visit you."

Elinor nodded.

"Then I'm certain you realize Reggie is not a child who

makes friends with other young ladies—she's not a girl who fancies learning how to set a proper table or dress in the latest fashions. She likely would choose to stay with the Houston family, but they've already departed Lowell. Besides, I probably would not have made such a request of folks who aren't members of the church. To do such a thing would surely have caused tongues to wag," he said with a weary expression.

"Having difficulty with a few of our opinionated church members, Pastor?" She smiled.

"Some of the good ladies of the church think Reggie lacks the proper social graces. And I must admit they are probably correct. I hadn't given much thought to the fact that she's growing up and some of her behavior is inappropriate for a young lady."

Elinor brushed a smudge of flour from the skirt of her utilitarian gray cotton dress. "Don't permit Martha Emory or Nancy Sanders to force their rigid standards upon you. Childhood is precious. Reggie has ample time to learn the etiquette of a proper young lady. She'll develop an interest when the time is right for her."

"I suppose you're correct, but Reggie can be quite a handful from time to time."

"Are you attempting to convince me I should tell you no?" she asked with a broad smile.

"No, not at all. Yet I don't want to . . . well, take ad-advantage of you, as I know you've truly m-more than enough to keep you busy," he stammered.

"'Tis true I tend to keep busy," she replied. "However, one more girl in the house ought not pose a great deal more work. I have time in the evenings when I can assist Reggie with her school lessons, and I think hearing about the mills from my boarders will interest her."

"So you're agreeable to the arrangement?"

"Only if you gain Reggie's approval. I do understand that you're faced with a difficult predicament, but if Reggie is forced to come live with me, I fear we'll both be unhappy. However, you may tell her that I would be most delighted if she would agree to come visit for the duration of your journey. In fact, if it will relieve any anxiety she may have, tell her that she is welcome to stop by and visit with me about the arrangement."

Justin beamed and exhaled a deep breath. "I'm relieved to know you are willing to entertain the possibility. And I'll pay you the rate you would receive for a boarder and an extra five cents a day for checking her schoolwork," he added hastily.

"No need to match a boarder's rate, Pastor. I'll have Reggie reside in my rooms. Otherwise, I'd be required to seek permission from the Corporation to have her stay in the house. This way, I'll neither be giving up boarding space nor be required to obtain consent from anyone."

"Yet you'll be preparing her food and seeing to her laundry and other needs. I insist."

Elinor glanced at the clock. "First we must gain Regina's approval. Then we can decide upon the remaining details. However, the girls will soon be arriving for the noonday meal, and I must see to my hair and finish preparing their food."

The words had barely been uttered when Justin jumped up from the settee as though he'd been struck by a volley of buckshot. "Forgive me. Not only have I come to your home uninvited and unannounced, but I've also detained you far beyond any reasonable expectation."

A laugh escaped Elinor's lips. "No need to rebuke yourself so harshly. I've enjoyed our visit and look forward to Reggie's answer. When would you plan to depart for Maine?" She followed him to the door.

"If at all possible, I'd like to leave immediately following church services next week. I haven't mentioned my departure to the church elders, but I've been in contact with a Congregational preacher, Arthur Conklin, who will be arriving in Lowell next Friday. He sent me a letter shortly after I arrived in Lowell and stated he's interested in spending time in our fair city. Seems he's visited England and now wants to draw some comparisons between our textile community and some of those he toured while across the sea—says he's writing an essay regarding the impact of the textile mills on homes in America and abroad."

"Doesn't sound like overly fascinating reading material," Elinor said with a giggle.

"No, I don't suppose it does. However, he's agreed to preach in my stead in exchange for use of the parsonage during my absence, and I am in hopes the elders will be agreeable to the idea. Of course, I wanted to have proper arrangements for Reggie before firming up the plans with the elders, although I've told Reverend Conklin he's welcome to come and stay at the parsonage in any event," Justin said as he opened the front door.

"That's most kind of you. I'll look forward to hearing Reggie's decision."

Elinor closed the front door and raced through her sitting room and into the bedroom, pulling the ribbon from her hair as she ran. One glance in the small mirror that hung over her dressing table gave her a start. She looked a fright. Damp strands of hair clung to her forehead, and a streak of flour lined her cheek. Too late to fret, she silently admonished herself. If she didn't hurry, her bread would be ruined and there would be no food on the table for the noonday meal.

"You seem happy," Lucinda said as she hurried into the house a short time later.

Elinor agreed. "Indeed! It's a beautiful day, and all is well with the world," she said while rushing back and forth, retrieving bowls of food from the kitchen.

Lucinda and Ardith stared at her as though she'd gone daft, but Elinor didn't care. She continued to smile and was singing when the girls left the house to return to work. Perhaps it was the thought of having Reggie come and stay with her. The child would break the monotonous routine of her life, and that prospect held great appeal.

"Please make her anxious to come and spend time with me, Lord," she uttered aloud before she continued singing the first stanza of "All Hail the Power of Jesus' Name."

Jasmine sighed as she settled into her mother's beloved rocking chair in the parlor. The journey to Mississippi had taken its toll on all of them—especially the children. They hadn't adapted to their new surroundings as smoothly as Jasmine and Nolan had hoped. Many tears had been shed since departing Massachusetts, but Jasmine continued to believe they would soon adjust.

Shadows were growing long across the willow-lined driveway leading to the Wainwright mansion when a knock sounded at the front door. Jasmine placed her mending in the basket beside her chair and hurried to the door.

She squinted in the early evening dimness. "Rupert Hesston? Is that you?"

"Has it been so long you've forgotten what I look like?"

She laughed and stepped back to permit him entry. "It *has* been a long time, but you haven't changed so much that I wouldn't recognize you. The lighting is inadequate," she added.

"Well, I must say that *you* have changed dramatically. The years have been very good to you, Jasmine. But you always were a beauty. Did you know that when I was around eighteen years old, I attempted to convince our mothers we weren't truly related so that I could call on you?"

"No, Mother never mentioned such a thing."

For some reason, Rupert's remark made her feel uncomfortable. Perhaps because Nolan had gone to visit with their overseer, Mr. Draper, and hadn't yet returned. Silly! Rupert was, after all, a distant cousin on her mother's side and McKinley's closest friend during their childhood years. In fact, he was now related to her on both sides of the family, for he had married Lydia Wainwright, one of Uncle Franklin's daughters and Jasmine's full cousin.

"Come join me in the parlor. Nolan and I were going to visit you once we were a bit more settled here at The Willows. I apologize for my tardiness. There's no excuse for not immediately calling upon you to express my condolences. Please forgive me."

"No need for an apology. I can only imagine the difficulty of having to return under these circumstances. The harshness of this epidemic has been dramatic among our families and friends. Thankfully, Lydia was in Europe and escaped the illness, and I suppose I'm just too ornery to die."

"Are there any other family members who survived?"

"Lydia is your uncle Franklin's only survivor, though one of your uncle Harry's grandchildren lived. I believe the boy has gone to make his home with a relative in Tennessee. Lydia might have been delighted to rear the child had she been here to make her wishes known. I truly despair over the thought of delivering so much bad news."

"She doesn't know?"

"She sailed for Europe in early June. She had no set itinerary, and although she has written to me, it's impossible to send word back. There is nothing she could have done, and had she returned home earlier, she might have contracted the fever herself. Like you, she'll have to deal with the shock, yet she won't be forced to feel helpless and watch as her family dies."

His words were a painful reminder of the horror Jasmine had been attempting to set aside ever since she'd arrived at The Willows. "I'll look forward to seeing Lydia upon her return. Please tell her to call on me or send word if there is anything she needs," Jasmine offered.

"That's very kind of you. And what of my good friend and cousin McKinley? Did he return to Mississippi with you?"

"No. Like you, I had hoped he would accompany us. However, he found it impossible to do so at this time. His position and family . . ." Her words trailed off into silence.

Rupert stared at her as though he expected her to say more, but when she remained silent, he said, "I recall your father telling me McKinley had married into the textile industry."

Jasmine was taken aback by the comment. "Married into the textile industry? I find it hard to believe my father would make such a comment."

He brushed the end of his dark brown mustache with his fingers. "Not exactly his words, I suppose, but I do recall Malcolm mentioning the fact that McKinley's father-in-law held a lofty standing within the textile industry and that McKinley had accepted a position with the mills. Hard to believe."

Had she detected a note of disdain in his voice? Rupert had always been judgmental and derisive, even as a young boy.

"How so?" she inquired. "Do you think McKinley ill-equipped for such responsibility?"

"Not at all. He is bright—there was never a question of his intelligence. In fact, he made the rest of us look like dolts.

What surprises me is his ability to embrace Northern ideals and attitudes. Of course, he had the influence of both you and his grandmother Wainwright. And I suppose when he fell in love with a Northern girl, it became easier to turn against his Southern heritage. He's probably embarrassed to return."

Jasmine narrowed her eyes as she attempted to keep her anger in check. "Neither McKinley nor I have turned against our Southern heritage. There are aspects of Southern life we do not embrace. However, we are not embarrassed by our beliefs. Rather, we are proud of them, Rupert."

The sound of the children clattering down the stairs caused Jasmine to turn her attention away from her guest. The diversion gave her a moment to calm herself. She needed to control her temper. Nolan had cautioned her they would be better served by remaining friendly with their Southern neighbors and divulging as little information as possible regarding their future plans.

"Come here, children. I'd like you to meet one of our relatives," she said as the three children were escorted into the parlor by Martha and Henrietta.

"Rupert, these are our children, Spencer, Alice Ann, and Clara. This is my cousin Rupert Hesston," she told the children.

Rupert smiled at the girls and shook Spencer's hand as though he were a grown man. Spencer's chest swelled beneath his cotton nightshirt.

"We're off to the kitchen for some milk," Martha said.

"And cookies," Alice Ann added with a broad smile that dimpled her cheeks.

"Lovely family," Rupert said as he watched the children leave with the two women. "Only whites working in the house now? What's happened to your father's house slaves?"

Jasmine dug the tips of her fingernails deep into her

palms and forced a demure expression. "Many of the house slaves died during the epidemic. Martha and Henrietta accompanied us from our home in Lowell. They have been in our employ for many years, and our children are comfortable in their care."

"But what of the others? I know there were some who survived, for I visited The Willows both while your father was ill and after his death. Did you relegate them to the slave quarters?"

Before she could answer, Nolan bounded through the front door and strode into the parlor. "I saw the horse out front and wondered who had come calling," he said, looking first at Rupert and then at his wife.

"Nolan," she sighed, relieved to have an ally. "I don't believe you've ever met Rupert Hesston, a distant cousin and Lydia's husband."

Nolan stepped forward and shook hands with their guest. "No, I don't believe I've had the pleasure. Although I do recall hearing your name mentioned. You and McKinley were friends as young boys, weren't you?"

"Indeed! We were inseparable, though different as night and day. I was in town earlier today and one of the locals mentioned some of the family had returned from up North. I hurried over, hoping that McKinley had returned. Of course, I'm pleased to see Jasmine also," he hastily added.

Nolan gave a hearty laugh. "I understand completely. I know McKinley would be pleased to see you also, but circumstances prevented him from being here. And how is Lydia faring?"

"I was telling your wife a bit earlier that Lydia will be returning from Europe in the very near future. I know she'll be pleased to see Jasmine, as they were dear friends during their younger years. How are you managing with your crop? Any problems getting the slaves to work for Mr. Draper?

Always difficult when you have to put a new overseer in place, especially during a crisis," he said.

"Things are going as well as can be expected under the circumstances. Mr. Draper is trying his best to meet my expectations."

Rupert nodded and stood up. "I didn't plan to stay long this evening but wanted to come by and see if there was anything I could do to help."

"That's kind of you. I'll be certain to send word if we need assistance," Nolan said as he grasped Jasmine by the arm and walked to the foyer.

"Thank you for calling on us, and please tell Lydia to send word when she arrives home," Jasmine said as they bid her cousin good-bye.

The twosome remained on the front porch until Rupert was well out of sight and they could no longer hear the sound of galloping hooves.

"There's something about him," Jasmine told her husband. "Something that sets my teeth on edge."

"Are you sure it's not the setting you've been forced to deal with?" he questioned sympathetically.

She shook her head, her focus still fixed to the road. "No, it's not just that. Rupert embodies an attitude that we shall be forced to face head-on before long. Once the community gives us time to settle in and mourn, they will descend upon us with their comments and reprimands," she said sadly. She drew a deep breath and blew it out again. "Mark my words. We shall soon reap their judgment."

Jasmine leaned down and pulled several weeds from the mound of dry dirt covering her father's grave before she placed a bouquet of wild flowers near the joint headstone. The marker had been carved and set in place at the time of her mother's death and forced her to accept the reality that both of her parents were now gone from this world.

"We'll need to have the engraver carve the date of death," Jasmine told her family in a trembling voice as she wiped a tear from her cheek.

"Why are you crying, Mama?" Alice Ann's lips quivered as she asked the question.

"I'm sad because your grandpa Wainwright died and I won't see him again," she said, feeling the sting of her words.

"But we'll see him in heaven, won't we?"

"Yes, dear. My sadness is that I must wait until then to see him again."

"But you always tell me that I'll be more grateful when I must wait for something."

Nolan and Jasmine exchanged a smile. "You are exactly right," Jasmine said. "Enough of this sadness. Let's go back to the house."

"Can I go fishing?" Spencer asked.

The journey to Mississippi had been exhausting, and Spencer's attitude since their arrival had improved little. He refused to be happy, except when he was at the small pond with his fishing pole. Thus far, school in Lorman was a fiasco. The school term had started nearly two weeks earlier than it would in Lowell. As if to punctuate his unhappiness, Spencer had become a constant source of trouble for the schoolmaster, and Jasmine and Nolan were daily receiving reports of his mischievous behavior.

"Be sure you return in time to wash up for supper," Jasmine instructed, thankful it was Saturday and she wasn't forced to deny his request.

He ran off without a reply, his feet pounding through the grassy meadow that surrounded the family cemetery. Jasmine took Alice Ann's hand and strode alongside her husband, who had hoisted Clara into his arms.

"I'm concerned about Spencer," she said to her husband. "He seems to be intent upon remaining unhappy."

"And making the rest of us unhappy in the process," Nolan agreed. "Yet I must admit, with all of the problems we've encountered here at the plantation, I've had little time to listen to his woes, which I fear only adds to his anger. It seems the little time I have with him is spent chastising him about his unpleasant behavior and poor performance in school."

"I'm hoping that once we've finalized arrangements for the additional workers and actually begun the harvest, things will slow down somewhat."

Nolan gave her a feeble smile and nodded. "I've asked the overseer to assemble the slaves Monday morning to tell them of our decision. I think it would be good if you were with me so they know that we are in agreement."

"Yes, of course. Martha can look after Alice Ann and Clara, and I'll have Henrietta make sure Spencer gets off to school on time. Have you advised Mr. Draper of our plans?"

Clara struggled to free herself from Nolan's arms and he soon stooped down and set her on her feet. She toddled alongside him while holding tightly to his finger. "No. I haven't decided if I can trust him to keep a confidence, and it's best the slaves hear the plans from us first."

"No doubt Mr. Draper will be as surprised as the slaves."

"Probably more so," Nolan said. "While Mr. Draper realizes we don't believe in slavery, I'm sure he has no idea we would actually free all of them."

"I only hope they'll agree to what we're offering. Otherwise, there's no way we'll be able to get the cotton harvested."

Clara released her father's finger, plopped down on the grass, and then raised her outstretched arms. "Tired of walking, are you?" he asked, lifting her high in the air and circling around until she giggled before setting her back on the grass. Nolan turned toward Jasmine, his countenance now more serious. "And what is the worst thing that could happen if we failed to bring in the crop?"

"I'd feel as though I'd failed to carry out my father's last wish," she ruefully admitted.

Nolan wrapped her in an embrace. "I don't believe your father would be supportive of our plans to free the slaves, so it's time you ceased being so hard on yourself. Nothing in our lives is dependent upon this crop."

Jasmine leaned back and looked into her husband's eyes. "Perhaps not, but if we are to carry out our plan and give the slaves their freedom, they'll need the money to establish themselves up north. Giving them freedom without any means to support themselves as they attempt to begin a new life is tantamount to setting them up for failure. Wouldn't you agree?"

"Of course. However, worrying is not going to change one thing. I believe the slaves will quickly realize that they are actually working as freed men to bring in this crop. I don't think there will be many who will choose to immediately leave the plantation. If they do, we can point out the difficulties they'll face and wish them well. And there may even be some who will be afraid to leave, especially the house servants."

She knew her husband was correct. Worry would serve no purpose but to render her useless. They were, after all, doing the proper thing by freeing their slaves. Surely God would see them through any difficulties that might lie ahead.

Alice Ann skipped off toward the house, and her younger sister raced on her chubby legs to catch up.

"After the announcement is made tomorrow, I'll talk to Prissy," Jasmine said as the two followed their children. "Since the day we arrived in Mississippi, she's talked openly with me. Perhaps she'll be willing to tell me what the reaction is in the slave quarters—especially if there's any backlash from the other plantations. By the way, did I tell you she and Toby plan to marry?"

"No. Somehow, it doesn't seem possible Toby should be old enough to wed."

"He was small for his age when he was young," she said, "but he's come into his own as a young man. He's eighteen now."

"Interestingly, Toby made a deep impression upon me when I visited Mississippi for the very first time. More than anyone other than you, I remember the first time I saw Toby here at The Willows."

"Truly? Tell me," Jasmine said.

"At supper the evening my brother and I arrived at the plantation, Toby was—"

"On the swing above the table stirring a breeze and fanning away the flies."

"Exactly. And I recall how he waved to you and flashed his big toothy grin from his perch."

"And how he'd fall asleep on that swing. Yet I recall only one time when he dropped his fan. Thinking back on his young life saddens me. How irresponsible and unfeeling to have a young child performing such a task. Can you imagine one of our children relegated to such a duty?"

"I truly cannot. However, we can't change what's happened in the past. All we can do is hope to change the future. It pleases me to know Toby has found someone to love, and Prissy seems a fine choice. If our decision to free the slaves should cause problems among the slaves on other plantations, I believe we can rely upon both Toby and Prissy to advise us."

As they rode side-by-side to the slave quarters on Monday morning, Nolan gave his wife a sidelong glance. She rode with a beauty and grace that made any horse appear stately.

"Not quite like riding one of our own horses," he said, hoping she would relax if he talked about horses rather than the announcement they would shortly make to the slaves.

"No, but she's a good animal with fine lines," Jasmine replied. "Father always bought good horseflesh—not Arabians like ours, but good stock all the same."

They rode on in silence until they reached the overseer's home, where the slaves stood congregated in one giant huddle. Most—especially the women—appeared frightened. A few angry faces peered at them as they dismounted, and the remainder seemed completely indifferent.

Nolan and Jasmine walked up the steps of the overseer's house and stood on the porch in order to be more easily seen and heard.

"Are you certain you want me to speak?" Nolan asked as they moved to the railing along the porch.

"Yes. If I speak, they'll still wonder if you are truly in agreement with my decision. There would be fear you might convince me to change my mind."

"Then stand beside me as I speak so they know we are united," Nolan said before turning to look into the sea of dark faces. "Thank you for coming out here this morning."

The overseer leaned toward Nolan. "They wasn't given no choice 'bout where they'd be this morning or any other morning," he said before spitting a stream of tobacco juice over the railing.

Nolan ignored the remark. "We asked Mr. Draper to have you assemble here this morning because we have an announcement to make. We know you've been concerned about what will happen to The Willows and to you and your families since Mr. Wainwright's death."

He scanned the assembled group but saw nothing except wary eyes staring back in return. No one said a word—they simply watched him and waited.

"As you may or may not know, neither Mrs. Houston nor I believe in slavery. In addition, her brother, McKinley Wainwright, who is the joint heir to The Willows, does not believe in owning slaves either. It's for that reason we've asked you to assemble here today. First, we want you to know that we are going to sign your papers, and all of you will become freed men, women, and children."

There was a gasp and a low rumbling among the group, but when Nolan motioned with one hand, the group again fell silent.

"You also realize there is a cotton crop that needs to be harvested. This leaves us in something of a dilemma, but we hope we've found a solution that will be acceptable to you. Each person who chooses to remain at The Willows and help pick the cotton will receive payment for his work so that when you leave here, you can travel north and have enough money to sustain you until you find some form of employment. Please understand that you are not required to remain. You will be freed whether you choose to stay or leave, but we hope you will see it is in your best interest to remain until the crop is harvested. Do you have any questions?"

No one spoke.

"Surely you must have some questions. Please don't be afraid to ask—there will be no more whips or dogs on this plantation. You have the right to inquire about your future."

"If we don' wanna stay and help with da cotton, when you gonna give us dis here freedom?" one of the men shouted from among the crowd.

"Miss Jasmine has already signed your papers. We will be

giving them to you before you walk away from this gathering. What you decide to do about your future is then in your own hands," Nolan replied.

Jasmine motioned for the overseer to move a wooden table off the porch. Nolan carried a bench, and Jasmine followed the two men as they situated the table in front of the crowd. Nolan pulled a sheaf of papers from his satchel and handed them to his wife.

"As I call your name," she told them, "please come forward and I'll hand you your papers. I apologize if I call the names of the deceased, but I do not have a list of those who were struck by the epidemic. However, a family member is entitled to the papers of any deceased relative."

"John Marcus," she called.

A muscular broad-shouldered slave stepped forward and neared the table.

"I need you to place your mark on this ledger page, which shows I have released you. That way we both have a record that you once were a slave at The Willows but are now free," Jasmine explained.

Nolan watched as the slave leaned over the table and made his mark. John's eyes were filled with disbelief and anticipation as Jasmine handed him a paper stating he was now a freed man.

"I's mighty thankful, Missus," he said, clasping the paper to his powerful chest. He held the paper high in the air and the crowd roared their approval. "I be stayin' to help with dat cotton," he said with a wide grin.

One by one, the slaves stepped forward, received their papers, and returned to the crowd as freed men and women—no longer subject to the whims of a white master. When the last paper had been signed, Nolan asked for a show of hands of those who planned to immediately leave. There were only two—a young man and woman who said they'd take their chances without the additional money.

"You can either begin work today or wait until tomorrow morning. It's your choice," Nolan said.

"Is you gonna keep count on how much we pick an' pay us accordin' to our work?" one of the men inquired.

"Yes. Since Mr. Draper won't be needed to oversee you in the fields, he'll weigh what you pick and keep a ledger account of it—and please don't put any rocks in your bags," Nolan said. "It won't be me but your fellow workers who will find your actions unfair. You'll be cheating them by receiving more than your share of the money."

"I's goin' out there and get started right now," John Marcus announced.

They watched the crowd disassemble, most of them hurrying off to retrieve their canvas picking bags.

Wendell Draper carried the table and chair back up the steps to the porch. "May I speak freely, Mr. Houston?"

"Of course."

"Old Mr. Wainwright was a good man. He treated his slaves better than most. Personally, I think you're making a mistake by setting these slaves free. Ain't my decision, of course, but they're better off right here than they'll be trying to make it on their own up north. That problem aside, you're going to be in mighty deep water when word spreads of what you're doing here."

"You planning to start the trouble?" Nolan inquired.

The overseer slowly shook his head. "I wouldn't do such a thing, Mr. Houston. You're misunderstanding my concern. I have no intention of saying anything to anybody, but slaves talk among themselves, just like you and I."

Nolan shrugged. "I don't expect them to keep their freedom a secret. It would be too much to ask."

"You could have waited until the crop was in to tell them."

"I won't use slave labor to bring in a crop. And why should I care if the slaves talk among themselves? It's human nature to discuss and make plans with your fellow man."

Draper leaned against the porch railing. "No offense, Mr. Houston, but you're a Northerner. I'm talking about word spreading to the other plantations. Our slaves—"

"Freed men," Nolan corrected.

"Our *freed men* are going to go over to those other plantations and tell the slaves you've given them their freedom. Believe me, it won't take long till word gets to the big house, and once word reaches the big house, the master knows. I'm afraid you're going to be in for more trouble than you bargained for."

"And I think you're borrowing trouble," Nolan replied.

CHAPTER · 6

September 1857

WITH MUCH LESS grace and decorum than her father who was following behind her, Reggie Chamberlain bounded up the two steps of Elinor Brighton's boardinghouse carrying a satchel stuffed with clothing and other miscellaneous belongings she believed to be the necessities of life.

"I thought perhaps you'd decided not to come and stay with me," Elinor said from the open doorway.

"Why would you think that? I told you I wanted to come," the girl casually replied.

Justin shrugged his shoulders and flashed an apologetic expression in Elinor's direction. "I told her you were going to be anxious. Especially since I advised you we'd be arriving as soon as Reggie tossed a few belongings in her bag."

"I did think you would arrive in time to join us for dinner. Have you eaten?"

"No, but Reggie had enough breakfast to hold her until supper, didn't you, Reggie?"

The girl wagged her head back and forth. "No. I told you I was hungry when we left the house."

Justin shifted his gaze back and forth between his daughter and Elinor. "It appears I'm incorrect. We'll go to the Merrimack House and have a meal together. Then I'll return with Reggie and be on my way."

"There's more than enough food left from dinner to feed both of you—if you have sufficient time, that is," she offered. "You can put your satchel in the bedroom," she said to the child.

Justin glanced at the clock. "I'm already getting a late start. I'd best be on my way. You can have Reggie eat an extra helping for me."

"Give me a moment," Elinor said, hurrying down the hall before he could object.

Her efficiency in the kitchen proved helpful. Within only a few minutes she had placed a loaf of bread, a hunk of cheese, two pieces of fried chicken, and a piece of cake in an old metal pail. She hurried back to the door and handed the tin to the pastor.

"I wouldn't want you leaving town on an empty stomach. You can eat this along the way."

"It's little wonder Reggie is so fond of you," he said.

She didn't know exactly why, but it pleased Elinor to know Reggie had spoken kindly of her.

"I put my satchel under your bed," Reggie announced as she skipped back into the hallway.

"And where did you place all your belongings?"

Reggie gave her a confused look. "They're in the satchel."

Elinor and Justin laughed aloud, but Reggie appeared vexed. "I don't know what's so funny."

"I'll explain later. Why don't you walk your father out to the wagon and bid him good-bye. I'll wait for you here."

Elinor watched from the doorway as Justin leaned down and embraced his daughter. He kissed her; then they appeared to exchange a few words. Soon Reggie was running back to the house. She stopped outside the door and waved until her father was out of sight.

"Come right this way and we'll find you something to eat," Elinor suggested as Reggie walked back inside the house.

"Chicken would be good."

"Then you're in luck—because chicken is what I served for dinner today."

Reggie giggled. "I know—my father told me."

While the child ate her dinner, Elinor took up her needlework and began stitching.

"What are you making?"

"A sampler," Elinor replied.

"What's a sampler?"

"It's a piece of needlework that is made using a variety of stitches—some difficult and some simple," she explained. "Many times young girls make them when they first begin to sew. My first sampler is hanging in the bedroom. My grandmother taught me the stitches."

"How come you're making another if you already have one?"

Elinor laughed. "I think there's plenty of space in a house for more than one sampler. However, I'm making this one for a raffle the Ladies' Aid Society will be hosting next month—if I complete it in time."

Reggie peered across the table. "Looks like you're about finished. Think we could go fishing?" she asked.

"Well, I don't know why not. It seems a perfect day, and we've several hours of daylight left. Did you bring your fishing pole?"

The girl bobbed her head up and down. "I put it out behind the house by your shed. I'll go and get it," she said, obviously delighted.

"I'll meet you in front of the house." Elinor tucked her stitching into a small basket, deciding to carry it along with her to the river.

"Do your boarders know I'm going to live with you?" Reggie asked as they neared the Merrimack River.

Elinor straightened the folds of her blue-and-cream-striped day dress, then settled on the grass a short distance from the water's edge. "I believe I've told all of them. Why do you ask?" she inquired as she pulled her needlework from the basket.

Reggie glanced over her shoulder and met Elinor's inquiring gaze. "Were they angry?"

"No, of course not. Besides, except for breakfast and dinner, they're gone from early in the morning until supper-time. In the evening some of them go to town or to the library, and there might be one or two who visit in the parlor with their friends. I think you'll find most of them nice enough."

"Do any of them fish?" Reggie inquired as she tossed her line into the water.

"I don't believe I've heard any of them mention fishing, so it appears you may be stuck with me—and perhaps Moses. Have you talked to Moses since Spencer's departure?"

"Only once. He said since Spencer's gone, his mama doesn't let him come down to the river."

"Then where did you see him?"

"At the river, but don't tell," Reggie said.

"I promise."

"Spencer was mighty unhappy about going to Missis-sippi. We promised to write to each other."

"And have you?" Elinor asked.

"Not yet—but he hasn't written to me either."

"Perhaps that's something you can do tonight while I'm working in the kitchen. Then I can post the letter for you tomorrow. What do you think?"

"I like that idea. I wish he were here so we could go to school together."

"What about Moses? I'm certain he's lonely without Spencer also. Maybe the two of you can begin walking to school together. We could go and talk to his parents and see if that would work."

"Sure would be better than having to walk into that school all by myself every day. I never saw a school quite so big as that one. I'm always scared I'll get lost just trying to find my way around."

Elinor laughed. "It's not all that big, Reggie. But it is a very nice school."

"Did you know Moses is colored?" she inquired absently.

"Yes, as a matter of fact, I did know that."

"He doesn't look colored. He looks white. But he says he's truly colored, so I believe him. Even Spencer says it's the truth. At my school in Maine, they don't let the Negroes go to school with the whites. We had a colored family in our town," she said in a whisper, as though it were a secret, "and Father said they should let the children go to school with us, but they wouldn't."

"That's true in many places here in the North, Reggie. Even though most Northerners oppose slavery, they still want to keep people divided."

"Seems silly, doesn't it? Moses is just a boy. He's no different than me."

"Indeed it is silly," Elinor replied with a warm smile. "And just as you said, Moses is a boy. But you, Miss Reggie, are not."

Reggie frowned. "Well, I know that. But . . . well . . . you know what I mean."

She nodded in complete understanding. "Of course I do."

The men's voices were escalating out of control in their upstairs meeting room at the National Building. McKinley realized that if Nathan or Matthew didn't soon bring the group to order, pandemonium would rule.

"Gentlemen! Gentlemen!" Nathan shouted while rapping a wooden gavel on a podium at the front of the room.

But they paid him no heed. McKinley was certain that few could hear him above the clamoring din that now filled the room. Matthew motioned to McKinley. "Nathan tells me there is a bell tower above this room. The stairway is out that door," he said while pointing toward the rear of the room. "Do you think you could make your way up there and ring the bell? It's the only way we're going to settle this group."

McKinley nodded before wending his way through the crowd. The stairway proved dark and dusty, and he wondered how many years had passed since the bell had been used. He carefully made his way across the platform and unwound the rope. With a mighty heave, he pulled the rope and then spun backward and fell to the platform as the frayed rope broke off in his hand. The bell swung, and the heavy clapper fell against the iron with a mighty gong that shook the platform. Even with his ears covered, McKinley flinched at the reverberation. He edged his way back to the stairs as the momentum caused the bell to swing back and sound once again.

Silence prevailed when he reentered the meeting room with the rope still hanging from one hand.

"Thank you, McKinley," Nathan said. "And now that I've been able to gain your attention and bring this meeting to some semblance of order, I would request your cooperation in maintaining this order until the meeting is adjourned.

I understand emotion runs high at this moment, and I am prepared for discussion regarding the tragic sinking of the SS *Central America*. However, chaos serves no purpose in this meeting."

McKinley had anticipated heightened emotions this evening, but he had expected the same decorum he'd always observed among the Associates in the past. Although Nathan Appleton appeared calm, McKinley realized the scene he had observed in this room was a true gauge of the catastrophe that would challenge the entire country. He wanted to remain calm, yet he knew that the hurricane that had sent a million dollars in commercial gold to the ocean floor would cause financial repercussions throughout the country.

Josiah Baines waved his hand in the air and then stood. "Is there any additional word on the ship or its contents? I've heard the entire fifteen tons of federal gold intended for our eastern banks was on that ship."

"Unfortunately, I'm told that is true," Nathan said. "As most of you know, the *Central America* sailed directly into the path of a severe hurricane off the coast of South Carolina. The passengers made a valiant effort for four days, bailing water and carrying coal to keep the iron boilers lit. Distress rockets attracted a small Boston brig, and the women and children were transferred and saved. A few men were later rescued after the ship went down, but over four hundred perished—a much greater loss than fifteen tons of gold."

"I doubt the banks or our creditors will think so," one of the men called out.

"I realize there are widespread reports of financial instability being carried between cities by telegraph message, but we must not let emotion rule our decisions, gentlemen. When a small group of us met several weeks ago, we were distressed by news of embezzlement in the New York branch of the Ohio Life Insurance and Trust Company. We did take it upon ourselves to protect as much of the corporate funds as possible. You must remember, however, that there was a rush on the banks and we were able to withdraw only a third of our corporate investment."

McKinley knew the men should offer up a prayer of thanksgiving that Nathan and the others had shared their insight and taken immediate action. If it had not been for political friends directing them to bankers sympathetic to future and continued industrial growth, the Associates would have lost much more. For in less than one month's time, the financial backbone of the country had been affected in a monumental way.

"We're thankful for what you accomplished," Thomas Clayborn commented. "Josiah tells me there are problems with the Southern cotton growers to add to our list of concerns. Can you give us the details?"

For the next half hour, Nathan outlined the epidemic that had plagued the South, along with the remaining details gathered by Matthew over the past several weeks.

"We expect a further report from Jarrod Forbes by the end of the month advising of any shortfall in the crop," Matthew added. "However, given the recent turn of events, we may see a marked decrease in sales. If that's the case, we'll need to decrease production and may not need the volume of cotton we had previously contracted to purchase. With luck and proper oversight, this may work out in the end."

"Are you anticipating layoffs?" Wilson inquired.

Matthew hiked his shoulders in an exaggerated shrug. "Who can say for certain. If we decrease production, you can be sure there will be layoffs. In fact, we may be forced to temporarily close several of the mills. Time will tell. I will keep you informed, and any of you are more than welcome to visit my offices and go over the ledgers and reports whenever you are in Lowell. I will, of course, continue sending written reports on a regular basis."

"I know all of you concur that Matthew can be counted upon to maintain our best interests as he makes his decisions in Lowell," Nathan said. "This is going to prove to be a trying time, gentlemen. I trust you have all invested wisely."

———

"Will ya soon be ready, lass?" Rogan called to his wife. "We need to be gettin' loaded into the buggy if we're to make it to the church before the weddin' begins. I do na think Bridgett is gonna be happy if ya do na have her veil there by the time she's due to walk down the aisle."

"See to Nevan and Katherine. They're dressed and ya can load them into the buggy. There's plenty of time. Bridgett told me the bishop insisted on the Mass commemorating Michaelmas before the weddin'. Them that's invited to the weddin' can remain in the church whilst the others go on about their celebratin'."

"I do na think Bishop Fenwick will look kindly upon our strollin' into the church in the middle of Mass," Rogan called up the stairs. "Why the lass decided to have her weddin' today is beyond my understandin'. If it's good luck she's lookin' fer, then she should be havin' the weddin' on St. Patrick's Day or Shrove Tuesday, not September twenty-ninth."

With expert ease, Kiara adjusted her cluster of dark auburn curls and then added the gem-studded comb Jasmine Houston had given her as a gift on her own wedding day. She gave herself one final look in the mirror before descending the stairs in a pale blue wool gown that highlighted her creamy complexion.

"She chose the day because it's a Saturday and most of their friends do na work so late on Saturday. Also, she knew Bishop Fenwick would be in Lowell, and she's considerin' it an honor to be married by the bishop—as would most," she added.

"Ya look as lovely as the day I married ya, lass," Rogan said with a twinkle in his eye. He leaned down and brushed her lips with a fleeting kiss.

With his blarney and warm kisses, the man could still cause her heart to flutter. "Go on with ya, Rogan Sheehan, or we'll be late to the church for sure."

"Is that a fact?" he asked as they stepped out onto the porch. With a hearty laugh, Rogan pulled her into a tight embrace and kissed her soundly while the children watched from the buggy.

"Da!" Nevan hollered, then covered his face with both hands.

"Am I causin' ya a bit of embarrassment, lad?" Rogan asked with another laugh before assisting Kiara into the buggy.

"Is Paddy comin' with us?" Kiara asked.

"He left more than an hour ago. I had him take Bridgett's veil with him," he said with a broad grin.

"Ya were rushin' me when me brother's already delivered Bridgett's veil?" She gave him a playful slap on the arm.

"Aye, and ya should be thankin' me instead of abusin' me," he replied while vigorously rubbing his arm.

Kiara laughed at his antics and settled beside her husband for the short ride to the church. She was pleased for the diversion Bridgett and Cullen's wedding would provide. What with the wedding and the private Michaelmas celebrations, the Irish citizens of Lowell would be celebrating until the wee hours of the night, though many would likely suffer the consequences come morning.

"Can ya tell me why Bridgett decided to be married at St. Peter's instead of St. Patrick's, where she's been attendin' church since she set foot in this country?" Rogan asked. "I do na think she made a wise decision. St. Patrick's was good enough for our weddin'."

"The bishop agreed to officiate if they held the weddin' as soon as he completed the Mass for Michaelmas. And ya can na deny that St. Peter's is much bigger and much prettier than St. Patrick's. Now ya need to quit finding fault with Bridgett's decisions."

"'Tis a sad day when a man's forced to give up a supper of goose with sage and onion stuffing. Especially when he's been looking forward to such a meal since last Michaelmas Day." He hesitated for a moment, his brows knit in a frown. "I do na recall any problem fittin' our guests into the pews at St. Patrick's on our weddin' day."

"Ya need to be rememberin' that when we took our vows, I did na have any relatives except for Paddy, and very few friends either. Bridgett and Cullen both have many friends from church and the Acre, as well as the people they work with. I'm thinkin' that will make for a mighty large group of guests—more than ya could comfortably seat at St. Patrick's.

"And if it's yar stomach ya're worried about," Kiara continued, "ya can be sure there will be plenty of food. Granna Murphy's been cookin' for days, and if I know yar granna, there will be a fat goose with sage stuffin' and plum sauce waitin' fer ya."

"And I'm hopin' she'll add some apples to the stuffin', too," he said with a lopsided grin as he pulled back on the reins and the horses came to a halt near the corner of Gorham and Appleton streets, where the wedding guests had begun to congregate.

"Paddy!" Rogan called as he waved his young brother-in-law forward. "Did ya deliver the lace?" he whispered. "Yar sister will na be forgivin' me if the delivery went amiss."

"Aye, that I did. And glad Bridgett was to get it too. I think Granna Murphy was as worried as Bridgett. The two of them could na get the veil out of me hands and shoo me out of the house fast enough."

Rogan laughed as he gave Paddy an enthusiastic slap on the back. "I'm thinkin' Granna was breathin' a sigh of relief when she saw ya with that veil. She was likely worried she would na get Bridgett married off as planned."

"Come on with ya," Kiara said as she took hold of Rogan's arm. "We need to be getting inside or Bridgett will think ya've forgotten ya're to walk her down the aisle."

"How could I be forgettin' such a thing when I've my wife to remind me?" he asked with a wink.

A short time later, Rogan walked down the aisle with Bridgett tightly clasping his arm. The bodice and sleeves of her flounced heather gown were edged with the intricate lace Kiara had created to perfectly match the lace adorning her veil.

"She looks quite beautiful," Kiara said once Rogan sat down beside her.

"Aye, but shaking like a leaf, she was. Likely worried about what's to come on her weddin' night."

A quick jab of Kiara's elbow wiped the smile from his face. "Careful, lass, or ya're gonna be causing me permanent injury."

"I doubt that. Now hush before the bishop throws ya out on yar ear," she whispered.

After leading the couple in the recitation of their vows, Bishop Fenwick peered over his expansive girth, read a prayer from his missal, and pronounced Cullen and Bridgett McLaughlin husband and wife.

Fiddle and accordion music wafted through the cool September air, and the wedding guests soon began to wander from Granna Murphy's congested house and out into the streets of the Acre. Paddy walked alongside a small group as they meandered down the street and then stopped for a moment to watch the cheerful crowd. He breathed deeply. It had been far too long since he'd had time to actually enjoy himself. Nolan Houston's departure for Mississippi had resulted in little time for Paddy to socialize, and he hadn't realized until this evening how much he missed being among his friends.

He slowly downed a cup of wedding punch and leaned against the clapboard wall of Kevin McCurty's pub as couples paired off and began to dance.

Liam and Daughtie Donohue laughed and bowed to each other as they finished their dance. "Good to see ya, Paddy," Liam said as he and Daughtie drew near. "I've been wonderin' how ya're managin' at the farm without Mr. Houston."

"I find I do na have much time to relax anymore, so I was mighty pleased to have an excuse fer a night to enjoy myself."

Liam patted him on the back. "Ya can be mighty proud of yarself, Paddy, to have Mr. Houston trust ya running his stables at yar young age—and Irish to boot. Not many could boast of such an accomplishment."

"Thank ya, Liam. I must admit there are times when all the responsibility is worrisome. Right now, I've got me a beauty of a horse—not a Shagya, but still a fine animal we acquired specially for an instructor at the Virginia Institute. Training the mare was going very well until I attempted to get her to lead off with the right foot." He raked one hand through his curly hair. "Now she's proving to be the most stubborn animal I've ever encountered."

Liam shook his head. "Then let her lead off with the left. What difference does it make to ya, lad?"

"The Institute wants all of their horses to lead off with the right foot so when they march in a line, they're synchronized. I've had everyone at the farm attempting to work with her, but no one's been able to succeed."

"Ya should be tryin' Baucher's method."

The three of them turned to see who was speaking.

"Well, if it isn't Mary Margaret O'Flannery," Paddy said. "Have ya met Mary Margaret?" he asked, turning toward Liam and Daughtie.

"I don't believe we've had the pleasure," Daughtie replied. "Are you new to Lowell?"

"Yes. I work with Bridgett over at number five—at the Boott mills," she added.

"How is it that we haven't met you before now?" Daughtie asked.

"I have na been here but a short time, and I do na know many folks yet. But I attend St. Peter's every Sunday. Bridgett says once I become more accustomed to the work hours, I'll have more energy and want to become more involved in activities. Right now I'm content to do my work and little more," she commented.

"Bridgett is correct. It takes time to adjust. Even though it's been many years since I worked in the mills, I well remember the weariness of those first months. Ah, Liam, there's Kiara and Rogan. I haven't had an opportunity to speak to them this evening. It was a pleasure to meet you, Mary Margaret—and good luck with that horse," Daughtie added.

Liam grinned at Mary Margaret. "I believe you were going to tell Paddy how to correct that problem with his horse, weren't you?"

"Aye—that I was," she responded sweetly. " 'Twas a

lovely weddin', don't ya think?" she asked, turning her attention back to Paddy.

"Aye. Bridgett's a lovely lass, and Cullen's a lucky man to be havin' her as his wife. Did Bridgett happen to tell ya that she sailed to America on the same ship as Kiara and me?"

Mary Margaret tilted her head, and he noticed a sparkle in her bright blue eyes. "She told me Rogan saved his money to pay her passage and that Lowell has been the only place she's lived since comin' to America, but she did na tell me about the voyage."

"Then sit yarself down, lass, and I'll tell ya what Bridgett was like when she was a very young lass."

Liam stepped away from the couple to greet some friends with a slap on the back.

For a brief time, as Paddy regaled Mary Margaret with stories of life aboard the ship with Bridgett and Kiara, he was transported back to his youth. Back to a time he'd not thought about for many years—a time when death had crept into their home and snuffed out the lives of his ma and da, and then hovered nearby, eager to claim his life also. Those were days filled with despair. Paddy knew that had it not been for Kiara, he would have perished on the Emerald Isle. He always dreaded such memories, but somehow sharing them with Mary Margaret made them seem less worrisome.

"So ya see, 'twas Bridgett who made the match between Kiara and Rogan," Paddy explained.

"What's that I hear ya tellin' the lass? That yar hopin' I'll find ya a match?" Rogan teased as he approached the couple.

Paddy's cheeks flushed at the comment. Once again, Rogan had embarrassed him in front of Mary Margaret.

"When the time comes that I'm lookin' for a match, I do na think I'll be needin' someone to help me," Paddy retorted.

Rogan emitted a loud guffaw and slapped his thigh,

obviously enjoying Paddy's discomfort. Mary Margaret remained silent, her gaze fixed upon Paddy. Had the lass not been within hearing distance, Paddy would have given Rogan Sheehan an earful.

"If ya act as though his teasin' does na bother ya," Mary Margaret whispered, "he's more apt to stop. Next time, just give him a smile and tell him ya'll be sure to let him know when ya're ready."

"Should there be a next time, I may be forced to give him a taste of his own medicine!"

"Do ya na realize that's exactly what he wants? To get ya all riled up?"

Rogan ceased his laughter and turned his attention back to the young couple. "Liam tells me the lass appears to know all about trainin' horses and is willin' to give ya some lessons."

Before Paddy could reply, Mary Margaret jumped to her feet. "Now ya would na be exaggeratin' a wee bit, would ya?"

"Ah, lass, so ya're catchin' on to me tricks, are ya? Though I may have overstated the facts a bit, 'tis the truth that Liam said ya're talkin' like a lass who knows her way around horses," Rogan countered.

"Me master in Boston owned horses—I cared for his children except when their tutor had them for lessons. Ornery lot of youngsters, they was. Their ma died, and instead of spendin' time with his children, their father bought them gifts. They all had horses, and it's many an hour I spent waitin' at the stables while they was riding or taking their lessons."

"So are ya then considerin' yarself an expert? Because, if it's an expert ya are, I'm thinkin' Paddy could put ya to work at the Houston stables," Rogan prodded while directing an exaggerated wink at Paddy.

Mary Margaret shook her head, causing her soft curls to swing to and fro. "I'm na an expert, but I do know Baucher's method works, for I've watched it used on horses meself."

"And what *is* this Baucher's method?" Paddy asked.

" 'Tis a whole system of trainin' a horse. But for gettin' the horse to lead off with his right foot like ya were mentionin' earlier, ya must first get the animal well in hand, with his head in an easy position. Then ya need to make certain his hind legs are well under his body. Once ya have done that, ya bear yar hand to the left and give an increased pressure to the animal's right leg."

Paddy scratched his head as he attempted to process the method Mary Margaret had just explained. He gave a gentle shrug of his shoulders. " 'Twould be worth a try since nothin' else has worked."

"And would ya na be willin' to try it otherwise?" she asked.

He detected a flash of anger in her blue eyes. "I do na know. I'm na a man to change my way of doing things if they're workin'. Does na make any sense."

"Have ya never considered there might be an easier or better way to perform a task? Is that na reason enough to change?"

"I suppose 'twould be cause enough," he agreed. "But if ya're sayin' ya think I should be shiftin' the entire way we train our horses to this Baucher method ya're talkin' about, I do na think that will happen. We pride ourselves on selling the finest, best-trained horses in the country."

"Aye," Liam said as he rejoined the conversation. "Even West Point and the Virginia Institute buy Arabians from the Houston Stables."

"The Shagyas?" Mary Margaret asked, recognition shining in her eyes.

Paddy squared his shoulders and his chest swelled. "Ya know of our horses?"

"I heard me master speak of them at the time he was buying another horse. He said he had seen the Shagyas, and though they were beautiful animals, he found them to be far too costly."

"Ha! The man is a fool. Ya need to come to the stables and have a look fer yarself," Paddy said.

Liam waved at Rogan as he and Kiara approached. "Our young Paddy has invited Miss O'Flannery fer an outin'," he told them. "Say, Paddy, when was it ya were gonna be comin' to escort Mary Margaret to the farm?"

Paddy glanced at Mary Margaret, uncertain what he should do. If he set a time, the lass might tell him she had no interest in keeping company with the likes of him. And if he said Liam had twisted his words, Mary Margaret might be insulted and think he didn't find her attractive. Of course, it would be altogether impossible to find the lass undesirable, with her piercing blue eyes and hair the shade of gingered carrots.

"I'm thinkin' we can arrange the time fer ourselves. Would ya like to dance, Mary Margaret?" Paddy asked, anxious to escape Liam and Rogan's antics.

"Aye, that I would," she replied.

Before there was opportunity for further discussion, Paddy led the slender beauty off toward the assembled dancers.

"Have ya found a good Irish family to live with here in the Acre?" Paddy asked as he put his arm on her waist.

"The Corporation put me in one of the boarding-houses," she explained.

His eyebrows raised to resemble twin peaks. "In one of the boardinghouses?"

The flounce of her deep green dress shimmered as they

twirled in time to the spirited music. "Aye. And why is that surprisin' ya?"

"I would think ya would prefer livin' among yar own people," he said. "Na many of the Irish lasses live in the boardinghouses, and them that do say they're treated poorly. I'll talk to Bridgett. I'm sure ya could live with Granna Murphy, who's a fine cook."

Mary Margaret's dancing came to an abrupt halt. "And why would ya be thinkin' to take it upon yarself to talk to Granna Murphy? I've got a perfectly good voice, and if I want to move to the Acre, I'm more than capable of doing so without yar help. And I have na been treated poorly at the boardinghouse. Mrs. Brighton keeps a good house and will na tolerate foolishness," she retorted.

"Are ya feelin' a wee bit too good to live with yar own people?" Paddy asked.

Mary Margaret's eyes flashed with anger. "Who do ya think ya are to be sittin' in judgment of me and where I choose to live?"

"Ya have more than yar share of a temper, Mary Margaret O'Flannery."

"So I've been told!" She gave a small stomp of her foot for emphasis.

Paddy narrowed his eyes as he glanced at her foot and then met her angry gaze. "Ya should na take offense so quickly."

She put her hands on her hips, her elbows pointed outward like two triangular blockades. "And you should na be attemptin' to pass yarself off as a horse trainer when ya do na even know anything of Baucher's method!"

She marched away, her hair flying as she threaded her way through the crowd. The lass had a sharp tongue and more than her share of pride! Who did she think she was, questioning his ability to train a horse? He crossed his arms and leaned against the wall, continuing to track her every move. She had stopped to talk to someone. He elevated himself to full height and strained to see above the crowd. Timothy Rourke! Why would she want to speak with *him*? Everyone in the Acre knew Timothy traded one lass for another at the drop of a hat. Yet even the brokenhearted continued to tag after him, seeking attention. What special charm did Timothy Rourke possess?

Paddy ignored Rogan, who was pointing his thumb in Mary Margaret's direction as he approached. "Why did ya let that bonny lass escape? Can ya not see she's talking to Timothy? Get yarself over there before he offers to walk her home."

"If it's the likes of Timothy Rourke that interests her, then she's na the lass for me," Paddy said while still keeping Mary Margaret in his sights.

"Then why are ya still staring after her like a lovesick pup?" Rogan asked. "If it's fear that's holdin' ya back, I'll go and fetch her back here for ya."

"I do na need yar help," he said, breaking loose of the firm clasp Rogan held on his arm and striding off.

He could hear Rogan's deep belly laugh as he approached Mary Margaret. He gave momentary thought to walking past her and pretending he didn't see her standing with Timothy Rourke. But if he did such a thing, Rogan would find some other way to embarrass him.

He approached the lass feeling a combination of fear, hope, and discomfiture. "I was wonderin' if I might escort ya home this evening," Paddy inquired.

"She already has an escort home," Timothy said.

" 'Twas Mary Margaret I was askin'."

She met his expectant gaze. "And why would ya want to escort the likes of me? A lass with a dreadful temper?" she inquired sweetly.

"I'll explain while I'm seeing ya home," he replied, now feeling somewhat more confident.

"If ya want to wait until I'm ready to go home, then ya may escort me. But I do na have to be in the boardinghouse until ten o'clock, so until then, I believe I'll accept Timothy's offer to dance."

Tim Rourke grasped Mary Margaret around the waist. As he began to lead her off, he whispered to Paddy, "No need to wait—I'll see the lass to her boardinghouse."

Paddy scowled at his rival. "I'll na be leaving without her. It's *me* that'll be seein' her home."

Filled with envy, Paddy watched Mary Margaret and Timothy. The man would not turn her loose for even a moment.

"He hangs on her arm as though he's afraid I'll steal her away," Paddy muttered aloud, angry he hadn't insisted upon dancing with Mary Margaret himself. Instead, he stood idly by while Timothy held her and danced another eight-handed reel.

"Come join us for a game of kick the turnip," Johnny Kelly urged as he tugged on Paddy's sleeve.

"I do na want to play games," Paddy retorted. There was more irritation in his voice than he'd intended, and Johnny's smile quickly changed to a frown. "I'm sorry if I hurt yar feelings," Paddy called out as the boy hurried away without another word.

It seemed as though hours had passed before the musicians finally set their instruments down and cited the need for something cool to drink. Paddy quickly stepped forward to claim Mary Margaret. "If ya're to be home by ten o'clock, we best be leaving," he said.

Her face was flushed from the dancing, and damp curls clung to her forehead, forming an auburn frame around her creamy complexion. "I'm having such fun I now am wishin'

I would have asked Mrs. Brighton for special permission to return later than ten o'clock," she said.

He raised an eyebrow. "So ya find Timothy Rourke pleasant company?"

"He's a lively sort of fella and can dance better than most. He did na miss a step on the jigs nor the hornpipe, though I do na think he can step dance as well as I. He said I should wait until the fiddlers returned and give him a chance to outshine me," she said with a cheery smile.

"I do na doubt he's tryin' to talk ya into staying a wee bit longer. If the fiddlers hadn't stopped for a drink, he'd still be fightin' to keep ya by his side. And then what would Mrs. Brighton say when ya returned home late?"

Mary Margaret's laughter filled the air like the soothing sound of a rippling brook. "I do na know, but I'd like to think she'd be understandin'."

"My buggy is at the end of the street," he said, leading her through the crowd.

"Timothy said there would be some strawboys comin' to call at Granna Murphy's later this evenin'. I do wish I could stay and see that bit of fun," Mary Margaret said as they reached the buggy.

"I do na know who told him there would be strawboys, but I've heard nothin' of it. The custom of going strawing is not often practiced in the Acre."

Mary Margaret's eyes shone with excitement. "I've never seen strawboys, and I'm thinkin' it would be amusing to see the young men dressed in their straw costumes while performing a jig or singing a song. Of course, I would na be able to guess their identity, but all the same, 'twould be fun trying."

"Aye. 'Tis true that the performance of a group of strawboys can add much to the weddin' festivities, but I think Timothy Rourke was speaking out of turn. I do na think ya'll be seeing any special performances this evenin'. Timothy would say whatever words he thought might entice ya to remain in his company a little longer."

"Ya seem mighty anxious to discredit him."

"I'm only speakin' the truth. Ya can ask any of the lasses he's trifled with," Paddy said as he helped her into the buggy.

"So ya think I'm a lass whose head is easily turned by the smooth talk of an Irishman?"

He thought for a moment as he pulled on the reins to direct the horses into a right turn down John Street. "I canna say for certain, but it appears ya might be."

Her lips tightened and her eyes narrowed. "Ya are an incorrigible man, Padraig O'Neill. Since the first time I set eyes upon ya, ya've done nothing but find fault with me."

"I'm merely attemptin' to direct ya down the right path," he explained.

She bristled at his reply, and her eyes darkened with anger. "When I need help making my decisions, I'll ask. Until then, I'll thank ya to keep yar opinions to yarself."

They rode in silence, Paddy's gaze firmly fixed upon the horses and Mary Margaret's back to him and her arms crossed tightly across her chest. Once again he'd managed to alienate the lass. Why couldn't she see that he was merely attempting to look out for her best interests?

"Like I told ya earlier, if ya ever plan to wed, ya're going to have to learn to control yar temper," Paddy finally said as he pulled back on the reins and they came to a stop in front of her boardinghouse.

Her lips puckered into a tight knot as she turned to face him. "Plan to wed? Is *that* what ya think? That the only thing I have to look forward to in my entire life is finding a man to marry? Ya flatter yarself, Padraig O'Neill!"

Before he could make his way around the buggy, Mary Margaret had jumped down and rushed toward the boardinghouse. She vanished behind the front door before he could say another word.

CHAPTER · 7

October 1857

NOLAN LEANED back in his chair and rubbed his weary eyes. He'd been staring at the ledgers, bills, and records of the plantation all morning. Fortunately, Malcolm Wainwright had been a meticulous man when it came to his holdings. Any information Nolan needed was at his fingertips—including papers of ownership for every slave now living at The Willows, along with a ledger listing personal facts about each one. The slave's name was followed by notations for medical treatment, type of clothing supplied, Christmas gifts, and a listing of special abilities and characteristics. A carefully inscribed date of entry preceded each detailed fact.

The swishing sound of Jasmine's skirt caused him to turn as she entered the library. "You look particularly lovely today," he said, enjoying the sight of her even more than he had years ago when they'd first wed.

"You are becoming quite the Southern charmer, Mr. Houston," she said with an exaggerated drawl.

"What I say is entirely true—I've always said you look stunning in yellow. You're like a ray of sunshine on a dreary day."

Jasmine laughed as she drew closer. "I believe the South has also rekindled your desire to write poetry. What have you been doing in here all morning? The children were hoping you might join us outdoors for a noonday picnic under the trees."

"Going through this paper work."

"I told you I would take care of the ledgers, my dear. I don't expect you to assist Mr. Draper and do the bookwork as well."

"Wendell doesn't need my assistance at this point. Besides, your father's slaves are now freed men. They can come and go, work or not—it's their own choice. Mr. Draper no longer makes their decisions; he merely directs those wanting to work to the tasks that must be accomplished."

"Miz Jasmine?" Prissy stood in the library doorway, twisting her hands.

"Yes, Prissy? Is something wrong?"

"Massa Wade from Bedford Plantation has come calling. I had him wait in da parlor. He says he has business wib Massa Nolan. Should I show him in?" The girl's voice quivered as she spoke.

"Did he say something to frighten you, Prissy?" Jasmine inquired.

"No, ma'am. But yo' daddy bought some slaves from Massa Wade one time. He treats his people real bad—likes to use da whip."

"There's no need to worry, Prissy. We'll not let anything happen to you or any of the others. You go back to what you were doing, and I'll see to Mr. Wade."

The girl's even ivory teeth shone like a string of fine pearls as she beamed at Jasmine. "Thank you, Missus," she said before hurrying off toward the back of the house.

Nolan arched his eyebrows. "I assume you know Mr. Wade?"

"The Bedford Plantation has been in Harold Wade's family for years. None of the Wainwrights have had a close association with the Wade family, however, because Father didn't particularly like Harold. I can't imagine why he's come. Do you want to see him here in the library, or do you prefer to entertain him in the parlor?"

Nolan stood and walked around the desk. "Why don't *we* entertain him in the parlor. Perhaps he won't stay long, and we'll be able to join the children for their picnic."

She clasped his arm and gave him a winsome smile. "And here I thought you'd completely forgotten the picnic."

Harold Wade stood with his elbow perched on the fireplace and his gaze fixed upon the foyer. Except for turning toward the young couple as they entered the room, he remained motionless.

"Mr. Wade. It has been some time since I've seen you," Jasmine said. "I don't believe you've met my husband, Nolan Houston."

Mr. Wade gave a slight nod of his head and finally stepped away from the fireplace to shake hands with Nolan. "My pleasure, Mr. Houston. Sorry about your family, Jasmine. We were never close, but I always respected your father."

"Thank you, Mr. Wade," she said. "Won't you be seated?"

"I prefer to stand—problems with my back. Besides, my business shouldn't take long. I've come to make a proposition, Mr. Houston."

Nolan sat beside Jasmine on the brocade-upholstered settee. "What kind of proposition might that be?"

"Like most everyone in these parts, I lost slaves to the fever. From what I'm told, I lost more than the rest of you. Then, to make matters worse, a lot of my field slaves aren't recovering as quickly as I had hoped. I thought it was probably their usual laziness, but the doctor tells me they need more time to fully recover. Says I'll never get another good day's work out of any of them if they go back to the fields before they're back to full strength," he complained.

"Perhaps if your slaves had been healthy and well fed before the fever hit, they would have fared better throughout the epidemic," Jasmine said.

Mr. Wade ignored her remark and turned his attention to Nolan. "I'm wondering if you'd consider striking up a bargain with me whereby we would share the use of our slaves until the cotton crop has been harvested. Some of the other owners have worked out such an arrangement, and I thought you might be interested in doing the same. Or have you already made such an arrangement with others?"

"No, I haven't entered into an agreement with any of the other owners. I understand your dilemma, Mr. Wade, but I doubt we'd be interested in doing such a thing for the entire harvest. If you're in dire straits at the present time, I can ask our folks if they'd be willing to go and help out for a short time."

Mr. Wade looked at Nolan as though he'd taken leave of his senses. "Ask your folks if they'd be willing?" he asked before emitting a harsh laugh. "Those *folks,* as you call them, are *slaves.* And they've got no say in whether they'd be willing or not. They do *what* they're told, *when* they're told, and *how* they're told. Now, I realize you live up north, and likely you don't hold with the idea of slavery, but you need to readjust your thinking while you're in Mississippi."

"Thank you for your suggestion, Mr. Wade, but we appear to be doing just fine with our own method. If you'd care to ride out to the fields with me, we can inquire about your proposition. However, I don't anticipate a large number will agree."

Harold Wade looked at Jasmine as though he expected

her to explain Nolan's behavior, but she merely smiled and nodded at him.

"We shan't be long, my dear. Please tell the children that if they are willing to wait a little longer, I'll join you for that picnic you mentioned."

Nolan realized their visitor thought he was completely daft. Men such as Harold Wade didn't stop to have picnics with their wives and children during the harvest, and they certainly didn't inquire whether their slaves were willing to work. But Harold didn't realize the men, women, and children harvesting the crop at The Willows were no longer slaves. And this was a fact Nolan didn't wish to divulge at this juncture.

"I got about ten healthy men and maybe five women that I could trade off with you," Mr. Wade said. "They're all good pickers. Overseer might have to take a whip to one or two to keep them moving, but otherwise they're well trained. You think you could spare that many of your *folks*?" he asked as they rode to the cotton fields.

Nolan gave the man a sidelong glance. "I can spare as many as are willing to go," he said while waving at Mr. Draper.

"Something wrong?" Wendell Draper asked as he pulled on his reins and brought his horse alongside Nolan.

"Would you gather together everyone working in the fields so we can talk to them for a few minutes?"

Mr. Draper tipped his hat and then bounced his heels into the horse's shanks, signaling his animal into a gallop. When Nolan and Harold Wade reached the south cotton field, all of the hands were awaiting them, their heavy canvas bags bulging with the morning's pickings.

"I apologize for taking you away from your work," Nolan started, "but Mr. Wade from over at Bedford Plantation is wondering if any of you would be interested in helping him bring in his crop. He wants to trade off workers. I told him I didn't think any of you would be interested, but it's up to you."

Mr. Wade rolled his eyes heavenward and shook his head. "Craziest thing I've ever seen in my life. One of these mornings you're going to come down here and every one of these darkies is going to be gone."

Nolan shrugged. "Guess that could happen." The two men watched as the workers gathered into small groups to discuss the proposal.

"Massa Nolan," one of the men said as he approached.

"Yes, Henry?"

"There's twenty of us men who's willin' to go over an' work at the Bedford place, but how's that gonna work when you do the weighin' here at The Willows?"

"You won't get anything on the days you're at Mr. Wade's, but I'll give you double what you pick on the days when Mr. Wade's men are here. Does that sound reasonable?"

Henry nodded. "Can we stop going over there any time we decide we'd rather stay here and work?"

"Absolutely. You can go for half a day, every other day, or however you decide, and you can quit whenever you decide."

Mr. Wade motioned to Nolan. "You can't do it that way—you'll need an overseer to bring them back and forth. They need to be on a schedule."

"For their own protection, I'll write out a pass for each of them to travel back and forth, and I'll furnish a wagon for those who want to travel to your place as a group. If they decide to leave without the group, they can walk back on their own. It won't take any additional overseer. I wouldn't say anything to discourage them, or they may decide not to help at all."

"If it's not overstepping my bounds, Henry, can you tell me when you think you and the others will come to the Bedford?" Mr. Wade asked between clenched teeth.

"We's thinkin' on comin' tomorrow mornin', unless it's rainin'. Iffen it's rainin', we be stayin' here."

"Absolutely! After all, I wouldn't want any of you to get wet," Wade retorted sourly before turning his attention back to Nolan. "I keep thinking this entire ordeal must be a bad dream and that any moment, I'm going to awaken."

"Bad dream? You should ask these people about bad dreams, Mr. Wade. They've been living a nightmare for years!" Nolan considered something for a moment, then added, "One more thing: you may not lay the whip to any of these men nor discipline them in any fashion."

Wade pulled his hat low on his forehead. "Very well. I'll plan on seeing your folks in the morning—if it doesn't rain, and if it isn't too hot, and they don't decide they'd rather sleep," he replied dryly before riding off.

———————

Nolan took the plate of food Alice Ann offered and sat down on one of the quilts Jasmine and Prissy had spread on the neatly manicured lawn. He wrapped a piece of thick ham in a slice of crusty bread that had been slathered with fresh churned butter and helped himself to a cup of lemonade.

"Are you going to come sit with me, Allie?" he asked.

"Me and Clara want to sit with Prissy. Mama can sit beside you," she said.

Nolan laughed. "What if Mama wants to sit beside Prissy?" he teased.

"Mama always sits with *you*," Alice Ann said matter-of-factly.

Jasmine and Spencer sat down on either side of Nolan. "I received a brief letter from McKinley," Jasmine said. "He says Violet continues to do well. The baby is still expected in early December, though he says Violet is hoping for late November. If it's a girl, they've decided to name her Madelaine Rose."

"A girl?" Spencer shook his head. "I'm hoping the baby will be a boy."

"I know you are, dear," his mother replied. "You are rather surrounded by girls. However, if it's a girl, it appears they've decided to name the child after my mother, although McKinley did say they plan to actually call the child Mattie Rose. I've never quite understood why you would christen a child with one name and then use another," she said to Nolan. "If they don't want to refer to the baby as Madelaine, why not simply name her Mattie?"

"But what if it's a boy?" Spencer insisted.

"They've decided upon Samuel Malcolm Wainwright should they have a boy."

Spencer nodded his agreement. "Sam. I like that much better than Mattie."

Jasmine smiled at her son. "I'm certain you do." She handed her husband a glass of lemonade. "I suppose this is McKinley and Violet's way of paying respect to the family, though I would have viewed his help here at The Willows as a greater tribute. I even thought to write and tell him so but knew it would only serve to further anger him."

"I'm pleased you restrained yourself," Nolan said. "Your brother is acutely aware you're unhappy he didn't come along to assist us—no need to cause a breach you would later regret. Any other news from Lowell?" he inquired before taking a bite of the thick ham sandwich.

"No. His letter was brief—merely an update of Violet's condition and the names they had chosen for the child." Jasmine took a drink of the cool lemonade. "I'm interested in hearing how things ended with Mr. Wade."

"Surprisingly, a number of the field hands agreed to go to Bedford and help with his crop. I truly didn't expect any of them to entertain his request," he replied. "For the life of me, I still cannot understand why they're willing to go over there. Surely they realize Wade will treat them no better than his own slaves."

"I thought they'd prefer to be here where they would earn their picking money. How are you going to handle the situation when Mr. Wade's slaves are here?"

"I'm going to pay double on those days. I doubt whether any of Wade's slaves are as motivated to pick as our field hands, so I offered to weigh out and pay double to our men."

"That was kind of you, yet it doesn't seem like enough of an incentive to make them want to go. I am truly baffled," she said. "What do you think, Prissy? Why would they want to go to Bedford?"

The girl shuddered at the question. "Um, I don' know, Miz Jasmine, 'cause that's one of dem places I'd never even want to visit. That massa Wade is a bad one. But iffen you wanna know, me and Toby can ask around and find out what dem men down in the quarter is thinkin'."

"Just so long as they don't feel obligated to go over there because of us. We don't want any of them feeling they must help Mr. Wade," Jasmine said.

"Never know what some people is thinkin'," Prissy said as she lifted a cup of milk to Clara's lips and helped the child with her drink.

———

By week's end, all of the men who had volunteered to assist at the Bedford Plantation stated they had erred and no longer wished to continue the trade. Nolan did not question their decision but was content to have the arrangement cease. He didn't like dealing with Harold Wade or the man's overseer and was pleased when their final labor exchange had been completed.

Accordingly, he was surprised to see Harold Wade and John Woodson, the owner of Rosewood, approaching the mansion on a cool evening some ten days later. He sat on the upper veranda and watched as plumes of dust kicked up around the horses' hooves.

"Gentlemen," Nolan greeted as he stood between two of the large columns forming the decorative colonnade that fronted the house.

"May we join you?" John Woodson inquired.

"Of course," Nolan replied. He waited at the top of the outer stairway that led directly to the veranda. "What brings you to The Willows?" he asked as they reached the gallery.

"Distressing news," Wade said.

Nolan noted the warning look Woodson directed at his companion.

"Why don't we sit down?" Mr. Woodson inquired in his thick, syrupy drawl.

"Something I can help with?" Nolan asked when the men had finally made themselves comfortable.

"I'm certain that you can, Mr. Houston. I told Harold on the way over here that I've heard you're a man of reason, and I know you're going to make a sound decision," Woodson said.

"Decision about what?"

"Seems the reason your *folks* were so willing to come over to my place and work is because they wanted to tell my slaves about what's going on over here. They've created chaos for me and many other owners," Harold said, his face now contorted in anger.

"Now, Harold, don't get all riled up. We've come to talk like gentlemen," John said. "You see, Mr. Houston, while you find nothing wrong in what you're doing, your actions have caused unrest among our slaves. Coupled with the difficulties caused by the epidemic, this unwitting action on your part has changed a problematic situation into something much more complex."

"I truly don't understand why you are placing blame upon me. I sent no one to Mr. Wade's plantation except at his express request. And I might add that he received more than he gave in the bargain. I did not complain, nor did the field hands. Mr. Wade was aware my hands were working without supervision and as freed men."

"No! I did *not* know you considered them freed men. You told me they did not need supervision as you let them work whatever hours they desired. Now they've told our slaves that they're going to receive money for their pickings and that you're going to set all of them free once you bring in your crop."

"It seems they secretly made their way onto other plantations while they were out with the passes you gave them and have now spread word throughout southern Mississippi and Louisiana," Mr. Woodson added.

"I imagine this is somewhat exaggerated, gentlemen, but I'll not deny what you've heard is true. My wife and I do not believe in slavery, and I'll not apologize for our beliefs or what we're doing. We're bringing in the crop only because it was one of Malcolm's final requests. Jasmine wanted to honor his wish, and we saw it as a way to provide funds for the freed slaves to begin their new lives."

"New lives!" Wade spat as he shot to his feet. "I *told* you he's crazed and that we'd get nowhere attempting to talk to him."

"Sit down, Harold," Mr. Woodson ordered. "Surely you can understand our concern, Mr. Houston. We not only fear unrest among our slaves but also believe they will begin to run away. And where do you think they are going to run to?"

"I have no idea," Nolan replied.

"Why, they're going to come *here,* where they believe they will receive safe haven. They think that if they can make it as far as The Willows, you'll protect them and grant them the same freedom and funds as you've promised your own slaves."

Nolan leaned back in his chair and folded his fingers to form a tent. "Though I would like nothing better, I cannot grant freedom if I don't hold their papers. You need only explain that fact to them."

"Do you think we are so naïve that we believe you? Papers mean little to those of you who are intent on giving the colored man his freedom," Wade snarled.

Woodson motioned for Wade to cease talking. "If you insist upon this foolishness," he asked Nolan, "would you at least consider telling your slaves you are reneging on your offer so that word will spread and we can once again control our slaves? You can later tell them the truth when you actually set them free."

"I'm sorry, but I can't do that. I believe you men are worrying needlessly, and I suggest you tell your slaves the truth: I can free only the slaves that belonged to Malcolm Wainwright."

———

Prissy waited anxiously at the end of the driveway, watching the road for any sign of Spencer Houston. He should have been home from school two hours ago, and now the missus was fretting something awful. She danced from foot to foot, uncertain if she should report back to the big house or continue watching. Surely the missus would realize she was still waiting at her assigned post. Maybe she should edge her way down the road a ways so she could see over the small rise in the roadway. Fear gripped her as she attempted to make a decision. She'd never gone off on her own. What if the missus thought she was trying to escape and run away?

A nervous giggle escaped her lips as she remembered she was now allowed to run away if she wanted. Slowly at first and then with a more determined step, she walked down the dusty road and up the small hillock. It was there she thought she saw something—or someone.

She moved more quickly and then began to run as she realized what she was seeing. "Spencer!" she screamed. "I'm coming, chile!"

Spencer was struggling to get to his feet when she reached his side. She tried to hide her horror. The boy's face was swollen and bleeding, and there were cuts and bruises on his legs and arms.

"You lay still, Spencer. I'm gonna go get your pappy so's he can carry you back home," Prissy said.

The boy nodded his agreement.

"Who did this to you?" she asked before hurrying off.

"Boys at school," he whispered. "They hate us 'cause we don't believe in slavery."

Prissy jumped to her feet. "I be right back with help." She raced down the road with white-hot fear rising inside her—a fear of what had happened to Spencer Houston and a fear of the future.

CHAPTER · 8

HUMMING UNDER her breath, Prissy worked the cloth back and forth on the mahogany table in an easy rhythm, then suddenly brought her work to a halt. Had she heard something banging on the house? She cocked her head to one side and listened. With a shrug, she returned to her polishing but then a persistent knock sounded at the front door.

"Who could that be?" she muttered while shoving the cloth into her waistband and scurrying down the hall. "Them young'uns best not be playing tricks with me."

Since Master Nolan had made his announcement to the slaves that he was giving them their freedom, not many folks had come calling at The Willows. In fact, since young Spencer's incident after school, there hadn't been *any* visitors. Of course, it didn't seem to bother Master Nolan none, 'cause he said they was all gonna leave Mississippi once the cotton crop was harvested. Prissy wasn't so sure that was going to happen. Talk of leaving frightened her. All she wanted to do was marry Toby—and the sooner the better. She didn't want no more trouble in her life, and with all this talk of freedom, there was bound to be trouble. She could feel it coming, just like a summer storm filled with jagged lightning.

Her eyes widened when she reached the front door, and she froze in place.

"Are you going to open the door, or must we do it for ourselves?" Lydia Hesston inquired irritably from across the threshold.

"Afternoon, Prissy," Rupert said. "Why don't you show us into the parlor and then tell your mistress she has company. Think you can manage to do that?" he asked with a sneer curling his lips.

Lydia pulled off her gloves as she leveled an arrogant glare in Prissy's direction. "I can find my way into the parlor. Go and tell my cousin I've come to call on her."

"Yessum." In her haste to depart the room, Prissy tripped on the edge of the patterned red and black carpet, nearly landing flat in front of Rupert.

"Clumsy girl," Lydia chided while Prissy regained her balance and rushed from sight.

"Mean-spirited woman," Prissy whispered.

Perhaps it *would* be worth leaving the South if she didn't have to put up with the likes of Mr. and Mrs. Rupert Hesston, she thought. How Miss Lydia and Miss Jasmine could be cousins—blood-related—and act so different was beyond Prissy's imagination. Both from the same family . . . one was filled with meanness and the other with love.

"Hard to unnerstand," she muttered.

"What's hard to understand?"

Prissy startled at the sound of her mistress's voice. "I thought you was outside in da garden," she replied. "You got company, Miz Jasmine. Yo' cousin Miss Lydia and her husband is come to call. They's in the parlor."

"Lydia has returned? How wonderful! Would you fix some tea and bring it to us in the parlor, Prissy?"

She hesitated. The last thing she wanted to do was go

back in the parlor and serve tea, yet she wouldn't refuse Miss Jasmine. "Yessum. I be bringing it ta you directly."

She considered asking Martha or Henrietta if they would serve tea and then offer to look after the children, but she thought better of the idea. Miss Jasmine might question why she would do such a thing. Prissy didn't want to lie to the mistress, but she could hardly tell Miss Jasmine what she thought of her relatives. Best to serve tea and remain silent, she decided.

Being careful to watch her step, Prissy carried the tray to the parlor, placed it on the walnut serving table beside Miss Jasmine, and turned to leave.

"Why don't you remain, Prissy? You know, Lydia, it's Prissy we have to thank for finding our Spencer, who was injured on his way home from school. She bravely went searching for him and then came running for help once she saw his tragic condition," Jasmine related while patting Prissy's hand.

"I's got silver that needs polishin'," Prissy said while backing toward the door.

"The silver will wait. Sit down here and have a cup of tea while I tell of your heroics," her mistress insisted.

Mrs. Hesston's mouth gaped open, and if Prissy hadn't been so frightened, she would have laughed aloud at the sight.

"Jasmine! Whatever are you thinking, inviting *her* to have tea with *us*? Have you taken leave of your senses?"

Rupert gave his wife a knowing look. "You see? I told you she's become completely irrational."

"*I'm* irrational? It's *you* people who are irrational. You won't tolerate *anyone* who doesn't believe exactly as you do. Spencer is evidence of that! Even though I disagree with slavery, I would never teach my child to hate those whose views differ. And I am not hesitant to say that evil permeates people who would teach such behavior."

Prissy shrunk back, wishing she could make herself invisible. Mrs. Hesston had pulled a handkerchief from her reticule and was dabbing her eyes as she looked to her husband for consolation.

"I cannot believe any of this," Mrs. Hesston said. "I came here seeking comfort from one I remembered fondly. Since my return from abroad, I've been surrounded by tragedy. First I discover my immediate family has perished, and now I find that one of my few living relatives has turned against me in my time of grief."

Jasmine set her cup down with an authoritative clunk. "Don't be overly dramatic, cousin. We've all suffered. I, too, lost my family members and have suffered grief. However, life goes on. We must each move forward in the way that God leads. Fortunately for me, I find that He is leading my family away from this place!"

***

It was midafternoon when Justin Chamberlain's horse-drawn wagon lumbered to a stop in front of the boarding-house on Dutton Street. He set the brake and jumped down, pleased to finally be back in Lowell. Packing the dishes and glassware had taken a fair amount of skill and patience, and then arranging all of their household goods into the wagon had proven more of a chore than he had ever imagined. He'd soon grown weary of the task. As he now surveyed the loaded wagon, he realized his lack of enthusiasm was apparent.

Louise would be appalled to see her carefully stitched quilts shoved atop the rough-edged barrels and crates—containers that would likely snag and rip her painstaking handiwork. But he had needed something to tightly pack the dishes and glassware, and the quilts were at hand. Besides,

Louise wasn't alive to see what he had done, and Reggie wouldn't care.

"Father!" Reggie squealed as she bounded out the door and threw herself into his arms. "You've finally come home!"

Justin firmly wrapped his arms around the gangly ten-year-old and kissed the top of her head. "I believe you've grown at least an inch during my absence."

"Then you should have returned more quickly," she said, tightening her chokehold.

He loosened his daughter's clenched fingers and took a step back while gently grasping her waiflike shoulders. She looked amazingly ladylike, wearing a bright blue print dress accentuated by rows of tiny pin tucks. Her soft brown hair was neatly combed and tied with a matching blue ribbon, and instead of dirt smudges, she bore a dusting of flour on one cheek.

"You look quite charming. Tell me how you've been," he said as they entered the front door.

"I've been wonderful—except for school. If I could have stayed at the boardinghouse and helped Mrs. Brighton all day, I would have been *very* happy."

"Pastor Chamberlain! When did you arrive?" Elinor inquired as she came down the hallway from the kitchen.

"Just now. I came straight to the boardinghouse. I couldn't wait any longer to see Reggie," he said, giving his daughter a bright smile.

"Do come in and sit down. I must say that I'm almost sorry that you've returned. Having Reggie with me has been most enjoyable."

Justin's eyebrows arched. "Truly?"

Reggie folded her arms across her chest and gave her father a look of mock indignation. "Why are you acting surprised?"

"Who says I'm acting?" he retorted, wrapping his arm around Reggie and drawing her closer.

"I know you're only teasing," she said. "You missed me bunches."

"You are absolutely correct on that account. And all of your friends from back home said to tell you hello. I even have some letters for you, but I promised I wouldn't turn them over until you agreed to answer each one."

Reggie's eyes sparkled with delight. "Is there one from Peter?"

"I believe there is. However, I want to hear all about your new school before I give you the letters. Otherwise, I'll not be able to pry a word from you."

"I'm doing fine in my classes. Aren't I," she said to Elinor.

"Indeed she is. I can't say that Reggie is thrilled with the school or her classmates, but she does her lessons as soon as she returns to the boardinghouse, and her teacher has written several notes praising her work. I've saved all of her papers for you to review."

"That was very thoughtful," Justin said before turning his attention back to his daughter. "And what is it you dislike about your classmates and the school, young lady?"

"The school is much larger than the ones I've attended. I like smaller schools."

"And your classmates?" he urged.

"The girls are very persnickety and the boys don't want to play with a girl, so they're mean—except for Moses. He's still nice to me."

"I see. Then it sounds as though you have your work cut out for you if you're going to make friends, and it appears you've already taken the proper steps with that new dress and ribbon in your hair."

"I didn't wear this dress to please any of those girls. One

of Mrs. Brighton's boarders gave me several dresses. She said they were more appropriate for a schoolgirl than a woman of her years."

"Yes, Ardith is nearly an old maid—she must be all of ten years older than Reggie," Elinor teased.

"Perhaps I should offer her a few coins for the dress," Justin suggested.

Elinor shook her head. "She was pleased Reggie was willing to wear the dresses. I think it would spoil her gift if you offered to pay her. Do tell us about your journey. Reggie was worried you had fallen victim to some difficulty. But I attempted to reassure her that all was well."

"There is no denying I was gone longer than I anticipated, and I do apologize for my delay. Both the packing and the journey were more difficult than I expected. There was a great deal of rain on my return, and with the weight of the wagon, I made little progress each day. Also, I stopped in Portland for a brief visit with the church leader who appointed me to the position here in Lowell. He and his wife are fine people, and since I was passing nearby, I decided to stop and see them. Rather thoughtless of me, now that I think about it," he said apologetically.

"Not at all. We've been having a grand time, haven't we, Reggie?" Elinor said enthusiastically.

"I learned how to bake bread while you were gone," Reggie proudly announced.

"Now that is truly an accomplishment," Justin replied. "And when will you be baking some of this fine bread for your father?"

"You can take a loaf home and have a taste this very evening," Elinor suggested.

Justin rubbed his hands together. "I can hardly wait to sink my teeth into it. But be prepared, young lady: I'm a harsh judge of bread, and you'll not be getting any praise unless it's justly deserved," he teased.

Reggie giggled at his remark. "I'm not worried. If the bread suits the girls who live here, I believe you'll find it passable."

"Harsh critics, are they?"

Reggie bobbed her head up and down. "Some of them like to complain about most everything. If the soup is a little too cool or a little too hot, if they hoped for white bread and Mrs. Brighton serves corn bread instead, if they have to work three looms instead of two at the mill, or if they must share their bed with two girls instead of one. Mrs. Brighton says not to pay them any mind when they're short-tempered. She says they complain because they're tired, but I think they're spoiled by Mrs. Brighton's fine food and good treatment."

Elinor blushed at Reggie's praise. "The girls receive fine treatment at all of the boardinghouses," she said with obvious embarrassment.

"I'm sure Reggie speaks with great authority regarding your abilities. I would like to remain and visit, but I believe we had best get the wagon home. I hope to unload at least a portion of the goods tonight and then finish tomorrow—especially since it will be Saturday and I'll have Reggie there to assist," he said, winking at his daughter.

"Let me get your loaf of bread. Do you want to pack your clothes tonight or come back and get them tomorrow, Reggie?" Elinor asked as she began to rise from her chair.

"I'll come back and see you tomorrow. I'll fetch the bread," she said, jumping to her feet.

"Wrap it in one of the linen cloths in the far drawer."

"I will," Reggie called over her shoulder as she raced off to the kitchen.

Justin shook his head. "I can't believe how much she's

changed. She appears much . . ." He hesitated and then shrugged his shoulders.

"Happier?" Elinor ventured.

"That too," he said. "I insist upon paying you for all you've done," he said as Reggie hurried back into the room, carrying the linen-wrapped bundle.

"We can discuss that matter at another time. And don't you forget to come back for your belongings, Reggie," she instructed as she gave the girl a hug.

"I won't. Thank you for letting me stay with you."

"You are most welcome," she said warmly.

The trio made their way out to the wagon, and Justin lifted Reggie up onto the seat. "I'll let you know what I think of Reggie's baking," he called out as he slapped the reins and flashed a smile at Elinor.

The sun had not yet crested the ridge of hills along the eastern fringes of the city when Justin Chamberlain forced himself from a sound sleep and settled his feet on the rough and splintered floorboards of his small bedroom.

He rubbed his eyes and raked one hand through his mop of disheveled hair in an attempt to pat down the errant strands that circled his head like ruffled chicken feathers. "Good enough," he muttered.

The previous night's work had continued until the cover of darkness made it impossible to safely continue unloading the household goods. He had secured the tarp-covered wagon in the barnlike storage shed at the rear of his house and then spent the next hour caring for his horses.

He'd gone to bed promising himself he would arise early the next day and finish unloading the wagon before Reggie awakened. That way they would have the entire day to uncrate and arrange the goods. Granted, it would take more than one day, but with an early start, he hoped to accomplish a great deal.

He was carrying the last of the crates into the front room when Reggie bounded down the stairs and met him in the parlor. She stood before him in an old cotton nightgown that had belonged to her mother. Wild wisps of hair flew in all directions as they escaped the long braid hanging down her back.

"You began without me," she accused.

"You need not worry. I haven't unpacked one thing, so there is still plenty to do. In fact, we'll be fortunate if we have everything unpacked by this time next week."

"I could remain at home all next week and help you," she volunteered.

Justin laughed aloud. "I think not, young lady. If the choice comes down to our living in chaos or your attending school, we'll live in chaos. We'll complete what we can today and work on it each evening next week."

"If you ask the teacher, I'm certain she'll send my work home."

"It's more important that you attend school than unpack boxes," he replied. "Now why don't you run upstairs and get dressed while I fix us some breakfast. Once we've finished our meal, we'll begin."

His daughter grumbled under her breath as she shuffled out of the room and up the steep flight of stairs, her feet slapping heavily on the wooden steps in a childlike display of irritation. Justin ignored the exhibition, knowing Reggie would be sorely disappointed that her actions failed to annoy him.

A hearty breakfast of eggs, bacon, and Reggie's home-made bread, along with a crock of raspberry jam supplied by Elinor, was waiting on the table when Reggie entered the kitchen in an old, faded dress that was too short.

"It appears you've grown since you last wore that dress," her father remarked as she plopped down on the wooden chair.

"The skirt may be a little too short, but it's plenty good enough to wear while I'm unpacking boxes."

"You're right about that. Incidentally, this bread is excellent." He waved the jam-laden slice he held in one hand.

Her eyes brightened at the praise. "Thank you. I'm pleased you like it. I'm going to attempt making some all by myself next Saturday. I'd like to make some on Monday, but since I must go to school . . ." Her voice trailed off as she gave her father a questioning look.

"Next Saturday it shall be. And I'll look forward to it with great anticipation," he replied. "Shall we get to those boxes?" he asked as he picked up their plates and cleared the table.

Reggie nodded. "It's nice to have all of our furniture again, isn't it?" Reggie asked as they began opening boxes.

He agreed. The furniture was scattered about the rooms in complete disarray, and yet there was comfort in being surrounded by their own belongings.

"I never saw this before. Who made it?" Reggie inquired, holding up an intricately stitched sampler.

"Your mother made it the year before we married."

"It's beautiful. May I have it?" she asked, tracing her finger over the raised stitching.

Justin was surprised by his daughter's request. "Of course. You can have anything of your mother's you desire. In fact, I know she would be delighted that you appreciate her handwork."

"Can I take it over to Mrs. Brighton's and show her?"

Justin mumbled his agreement while unwrapping the hastily packed dishes. "It appears I didn't secure these as well as I thought."

Reggie surveyed the broken plate and grinned. "So long as three of them remain unbroken, we'll do fine."

"Three?"

She gave him a look of surprise. "We'll need to invite Mrs. Brighton for supper, don't you think?"

Her father was kneeling on the floor, reaching deep into one of the crates. "Oh yes, of course."

Once again she had surprised him. Reggie, so slow to make friends, especially with adults, had apparently grown quite fond of Elinor Brighton during his absence. The thought pleased him. After the incident at the church, he was acutely aware his daughter could use the guidance of a woman.

"Were you expecting company?" Reggie inquired as a knock sounded at the door. She stood up and peeked out through a small opening in the parlor drapes.

The knocking continued and Justin sat back on his heels. "Are you going . . ."

"It's them!" Reggie hissed. She tiptoed back to her father.

"Them? Who is *them*?"

"The church ladies!" she whispered. She leaned closer to her father's ear as the knocking grew more insistent. "We need to hide."

"Pastor Chamberlain!" Winifred Mason's shrill voice called from the other side of the door. "Try the back door. I know he's in there! I'll look through the parlor windows and see if anyone's in there." She had apparently taken charge of the group.

Justin rose to his feet. "We can't hide in here, Reggie. I'll tell them we're busy and ask them to return at another time."

"On a school day," she said quickly.

He smiled and nodded while walking to the door.

"Ladies!" he greeted, positioning himself to block their entry.

"My dear husband saw your wagon in front of Mrs. Brighton's boardinghouse yesterday and told me you had returned with your furniture and household goods," Winifred said, the frightfully large feather on her hat bobbing back and forth in time with her exaggerated movements. "Believe me, it didn't take long before I spread the word to the other ladies that we must come over here today and assist you."

"You are very kind to offer, but Reggie and I have the situation under control. We've already unpacked most of the crates and boxes," he explained.

"Tut, tut, this is women's work," Martha Emory said. "You and that young child can't properly arrange a household. Come along, ladies," she commanded as she gave the door a hefty shove.

Justin flattened himself against the wall as the women stormed the house. They hesitated in the foyer for only a moment before turning their attention to the parlor. The chaos and disorder beckoned them onward like soldiers who had glimpsed the enemy. They charged into the room with fierce determination etched upon their faces. They had observed their obstacle, and they would conquer!

Martha placed her parasol in the umbrella stand with a definitive thunk. "You were gone for so long we thought perhaps you'd return with a wife. You *didn't*, did you?"

"No," Justin replied softly while watching the remaining ladies begin digging through their belongings. "As I said, Reggie and I are quite capable of completing this task without assistance," he insisted, though no one except his daughter appeared to hear him.

"You see? There's no need to worry, Caroline," Martha remarked to her very eligible daughter.

Caroline's face reddened, and she quickly turned a dagger-filled glare upon her mother.

Reggie edged close to her father's side. "Tell them to leave," she pleaded as the women began rearranging the parlor furniture.

He shrugged his shoulders. "I don't believe there's any way to get them out," he said, now resigned to his fate.

"Do *something!*" Reggie implored.

"Ladies! Please don't move the furniture. I'm quite happy with it just the way it is," he requested feebly.

Winifred looked at him as though he'd lost his mind. "You can't have the divan sitting in front of the window. The sun will fade the fabric."

"Indeed!" Caroline agreed.

"I'll close the draperies," he argued.

"You'll forget after one or two days," Martha insisted. "If there were a woman—a *wife*—to attend to such matters on a daily basis, then such an arrangement might be acceptable."

Although Justin and Reggie made several more attempts to halt the women's ministrations, their suggestions went ignored. Finally, Justin sat down and watched while Reggie paced back and forth behind him, muttering words of irritation and disgust. When the group had the parlor arranged to their satisfaction, they clumped up the stairs to accomplish their next mission.

"Who could *that* be?" Justin asked as another knock sounded at the front door.

He pulled open the door and was greeted by the unremitting chatter of another group of women from the church. The thought of slamming the door was tempting, yet he maintained his dignity.

"Ladies! I do believe I have all the assistance I can stand for one day."

"You can never have enough help when it comes to settling into a new house," Cecile Turnvall remarked as she, Abigail Mitchell, and Charlotte Brown bustled into the parlor.

There was no stopping Cecile. She and her comrades immediately set about moving all of the furniture the first group had arranged only a short time earlier. They tugged and pulled and huffed and puffed until the furniture was settled into a display that met with her satisfaction.

"That is *so* much better," she triumphantly announced. "Men have no sense of design and balance."

Justin stared into the room. This group had returned the furniture to much the way he'd arranged it earlier in the day.

"Well, I have never been so insulted!" Winifred remarked as her small group came down the stairway in time to hear Cecile's pronouncement. Winifred marched into the parlor with her mouth agape as she viewed the change that had taken place during her absence. "The furniture was perfectly arranged when we went upstairs. What have you done, Cecile?"

Cecile's eyebrows furrowed. The woman was obviously confused. "I have set things aright in this parlor," she answered calmly.

Winfred turned to her companions. "Gather your belongings, ladies. We're not wanted here, and I'll not be a part of making the pastor's home into a gaudy facsimile of how a genteel home should appear."

Justin stood helpless as Winifred, Martha, Caroline, and the other ladies who were members of the first contingency pinned their hats in place, yanked their parasols from the umbrella stand, and marched out the front door with the same vigor and determination with which they'd entered earlier.

"Now let's get started in the dining room," Cecile said to her collaborators.

Reggie tugged on her father's sleeve. "Are you going to let them continue changing things around? Soon another group will show up and then another."

Justin shrugged in confusion. "There's no way to stop them. You know I've already tried."

"Well, these ladies wouldn't get away with this in Mrs. Brighton's house. Sometimes the girls try to rearrange the furniture in the parlor or dining room, but Mrs. Brighton puts her foot down and immediately calls a halt to such activity. She would never allow such behavior in *her* house."

"It's too bad Mrs. Brighton isn't here right now," he said wearily. "Perhaps she would help us do the same. I believe I'll go make sure the door to my study is locked. I don't want them in there rearranging my books."

Justin searched for his daughter a short time later, thinking perhaps the two of them should take their fishing poles and head off to the river. If the good church ladies were determined to occupy his house, then he and Reggie might as well enjoy themselves for the remainder of the day. But Reggie was nowhere to be found. Finally he remembered the secret opening in her upstairs closet and thought maybe she'd gone to hide in her room.

"Reggie?" He knocked on the door before entering her room, but she wasn't there and the secret opening in the floor was securely covered.

He sat down on her bed but jumped to his feet when a burst of commotion erupted from downstairs. He hurried down the steps and stopped in the hallway. Elinor Brighton was standing beside Reggie, loudly clapping her hands.

"Ladies! Give me your immediate attention," she commanded in an urgent tone before once again clapping her hands together.

A distinct look of irritation crossed Cecile's face. "What is it?" she asked.

Unwavering, Elinor met Cecile's formidable gaze. "You must *all* leave—immediately."

"And might I ask just what authority you have in this matter?" Charlotte inquired.

"Exactly my question also," Cecile added.

"I have been asked to arrange the house in a manner that will be most beneficial for Reggie as she undertakes her duties in the house. With all due respect, I must request that you leave, or I'll be forced to use Pastor Chamberlain's broom and sweep you out," she said with a lopsided grin.

Elinor watched as Cecile Turnvall picked up a vase and crocheted scarf and began to arrange them on a side table. "Get the broom, Reggie!"

Cecile's mouth opened into a wide oval. "You're serious!"

"That I am," Elinor replied as Reggie reappeared with a straw turkey broom. "I know your hearts are in the proper place and that your intentions are well founded. However, the pastor has asked you to leave, but you've not done so." She waved the broom back and forth above her head. "Will you now leave peaceably, or must I put this broom to a use for which it was never intended?"

The women cast unhappy glances at Elinor, but she didn't waver. Instead, she remained in place, wearing a pleasant expression on her face while they prepared for their departure.

"How *dare* she act in such a bold manner! Why, she's simply trying to snag him for herself," Charlotte whispered to Cecile.

"We'll see about that! I know Martha Emory has plans for her Caroline and the preacher. I'm going to tell Caroline that she had best get busy, as she has some obvious competition," Cecile said loudly enough for all to hear. "Although at her age, Elinor Brighton hardly seems competition."

"She's merely using the girl in order to win him over for herself," Abigail agreed.

Elinor remained steadfast and didn't say a word until the last of the visitors exited the house. "I believe they're gone for good," she said as she closed the door. "From what they said, I imagine they'll be quick to tell the others what's occurred."

"I can't believe you actually succeeded in forcing their departure," Justin said with a hearty laugh. "And to think they actually believe you came here because you're interested in finding a husband."

"And not just any husband, but you. The very idea!" The two of them burst into gales of rippling laughter, not stopping until they were breathless.

Justin glanced at his daughter, who was staring at the two of them with a strange look in her eyes. "Good job, Reggie," he said. "Thank you for fetching Mrs. Brighton."

"You're welcome."

A strange faraway look remained in Reggie's eyes. Justin tilted his head to one side, attempting to discern just what his daughter could be thinking. Perhaps she was coming down with a cold. He shook his head and uttered a silent prayer that this would not be the case.

CHAPTER · 9

MCKINLEY FOLLOWED behind Matthew as the two entered the home of Nathan Appleton. The gathering this evening would likely reveal the same behavior that was being exhibited throughout the entire Northeast. An ominous apprehension shrouded the room like a proclamation of death. McKinley shuddered as he inhaled a deep breath. The air was thick with fear.

"They've prepared themselves for the worst, and that is good," Nathan whispered.

"For once I wish I could disappoint them," Matthew replied with a look of weariness.

Nathan nodded and moved to his desk. "Gentlemen, we'll not keep you waiting. Matthew has brought a report and his recommendations."

McKinley accompanied Matthew to the desk and began to arrange the sheaf of papers in his case while Matthew greeted the members of the Boston Associates.

"We are all acutely aware the banks have been closed since the thirteenth of October. To date, there is no indication when they may reopen. Already there is a rise in unemployment. Real estate and grain prices have begun to decrease, although there are predictions the South will not suffer as greatly as the rest of the country due to their slave economy. Personally, I fear that if some means isn't found to slow down the panic, we will find ourselves in a deep recession."

"I agree," Nathan said. "However, a financial panic can be like a malignant epidemic that kills more by terror than by real disease. Consequently we must remain level-headed."

Matthew nodded his agreement. "But we must also be prepared for a tumultuous period, especially here in the North. We must have a definitive plan of action. From the reports I've received to date, we will continue to receive the cotton shipments as contracted from all of our Southern growers. I anticipate little shortage due to the yellow fever outbreak among our largest producers. However, if we don't employ a replacement for Samuel Wainwright in the near future, we may face difficulty next year. Most of our contracts are due for renewal, and we'll need someone to negotiate with the Southerners—unless we look elsewhere," he hesitantly added.

A hush fell over the room. Even McKinley ceased shuffling through the paper work and directed his full attention to his father-in-law.

Finally breaking the silence, Thomas Clayborn rose to his feet. "Whatever do you mean by that remark, Matthew?"

"I've been contacted by an envoy representing the Russian cotton producers. They are very interested in wooing us back—their prices are certainly more competitive . . ."

"I thought we decided a number of years ago that the Russian cotton was inferior and we were not going to use substandard raw materials," Leonard Montrose said.

"It appears the quality, at least what I saw, was equal to

what we've been receiving," Matthew replied. "If the Russian prices continue to drop and the economy doesn't quickly recover, I believe this is an option we'll need to seriously consider."

"What they show you and what they actually deliver will likely be entirely different," McKinley put in. "And what of our loyalty to the growers who have so capably supplied you through the years? If the country is to survive, should we not continue doing business within our own borders when products are available?" He was unable to keep his anger in check.

"You have a valid point, my boy," Nathan said. "However, our first duty is to our investors. If the recession continues, we may want to consider the Russian cotton, but we should first give our Southern growers an opportunity to meet an equal price, don't you think?"

The men muttered among themselves as a haze of cigar smoke floated upward and layered the room.

Matthew leaned forward. "I'm more than willing to give all of our suppliers equal opportunity, but if we sign contracts with the Southern growers, we will be bound and it will matter little what price the Russians offer. How do you plan to overcome such an obstacle? As in the past, I believe the Southerners will insist upon contracts."

Nathan took a sip from his glass of port. "Once again, present them with an option. Tell them we will make every effort to purchase their cotton, but we'll not be signing contracts at this time. It will be their choice."

"You're gambling with our future, Nathan," Robert Woolsey cautioned.

"The South will likely pursue and win the English market. If the Russians don't actually come through or if their product is inferior, we could be left without any cotton whatsoever. I believe we should contract with at least half of the Southern growers in the event this plan with Russia proves foolhardy," Matthew suggested.

Nathan nodded his agreement. "All of life is a gamble, Robert. Fortunes are made and lost in the blink of an eye. Only the brave weather the storm."

"Or drown," Robert countered. "To lose my own investment is one thing—I have a vote in the matter. But we are responsible for the futures of more than ourselves. Give pause to think about the vast number of employees and suppliers who work for us and will be affected by the decisions we make this night as well as in the future."

"No need to become maudlin," Josiah Baines said. "We all realize these are weighty issues we're settling upon."

"And we do have time to wrestle with some, but Matthew cannot be expected to move forward without direction," Nathan said.

Robert Woolsey stood to be recognized. "What is the situation regarding layoffs in the mills?"

"Layoffs will begin within the next month, and I surmise several of the mills will be closed down," Matthew answered. "I truly dislike being the bearer of bad tidings, but all of you are intelligent men who understand what has happened as well as I do. The system of paper currency and bank credits in this country has caused wild speculation and gambling in stocks. Even President Buchanan has reported that the fourteen hundred banks in this country have been irresponsible and are deferring to the interests of their stockholders rather than the public welfare. Until there are restrictions forcing the banks to back their paper currency with gold and silver, these problems will continue. Let us hope Congress will finally take definitive action."

"Well said, Matthew," Nathan exclaimed. "Even those of us who own stock in many of these banks want to see matters handled in a more appropriate fashion."

McKinley surveyed the room and wondered what these men must be thinking. His investments were of a much lesser value than the holdings of these men, yet he knew he stood on the brink of financial ruin. Fear had become McKinley's constant companion, and he wondered if the calm appearance of these men was merely a façade. He longed to confide in his father-in-law, though his pride prohibited him from speaking.

Samuel had been his one confidant throughout the last several years. He had looked to his older brother as a mentor and a refuge where his secrets would be protected. Only Samuel had known McKinley's financial woes. Only Samuel had known that, in his haste to provide Violet with the same worldly possessions she'd enjoyed in her father's home, he had overextended himself—and he had continued down the same path even to this day, contracting and beginning to build an ever bigger and more lavish home for his family. He'd borrowed well beyond the worth of his investments. The only thing that could possibly pull him from his financial abyss was the sale of The Willows. He could only hope Jasmine would bargain well for its sale.

"For now, what say you in regard to new contracts, hiring a replacement for Samuel Wainwright, layoffs, and the many other issues bearing down upon us?" Matthew inquired.

"I suggest we empower you to cautiously move forward with layoffs where needed. In regard to the contracts, we have several months before we need make a final decision. Let's give that topic additional thought." Nathan scratched his beard. "I know if Samuel were alive, he would already be negotiating with the growers to secure their new contracts. However, I believe we should refrain from hiring a replacement at this juncture. If questions arise regarding contracts, we can then truthfully say we've been slowed down in the process due to Samuel's untimely death. What say you?" he inquired.

Once again murmurs filled the room, like the annoying hum of mating cicadas. Each man was intent upon discussing his view with a neighbor before reaching a final decision. Each one was hopeful he could sway a comrade to his own particular viewpoint. After waiting several minutes, Nathan pounded a gavel and restored order to the group.

"We can talk *after* the meeting. For now let's vote so those who need to return home may do so."

McKinley was not surprised when an overwhelming majority agreed with Nathan's proposal. They were usually in accord with his directives. Even those who voiced opposition during the meetings usually succumbed to the pressure to go along with the group. Like sheep, they nearly always followed their shepherd.

CHAPTER · 10

Early November 1857

JASMINE STEPPED into the library, her white kid slippers gliding across the carpet without a sound. Nolan's chair was turned toward the garden, but he was obviously engrossed in the letter he held in one hand.

"A letter from home or a business matter?" Jasmine inquired as she drew near his chair and gently grasped his shoulder.

Nolan started at her touch. "I didn't hear you approach," he said, placing the letter on his desk. "The letter is from Albert Cameron at the Lowell Savings Bank, along with a note from Paddy that he included."

"Is Paddy having problems with the farm?" she asked, taking a seat opposite her husband.

"No, nothing like that. Paddy could care for the farm and horses without a second thought. However, it seems the economy is much worse in the North—at least for the present time. Albert explains problems that have occurred and his prospects for the future. . . . It's rather dim, I fear. He says he recently reviewed a number of Southern newspapers and was surprised at the lack of coverage regarding what he describes as a full-blown panic that has now thrown large portions of the country into a recession."

"I've not heard or read anything that indicated the country was in a recession. Are we so far removed from the rest of the country that we have no idea what is transpiring at home? Surely Albert is exaggerating," she said.

"He isn't one to overstate his concerns, so I seriously doubt he would write unless he perceived this as a genuine problem. He says predictions of a quick recovery aren't forthcoming, and he also states that President Buchanan referred to the country's monetary interests as being in deplorable condition, though he does believe we'll make a complete recovery."

Jasmine stood up and moved to Nolan's side. "This makes no sense. Why would this information not be important to the Southern community? For the life of me, I cannot understand why such matters would be hidden beneath a cloak of silence."

Nolan smiled and patted her hand. "I don't imagine anyone is making a concerted effort to hide these issues. The newspaper editors have likely decided that since the Southern economy has not yet been affected, there is no reason to create panic among the gentry."

"So they're going to bury their heads until disaster swoops down upon them rather than preparing when they have the opportunity?"

"I believe they prefer to think the problem will not filter into the Deep South. And though I have serious doubts, they may be correct in their thinking."

"Oh, pshaw! There must be more to this than meets the eye. I'd guess someone in power made a decision to withhold the information from the South for as long as possible and for whatever reason. I would speculate that favors are being exchanged among the powerful and at the expense of the citizens."

Nolan gave a hearty laugh. "I believe your analysis of the situation may be more dramatic than the actual truth—whatever that may be."

Jasmine removed a small watch from the tiny pocket set in the seam of her violet day dress. "I didn't realize it was getting so late. I had best check on Spencer. I told Henrietta I would see that he completed his sums." She kissed him on the cheek. "I'd like to discuss this matter further when I've finished. I haven't yet heard what Paddy had to say in his note to you, and I want to read Albert's letter," she called over her shoulder.

The violet and gray silk fringe that edged the bodice and sleeves of the wool dress swayed in time with her steps as Jasmine hurried up the steps to the small room she had converted into a schoolroom for her son.

Spencer was leaning out the single window in the tiny room with only his lower body remaining inside the framework.

"That's a dangerous position, Spencer. Come back inside before you fall and hurt yourself," Jasmine warned. "Have you finished your lessons?"

"On the table," he replied as he wriggled his upper torso back inside. "Can I go fishing if they're all correct?"

"Do you never tire of fishing?" she inquired with a soft smile.

"It's the only good thing about being in Mississippi. It remains warm enough to fish nearly all year long, doesn't it?"

"Sometimes nature will play a trick upon us and we'll have unpleasant weather for a good deal of the winter," she said absently as she checked his figures.

"Will we be home for Christmas?" he asked.

"You know that's impossible, Spencer. I don't know why

you'd even entertain such a notion. Even if all of the cotton had been picked, we couldn't possibly prepare to return to Massachusetts by year's end."

His head drooped until it nearly rested upon his narrow chest. "I know, but I want to go home."

His plea wrenched Jasmine's heart. She knew her son was unhappy, and she couldn't blame him. Since the incident at school he'd become reluctant to leave The Willows. Even attending church had become a battle. Forcing him to sit in the same pew with some of those same boys who had raised their fists against him seemed cruel.

She tousled his brown waves and pulled him close. "I want to go home too. This is a difficult time for all of us, but we must complete what we came here to do. Once we return home, all of this will soon be forgotten."

The look in Spencer's eyes revealed he wouldn't soon forget the beating he'd taken, yet Jasmine knew both prayer and time could heal his internal wounds and make him an even stronger person. Suffering at Bradley's hands had made her stronger, and now she seldom thought of those frightful years when she was his wife. The same transformation could happen to Spencer.

"I miss Moses. I tried making friends with some of the slave boys, but they don't want to be my friend."

"They are no longer slaves," Jasmine corrected. "Most likely they are skeptical of your motives. Don't take it to heart. They will come around in time."

He didn't seem to hear her. Jasmine ached for her son's misery. She went to the table and quickly scanned his arithmetic.

"Wonderful!" she exclaimed as she wiped the slate clean. "If time at the pond is what you want, then off with you. But promise me you'll be home in time for supper."

His face brightened. "I promise. And maybe I'll bring some fish home with me."

The two of them walked downstairs together. Jasmine watched as Spencer ran off to fetch his fishing pole, and once he was out of sight, she returned to the library.

Nolan glanced up as she walked into the room. "That was a quick lesson."

"I was merely checking his work, not giving him a lesson. His answers were all correct, so now he's off to the pond to catch some fish. He's terribly unhappy and longs to go home," she said, sitting down opposite the mahogany desk that had belonged to her father.

Nolan tilted his head to one side. "I believe that's true for all of us."

"That's what I told him, but that fact doesn't lessen his own misery. He misses Moses and being in school with his other friends, not to mention being in familiar surroundings. He's been isolated since the episode at school. Even the former slave children want nothing to do with him."

"I realize that, my dear, but we can't change what is in the past or force friendships. Like most children, Spencer is resilient."

"He deeply resents that we brought him here," she said in a faint whisper.

"And you're now feeling blameworthy for what happened at school. We made the proper decision, Jasmine. The event at school does not change the fact that Spencer belongs with us. Please promise me that you won't continue down this path of self-recrimination."

"I promise—but it won't be easy." Her gaze fell upon the missive lying open upon the desk.

"What did Paddy have to say? Any good news?"

Nolan laughed. "It seems he's met a girl. He says she fancies herself quite the expert on horses. From the sound of things, he may have met his match, though he says she's a bit too high and mighty for his liking. Apparently she lives at Elinor's boardinghouse instead of in the Acre. When he offered to help her find a place in the Acre, she told him she'd live where she pleased and it wasn't in the Acre."

"Dear me! I can't imagine Paddy taking it upon himself to tell a young lady where she should live. No wonder the girl spoke her mind."

Nolan laughed. "That's not the worst of it. Seems he was having difficulty with one of the horses, and she told him how to correct the problem using Baucher's method. He had never heard of the technique, and she quickly put him in his place."

"And did he take her advice?"

"He did. And it worked! However, it seems she may have taken a liking to Timothy Rourke. Who knows? Our Paddy may be wed by the time we return to Lowell."

Jasmine clasped the fringed bodice of her dress. "Don't even think such a thing! We'll be home much too soon for any weddings to occur. In fact, given the tenor of Albert Cameron's letter, I think we should truly consider leaving at the earliest opportunity. I'm afraid we are going to be dramatically impacted by the events occurring at home. There are likely matters that need our attention even as we speak."

"What would you have me do? I see no alternative other than to complete the task at hand. Once the cotton is ready for shipment, we'll leave—even if we haven't sold The Willows. I know McKinley will object, but if selling the plantation is the only thing that prohibits our return home, we'll place it in the hands of someone we trust. Someone who will bargain for the best possible price."

"I am in complete agreement. And should McKinley find fault with our decision, then he may handle the sale himself. My hope is that we can return by spring. Poor Alice

Ann believes her pony will be all grown up before she returns home to ride the animal again."

"Yes. She's mentioned her concern to me on several occasions. But I told her she was going to have many years to ride her horse." Nolan walked around the desk and gently pulled Jasmine from her seat and into his arms. "Please don't fret about the children. Once we return home, their bad memories will fade. We've done the proper thing by coming here. Giving your father's slaves their freedom and enough money to begin a new life is worth the few sacrifices we've been forced to make."

Jasmine lifted her face and looked into Nolan's deep blue eyes. "Who could ever ask for a better man than you? No wonder I love you so much."

She closed her eyes and felt the warmth of his arms as they tightened around her waist. He captured her lips in a long, lingering kiss, and she knew she could never love another.

———

Elinor poured two cups of tea—one for herself and one for Justin Chamberlain. Since his return from Maine, he had begun stopping by the boardinghouse regularly—once or twice a week—generally seeking advice regarding Reggie's behavior or requesting Elinor's assistance with a church function.

Through the weeks, they had formed a comfortable companionship, and Elinor now looked forward to his visits, particularly when they were discussing an idea for one of his sermons. Justin's visits helped provide balance to her life, an escape from her routine housework and meal preparation.

"You appear preoccupied," Elinor remarked after Justin had failed to answer her question.

"What? I'm sorry . . . my mind was elsewhere."

She laughed. "That's what I said—you appear pre-occupied. Is it something you'd care to discuss?"

Justin appeared rather sheepish as he looked up from his cup of tea. "Actually, I've come to ask another favor of you, and I've been searching for some way to broach the topic."

"There's no need for such tactics between friends. You merely need ask. If I can help, I will be pleased to do so," she said in her no-nonsense manner.

He gave a nervous laugh. "I need a place for Reggie to stay all next week."

"Why would you hesitate to ask? You know I'm fond of Reggie. If we didn't enjoy one another's company, she wouldn't stop here on her way home from school each day," Elinor said. "You need only tell me when she'll arrive."

"You are very kind. I must leave for Boston early Monday morning and hope to return Friday evening."

"In that event, it would be best if she stayed with me Sunday night. That way you can leave on the early train. In fact, why don't you and Reggie join me for supper Sunday evening—if you have no other plans," she added hastily.

"I fear your kindness causes me to impose upon you," he said sheepishly. "However, joining you for supper is very appealing. Are you certain you'll go to no trouble on our account?"

"I promise," she replied. "May I tell Reggie of our plan when she stops to see me after school today, or would you prefer to tell her yourself?"

Justin gave her a feeble smile. "She knows I must go to Boston. She said that if I didn't come and ask you today, she would do so herself. There was little doubt in my mind she would carry through with her promise."

"Then I will tell her the arrangements have been completed."

Reggie yanked on the needle and then emitted an exasperated sigh. "My thread knotted again," she lamented as she turned over the sampler and glared at the tangled thread.

"You try to save time by using a piece of thread that's much too long—that's what causes it to knot," Elinor quietly informed her as she sat down beside the girl and examined her handiwork.

"I use a longer piece because I don't like threading the needle."

"Is it because you don't like threading the needle or because you think it's quicker if you use a longer thread and don't have to stop so frequently?"

"Because it's quicker," Reggie replied with a giggle.

"But only if the thread doesn't knot, and usually—"

"The thread knots," she said, completing the sentence.

"Making a sampler isn't a test of speed, Reggie. Rather, it's intended to teach you the variety of stitches you can use in future fancywork. There! I think I've untangled it for you," Elinor said as she handed the piece of stitching back to the girl. "Your stitches have improved greatly. You should be very proud of what you've accomplished thus far."

Reggie ran her finger across the stitching. "Do you think my father will believe I made this all by myself?"

"Well, if he doesn't, I'll be the first one to come to your defense. I do believe your father is going to be *very* proud of you."

Shortly after Justin Chamberlain returned from Maine, Reggie had shown Elinor the sampler her mother had made before her marriage. The child was enchanted by the piece and expressed a desire to make one of her own. "So they can hang on the wall side-by-side," she had told Elinor before expounding upon the fact that Elinor would need to teach her well. After all, the stitching would need to be of a fine quality, for people would surely compare the two pieces of handwork, Reggie had advised.

And so they had begun the project. Each evening when Reggie stopped by the boardinghouse, she worked on the sampler while Elinor prepared supper and the two of them visited about their day—Reggie's ongoing struggle to fit in at school and Elinor's efforts to keep her house running smoothly.

Now, without the necessity of going home for the next week, Reggie was certain she could accomplish a great deal on her sampler while her father was away in Boston—at least that was the hope she had expressed to Elinor.

So while Elinor pared potatoes for the stew she would later be serving for supper, Reggie pushed her needle through the tightly woven muslin and then gently pulled the length of thread to the opposite side of the fabric. "I heard the girls talking last night," Reggie told her. "Ardith and Lucinda were crying. They're afraid they're going to lose their positions at the mill. Lucinda said the overseer in the weaving room told six girls to go to the office and collect their final pay yesterday. She thinks she'll be next. What do you think?"

"The only thing I know is that many of the girls are losing their jobs. Thus far, we've been most fortunate. There are very few boardinghouses where at least one or two girls haven't lost their positions. I suppose it was bound to happen, yet I've been fervently praying that those who are most in need of their wages will be protected."

"Lucinda said she didn't know how her family would survive without the money she sends them. Then Janet laughed and said she didn't know how she would survive without money to buy new shoes and jewelry, but she knew she wouldn't lose her position. Next, Ardith told Janet to

182

keep quiet or leave the room, and then Janet said she didn't have to and then—"

"I believe I understand the gist of the discussion," Elinor said with a faint smile. "All the girls are concerned about losing their livelihood."

"Aren't you afraid? What happens if they all leave your boardinghouse? What will *you* do?" Reggie asked.

"Eventually I would be forced to speak to my brother, Taylor, and request his assistance, I suppose. However, I pray the financial problems of our country will be resolved before I'm required to take such a step."

"I thought you told Father your brother was moving to Maine."

"Yes. In fact, he's already done so. He bought part interest in a milling operation. I'm not sure his timing was the very best, but one never knows about such things."

Reggie's eyes opened wide. "You mean you would move away from Lowell?"

"If necessary, I would have to."

"But what would I do without you?" she asked, her eyes filled with concern.

"No need to begin worrying, Reggie. I'm confident this will all work out for the best."

The girl bobbed her head up and down, though she didn't appear convinced. "I don't like Janet—she's mean."

"Well, that was a quick turn in our discussion," Elinor commented as she removed the heavy white dinner plates from a shelf in the kitchen.

"I don't want to hear about you moving away, so I decided to talk about something else."

Elinor was touched by Reggie's reply. Knowing the girl had suffered through a lifetime of missing a mother gave her pause. She now questioned why she had been so forthright with the child. After all, Elinor had suffered through the same feelings as a young child, and there was no need to cause the girl unjustified concern. Yet truth was truth, and if matters continued to spiral downward, she would have no choice but to move. There would be far too many women in Lowell seeking employment for her to remain.

"So you've decided you don't like Janet because of her remarks to Ardith and Lucinda?" Elinor inquired.

"Not just that. She appears to enjoy herself the very most when others are suffering. Have you noticed that about her? The last time I stayed here, Sarah received a letter from home saying her father had been severely injured in a farming accident. As she was reading the missive, Sarah began to weep. Without even asking permission, Janet took the letter from Sarah and began to read aloud all the terrible details contained in the letter. Even when Sarah covered her ears and begged Janet to stop, she continued. And all the time she had a cruel look on her face. I waited for a few moments and when no one else did anything, I grabbed the letter from Janet's hands and gave it back to Sarah. That's why Janet is always saying mean things to me."

Elinor dropped into the chair opposite Reggie. "How is it that I know nothing about any of this?"

Reggie shrugged. "I suppose because Janet always threatens the girls, and they're afraid to tell you what she's really like. Janet told Sarah she had better not complain to anyone or she'd be sorry."

"But what threat would Janet pose? The girls are all equal in this house."

"But not at the mill. That night Sarah said she didn't care what Janet said, for she was going to tell you about her improper behavior. Janet pushed me out of the room and told me to go downstairs. After she closed the door to their room, I clacked my feet on the top two steps like I was going downstairs, but instead I listened outside the door. I heard

Janet tell Sarah that if she said one word to anyone, she would tell the overseer and he would terminate Sarah," Reggie explained.

"Surely Sarah didn't believe such nonsense. The overseer isn't going to terminate Sarah merely because Janet makes such a request."

"From what I heard, it appears Janet and the overseer are very close friends. The girls said she receives special treatment all the time. Even Mary Margaret said it was true, and she rarely says much about any of the girls. Did you know Janet doesn't have to operate as many looms as the other girls? Mary Margaret says it's because she's friends with Mr. Wingate, the overseer."

"I am taken aback to think that Mary Margaret would relate such delicate information to a girl of your tender years," Elinor said.

"Oh, she didn't tell *me*. I heard her whispering with Lucinda and Ardith in the parlor one evening after the incident with Sarah. Janet is always making unkind remarks to Mary Margaret because she's Irish. Janet says Irish people shouldn't be permitted to live in the boardinghouses, and as soon as she can move to another room, she's going to do so."

Elinor tilted her head and began to rub her forehead. "You are a true fount of information, Reggie. However, I'm afraid the details you've related are not very heartening. I thought the girls were all quite happy, yet trouble has been brewing right beneath my nose and I didn't even smell a whiff. And I have always considered myself a relatively good judge of character."

Reggie laid her stitching on the edge of the table. "You must promise you won't breathe a word of what I've told you. Otherwise, I'll never be able to sneak about and hear their conversations again."

Elinor tucked a loose strand of Reggie's hair behind the

girl's ear. "I won't divulge your secret, but you must call a halt to your spying activities. You know such behavior is inappropriate, don't you?"

"Yes," Reggie replied in a disappointed voice. "But it *is* fun," she added with a sparkle in her eyes.

Elinor bit her lower lip so she wouldn't laugh at the girl's reply. "But you promise to stop?"

Her head bobbed up and down.

"Good! Now that we've settled that issue, I had best get back to supper preparations. The girls will be arriving within the hour."

"Would you like me to help you in the kitchen?"

"I believe I have everything under control. Why don't you continue stitching on your sampler."

"May I go outside for just a short time? I promise I won't go far, and I'll start home when I hear the final bell ring at the mills."

"That's fine," Elinor said. "There's a cool breeze. Be certain to wear your bonnet!"

The fresh air would do Reggie good, and Elinor needed a bit of time to digest the discomfiting news. Exasperated by what she'd been told, Elinor slapped her hand upon the table. How had she overlooked the manipulation and cruel behavior that bubbled beneath the surface of the girls' smiles and polite table conversation? And how long had Janet's meanspirited behavior been going on? She wrestled with the thought momentarily until she remembered Janet mentioning she was going to be promoted. When was that? At least a year ago. Elinor had been surprised when Janet made the announcement—especially since Janet had moved to Mr. Wingate's weaving room only a few weeks earlier. From all appearances, Janet had taken the wrong path when she accepted her new position.

Elinor had heard the stories of mill girls succumbing to

the advances of their superiors for special favors, yet she
didn't think any of her girls would ever compromise themselves. Obviously, she had been incorrect. Now that she was
aware of what was happening, she would be more observant.
Deep inside she harbored the thought of greeting Janet with
a notice to vacate her house this very evening. But she
couldn't keep her word to Reggie and force Janet from the
boardinghouse without furnishing a reason for her action.
Janet was shrewd and would likely assume Elinor had learned
of her behavior. If Elinor wasn't careful, Janet would blame
one of the other girls, who would soon suffer her wrath.

As the girls entered the house after work, Elinor
reminded herself to remain silent regarding the discoveries
made this afternoon. She must bide her time with a listening
ear and a watchful eye.

Except for Reggie, who for some unknown reason
appeared particularly jovial, the mood around the supper
table was somber.

"I pray that all went well at work today?" Elinor inquired
as she passed the plate of bread.

Janet ladled a heaping portion of stew onto her plate.
"No one was laid off today, though I believe there will be
several tomorrow."

"Truly? And why would you think so?" Elinor inquired.

Janet glanced about the table with a self-satisfied look on
her face. "I overheard some of the *men* talking today."

Elinor digested the reply before speaking. "I would think
it very difficult to overhear a conversation while operating
those noisy looms."

The girls smiled at Elinor's remark but said nothing.
They watched Janet, obviously curious about how she would
reply.

"I waited a brief time after the noonday bell had
sounded—when the machinery was shut down for dinner

break. Consequently, I had no difficulty whatsoever."

"I see," Elinor said, remembering that Janet hadn't appeared with the other girls for the noonday meal.

In fact, now that Elinor thought about it, there had been any number of days when Janet hadn't arrived for the noonday meal. This would provide a perfect opportunity for her to meet with Mr. Wingate, who was, after all, a married man. One who likely carried a lunch pail for his dinner yet would be expected home on time for supper.

"Where did you eat your dinner today, Janet? I missed you around the table," Elinor casually remarked.

"I took some ham and bread left over from breakfast. I wanted to spend the time visiting with some of my friends from the number four mill."

"I see. In that case, I hope you had an enjoyable visit."

"Yes, I did," she replied curtly. "Now if you'll excuse me, I want to fix my hair before I go into town. I saw a perfectly charming pair of earbobs at Whidden's. I don't believe I'll be able to sleep until I've purchased them."

A look of disgust was exchanged among the remaining girls, who soon excused themselves and moved to the parlor with Reggie following along behind.

"Come help me in the kitchen, Reggie. I think it's best if you remain with me."

"If Mrs. Brighton doesn't object," Mary Margaret said, "you can come up and visit with us after you've finished your chores. Would that be all right, Mrs. Brighton?"

"Yes, of course," Elinor agreed.

Although she was ready for bed by nine o'clock, Elinor sat reading a book in her small parlor near the front door. She never went to bed until all of the girls had returned from their evening outings, and Janet had not yet come home.

She looked up from her book as Reggie came running into the parlor with her nightgown flying about her legs.

"Janet's coming down the sidewalk," she announced.

"And how do you know that?"

"I was watching from the upstairs bedroom window," she replied with a giggle.

The words had no more than escaped Reggie's lips when the latch on the front door clicked.

"See! I told you," the girl whispered with a smug grin. "I believe I'll go to bed. Shall we say our prayers?"

During Reggie's previous visit, they had begun a ritual of saying their prayers aloud each night before going to bed, and Elinor was pleased Reggie wished to continue the practice. Elinor prayed and then nodded to Reggie to begin. Her prayer was much briefer than usual, and Elinor decided the child must be completely exhausted from the day's activities.

"I'll be back as soon as I make sure the front door is locked and there are no candles burning. You go ahead and get into bed."

After completing the nightly ritual, Elinor returned to her rooms. Reggie had followed her instructions and was already in bed with her eyes tightly closed. Using the brass candlesnuffer by her bed, Elinor extinguished the flame and slid between the bedcovers. Her thoughts wandered aimlessly, and exhaustion soon gave way to sleep.

"What was that?" Elinor shrieked, sitting straight up in her bed. Something had startled her out of a sound sleep. She covered her mouth and waited a moment.

A shrill scream sounded from upstairs. Fear gripped her and she grabbed her robe from the foot of the bed. It was then she heard Reggie giggle.

"You don't need to hurry upstairs—it's only a toad," she said. "I put it in Janet's bed."

"Who did this?" Janet screamed, her voice piercing the

quiet night. "Catch it! Somebody do something!"

Reggie lifted her knees to her chest and giggled until tears ran down her cheeks. "I knew she'd be afraid of a silly toad. I told Lucinda to sleep with Mary Margaret so Janet would be the only one getting into the bed. Then I put the toad in her bed before I came downstairs," she admitted.

"And that's why you were watching to see when she was coming home."

"Yes. I didn't want the toad to be frightened for too long," she said, stifling her laughter.

"It's good to hear you were at least concerned about the toad's welfare," Elinor said.

"Please don't be angry. We all thought it a fine joke and nobody got hurt. I'll apologize and tell her I'm responsible so she won't become upset with the others."

Elinor nodded. "I think catching the toad would set things aright even more than an apology. Let's go upstairs and see if we can find it."

By the time they reached the upstairs room, Janet was sitting atop one of the trunks with her feet drawn up underneath her. "You did this, didn't you? You are the most unpleasant child I've ever encountered."

"Truly? Then I must introduce you to some of those who would put me to shame," Reggie said. "I put the toad in your bed and I was going to say I'm sorry, but I'm not. If it weren't for Mrs. Brighton, I'd leave it here to frighten you all night."

Elinor pointed at the toad and Reggie quickly retrieved the creature. "Did it touch you?" Reggie inquired.

"Yes! It got on my legs and my hand."

"Then you'd best watch for warts. Toads are known to cause warts on people of foul disposition—such as yourself."

"And you!" Janet screeched. "You're holding it in your hand and you are a horrid little person, so you will surely get warts also," she said in a gleeful tone.

"But I don't care if I get warts, and you do," the child countered, then lifted the toad in front of her face and whispered words of praise to the creature while walking down the stairs. "I have to put you outside now. But if Janet is mean, I'll be sure to find you again," she promised.

Once the toad had been placed outside, Elinor pointed Reggie toward one of the chairs in her parlor. "We need to talk," she said as she gently closed the door.

"Are you going to tell Father?" she asked. "He'll never let me come and stay again if you do. Please don't tell him."

"I'm not going to tell him, but I think I have a better solution to the problem with Janet. Not as much fun perhaps, but I think it will prove much more beneficial to all of us."

"What is it?" Reggie asked, her eyes wide with anticipation.

"We need to pray for Janet."

"What? I don't want to pray for Janet. I don't like her."

"I know, and that's all the more reason we must do so. We need to pray that Janet will have a change of heart, and we need show her kindness. Only that way will we see a change in her."

Reggie frowned as she contemplated the suggestion. "I suppose I could *try*. But I think you'll need to pray for me too. Otherwise, I'll fail and have thoughts of placing a snake in her bed."

"In that case, I'll be praying very hard!"

When Justin arrived in Lowell late Friday afternoon, he was several hours ahead of schedule. At least as far as Reggie was concerned. A single row of stitching along the bottom of her sampler required completion, and she was intent upon completing the project. Consequently, his daughter had greeted him at the front door of the boardinghouse with an accusatory "You're early!"

"I thought you would be pleased to see me," he said, surprised by her outburst.

"But I thought you wouldn't be back until later in the evening."

Justin stood in the doorway, hat in hand, uncertain how he should respond. "Would you like me to leave and come back later?" he finally inquired when she didn't invite him inside.

Before Reggie could reply, Elinor strode down the hall, wiping her hands on a linen dish towel. "Pastor Chamberlain! How nice to see you. I trust you had a pleasant journey. Step aside so your father can come inside, Reggie," she said in an authoritative manner.

Reggie moved to one side and inched the door open for her father. "I'm not ready to go home," she announced. "I have *things* to finish."

"I see," Justin said, looking to Elinor for assistance.

"Why don't you see to your chores while your father and I visit in the parlor? Perhaps you'll be finished by the time he's ready to leave. If not, I'm sure he won't mind if you come home after supper."

Elinor's words seemed to resolve matters for Reggie, and Justin watched his daughter stride down the hallway as though she were on a mission of great importance.

"I can't believe the changes in Reggie since we've moved to Lowell. It's amazing. Now she voluntarily wears a dress and combs her hair, and her schoolwork is much improved. I must admit that you've had an astonishing influence upon her. I am most grateful."

"Reggie is an easy child to love," Elinor replied.

Justin laughed and shook his head. "That's not what most people say!"

"Then most people haven't taken the time to get to know her. Besides, Reggie and I share much in common. I think that's why I'm so easily able to influence her behavior."

Justin leaned back in the chair and gave his full attention to Elinor. "You've never mentioned having a common bond with Reggie in our previous discussions."

"I suppose I haven't, but Reggie and I have discussed it. You see, like Reggie, my mother died when I was but an infant. Unlike Reggie, I had my grandmother and other family members to help raise me, but I always felt different from the other children. Especially the girls when they would speak of their mothers taking them shopping or teaching them how to do a special embroidery stitch. . . . I felt set apart from them. So I began playing with my brother and his friends, doing the things they enjoyed: climbing trees, fishing, capturing snakes and spiders to scare the girls. The boys didn't judge me—they didn't care whether I had a mother teaching me how to sew and shop."

"And so that worked for you?"

"Until I began school. Once again I became an outcast because I didn't want to dress or act like a girl—until I met Bella, Taylor's wife. Taylor brought her to England after they married, and I thought her quite wonderful. As you know, they brought me here to America and I lived with them. Bella quickly influenced my behavior."

"Were you unhappy when she forced you to change?"

"Oh, she didn't force me. I admired Bella, so I attempted to emulate her in every way. Of course, I don't believe Reggie has changed because she wants to imitate me, but rather because I can relate to her experiences. I've not attempted to transform Reggie—merely offered her different options. And for the most part, she has been quite receptive. Now why don't you relax while I go to the kitchen and prepare a pot of tea."

Justin nodded and smiled as Elinor rose from her chair. She was an extraordinary woman, tender and kind yet filled with a strength he hadn't observed in most women—likely due to the losses she had suffered. One would be forced to develop inner fortitude in order to survive so many difficulties, he decided. And she had worked wonders in his daughter's life, and for that he would be eternally grateful.

With a practiced ease, Elinor placed the tea tray on the table in front of her and began to pour. "Biscuit?" she offered.

"Yes, thank you," Justin replied as he pulled a handful of coins from his pocket. "I am going to insist upon paying for Reggie's care. If you won't agree, then I'll have to make other arrangements in the future. In these difficult times, I will not add to your financial burden."

"My finances have not changed in the least. I have, in fact, been much more fortunate than many of the keepers. None of my boarders has lost her job, though I've heard talk of additional layoffs in the future. As for Reggie, having her here is my pleasure. Should her time with me ever become a financial burden in the future, I will surely tell you. For now, however, I simply cannot accept your money."

Justin placed the coins on the table. "I insist!" he said while maintaining a steady gaze into Elinor's thoughtful eyes.

"May I suggest we place the money in a benevolence fund? One that can be used solely for aiding the girls who lose their positions at the mills? There are many who help support their families with their wages, and losing their jobs will be devastating. If we could help in some small measure, I believe it would be a fine way to exhibit our Christian charity. What do you think?" she asked, scooting to the edge of her chair.

Her enthusiasm was contagious. "I believe a benevolence fund is a wonderful idea. The fund could be handled through the church, and I believe you would be the ideal person to take charge!" He leaned forward and took both of her hands in his own. "Would you be willing to accept such a challenge?"

"Yes, of course. I would be honored to do so."

"Look what I—" Reggie's words stopped midsentence.

Justin turned toward his daughter. Her gaze was fastened upon his hands tightly wrapped around those of Elinor Brighton. He froze in place, unable to move. There was a look of accusation in Reggie's eyes that forced him to remain transfixed. Fortunately, Elinor pulled back.

"You've finished?" she asked, her attention moving to the fabric in Reggie's hand.

She nodded. "Look what I made," she said, proudly holding up the sampler for her father's inspection.

"Bring it closer and let me see," he said. He took the sampler and carefully examined her sewing. "Am I to believe you made this all by yourself?"

"Mrs. Brighton taught me the stitches, but I did all of them myself, didn't I?"

"Every single stitch—and some of them twice."

Reggie edged onto her father's knee. "I want to put it in a frame and hang it on the wall."

"That's a fine idea. We'll put it in the parlor, where all our guests can see it when they come to visit."

"I want to hang Mama's sampler in the parlor too," she said carefully.

Justin knew she was watching for his reaction. Was it because he'd been holding Elinor's hands and she thought him disloyal to her mother's memory?

———

Reggie wriggled under the bedcovers, hoping to find a comfortable depression in the lumpy mattress. She'd been in bed for over an hour, yet no matter how she repositioned herself, sleep wouldn't come. Perhaps because it was the first night back in her own bed after a week at the boarding-house . . . or perhaps it was because she couldn't forget her father holding Mrs. Brighton's hands when she had walked into the parlor earlier this evening.

Oh, she liked Mrs. Brighton—in fact, she was quite fond of the boardinghouse keeper. Yet a troublesome suspicion had begun to grow ever since she walked into the parlor. She tucked the quilt under her chin and wished she could push the thought from her mind. Surely Mrs. Brighton's friend-ship was genuine. Reggie didn't want Mrs. Brighton to be another one of those women who used her in order to win her father's attention. Before coming to Lowell, she'd had her fill of women befriending her as a means to snag a hus-band for themselves.

"Please don't let her be like all the rest," she murmured into the darkness, hoping to push the unpleasant thought from her mind.

Yet no matter how she tried, the scene in the parlor played in her memory over and over again, like a squeaky violin that could not be silenced.

"Just like the others, I shall put her to the test!" she finally muttered.

The decision made, she rolled over and drifted into a restless sleep.

CHAPTER · 11

PADDY SHADED his eyes from the early morning sun and squinted hard as he attempted to make out the riders approaching from the east—two of them. He couldn't make out the riders from this distance, but he didn't recognize the horses. Strange to have visitors arrive this early in the morning. He had planned to take several of the Arabians out for their morning exercise. Since Mr. Houston's departure for The Willows, he'd had scant time for riding, which he truly loved, and was looking forward to a morning spent with some of their finest animals

The riders were proceeding at a slow pace, so he would have time enough to retrieve one of the beauties from its stall and lead it into the corral adjacent to the barn. He stopped to pat the nose of Alice Ann's pony, Winnie, as he passed by. The pony would be a good animal for the girl—if she ever got a chance to ride her again.

"Sure and I wish they'd come home," he muttered as he gave the pony one final pat.

The riders were within a short distance of the barn when

he finally led Glory's Pride out of the barn.

"I do hope that's one of ours," the rider called out as he approached Paddy.

Paddy gave a hearty laugh, for he recognized the speaker. Leland Bradford was a captain at West Point who had been to the farm on previous occasions. However, Paddy had never seen his companion.

"I do na think so. Glory's Pride is one of our finest studs. This fine fellow will na be leaving the Houston farm."

"Can't blame me for trying. How are you, Paddy?" The captain swung down from his horse and pulled off his glove before reaching to shake Paddy's hand.

"Fine, but I must admit I was na expecting visitors this mornin'. What brings ya to Massachusetts on this fine day?"

"This is Captain Ira Payne. He's in our main offices at the Point—helps take care of the finances," Captain Bradford explained as he made the introduction.

Paddy nodded. "Pleased ta meet ya, Captain. How can I be helpin' ya?"

Captain Bradford removed his hat and surveyed the surrounding area. Paddy didn't know what the man was looking for, but he waited patiently. Mr. Houston had taught him to be patient with their customers—especially the military, for Mr. Houston believed these men needed to feel they were in control.

Glory's Pride nudged Paddy with his broad nose, and Paddy turned to pat the horse. "Just a minute, boy," he murmured in a soft voice.

"We're interested in seeing the horses you're to deliver to the academy in the spring," Captain Payne finally told him.

"I do na recall ya ever doing such a thing before. Is there some problem?"

"With the *Houston* horses? Of course not!" Bradford declared. "We've merely begun a new procedure that includes reviewing the stock approximately six months prior to delivery."

Paddy thought the idea a waste of their time, yet who was he to argue with these military men. If they wanted to see the stock, he would give them what they wanted. "Simon! Harry! Michael!" he shouted.

The three men came running from different directions, all lurching to a halt in front of Paddy. "I need the horses scheduled for spring delivery to West Point brought into the far corral."

"All of them?" Simon asked.

"Aye, all of them."

"Gonna take a little while. Some of them's out in the far pastures."

"We have all day," Captain Payne said.

Paddy signaled for the men to round up the horses before turning his attention back to the visitors. "Could I interest ya in a cup of coffee or some tea? Me sister and her husband live here on the property, and I'm sure she'd be happy to have a bit o' company."

"That's a kind offer, but we were planning to talk with Mr. Houston. Is he about?" Bradford inquired.

"I do wish ya would have sent a telegraph or written before ya made yar visit. I could have let ya know Mr. Houston is in Mississippi, sir. I do na have an exact date for his return. However, he has left me with the authority to oversee the operation of the farm."

The two men exchanged a glance. "What business could Mr. Houston possibly have in Mississippi? Off searching for some new breed of horse?" Bradford inquired with a chuckle.

"Family matters," Paddy replied simply.

Captain Bradford directed his puzzled gaze at Paddy. "Family? Houston isn't from the South. He told me his parents hailed from England but he was born and reared in this part of the country."

"'Tis *Mrs.* Houston that has roots in the South," Paddy explained, uncertain how much information he should be parceling out to these men.

Bradford led his horse to the corral and glanced over his shoulder at Paddy. "Do you mind if we turn the horses loose in your corral while we talk?"

"Sure and that would be fine. Let me unsaddle them for ya."

"Since Mr. Houston isn't here and it's going to be a while before your men return with all of the horses, perhaps we should have that cup of coffee you offered earlier," Captain Bradford remarked.

"Aye. If ya'll follow me, it's only a wee stroll from here. There's a bit of a nip to the air, but I imagine you gentlemen are accustomed to being out in all types of weather."

Paddy quickly unsaddled the mounts and turned them into the corral before joining their owners. He was careful to observe the men's actions as they walked toward Rogan and Kiara's house. Although he could have entertained them in the main house, where Maisie would have been more than willing to serve the officers their coffee, he would feel more comfortable in Kiara's home. And something told him he needed to level the playing field. He feared there was more to this visit than merely assessing horseflesh.

"How has your business been faring these past months?" Captain Payne inquired as the men settled themselves in the parlor.

Paddy didn't know if the captain was simply making polite conversation while they awaited their coffee or if he was on a fishing expedition and hoped to elicit vital information of some sort.

"As well as can be expected, I suppose—can always be

better, don't ya know," he said with a grin.

Payne hunched forward in his chair. "These are difficult times. The North is suffering particularly hard, and I imagine it won't be long before the South succumbs to the economic downturn also. We've all been forced to take monumental steps in order to preserve our financial security. Even institutions such as West Point have been dramatically impacted by this latest panic. No doubt you're suffering the same consequences—certainly nothing to be ashamed of. After all, the purchase of horses is something a man can delay until there's a turnaround in the economy."

They were playing a game of cat and mouse—waiting for him to say the wrong thing, yet Paddy didn't know what the wrong thing might be. Mr. Houston always said to play your cards close to your chest and above all, don't speak unless you speak the truth.

" 'Tis true most are sufferin'. The bank closures are difficult for all and that's a fact. Ah, here's our coffee," he said as Kiara came into the room. He was thankful he could turn their attention to something other than his reply.

Captain Bradford settled back on the divan with his cup of coffee and riveted his steely eyes upon Paddy. "Have you had any purchasers renege on their contracts?" he inquired boldly.

"I would na discuss your contract with others, sir, and I can do nothing less for our other patrons. I'm sure ya understand—'twould be improper to do such a thing. But if it's additional horses ya're needin', I do na think I can be of assistance."

"I think I can take that statement to mean that your business has suffered very little. Apparently, like us, your clients pay six months in advance of delivery or have managed to find another method to meet their obligation."

Paddy took a gulp of his coffee and placed the cup on

the table. "Ta tell ya the truth, gentlemen, I'm not a man who enjoys playin' games with words. I prefer spending me time with those horses you've contracted to purchase. And there's nothin' I'd like better than to go out riding one of them. So understand me when I say that I do na mean to insult ya, but I'd like ta know just what it is ya're wanting. I don't believe you came all this way just to take a wee look at the horses."

Captain Bradford chuckled. "You're right, Paddy. We know we can always count on excellent horses from this farm. You and Mr. Houston have never disappointed us—in fact, you always exceed our expectations. Unfortunately, we've come today because we need to renegotiate our contract with Mr. Houston."

"Renegotiate?" Paddy's heartbeat quickened. "The West Point contract is valid for another two years. What is it ya're hoping to renegotiate?"

"Much like every other institution in this country, West Point is suffering from the poor economy," Captain Payne explained. "I'm pleased to hear that at least your business hasn't felt the impact. Hopefully, that will work to our advantage."

Paddy inwardly cringed. He'd been cautious in his conversation, yet it seemed he'd given them enough facts to use against him. These men were shrewd. Moreover, they had a history of negotiating contracts, while he had none. He could send for Albert Cameron at the bank or even McKinley Wainwright, yet he doubted they would strengthen his position. In fact, such a tactic could weaken his ability to negotiate—especially if they didn't agree with his opinion on how to handle the situation.

"You gentlemen have taken my words and attempted to twist them to yar advantage. Just because we have no additional horses ta offer does not mean we've not been hurt by the financial crisis or that we are in a position to rewrite our contract with the academy. I understand that with the banks closed, ya've likely na been able to transfer the money for the horses, and we have no problem with that."

"This is more than a matter of transferring funds," Payne said. "And while I understand you must protect the interests of this business, given the difficulties we're suffering at West Point, it is imperative that we receive the horses at a lesser price. Now I realize lowering the selling price of your animals isn't something you're anxious to do. However, we simply have no choice."

Paddy stared at him. "No choice? Of *course* ya've got a choice, Captain. Ya can honor your contract and if ya can na do that, ya can do the respectable thing and tell me ya can na purchase the entire herd ya've contracted for. We're not anxious for that to happen, but we're better off to sell our horses elsewhere."

Bradford stood up and began pacing in front of the divan. "The fact of the matter is we *need* all of the horses."

"But ya can na afford them. So tell me how many ya can pay for and that's what we'll deliver to ya come spring."

"West Point has done an excellent business with you in the past," Bradford pointed out. "I would think you'd be willing to accommodate us this one time."

"Then let me ask ya this, Captain Bradford. If I delivered all but ten of the horses you contracted for, would ya hand me money for a full herd? Would ya be thinkin' it didn't matter because I'd always met the terms of my contracts in the past? I do na think that's what would happen, yet it's exactly what ya're asking of me."

Bradford ceased his pacing and turned to face Paddy. "You are correct. I would not pay you for goods I did not receive. You, however, hold the power to help us equip men who will one day serve this country."

"I know ya're thinking I have no sympathy for yar situation. Nothing could be further from the truth. I wish there was some way I could help, but I can na sell the horses for less," Paddy replied quietly. "The truth is that the academy already receives the horses for less than anyone else we contract with—and I should na be tellin' ya that, but 'tis a fact. The profit we make on your horses is marginal at best, and we can na afford to be giving the animals away."

Captain Payne leaned forward and rested his elbows on his broad thighs. "And what would you do if we cancelled the entire contract and took none of your horses? Would you be equally willing to continue feeding and caring for all those horses, knowing you'll not find anyone to purchase them given the state of the economy? Now, we've told you we need those horses, and we've also told you we cannot afford to pay the entire price for them. We need something from you other than hearing there's nothing you can do!"

"To tell ya the truth, Captain, I could probably sell every one of those horses to the Virginia Military Institute for more money than we've ever received from West Point. But that's na what I want ta do. I understand ya need the horses and I want to provide them to ya, but yar threats do na serve ya well."

Captain Bradford sat down on the divan. "You're right. I apologize for our behavior, but we're placed in a difficult situation. We were told to return to the academy with a renegotiated contract for all of the horses."

"Would it ease yar financial problems if we agreed to accept payment for the horses in installments rather than in a lump sum? Payment is already past due on the herd, but I'd be willing to accept half now and half upon delivery in the spring. I'm hopeful Mr. Houston will return by spring, and if further negotiation is needed, he may be willin' to help ya further."

The two men exchanged a glance; then Payne nodded and smiled. "I apologize for my heated behavior. You've done less than we hoped for but more than we expected. You've a good head for business, and Mr. Houston is fortunate to have you in his employ."

Captain Bradford chuckled. "You should consider yourself highly complimented, Paddy. Captain Payne isn't liberal with his praise."

Paddy glanced toward the hallway and saw Kiara standing beside the parlor door. She winked and blew him a kiss. He could see the pride in his sister's eyes, and his heart swelled at the sight.

"Are ya certain Kiara won't mind if I'm comin' along uninvited?" Mary Margaret asked for the second time since they'd departed the outskirts of town.

Bridgett gave her friend a stern frown. "How many times must I tell ya the same thing, Mary Margaret? Kiara's not the type to think ya need an invitation in order to come visiting. Besides, it's not as though we're arriving unexpected. She knows Cullen and I are coming to pay a visit. She'll be pleased to see ya. Won't she, Cullen?"

"Aye," Cullen replied while keeping a tight hold on the reins and his eyes fastened upon the narrow path.

Cullen had borrowed the horse and buggy from one of the men at work, and from all appearances, he didn't have much experience handling either. The horse seemed to sense his anxiety and Mary Margaret thought the animal a wee bit skittish. She considered offering to take the reins, but Cullen might be offended by such a suggestion. So she clung to the side of the buggy and hoped the animal would trust its own instincts rather than Cullen's direction with the reins, which she noted he was holding much too firmly.

As they neared the house, Cullen yanked back on one of the reins with such fierceness the horse turned sharply, nearly overturning their buggy.

Without thinking, Mary Margaret began issuing orders. "Quit pulling back with your right hand and loosen your hold on the reins," she hollered, tempted to grab the reins from Cullen's hands. However, her good sense prevailed and she refrained from such unacceptable behavior. When the buggy was finally turned aright and the horse had settled, they stepped out of the wagon. Mary Margaret couldn't remember a time when she'd been so happy to be on solid ground.

"That didn't go so well, did it?" Cullen asked with a sheepish grin.

"I think ya did mighty fine, don't you, Mary Margaret?" Bridgett asked.

Mary Margaret knew she was expected to agree with her friend, yet she did not want to return to the city with Cullen McLaughlin handling the reins. "We've arrived safely, and for that I'm thankful. Are ya a wee bit afraid of horses, Cullen?" she inquired.

"I suppose ya can tell I've not been around animals very much."

"Aye, but there's no shame in that. Driving a horse takes a bit of instruction and practice, just like most things in life. I'd be pleased if ya'd consider permitting me to give you a bit of a lesson. In fact, if ya'd like, I could take the reins and teach you as we return."

"Could ya now? I did na know you were an expert with the horses."

"She's an expert and that's a fact," Paddy said as he drew near.

Mary Margaret couldn't tell if Paddy's words were spoken as a compliment or if he meant to ridicule her, so she kept her attention focused upon Cullen.

"Before I came to Lowell, I was around horses a great deal of the time," she told him. "My employer permitted me the use of his animals when I was not busy with my other duties, and I grew fond of them. I find them loyal and tolerant—unlike many humans."

She noted Cullen's glance toward Paddy before he answered. "I'd be pleased ta have ya give me a bit of instruction."

"Then it's settled," Mary Margaret said.

Paddy gave her a broad smile. "Bridgett, I believe my sister is expecting ya in the parlor. Cullen, I told Rogan we'd join him in the small barn out back. He's finishing up some carving for Liam. I believe he's nearly as good as Liam, but he denies there's any truth ta what I say."

Bridgett grasped Mary Margaret's hand, and they hurried toward the house while the men walked to the barn. Mary Margaret felt a sense of relief that the men were not joining them. She didn't want to spend her Sunday afternoon sparring with the likes of Padraig O'Neill.

"Where are Nevan and Katherine?" Bridgett asked as they entered the neatly appointed parlor.

Evidence of Kiara's skill with a needle adorned the room, and Mary Margaret wondered at the patience it must take to create such beautiful handwork.

"They've both gone to Simon and Maisie's to visit Moses. Poor Moses has been so lonely with Spencer gone that he comes almost every evening and asks if Nevan and Katherine can come for a visit. Although I believe it an imposition, Maisie insists her life is much easier when Moses has the children to play with."

"Children need one another for entertainment." Bridgett took a good look at her friend. "Ya're beginning to look a might uncomfortable."

"Aye. Only a few months until this babe is born, and none too soon for my liking. I'm ready to hold the wee one in my arms and be done with this," Kiara said, resting her arm atop her protruding stomach.

"And what do Nevan and Katherine think of having a new brother or sister? Are they excited?" Bridgett asked.

Kiara laughed. "Not nearly as eager as Paddy! I believe he's even more excited than he was when Nevan and Katherine were born—though I do na know how that's possible."

"Paddy?" Mary Margaret asked, stunned by the revelation. "I wouldn't think him a man who enjoyed children."

"Truly? I'm surprised you'd say that," Kiara said. "From the time he was a young lad, he's been caring and compassionate. He nearly died as a child, and then when we came to Lowell, we faced great adversity. Paddy and I came to this country as indentured servants, but through the grace of God we received our freedom. Know that I speak the truth when I tell you there is no finer man than Padraig O'Neill." Her eyes shone with pride.

Bridgett giggled. "And what would your husband be thinkin' of such a remark?"

Kiara blushed. "Other than my husband, of course."

"I do agree that Paddy is a fine man," Bridgett said. "It's with great fondness I remember sailing across the sea with you and Paddy."

"Aye. He wasn't afraid of anything then and he still isn't. I marvel at the man he's become. Why, only today I listened to him bargain with men from West Point concerning the fact that they couldn't afford to pay for the horses they'd already contracted to purchase. Once Paddy determined they were in financial difficulty and weren't attempting to take advantage of him, he offered a fair and compassionate compromise."

"Enough about Paddy now," Bridgett said. "I came here

to have ya show me how to correct the mistakes in the lace I've been making, and if we don't begin soon, Cullen will be telling me it's time to go home."

Kiara gave Bridgett a warm smile. "Let me see what ya've brought for me."

Bridgett pulled the piece of handwork from her bag and offered it to Kiara. Mary Margaret glanced at the lace and then at Kiara—she was certain she saw Kiara shudder at the sight.

"You'll be needing some help with this," Kiara said as she examined the stitches.

"There's no denying it's na a pretty sight, but for the life of me, I do na know what I've done wrong," Bridgett lamented.

"The weave is much too loose. Ya've used a pattern that's too large for this thread, and then ya've put too few twists between the stitches, making it even worse. Yar braids are not bad, though, so there's hope for ya. We'll get ya started with the proper thread. Would ya fetch me my basket?"

Mary Margaret listened closely as Kiara began the intricate lace-making instructions, but as the afternoon wore on, her thoughts wandered to Kiara's earlier discussion of her brother. Perhaps Mary Margaret had misjudged Paddy. Perhaps he really was a good person and she'd been overly distrustful. He was, after all, quite good looking, and by all accounts there were any number of girls who would be pleased to have him come calling. Truth be told, she might enjoy having him call on her!

CHAPTER · 12

REGGIE TAPPED lightly and then turned the doorknob of Mrs. Brighton's back door.

"Reggie! I was beginning to think you'd forgotten where I live. And you've come just in time to help me with these apple pies," Elinor said with a broad smile. "Take off your cloak. I'm happy to see you."

Reggie returned the smile before removing her cloak and hanging it on the iron hook by the door. "It doesn't appear you need any help," she said as she entered the kitchen. "The pies are ready to bake."

Five pies rested on the table, and Reggie knew from her stay at the boardinghouse that each piecrust was heaped full of tart apples mixed with sugar and cinnamon and then generously dotted with butter before being covered by the top crust.

"These are ready, but I have some extra dough and there's butter and cinnamon and sugar," she said, pointing at the crocks sitting on the table.

Unable to resist the temptation, Reggie lifted the ball of

dough from the bowl and slapped it onto the table. With the ease of someone who had been preparing piecrust for years, she began rolling the dough into a thin crust while Elinor set the pies to bake.

"I must say I'm impressed with how capably you've learned to roll a piecrust," Elinor said.

"Thank you." The compliment pleased her, but she forced herself to remain guarded.

Mrs. Brighton wiped her hands on the towel tucked at her waist, then turned her attention to the girl. "Where have you been all week? I've missed you."

"It's only Thursday," Reggie replied as she spread a thin layer of butter across the crust.

"But you usually come to see me every day after school. When I didn't see you for three days, I was beginning to think you must be ill. If you hadn't come today, I was going to come and check on you this evening after supper."

Reggie began to carefully sprinkle the sugar and cinnamon mixture over the buttered crust. "To see me or to see my father?" she asked with a sidelong glance, hoping to evaluate each word and look that the two of them now exchanged.

A frown creased Mrs. Brighton's face. "To see whoever could answer my questions about why you hadn't come to see me."

Without looking up, Reggie rolled the dough up into a long tube and carefully cut it into even slices, just as Mrs. Brighton had taught her. "Would you still want to see me if I told you my father has met a woman? I think he wants to marry her."

"Why would that change *our* friendship? Would you be leaving Lowell if he married?"

Mrs. Brighton appeared confused by the question, though Reggie thought it quite forthright.

"No. But I didn't know if you'd think I shouldn't come around if Father has a lady friend."

Mrs. Brighton cupped one hand under Reggie's chin and lifted her head until their gazes met. "I don't know why you would even ask me such a question, Reggie Chamberlain! You are always welcome here. But since we're revealing our thoughts, do you know what I thought when you didn't come to visit?"

"No," she replied as she neatly placed the circles of dough in a pan.

"That you'd wanted to be with me only until you completed your sampler. And since you had finished the sampler last week, you were finished with me also."

Reggie's eyes opened wide with surprise. "You thought *that*? How could you think such a thing?"

Mrs. Brighton shrugged. "It wasn't difficult. Each evening as I sat stitching, I wondered why you hadn't come by—it was the only thought that seemed plausible. However, it now makes sense. Your father wants you to spend time with his new friend so the two of you can become better acquainted."

A feeble smile was the most Reggie could muster. Now what? She didn't want to lie, yet she was still uncertain of Mrs. Brighton's motivation. This brief conversation was not enough to convince her of the older woman's loyalty. She'd learned long ago that she needed more than a few patronizing remarks—much more.

"I don't know if I want my father to marry anyone—not ever," she said, plopping down on one of the wooden kitchen chairs.

Mrs. Brighton sat down opposite her. "I understand the thought of another person becoming a part of your family could be frightening. After all, you don't want a stranger coming between you and your father. However, I don't think your father would be interested in a woman who wouldn't become a good mother for you. You need to give this lady an opportunity to become your friend. Show her the sweet young lady that you've shown me, and the two of you will become fast friends."

"My father isn't always the best judge of character. He doesn't know that people sometimes pretend to be something they're not. Besides, we're doing just fine without a woman in our house,"

"I suppose that's true enough, but you must remember that your father is probably lonely. I know he has you and he has the members of his congregation, but that's not the same as having a wife. You should think of his happiness also, Reggie," she said softly.

"Why should he want to get married again? I thought you said it wasn't so terrible being without a husband. Didn't you say that?"

"Yes, I did. And for me, that's true. However, that doesn't mean it's the same for your father. He may be very lonely and want to marry again. Trust God to provide you with the perfect mother and He won't disappoint you. If you like, we could pray about this each day when you come to visit me. We wouldn't need to tell anyone else. What do you think?"

"I suppose we could pray that if he marries, he marries the woman I choose," Reggie replied with a giggle.

"If he's already chosen someone, don't you think we should pray for you to accept *her* instead?"

"Possibly . . ." She paused. "In fact, I believe you're absolutely correct."

The front door opened, and Elinor could hear the girls chattering as they hung their capes in the hallway.

"Smells like apple pie. Again! I would prefer some variety myself. We had apple pie earlier in the week."

Reggie peeked around the doorway into the dining room. "If you're tired of apple pie, then don't have any. I'll be happy to eat your slice and mine too."

"There *is* no slice that belongs to you, Regina Louise. In case you've forgotten, *you* don't live here," Janet said.

Elinor slapped a serving spoon onto the table, her irritation mounting. "And *you* do not decide who eats at my table, Janet. If you're unhappy with the fare I serve, then you're free to seek a room elsewhere. I have no hold on you or where you live."

"Unlike you, there are many keepers who have already lost boarders due to the layoffs. You need only speak to one or two of them to realize they are feeling the pinch of making ends meet without a full house. I'd think you would be anxious to keep *all* of us happy."

There was little doubt Janet's reply was a veiled threat. She would make every effort to influence the other girls to follow if she decided to leave Elinor's boardinghouse. It was clear Janet was attempting to intimidate her, and the very thought was infuriating. Even though the girls disliked Janet's meanspirited behavior, in her absence, they whispered about her ability to influence the overseer, so Elinor knew they feared her.

"Don't worry, Mrs. Brighton, she won't leave," Reggie said quietly. "You keep the best boardinghouse for the Corporation and everyone knows it—especially Janet."

Elinor smiled and tousled Reggie's hair. "I'm not worried, Reggie. Janet knows I strive to give my best effort in order to provide the girls with a good house."

Obviously the comment served only to annoy Janet, for she leveled a look of disgust toward Reggie as the girls seated themselves around the supper table. An uncommon silence permeated the room as the girls filled their plates and began to eat. Had her comments to Janet caused the other girls discomfort? Surely not. Yet she wondered at their lack of conversation. Elinor had grown accustomed to their silence during the noonday meals. After all, they had but half an hour to hurry home, eat, and then rush back to the mill. However, during supper, when there was no need for haste, the girls usually recounted the day's activities, and the room was filled with the sounds of their chattering and laughter. This evening, however, the mood remained somber and unusually quiet.

It was shortly after Janet's exit out the front door that the girls finally began to talk. They had gathered in the parlor, and after clearing off and washing the dishes, Elinor and Reggie joined them.

"I'm pleased to hear a bit of chatter," Elinor said as she sat down. "You were all so quiet during supper that I feared I had affronted all of you with my harsh remarks to Janet."

"You weren't harsh, Mrs. Brighton. You spoke only the truth," Helen said while fidgeting with a strand of her thin, mousy brown hair.

"Thank you, Helen, but I fear I was lacking in both manners and Christian kindness toward Janet."

"She doesn't deserve either," Mary Margaret chimed in, her bright blue eyes flashing. "Janet needs to be fallin' to her knees and askin' forgiveness from the Almighty for her behavior."

"Yet Janet's actions don't excuse my own behavior, Mary Margaret. I fear I only made matters worse."

"I do not see how things can get much worse with Janet. She's filled to overflowing with the power she holds over us. It's ironic that she should need her position at the mill less than the rest of us, yet she'll likely be working long after the rest of us have lost our jobs," Ardith lamented.

Tears pooled in Sarah's eyes, and she withdrew a hand-kerchief from her skirt pocket. "I don't know what will happen to my family if I lose my position. My father was severely injured in a farming accident and he's not been able to work. In each letter I receive from home, my mother tells me how they're struggling. She fears they'll lose the place," she mournfully related. "Without the money I send, her fear will become a reality."

"Aye," Mary Margaret agreed. "While others toil to keep food on the table for their families, Janet's off to town purchasing new baubles for herself each payday. She's a cheeky one."

Sarah nodded. "I don't approve of Janet's behavior with the overseer, but I dare not say anything against her. Just today there were five layoffs in number three and seven in number five. It's utterly frightening. I can barely sleep at night; then I'm so weary I have difficulty remaining alert at my looms."

"I know all of you are deeply concerned about losing your jobs. However, you gain nothing by embracing an attitude of fear. I believe you'll do much better if you'll remain calm and adopt an optimistic attitude," Elinor encouraged.

"That's easy enough for you," Sarah said. "You don't have a family that's depending upon you."

Helen folded her lanky arms across her waist. Her eyes appeared to bulge from their deep-set sockets as she bobbed her head up and down in agreement. "She's right, Mrs. Brighton. It's a terrible load having your family waiting to receive money from you every week. My father's dead, and without the money I send home, my sisters and brothers will go hungry. The burden weighs heavy on me, and there's no one to help any of us if we lose our positions."

Elinor leaned forward and looked into the faces of each of the girls. "Now, I want you to listen carefully to what I'm going to tell you. I am not a wealthy woman, nor do I think my life has been one of particular ease. However, God has blessed me in many ways, and I've been able to set aside a portion of my wages throughout the years. If your hours are decreased or you lose your position, I want you to come to me and I will help you. In addition, Pastor Chamberlain has set up a benevolence fund at the church—one that is solely for those of you who find yourselves unemployed and in need of assistance. I am overseeing that fund. All you must do is exhibit your need for assistance.

"And I hope you girls know that I would permit you to remain in the house so long as the Corporation offered no objection. I'll do all I can to help you remain in Lowell until this crisis is over, if that is your decision. We may have to eat a bit more sparingly, but we'll make do and see each other through this difficult time."

Sarah began to sniffle again. "Thank you, Mrs. Brighton. You're most generous."

Elinor patted Sarah's hand. "I trust all of you are keeping the economic situation in our country and at the mills in your prayers. In times of difficulty, our true power comes through prayer. We must remember that we have a heavenly Father who cares deeply about our every need. When others flail about in worry and torment, we should be leaning upon God, knowing He will see us through our tribulation. Instead of showing others the strength we have in our Lord and Savior, we often emulate the behavior of nonbelievers."

"Aye. 'Tis true the good Lord above can help if He's a mind to," Mary Margaret remarked. "But there's many an Irish family lyin' in their graves because God turned a deaf ear during the potato famine."

"Our ways are not God's ways," Elinor reminded her. "Many times we don't understand why tragic things occur or why God doesn't step in and make things better each time we cry out to Him. When that has happened in my life, I try to remember that Jesus didn't want to die on the cross either. Even though Christ cried out to God, it didn't change His death on the cross. Nor did it take away His pain and suffering. However, God was still there—as strength and refuge— just as He's here for us. You may still lose your position at the mills, your families may go without food, and you may despair. But when all is said and done, if you have Jesus as your Savior, you have what is most important—your eternal salvation."

" 'Tis true, but watching those ya love die is a hard thing to do," Mary Margaret said.

Elinor nodded. "Indeed! And I can't even begin to fathom what it must have been like for God to observe His beloved Son put to death—especially knowing that Jesus was perfect and didn't deserve any of the cruelty heaped upon Him. He had never sinned, yet He willingly suffered so that we might have eternal life. It truly amazes me each time I pause to think of the depth of God's love for us."

"Ya're right, o' course, but sometimes 'tis difficult to remember anything but yar own pain," Mary Margaret said quietly.

"For all of us," Elinor agreed, patting her arm. "Now if you girls will excuse me, I believe I'd better walk Reggie home before her father begins to worry."

"He won't worry," the girl said. "I told him I was stopping after school and that you'd likely have me stay for supper."

"But I don't imagine he planned on your being away until this hour. It's nearly nine o'clock. Let's hurry to the kitchen and wrap up the sugar-and-cinnamon crusts. You can pack them in your tin for a treat with your noonday meal tomorrow."

Reggie brightened at the offer and jumped to her feet.

"I like that idea," she said while leading the way into the kitchen.

A short time later they were on their way. Although Reggie insisted she was quite capable of walking home by herself, Elinor accompanied the girl after explaining a walk would give her the opportunity for a much-needed breath of fresh air.

"You're very nice to everyone. I like that," Reggie said, grasping Elinor's hand as they walked down the street.

"I appreciate the compliment, though you seem to forget that only this evening I was less than kind to Janet."

Reggie giggled. "You're nice to people who *deserve* your kindness."

"That's just the thing, Reggie. Those who deserve our kindness the least are the very ones whom we're called to show the most compassion. Unfortunately, I failed miserably with Janet. But I'll try to do better next time. And here we are—you're safely home." She handed the sweetened pie-crusts to the girl.

Reggie kicked a pebble down the street as they stopped in front of the frame house. "Can I come back and visit tomorrow?"

"Why, of course. I thought we'd settled that issue. I'll be expecting you after school. I'm going to begin embroidering squares for a quilt. Perhaps you'd like to work on one of your own?"

"Oh, that would be grand. I'll see you tomorrow," Reggie said, hurrying up the path to the house.

Elinor watched until Reggie had safely entered the house. As she turned toward home, Elinor's thoughts returned to her earlier conversation with Reggie. She had longed to ask for the name of the woman who had captured Justin Chamberlain's heart. However, she had forced herself not to pry. Not knowing would make it easier to remain optimistic—more capable of encouraging Reggie. After all, had Reggie revealed that her father was enamored by someone like Caroline Emory or Sarah Sanders, Elinor would find it impossible to remain positive.

Yes, she decided, there were some things best left unknown.

CHAPTER · 13

THE ENTIRE DAY had been replete with problems. Clara had whined and cried throughout her waking hours, and on the few occasions when her tears ceased, Alice Ann teased her until the weeping again began in earnest. And Spencer's behavior had been no better. He had refused to complete his schoolwork, maintaining he was tired and didn't feel well.

Jasmine rocked Clara on her lap, hoping the child would take a nap. "Perhaps the children are ill. Have you heard whether there's any sickness on the other plantations?" she asked Prissy, who was rolling a ball across the floor to Alice Ann.

"You's worrying too much, Miz Jasmine. The plague's over with—we done with dat mess till next year," Prissy said as she tossed the ball back to Alice.

"There are illnesses other than yellow fever—ones that occur throughout the year," Jasmine replied as she rested her palm on Clara's forehead. "Come here, Spencer. Let me see if you're feverish."

Spencer placed his palm on his forehead. "I don't have a fever," he told her.

TRACIE PETERSON / JUDITH MILLER

"I'll be the judge of that. Come here, please."

With a grudging look upon his face, Spencer moved to her chair and leaned down while Jasmine placed her hand on his forehead. "You don't feel warm," his mother conceded. "I can't imagine what's wrong with the three of you today."

"We want to go home," Spencer said as he flopped down on the divan.

"So do I. And we will. Every last person on this plantation is going to leave. But first we must get picking the final crop, and once it is ginned and baled, we can ship the entire crop to New Orleans."

Spencer formed his lips into a taut line and narrowed his dark brown eyes. "When that's done, you'll say we must remain until you complete something else. We're never going to leave, and I don't want to live here."

"Your father and I are perfectly aware of your wishes, Spencer, and if you don't cease your unpleasant behavior, you may go to bed."

"We haven't even had supper yet."

"Exactly!" Jasmine replied, her retort filled with exasperation.

"So you think we's gonna be leaving soon, Miz Jasmine?" Prissy asked in a trembling whisper.

Jasmine nodded. "Mr. Houston agrees that we will leave by February at the latest—whether or not the plantation has sold."

Prissy wrapped her arms around her knees and began to rock back and forth. "I don' wanna leave here, Miz Jasmine. I done lived here long as I can 'member, and dis here's my home. Don't wanna be leaving it. I always been thinkin' me and Toby would jump the broom and we'd grow old on dis here place. Now ever'thing's changing."

"There's nothing to be concerned about, Prissy. You and Toby are going to be just fine. Surely you want your freedom more than you want to stay here."

"I don't care nothing 'bout no freedom if I can stay here and have ever'thing stay the same as always."

"But it can't, Prissy. The Willows is going to have a new owner, and we have no idea who it might be—possibly someone like Mr. Wade from the Bedford Plantation. You wouldn't want to be here if that happened, would you?"

"No, ma'am. I just want things to go back to the way they was before Massa Malcolm died. Ain't nobody up there in the North gonna hire me to do no work."

"Of course they will, Prissy. You're a wonderful house-keeper and have much to offer—and so does Toby."

"They ain't gonna want me when they find out I'm gonna have a baby," she whispered.

Jasmine met Prissy's intent, frightened gaze. "You're . . ."

"Yessum."

"You and Toby should be married immediately. Why didn't one of you come to me?"

"Toby don' know either," Prissy whispered. "I was skeered to tell him."

Jasmine grasped Prissy's hand. "There's no need to be afraid. Toby is an honorable man. He'll want to be respon-sible for his child—he was already planning to marry you."

"Yessum, that's true."

"Then we need to see to this matter immediately. Is there someone special you'd like to perform the ceremony?"

"Ol' Samuel down in the slave quarters—he do the preaching and marrying for us," she said.

"I want you to promise me you'll talk to Toby this very evening. Then tell him I want to speak to him."

"Oh no, ma'am. Please don't be giving Toby no talkin' to—he'll for sho' be angry with me if you do that."

"I wasn't going to scold him, Prissy. I want to tell him that I'll be willing to help in any way necessary so the two of you can be married as soon as possible," Jasmine said. "And I want you to cease your worrying about finding a place to work and live when we go North. Both you and Toby can live at the Houston farm. There's plenty of work on the farm that I'm certain Toby would enjoy, and you can continue to help with the children. Everything is going to be fine, Prissy."

"Yessum," she replied in a faltering voice.

Her agreement was unconvincing, and Jasmine knew nothing she said was going to convince Prissy her life would be better away from The Willows. The young woman would have to see for herself. Once they were in the North, her life would be filled with possibilities. There would be ample opportunities for her and Toby as well as the baby she was now expecting.

"I'm going to go downstairs and see if Mr. Houston has returned. He said he would be bringing a land agent home late this afternoon," Jasmine said as she placed Clara in Prissy's arms. She walked toward the door and then turned and glanced over her shoulder before exiting the room. "And don't forget I want to talk to Toby later this evening."

Prissy nodded her agreement. However, she looked as though she'd been told she was going to receive forty lashes.

Jasmine's friendship with Prissy had deepened since their arrival at The Willows, and Jasmine truly enjoyed the young woman's company. She wanted to believe Prissy trusted her, yet the girl remained unwilling to embrace the thought of moving North no matter what Jasmine said or did. Perhaps Prissy was afraid to trust anyone—even Toby. After all, Toby was more than anxious to leave the South and gain his freedom.

And why hadn't Prissy told Toby she was expecting his child before now? Surely she didn't intend to wait until they wed to tell him. Jasmine was certain Toby would have married Prissy the moment he discovered her condition. And though Jasmine hadn't expressed her surprise to Prissy, she was somewhat taken aback by Toby's behavior. From the time he was a young boy, he'd always attempted to act in an honorable manner.

"I see you've arrived home," Jasmine greeted Nolan as she walked into the library. She glanced about the room expecting to see the land agent.

"Yes—a short time ago. If Mr. Turner is a punctual man, he should be arriving within the hour." Her husband stood and kissed her cheek. "You look particularly lovely today."

A lilting ripple of laughter escaped her, and she sat down beside him on the divan. "You say that *every* day."

"Because it's true," he replied. "How has your day been?"

"Difficult. The children have been out of sorts. Clara crying, Alice Ann teasing, Spencer unwilling to do his school lessons—I don't know what's gotten into them. Spencer says it's because they're homesick, but that's his reasoning for everything."

Nolan pulled her closer in a warm embrace. "We'll be leaving soon. We're all anxious to return to the farm, but poor Spencer wants to believe he's the only one who's truly unhappy. I'm sorry your day has been trying."

"I haven't shared the most surprising news of all," she said, turning to face her husband.

"Did you know that when you become excited, the golden flecks in your eyes sparkle like brilliant gold nuggets?" he asked before leaning forward and brushing her lips with a kiss.

She giggled and pulled away from her husband's embrace. "Nolan, stop that! I have something I must tell you."

He immediately drew her back into his arms and kissed her with increasing passion. "So tell me . . . what is your news?" He pulled away only far enough to whisper his question.

His breath tickled her lips, and she smiled while pushing against his chest. "I can't speak if you continue to smother me with kisses."

"All right. I promise to stop—at least for a few moments. I do hope your news warrants my sacrifice," he said with a grin.

"When Spencer was lamenting his woes about returning home, I told him that we would all be leaving soon. Then, as she normally does, Prissy said she didn't want to depart The Willows. I made every attempt to convince her that she would find suitable employment and she and Toby would have a good life."

"I believe I've heard this all before," Nolan said, giving her a sidelong glance.

"But not this part! She said no one would be willing to employ her because she's going to have a baby."

Nolan turned to meet her gaze. "Well, that *is* news. If she's speaking the truth, I'm surprised Toby hasn't already married her."

"She hasn't told him!"

"Seems strange she wouldn't tell him immediately— especially since they plan to marry. Did she say why she hadn't spoken with him?"

"She said she was afraid to tell him, which made absolutely no sense to me. Toby is gentle and kind—I have no doubt he will accept responsibility for his actions. Though I must admit I'm disappointed by his behavior."

"Don't judge him too harshly, Jasmine. We don't know the circumstances, and it's unfair to place blame."

"You're correct. Blame won't change anything. I told Prissy she was to tell Toby about her condition today and that I wanted to talk with him this evening."

Shifting on the divan, Nolan turned to give her his full attention. "I don't believe this is a proper topic for you to discuss with Toby, my dear. Tell Prissy to have him come and see me."

"I was merely going to tell him I thought they should marry immediately and ask what I could do to assist them."

"Still, I think it would be more appropriate for him to talk with me. Besides, he'll likely be more at ease speaking to another man, don't you think?"

Jasmine nodded. "Yes, of course. I did tell Prissy that she and Toby could come and live on the farm and work for us if she was fearful about their welfare. I do hope you don't disapprove?"

He laughed. "Have I ever disapproved of your lending aid to others? There's more than sufficient work to keep them both busy at whatever work they might choose to do. However, I believe we should permit Toby to have a say in the matter. I don't want him to feel we're forcing them to come and live at the farm."

"No, of course not. I made the offer because of Prissy's concern about finding work. Should they choose to go somewhere else, that's perfectly acceptable."

The quiet was interrupted and Nolan stood and peered out the window.

"Ah, I believe that is Mr. Turner's carriage approaching in the driveway," he said as he pulled out his pocket watch and snapped open the lid. "I'll go out and greet him."

"I believe I'll go to the kitchen and ask Martha to serve refreshments. I shouldn't be long."

Jasmine walked down the hallway and into the empty kitchen, then realized the servants were likely in the detached summer kitchen. During the heat of summer, the kitchen contained within the walls of the house was used merely as a serving kitchen for preparing coffee, tea, or lemonade.

She waved to Martha as she drew near the other kitchen. "Are you busy preparing supper?" she asked.

"Oh, I don't do much, Miss Jasmine. These ladies tolerate me in their kitchen just because I miss cooking," she replied.

"Ain't true, Miz Jasmine. Miss Martha's a mighty big help," Esther said, her black face gleaming like ebony.

"Is there something I can do for you," Martha asked, "or did you want to oversee the supper preparations?"

"Could you possibly prepare light refreshments and serve them in the library? Mr. Nolan and I are meeting with a gentleman for a short time. Though it's near suppertime, I thought I should at least offer him a light repast."

Martha's head bobbed up and down. "You go and entertain your guest, and I'll be in shortly."

The meeting proceeded more quickly than Jasmine had anticipated. In fact, there seemed little to negotiate. Mr. Turner agreed to handle arrangements for the sale of The Willows, and if a buyer was not secured by the time they departed, he would handle matters in their absence.

"My wife is unwilling to give you final authority on the sale price, Mr. Turner, but if you telegraph any offers, we will make every effort to reply promptly," Nolan said. "Of course, we remain hopeful you might locate a qualified purchaser prior to our departure."

Mr. Turner nibbled on one of the molasses cookies he'd placed on his saucer. "As I said, there's little likelihood you'll have a buyer any time in the near future—however, one never knows. There may be a potential purchaser who is anxious to invest in this fine plantation. Bear in mind, however, that the market is depressed at this time. Even though we've not suffered losses such as those experienced in the

North, we're now beginning to feel the repercussions of this economic downturn, and there are fewer men willing to take risk with their capital."

"The Willows isn't a risk," Jasmine asserted. "It has always turned a fine profit for our family."

Mr. Turner gave her a perfunctory smile. "I'm sure that's a fact, Mrs. Houston, and I'm going to do my very best to secure the highest possible price for your family's home. I merely wanted to warn you in advance that the sale might take longer than you would normally anticipate. So long as we're clear on that issue, I believe we can sign the necessary papers and I can be on my way."

Nolan and Mr. Turner took care of the necessary paper work, and Mr. Turner wished them a good evening.

"I don't particularly like Mr. Turner," Jasmine said to her husband after the land agent had departed the house.

"He seems as trustworthy as the other agents I spoke with. He bears a good reputation in the area, though I suppose he is rather negative," Nolan replied.

"Truly? I barely noticed," she said with a glint in her eye. "Anyone listening to him for long would find himself in a state of utter despair."

Nolan glanced up from his desk and motioned Toby forward. "Come in and sit down," he said while pointing his pen toward the chair opposite the massive desk.

Toby hesitated for a moment but finally dropped into the chair and stared into Nolan's eyes. "You wanted to see me, suh?" he quietly inquired.

"Yes. Please understand I'm not passing judgment, Toby, but given the circumstances, I would highly recommend you and Prissy marry immediately."

"Yessuh. Prissy told me 'bout the situation this afternoon. I told her not to be worrying—that we'd get ol' Samuel to marry us. Ain't no need for nothing more'n the three of us to get things taken care of. I'm going down an' talk to him soon as we's finished with our talk."

Nolan nodded. "Miss Jasmine asked me to tell you we would be pleased to help with any wedding preparations. Surely Prissy would prefer something just a bit more elaborate than repeating your vows before Samuel."

"No, we's agreed 'bout the marriage. Everything should be taken care of by dis time tomorrow," he said. "It's better dis way."

"If that's what you prefer. And did Prissy tell you that if the two of you want to come to our farm in Lowell, we'd be pleased to have you come and work for us? You're not obligated, but Prissy was concerned about finding work and there's plenty at the horse farm. You could stay until after the baby is born, and if you then decide you want to leave, we'll not have any objection."

Toby began to fidget at the mention of Prissy's condition, and Nolan regretted going into detail.

"You and Miz Jasmine is very kind. When da time comes to go north, we'd be proud to work for you, Massa Nolan."

"Good. And if you need *anything* for the wedding, please—"

"No, suh, we ain't gonna be needing nothin'—nothin' at all," Toby said. "We's jest fine. If we's through, I believe I'll go on down to the quarter and talk to ol' Samuel."

"Yes, of course."

Nolan was deep in thought when Jasmine entered the library a short time later. "Did you talk to him? What did he say?"

"I talked to him. They don't want any type of large ceremony. Toby has gone to speak to Samuel, and he advised me that they will be wed by this time tomorrow. He said he and Prissy are in agreement about wanting just the three of them present when they say their vows."

His wife exhaled and she frowned. "And here I was hoping for something cheerful to focus upon."

"I'm not certain Toby shares your enthusiasm. However, he did accept our offer of employment, so at least that much should please you."

"Yes. It pleases me they'll be with us and I'll have the pleasure of seeing their child," Jasmine replied. "If only *all* of life's problems were so easily resolved!"

CHAPTER · 14

February 1858

NOLAN ADJUSTED his silk top hat before lifting Alice Ann into the carriage and onto Prissy's lap. "I believe we'll have ample room in the carriage. Especially since Henrietta and Martha decided they weren't feeling well enough to join us," he told Jasmine.

"I do hope you don't mind going along with us this evening, Prissy. With Henrietta and Martha both ailing, I thought we might be forced to remain at home," Jasmine said. "But the children wouldn't have forgiven us if we attended the festivities without them."

"It's fine, ma'am. I's glad to help." Prissy peered at the house. "Where's Henry? Ain't he gonna drive the coach?"

"Henry's ailing too," Nolan said. "I told him to remain abed and perhaps he'll be better by morning. Besides, I enjoy driving my own coach from time to time. It will give the gentry of Mississippi yet another grievance against me," he said with a grin.

Jasmine stroked Clara's soft hair. "Clara and Alice Ann will likely be asleep soon after we arrive."

"I won't sleep. I'll remain awake until we return home," Spencer promised. He was sitting beside his father and obviously feeling quite grown up.

"Personally, I would have been happy to remain at home," Jasmine told her husband. "Besides, I find it strange that we received an invitation to the gathering at Rosewood. After all, we've been excluded from every other social function since our arrival. Why would the Woodsons invite us to their party celebrating the final picking? After all, there's no denying the fact that John Woodson dislikes us intensely."

"He's extended an olive branch, my dear. The least we can do is reciprocate in kind. And the children haven't had an opportunity to participate in any festivities. Christmas, after all, was quite glum this year."

"You're right, but services at the church were quite nice, I thought," she said as they made their way down the lane. "And I'm completely surprised you want to attend tonight, Spencer. I feel certain some of your schoolmates will be among those invited."

Spencer flashed a smile at his mother. "Since we're leaving next week, this will give me a chance to tell all of them what I truly think of their deeds."

"Now, son, I expect you to be on your best behavior," Nolan warned. "No rowdiness."

He nodded. "Not unless they start it."

"No fighting whatsoever!" Jasmine insisted in a stern tone. "If you encounter any difficulty, you must come directly to your father or me for assistance."

"All right," he begrudgingly agreed. "Do you think it's snowing at home?"

"Probably so," she replied absently.

Spencer scooted around in his seat and directed his attention to Prissy. "Just wait until you move up north. One morning you'll wake up and look out your window, and you'll see piles and piles of white snow covering the ground."

"We had us some of dat white stuff one or two times. It come fallin' from da sky in little white flakes, but it melted to water when it hit the ground—didn't do no piling up," she said. "Massa Wainwright told us snow was for up north, where it be cold and unpleasant, an' rain is for in da South, where it be warm and agreeable."

"That sounds like something my father would say," Jasmine commented. "However, the North is not unpleasant, though it does grow cold in the winter. But you'll soon learn to love the North."

"I s'pose," Prissy said, although her voice lacked enthusiasm.

"Here we are," Nolan said as he pulled back on the reins and the horses brought the carriage to a halt outside the main entrance of Rosewood.

Festive decorations adorned the foyer of the big house, where both John and Ramona Woodson stood near the entrance greeting their guests. Mrs. Woodson immediately directed one of her house slaves to escort Prissy and the children upstairs, where they were to be entertained.

"We're pleased you accepted our invitation," Mr. Woodson said as he pointed to another slave to take their wraps.

Jasmine directed a dutiful smile toward their host. "We were pleased to be included."

Mrs. Woodson whispered to a butler, who stepped forward and ostentatiously announced their arrival to the many guests gathered in the loggia, where music was playing and the guests were beginning to dance.

"Shall we?" Nolan asked as he led Jasmine to the dance floor.

"Seems everyone in the area is in attendance," Jasmine said as they circled the floor. "It's been years since I've attended one of these parties, yet most of the faces remain familiar. It appears as if few of my generation have departed this area. You'd think they would want to strike out and see another part of the world."

Nolan led her in a wide circle toward the rear of the dance floor. "I'm certain they do see other parts of the world. Most everyone here is widely traveled. But unlike you and McKinley, they chose to return."

"They travel, yet they've not yet become enlightened," she remarked.

Nolan cocked one eyebrow. "I believe they would quite disagree with you, my dear. In fact, I believe you'd find they think *you* are the one who is unenlightened."

"No doubt."

The music proved quite delightful, and Jasmine spent much of the evening dancing with Nolan and a few of her schoolmates from years ago. Throughout the evening, she watched the doorway closely, almost expecting to see Spencer emerge with a bloody nose, but such was not the case. Instead, he remained ensconced upstairs until after midnight, when they were preparing to depart for home.

"From all appearances, you and the other boys got along well this evening," Jasmine commented as she settled Clara into a nest of blankets in the back of the carriage. Prissy helped Nolan settle Alice Ann in beside her sister.

"Yes. They were quite friendly—even apologized for their behavior and said the issue of slavery was one that should be settled by our parents."

"I'm pleased to hear their parents have spoken to them and explained their actions were inappropriate," she replied.

"Did you enjoy yourself, my dear?" Nolan inquired as the carriage rocked to and fro on the uneven road.

"The evening was tolerable, though I didn't find it as jovial as I remember from my childhood. And what happened to all of the men? One moment the dance floor was filled with more couples than one could imagine, and suddenly it seemed as if all of the men had disappeared and the women were standing about fanning themselves and drinking punch."

Nolan nodded. "I wondered at that myself. I even commented to Woodson about his missing guests. He said they'd gone into his library to conduct business of some sort. Rather rude, if you ask me. Seems they could conduct business somewhere other than a social gathering that occurs but once a year."

"Indeed you would think so. I thought Lydia looked quite lovely this evening, though she and Rupert both were somewhat aloof, didn't you think?" Jasmine asked.

"Jasmine! Look up ahead! Is that glow of red coming from the direction of The Willows?" Nolan's voice was an urgent plea begging for a denial from his wife.

She stretched to the side and leaned out the carriage window. "Oh, Nolan! The Willows is on fire! Hurry! Hurry! It appears to be the house. Martha, Henrietta, and the other house servants are in there."

Nolan flicked the reins and urged the horses into a gallop. "It's more than the house. The entire sky seems lit up. It's coming from all directions. It appears that nothing has been spared. I fear the entire plantation is afire."

"Surely not. Dear God, let this be a dream!" she cried out.

———

Jasmine leaned heavily against Nolan's chest, clutching his arm, as they surveyed the plantation, unable to believe the devastation that surrounded them. Fires burned in varying degrees throughout the plantation. Unremitting flames snaked across the acreage, licking and scorching every vestige of habitation lying in their destructive path. Smoke curled upward and spread across the sky like a giant blanket that had been unfolded to hide the starlit heavens. The heavy stench seeped downward and filled their nostrils—a continuous reminder of the fire's catastrophic obliteration.

Fear swelled through Jasmine, clawing at her with an unrelenting insistence. "We must see if anyone has survived. All of the servants were in the house, even Martha and Henrietta." Her voice was shrill and cut through the February air. "There doesn't appear to be anyone attempting to put out the fires."

Nolan wrapped her in a protective embrace. "We can't possibly contain these fires. It's much too late for that. The most we can hope for is to find the servants alive."

"Look over dere, Miz Jasmine," Prissy exclaimed. "Someone's wavin' a white cloth from behind da tree."

Nolan cupped his hands to his mouth. "Who's there? This is Nolan Houston—come out and show yourself."

Jasmine squinted as she attempted to make out the figure running toward them. "I believe it's . . . Yes! It's Henrietta. Henrietta!" she called. "Praise God, you are safe! Where are the others? Martha? The house servants? All of the former slaves that were down in the quarters? Can you tell us anything?"

Henrietta dropped to the ground and began to weep in deep inconsolable sobs, her body heaving up and down as she clung to the hem of Jasmine's gown.

Nolan hurried to where she sat and helped her to her feet. "Let me assist you into the carriage, where you and Jasmine may sit and talk," he urged.

"You're safe now, Henrietta," Jasmine whispered as she pulled the woman close and patted her back. "Please tell us what happened. You're the only person we've been able to locate."

Henrietta nodded her head up and down as she appeared to choke back her sobs. "It was terrible, Miss Jasmine, just terrible. Martha was overcome by the smoke. I pulled her out of the house, but I don't know if she's alive. I'm ashamed to say I was afraid to remain. After all, what could one woman do against all that? I ran out here to hide," she cried, beginning to weep once again.

"It's all right. You did the right thing, Henrietta. What about the others? Did any of them survive?"

"The men took all the colored folks from the house and the quarters. I heard a gunshot, and then someone yelled that they'd shot Mr. Draper. I don't know if it's true—I've been afraid to show myself for fear they would kill me too."

"What do you mean the men took all the colored folks?" Jasmine asked. "What men?"

"The men that started the fire," she gasped.

Jasmine and Nolan exchanged a worried look, but it was Nolan who spoke. "You say they took the coloreds—did they not put up a fight?"

"Those men had guns, Mr. Houston, and I heard them yelling back and forth. They put all of them in chains so they couldn't run off. I kept praying you would return or that one of the neighbors would come down the road on their way home. I kept praying someone, anyone, would come and help."

"What did these men look like, Henrietta. Did you know them?"

"They were white, riding horses—a few carriages too, but mostly on horseback. They were dressed in fine clothes, but I don't know folks from around these parts. I heard one of them laugh and say something about paying a neighborly visit."

Nolan slapped his top hat on his leg. "This is an outrage! There's no doubt these fires were set by the very men who were at that party this evening. I'd venture to guess they weren't in John Woodson's library at all—they were out setting fire to our plantation while they knew Woodson would keep us occupied at his party. Every one of them took part in this travesty."

Prissy leaned forward from the rear seat of the carriage, tears lining her cheeks. "D'ya know what happened to my Toby, Miz Henrietta?"

"They took him—they took all the house servants first and put them in chains. Some of the riders had gone to the slave quarters, and that's when I heard the gunshot. Soon after they brought all the others back to the main house, where they chained and put them in the wagons. I was still hidden near the house and knew I had to get away from there before they spotted me." A look of terror sparked in her eyes and she hesitated a moment. "Do you think they took Martha?"

Nolan slowly shook his head back and forth. "No. I don't think they would take a white woman. They came with shackles and chains in order to steal the coloreds and force them back into slavery. I'll go and see if I can find Martha. You say she was outside the rear of the house?"

"Yes, sir. Behind the big trees along the path to the water troughs."

Jasmine grasped Nolan's arm. "Wait a moment, please. It sounds as though a rider's approaching—or is it my imagination?"

"You're right; someone is coming down the road. I'd best wait and see who it is. I'd like to think it's someone coming to lend a hand, but I don't know who that would be since it appears as if all of our neighbors took part in this devastation."

"Looks like it might be Rupert—and I'd guess that he smells like smoke." Jasmine climbed out of the carriage at the same time that Prissy grabbed a blanket from off the front carriage seat and scooted into the far corner beside the children, being careful to pull the cover over herself. Fortunately, the girls were sound asleep, and Spencer was watching in wide-eyed silence.

"Are you cold, Prissy?" Jasmine asked.

"No, ma'am, just wantin' to stay out of the way," the girl meekly replied only moments before Rupert reined his horse to a halt beside the carriage.

He tipped his hat and directed a wide grin at Jasmine. "Cousin," he greeted. "Appears you've been forced out of this place."

"These fires were intentionally set, and we know that you and your friends are responsible," she accused, "and to think you call yourselves gentlemen. You're all a disgrace to mankind."

"Careful, Jasmine. You've already made enough enemies in these parts with your judgmental attitude and quick tongue. Just as these fires were meant to deliver a message, I'm here to enlighten you. You and your kind are not wanted in the South—it's best you realize that before it's too late." He reached into his coat pocket and pulled out some folded papers.

She emitted a wounded laugh. "Too late for *what?* There is nothing remaining, *cousin.* You and your legion of pathetic followers have already destroyed or taken everything we own, so you may feel free to tell your cohorts we will leave when we are ready and not a moment before. And merely as a matter of curiosity, what does Lydia think of your behavior? Even through the most difficult times, the Wainwrights have protected and defended one another. Does she know of your involvement in this unspeakable affair?"

"Indeed, Lydia *is* a Wainwright, and though both Lydia and I hold familial ties to you, our Southern heritage and beliefs go beyond a loyalty to family bloodlines—especially when the family members involved have pledged their allegiance to the abolitionist North. And you, my dear cousin, are no longer a Southern Wainwright—you are a Yankee Houston," Rupert retorted, his face now contorted with anger. "So far as we're concerned, you need to take your family and abolitionist ideas and return to where you came from."

Nolan stepped forward and positioned himself between Rupert and Jasmine. "You need to remember whom you're talking to, Rupert. I'll not tolerate any more of your abusive behavior. I demand the immediate return of the people you kidnapped from this plantation."

"*People? Kidnapped?* You mean those slaves? They've been taken to other plantations where they belong *and* where their labor is needed."

"They are *not* slaves. Jasmine has signed their papers—every one of them is free, and you have no more right to hold them than you would me."

"Don't tempt me, Nolan," Rupert sneered.

"If they are not immediately returned, I shall take this matter to the law. I intend to see each person who participated in this heinous deed prosecuted to the fullest extent possible."

Rupert's laughed was filled with a sadistic ring. "Do you now? Well, before you go and make a fool of yourself, let me tell you that it was the law that helped plan and carry out our strategy. You can rest assured you'll receive no help from any lawman in these parts."

"You've delivered your message. Now I'm telling you to leave our property."

"Well, that is another matter entirely. You see, I have papers here that show you've agreed to turn the property over to me. After all, the fire destroyed everything of value and you have no reason to hold the property any longer." Rupert grinned as he threw the papers at Nolan's feet.

"We've agreed to no such thing," Jasmine protested. "I'll not give you The Willows. Not now—not ever!"

"But my dear, you already have. I have witnesses who will vouch for that fact—testify under oath—that they saw you willingly sign those papers."

Nolan picked the papers up. It was impossible to read them, but Jasmine quickly went to see what they might say. "You won't get away with this. I'll go to town and tell the judge everything that has happened."

"You do that, cousin. You'll find, however, if you look those papers over, Judge Weston is one of the people who witnessed our transfer of ownership." Rupert gave a maniacal laugh.

"You've said what you wanted to say. Now leave," Nolan commanded.

"Not without Prissy. Come on out of there, girl," Rupert called. "I see you hiding under the cover. Don't be making me wait—get on out here."

"Prissy isn't going anywhere with you. Get out of here," Jasmine ordered, her fists balled in anger.

"Why don't you let Prissy answer for herself? Come on out, Prissy, and I'll take you to that fellow you're so fond of—Toby, isn't it? I know you don't want to see him take a lashing, so why don't you hurry out of there," Rupert said with a cruel smile curling his lips.

Jasmine rushed to the carriage as Prissy dropped the blanket and stepped out. "You're not thinking of going with him, are you?" she whispered while grasping the girl by her thin shoulders.

Tears streaked Prissy's cheeks. "I don' want Toby gettin' no lashing on my account," she murmured.

"Don't you see he's lying to you, Prissy? He's not going

to take you to Toby. He's not going to do what any of us want. He'll either keep you or sell you to the highest bidder, but he's not going to reunite you with Toby. Rupert Hesston isn't going to do anything that would please anyone except himself. Have I ever lied to you, Prissy?"

"No, ma'am, but iffen I can help Toby . . ."

"That's just it, Prissy. You can't help Toby. None of us can. Think of your baby," she whispered. "Toby wouldn't want his baby to grow up in slavery. Would he?"

"No. But I don' care nothing 'bout this child right now; I care 'bout Toby," Prissy insisted.

"There, you see—she wants to come with me. Let her be, Jasmine. You say she's free, yet you attempt to hold her against her will," Rupert said. "Apparently you haven't truly freed your slaves."

"We's free," Prissy hissed. "She's jest tryin' to make me see what's best."

"You know what's best, Prissy," Rupert said with an evil look in his eye. "Now get over here."

She stiffened. "No, suh, I ain't going, and you can't make me." Her voice was trembling with fear as she took cover behind Jasmine. "He can't, can he?" she whispered.

"I want you off this property immediately!" Nolan commanded. "Get out and don't ever return."

"Prissy belongs to me. I won't leave without her."

"You'll leave now." Nolan stepped forward, his hand going to the inside pocket of his coat. Jasmine wondered at his actions. Nolan never carried a gun, but it appeared he was about to draw one now.

"Very well. I'll leave, but I'll be back. And when I return, I'll have help with me. You think you have nothing left? Remember, you still have your children—but perhaps not for long. You have your lives as well. You're going to be sorry for your actions here tonight," he threatened. "You have my word. We'll be watching you. When you come to town, I'll get Prissy then and no threat of yours will stop me. You'll be lucky if you even make it as far as town."

He mounted the bay gelding, jerked on the reins, and kicked his heels into the horse's flanks. They stood watching as the horse carried him down the road at breakneck speed.

"Why is he so insistent upon having Prissy?" Jasmine asked. They both looked to the girl who was now backing up toward the carriage.

Jasmine realized there would be no answer from her and turned her gaze once again to her husband. "He's taken The Willows and everyone else. Nolan, he surely means to see us in complete defeat."

"No, I believe he very well means to see us dead," Nolan said in a whisper only Jasmine could hear.

CHAPTER · 15

JASMINE STARED into the carriage, where the girls were still sleeping soundly. Thankfully, Spencer had remained a silent observer. No telling what her cousin might have said or done had her son attempted to enter into the quarrel, especially in light of his final threat toward their children. Jasmine shivered as she recalled Rupert's parting words.

"I've failed miserably," she said as Nolan wrapped her in a comforting embrace. "Nothing has gone as we hoped. Because of me, every one of our former slaves has been forced back into slavery. And likely into the hands of owners and overseers who will abuse them for no other reason than the fact that they come from The Willows."

"I must go and check on Martha. Once we know her condition, we're going to need to formulate a plan. Stay here with the children, and I'll return as quickly as possible. If I attempt to take the horses any closer to the fire, they'll only become skittish. I don't want a runaway carriage—especially since it's our only means of transportation."

"Hurry, Nolan—and take Prissy with you, just in case

Rupert didn't actually leave. Should he return and you weren't here, there's no way I could protect her."

Jasmine climbed into the carriage and settled in beside Henrietta. They sat watching the roadway, both of them praying Nolan would return before they spied any sign of a rider coming in their direction. Jasmine tried to calculate what should be done next, but her mind refused to work. These past months had been the hardest of her life, losing first her father and brothers and now The Willows and all the people she had hoped to free.

"Can we hope to find the others?" Henrietta asked softly.

Jasmine saw Spencer watch her as if intent for the answer. "I don't think so. The law won't be any help to us, and other plantation owners will simply hide our people away until we give up. To push them for answers might even result in the death or removal of them all together." She shook her head. "I just wanted to do a good thing here." Spencer reached out and touched her hand, and Jasmine clung to it gratefully.

"I sure hope they won't take long to find Martha," Henrietta suddenly declared. "I don't know what might happen if they don't come right back."

"Don't be afraid, Henrietta. The Lord is with us. He is watching over all of us."

"Was He watching earlier when those men came?" Spencer asked seriously.

"Yes, I suppose He was," she said. "I believe He sees everything."

"Then why didn't He stop them?"

"I don't know, Spencer. I wish God would have stopped them, but apparently He has something else in mind."

"Maybe He just wants us to go home. There's nothing to stop us from going now."

Jasmine nodded. Her son was right on that account. In

fact, if they didn't go now, they might very well risk their lives.

They didn't have to wait long, for a short time later, Prissy and Nolan hurried toward them. Martha was very evidently absent.

"I'm sorry, dear, but Martha . . . was obviously overcome by the smoke." Nolan met Jasmine's gaze hesitantly. She felt sorry for her husband. He no doubt feared she might be unable to withstand yet another blow. She nodded at him, hoping it might ease his concern.

"If it helps at all," he continued, "she appeared peaceful, as if she'd merely fallen asleep. I would like to remain here and bury her, but I fear Rupert's threats were real. If so, he may return later tonight or at daybreak. We must leave, Jasmine. I can possibly return tomorrow and bury Martha, but right now we must get the children to safety."

"I agree," Jasmine managed to say, though she felt as if she were in a daze. How could things have appeared so peaceful, so good, only hours ago? "If Rupert returned, we would be defenseless against him and his treacherous friends."

"Think, my dear. Do you know *anybody* who would help us? Even if only for a short time, we need a place to hide until we can make arrangements to leave. If Rupert is determined to have Prissy, I'm convinced he'll follow us."

Jasmine realized there was no time to mourn any of the losses she'd sustained. There never really had been a time— had there? She squared her shoulders and pushed aside her grief. There had to be someone who might help.

Prissy began to weep. "I don't want yo' babies getting hurt, Miz Jasmine. You leave me here. I ain't gonna put them in harm's way. Massa Rupert will have to find me first, and I know some good hiding places 'round these parts."

"He'll put the hounds on you, Prissy. I'll not have that!

251

You're coming with us," Jasmine insisted.

"What about the preacher in Lorman?" Nolan asked. "Any chance he might help?"

Jasmine wrung a handkerchief through her fingers. "I doubt he'd be willing to chance losing his biggest contributors. Besides, he's pro-slavery and doesn't understand us or our beliefs. He thinks we're fools and he's told me so."

"Isn't there a soul you can think of?"

"Wait! When Mr. Forbes came to Lowell and talked to us, he mentioned my cousin Levi had survived. Now that winter is upon us, I'm guessing he should have returned home."

Nolan drew closer and took her hands in his own. "Can we trust him? Once he discovers our beliefs, will he betray us?"

"Levi has always been a free spirit—never one to conform to others' beliefs. Yet I haven't seen him in years and can't speak with authority on whether he'd be willing to lend aid. However, I don't see that we have any alternative other than to throw ourselves at his mercy."

Nolan nodded. "I'll approach him with the option of turning us away if he doesn't want to become embroiled in this matter. Of course, I'll seek his promise not to tell anyone we requested his assistance. However, if he agrees to help us, we'll have to trust that he is willing to embrace the cause. We have no other choice. How far is it to his home?"

"At least ten miles," Jasmine replied. "He doesn't live in Lorman."

"Although I dislike having to travel ten miles at this time of night and under these conditions, it's to our advantage Levi lives in a secluded area. Someone would surely see us if we were attempting to hide in town. We must leave and get as far from here as possible before daybreak."

Nolan and Prissy climbed into the carriage, and they

were soon on their way. Jasmine stared at The Willows until it was gone from her sight. She then focused on the road before her, attempting to remember the proper turns and directions that would best deliver them to Levi's door. She prayed he would be home. What if he was visiting relatives, or what if he turned them away? *Quit borrowing trouble,* she silently chastised herself, though it was difficult to push the disturbing thoughts from her mind.

"I believe we need to take the path that veers off to the right just up ahead," she told Nolan.

"You *believe?*" he asked, slowing the horses.

"I haven't been to Levi's home in years, and it's dark, Nolan. I'm doing the best I can," she replied while attempting to hide her own concern.

"I know you are, my dear. I'm sorry; the stress is beginning to wear on me. Forgive me?"

"Of course," she said as they turned down the road. They'd traveled only a short distance when Jasmine said, "Yes, this is right. I do remember. We'll take another right turn, and then it's only three or four miles."

"Good. It's soon going to be daybreak, and I'd like to have the carriage safely hidden and the family inside Levi's house before the sun rises."

"I do hope he remembers me," she said quietly.

"Of course he'll remember you."

"I haven't seen him for years. Since my marriage to Bradley—he attended the wedding."

Nolan gave her a lopsided grin. "At least your name remains Houston. Surely your father has visited with Levi throughout the years and informed him of the many happenings in your life."

She shrugged. "Who knows? Father would have willingly offered the information, but I don't know that Levi would have been interested. As I said, he's nothing like the rest of the family."

"Hopefully, that will be to our advantage."

"But being different doesn't ensure his help."

"Well, we will soon find out." Nolan pulled back on the reins and the team came to a halt near the front entrance of the hulking, poorly maintained frame house sitting a distance from the road. The house was surrounded by leafless oaks, and a substantial barn was located to the distant rear of the house.

"The rest of you remain in the carriage while we go up and speak with Cousin Levi," Jasmine said with a cheery smile. "We shan't be long."

The girls remained asleep and the others appeared quite content to remain in the carriage while someone else secured provision for their safety. Truth be told, Jasmine longed to remain in the buggy with them. She disliked having the group reliant upon her to find the proper accommodations; there was much at stake.

She tapped upon the door—lightly at first and then more forcefully. "I forgot that he's a bit hard of hearing," she said to Nolan as they stood on the wraparound front porch.

A frazzled-appearing servant finally answered the door after peering out from behind the lace curtains at the front windows. "May I help you?" she asked, opening the door only wide enough to extend her beak of a nose through the crack.

Jasmine nearly giggled at the sight. "Good morning. My name is Jasmine Wainwright Houston—I'm Levi's second cousin. Is he in?"

"You've come calling at this time of the day? He's not even had his breakfast."

"Well, nor have we, and we would be most happy to join him if you'd tell him we've arrived. Actually, there are seven of us. Our three children, two servants, and the two of us," she added with what she hoped was a pleasant smile.

"I'll go and tell Mister Levi you're here. You may wait on the porch."

"Perhaps we could at least enter the foyer," Jasmine said. "I assure you we're harmless." If they were already in the house, it would be much more difficult for Levi to send them on their way—or so she hoped.

The servant opened the door a bit farther and peered at the wagon with a frown on her face. "I suppose it wouldn't hurt," she conceded begrudgingly.

"Thank you. I'll go and fetch the others while my husband moves our carriage and horses into the barn," Jasmine said as she and Nolan turned and stepped from the porch.

"I'm not certain . . ."

"Not to worry—I'll explain to Cousin Levi," Jasmine said without giving the woman any further opportunity to protest.

"Handled quite nicely," Nolan complimented as they hurried to the carriage.

"Thank you. I hope the meeting with Levi goes as well. As I recall, he's fond of children—at least he always treated me well as a child. Let's hope he still looks kindly upon youngsters. Some older people don't, you know," she added in a hushed voice.

Nolan laughed. "Yes, I do know, my dear. My own father was one of them. I'll be in as soon as I've cared for the horses. Don't let him pitch you out on your ear before I return."

"I'll do my best. He may not be down for breakfast until after you join us," she hastily added as she helped the women, each one carrying a drowsy child, out of the carriage.

Although the notion gave her comfort, her hope was

dashed when the small group entered the front door. Cousin Levi stood at the bottom of the stairway with his hand resting upon the oak balustrade, looking as though he expected royalty to enter his presence.

The old man adjusted his spectacles and peered at the group, his eyes traveling from head to toe as he examined each one. "A bit overdressed for a morning call, aren't you?" he inquired as his gaze finally settled upon Jasmine, who was still attired in her ball gown.

Jasmine glanced at her mauve satin gown with its puffed trim across the bodice and hem. The silk roses and fichu adornment further served to make the gown appear completely inappropriate for morning wear. "Yes, we are. However, my family attended a gala at Rosewood Plantation last night, and we now find ourselves in quite a quandary. I'm hopeful you'll be willing to help. If I might have a few moments of your time, I can explain."

"Since the children are still in their party wear, may I assume they've not eaten breakfast, either?" he inquired.

"No, they haven't," Jasmine replied.

"Maude!"

The beak-nosed servant rushed into the foyer with her cap askew. "Yes, sir?"

"Take the children and servants and feed them breakfast."

"At the dining table?" she asked, her gaze clearly fixed upon Prissy.

"Yes, at the dining table, and quit staring. I'm certain the colored girl knows how to use a fork as well as you and I. Off with you now, and take them along."

"I's willin' to eat in da kitchen or even help prepare da food," Prissy offered.

"Nonsense. Go and eat," Levi ordered.

"You're very kind," Jasmine said.

"I'm a grumpy old man. Now come into the parlor and

let me hear your tale of woe." He slowly edged himself into one of the overstuffed chairs. "My rheumatism kicks up from time to time. Probably a storm moving in," he explained as he scratched his thinning white hair. "I'm trying to remember what it was your father told me about you. Ah, yes. Your first husband died and you married his brother, isn't that it?"

"Yes. And I live in Massachusetts," she added.

"Right . . . an abolitionist. Your father mentioned that too. I was surprised he'd come to accept the fact that you and McKinley had turned against the South."

Jasmine cringed at his characterization of her beliefs. "We didn't turn against the South, cousin. We are abolitionists, but we continue to love the South and many of the people who live here. However, we find it impossible to embrace slavery—which is what brings me here."

A startled look crossed his face. "I don't own any slaves, so you have no argument with me."

Jasmine smiled and leaned over to pat his hand. "This has nothing to do with whether you own slaves, Cousin Levi." Clearly and concisely, she explained their dilemma, leaving few details to the imagination. Levi gave her his full attention without once interrupting her explanation. She had nearly completed reciting the facts when Nolan entered the front door.

"Do permit me to introduce you to my husband, Nolan Houston."

"You're a fellow artist, I understand," Nolan said.

"Ah, you paint?" Levi inquired.

"In my early years I spent a great deal of my time writing and sketching. My passion, however, was poetry. Now, I no longer have time to indulge myself. Perhaps when the children are grown and life has settled a bit."

Levi laughed as he shook Nolan's hand. "Don't wait too

long, my boy, or you'll never return at all. I know many people frown upon artists. They think us lazy and unwilling to adhere to *their* idea of honorable work. Little do they realize how difficult it is to place paintbrush to canvas or pen to paper and deliver a work of beauty. But those of us who are blessed with creative gifts have an obligation to God and mankind to use that ability. Don't waste your talents! From what your wife tells me, you have been given much that you could write about."

"Unfortunately, none of it heartening," Nolan replied.

"True. Nonetheless, much art is communicated through pain and suffering. Remember that when you return to your home. However, the problem at hand is of greater import than your artistic endeavors. Jasmine says you need protection until you can formulate a plan for you and your family to flee back to the North."

"Are you willing to assist us? I'd like to say we won't be placing you in danger, but such a statement may not be truthful. Men who would threaten the lives of young children will care little if they injure you also. I want you to be fully aware of the possible harm that may befall you."

"I'm an old man, Nolan. Death does not frighten me. As for the slavery issue, I was born and raised in Mississippi, but unlike most folks around here, I've lived in other places. Certainly, some of my neighbors have traveled abroad or gone north for short periods of time, but they've never actually immersed themselves in other cultures and social settings. As I told your wife, I own no slaves. In fact, I never have. I hire servants to assist me as needed—white folks. There aren't many freed men around these parts or I'd be willing to hire them."

"Then you agree with our stand against slavery?" Nolan inquired.

"I don't participate in slavery, but I *do* believe in the right to make a choice. Not quite the same thing you folks believe. Let me add, however, that I strongly oppose the tactics being used by Rupert and his cronies. I stand willing to assist your family, though, if you believe Rupert's threats to be real. I suggest we reason together and develop a well-thought-out plan—after breakfast," he said with a broad grin. "Man cannot work on an empty stomach. Let's join the rest of your family in the dining room."

Once breakfast had been completed, Henrietta and Prissy were shown to a room where they could tend the children, and Levi escorted Nolan and Jasmine to his library.

"Why don't you specify your priorities and what you need from me so that we may begin to formulate a plan," Levi said, taking up his pen.

Jasmine sat opposite Nolan, grateful that the older man was taking charge. "We had given all of my father's slaves their freedom, cousin. They are now freed men and women. We told them we would divide the money we received for the crop they were harvesting so they would have enough to begin their lives and become established in the North."

"Mighty generous of you," Levi remarked.

"Perhaps, but none of that is now going to occur. The Willows has been stolen from me. Rupert has some forged documents that everyone for miles around will attest to being bona fide. The cotton, ready for shipping, has been burned, and worst of all, all of our former slaves have been hauled off by Rupert and his men and are being sold back into slavery. Do you think there's any way we can help them regain their freedom before we depart?" Jasmine asked as she attempted to hold her emotions in check.

"Now, it's not going to serve us well if you become distressed. We need to keep our wits about us if we're to accomplish our mission. Concerning the slaves . . . I don't know how your husband feels about this issue, but I believe our first priority should be getting all seven of you to safety," Levi said.

"But I fear if we leave the field hands, they'll never escape bondage," Jasmine said, dabbing her eyes with a lace handkerchief. "I know we don't have the law on our side, nor the sympathy of our neighbors, but it seems we should at least try."

Levi leaned back in his leather desk chair and clipped off the end of a cigar. "I'm not going to sit here and tell you I think you're going to have much success with such a venture either now or in the future. Frankly, your first responsibility is to those three children. Once they're safely returned home, use your own judgment about coming back and helping the others gain their freedom," he said while puffing on the cigar.

"Your cousin is absolutely correct, Jasmine. I abhor these ghastly happenings, but the children cannot remain in Mississippi while we go searching about the countryside. You know as well as I do that our chance of finding any of the former slaves is miniscule."

"And if you find them," Levi added, "your attempts to regain their freedom will be thwarted at every turn. These men are shrewd, and they'll quickly assist one another in their scheme."

"Yet our former slaves are depending upon us—I know they are," she lamented. "We'll be like all the rest: we'll leave them disappointed and reinforce their belief there are no whites who care for them."

Nolan leaned forward and grasped her by the shoulders. "Jasmine, we *cannot* remain here. You would never forgive yourself if something were to happen to our children."

"I know, I know," she finally conceded in a hoarse whisper. "Yet I feel as though I've betrayed all those people."

"No, my dear. You haven't betrayed them—it's Rupert and his cronies who have made a mockery of the law and justice. And one day he will pay dearly for his actions," Nolan assured her.

Levi leaned forward and rested his arms upon the massive desk, ocher spots showing prominently on his aging skin. "Now that we've settled the issue of the slaves, let's move on. Have you booked passage for your transportation home?"

"Yes. We should be able to exchange Martha's passage for Prissy's use. However, Rupert knows our plans. When he came to visit, he asked about our journey and then inquired if we would take the same route home. We told him that we had made arrangements with Captain Harmon to sail home on the *Mary Benjamin*," Nolan replied. "Knowing Rupert, he'll surely be on the lookout at the docks in Rodney. He and the rest of the men realize it's the ideal place for us to board a steamboat to New Orleans. And he did say he'd be watching us."

"I realize the journey would be difficult, but I think you'd be wise to travel north by foot for a time—get yourselves to Vicksburg, then take a steamboat north and make train connections for the remainder of your journey. If Rupert believes you're going to sail out of New Orleans, he'll have his men stationed in Rodney and Natchez."

"True," Nolan agreed. "And he'll be expecting us to sail south toward New Orleans rather than north. We can make our way along the river until it appears safe."

"Rupert is clever. He may send men in *both* directions, so your journey is going to be treacherous until you're safely beyond Vicksburg. I doubt they'll search any farther north than that," Levi said thoughtfully. "I can furnish you with food, and I'll have Maude see if she has something you can wear other than that . . . that . . ." He flitted his hand toward Jasmine's gown.

"Ball gown," she said, completing his sentence.

"Yes. You'll need something more substantial—and shoes made of something other than cloth, I suspect."

"Maude!" he shouted while ringing a small brass bell that had been resting on his desk.

"Yes, sir?" She edged into the room like a frightened bird.

"Mrs. Houston is going to need clothes in which to travel. This, of course, will not do." He once again waved his hand up and down. "Do you think you can be of assistance?"

The older woman's eyes traveled up and down Jasmine's body as though she were taking measurements. "My clothing would not fit her, sir. She has more meat on her bones than I, but I suppose I could go into town and make some purchases if you like."

"Would such purchases arouse suspicion, do you think?" Jasmine inquired.

"Why would anyone care if I was purchasing a traveling suit for Master Levi's relative?" she asked.

Jasmine flinched. "That's the point, Maude. We don't want anyone to know I'm here or that I'm leaving."

Maude stared at her as though she'd taken leave of her senses.

"It's private information, Maude. Not a word to anyone. Understand?"

"Indeed, sir."

"But will it cause suspicion?" Jasmine insisted.

"I sometimes make clothing purchases to send to my family. Should anyone inquire, I'll say my sister is in need of a traveling suit and there's nary a decent shop to be found near her home. 'Tis the truth anyway."

"Your sister is traveling?" Levi inquired.

"*No!* The part about having no decent shops in Kenwick," Maude said in an exasperated tone.

"I see," Levi said. "I want you to hasten off as soon as possible. Don't dally, but find both shoes and a dress, along with a change of clothes for the children, if possible. Put it on my account," he added.

Jasmine stood and motioned to Maude. "I'll go to the other room and give you some measurements, Maude. If you gentlemen will excuse me for a short time?"

"Of course," Nolan replied. "We'll work on the additional arrangements. We should likely plan to leave at first light, don't you agree?" he asked Levi.

"You may want to leave under cover of darkness. I'd suggest you leave well before daylight so you can be away from this area before sunrise. I'm concerned Rupert may come here searching for you—I want you to be well on your way if that should occur."

"Rupert calls on you?" Jasmine inquired as she and Maude reached the doorway.

"Not on a regular basis, but we see each other from time to time. And now that there is so little family remaining, he's bound to wonder if you thought to come here."

Jasmine frowned. "I suppose you're correct. I hadn't thought of Rupert considering we might come here, though I don't know where else we could have gone. Maude and I will see to the clothing while you assess our other needs—and I think we should travel to Vicksburg by wagon, not on foot."

Levi gave a brief laugh as he stubbed out his cigar. "I'm sure you do. However, you won't be safe traveling on any roads that will accommodate a wagon. You're going to need to keep to the woods if you're to stay out of sight. You may be able take a coach once you're twenty or thirty miles north, but remember—each person who sees you is one who may betray your whereabouts."

"There's one more thing," Nolan told Levi. "Our hired woman was killed in the fire. She still lies near the back door of the house. Can you see to her proper burial?"

He nodded. "Be assured of it."

Jasmine sighed. It would have to be enough. They had no other choice.

————

That night, with Clara hoisted into a sling on Nolan's back and each of them carrying provisions to sustain them until they reached Vicksburg, they stepped out into the crisp air.

"Thank you for everything! I pray we haven't placed you in any danger," Nolan said. "Make some arrangement to rid yourself of the carriage and horses; I'm afraid Rupert would recognize them."

Levi nodded. "Don't worry about me—you've got more than enough to concern yourself with. You'll all be in my prayers." Levi's eyes shone with emotion as he picked up his worn leather Bible and tucked it into Jasmine's satchel. "I want you to have my Bible as well as the money I placed inside the front cover. Don't refuse me; you'll need both the money and God's Word to sustain you throughout your journey."

Jasmine leaned forward and placed a kiss on her cousin's cheek. "Thank you for your kindness. I'll write once we've arrived home."

"Remember to keep to the woods. So long as you can hear the river and you're headed due north, you'll remain on course." Levi took hold of Jasmine's arm. "And don't fret about The Willows. I, too, have friends in these parts. I may not be able to get your slaves back, but I feel confident between my friends and what I know of Rupert Hesston, we'll secure The Willows for you and McKinley. Now hurry on."

Jasmine felt only moderately relieved at this thought. "Thank you so much."

Nolan waved, and their small band walked away from the house with Alice Ann holding tightly to Jasmine's hand. Henrietta and Prissy walked side by side. Spencer brought up the rear, listening for anyone advancing from that direction.

"I don't like this," Alice Ann whined as she tripped on a fallen branch.

"You're fine. You didn't fall. So long as you hold my hand, nothing will happen to you," Jasmine said in a reassuring voice. "We're on a great adventure, Alice Ann. One you can tell all your friends about once we get home."

"I'm going to tell Winnie first thing," she said.

"A horse can't understand you," Spencer told her.

"Shh!" Nolan warned. "Let's keep our voices down. We're close to Rodney, and there may be rowdies out and about in these woods."

Alice squeezed Jasmine's hand more tightly. "Is somebody going to hurt us?"

"No. Your papa won't let anything happen to you, Alice Ann, but you must do as you're told. Try to keep quiet unless it's very important."

They moved slowly, silently picking their way through the stand of woods that flourished not far from the banks of the Mississippi. The raw, fishy stench of the river mingled with the lapping sound of the water as it licked the dry riverbank—sounds and smells that directed their path when vision failed them. For a short time they floundered in the darkness, but their eyes quickly adjusted to the shadowy surroundings and they picked up their pace. All but Alice Ann, who was shifted to Nolan's back while Henrietta and

Jasmine took turns carrying Clara. There was little doubt this would be a grueling journey.

The night was filled with the sounds of croaking frogs and hooting owls while the distant moon cast eerie shadows in all directions. Giant tangles of Spanish moss hung from the trees like thick spider webs waiting to lure their prey. Jasmine swallowed her fear and followed closely behind Nolan as she wondered about the terror of all those runaway slaves who had stumbled through these woods before them. Runaways with dogs sniffing and yelping in the distance and then growing closer and closer, nipping at their heels until surely the bile of fear would rise in the throats of those slaves and nearly choke them. How did they manage to stop breathing and listen for the snap of a twig or the sound of a footstep on the forest floor when everything within them ached to run like the wind? How did they withstand the pure terror of being at the mercy of both the elements and their cruel captors? Though she feared for her family, her terror could be nothing compared to those brave slaves who dared to run for freedom.

"I think I hear something," Spencer hissed.

Nolan quickly gathered them together behind a growth of bushes. "Don't anyone say anything," he whispered.

Jasmine's heart hammered with the violence of pounding thunder on a stormy night as they hunkered behind the overgrowth. The voices were coming from the direction of the river—not from behind them, as Spencer had thought. Jasmine shrunk back as the voices grew louder.

"I'm not going any farther," a man said. "If Rupert wants to chase after that colored girl, then let him come and get her."

"He wants *all* of them—not just the darkie."

"Says he wants to prove to them that they've got to show him proper respect."

"This is mad. I'm not going to stay out here any longer just so Rupert can force someone to show him some respect. Besides, if they were headed north to Vicksburg, they would have been on the last boat. There's another one due in the morning. I say we go back to Rodney and, come daybreak, wait at the dock to see who boards the boat."

The other man grunted his agreement.

Nolan signaled them to remain where they were until long after the men could no longer be heard and then emitted a sigh. "I think it's safe for us to continue now," he whispered.

Jasmine clutched his arm. "From what those men said, I believe we'll be safe once we arrive at Grand Gulf. Let's pray we don't have to continue on foot to Vicksburg. I don't believe I could make it," she said wearily as she again wondered how runaways had endured their flight to freedom under circumstances much harsher than the conditions she was now being forced to experience. Suddenly she felt dreadfully inadequate.

CHAPTER · 16

MARY MARGARET hoisted her skirts a few inches and made her way across Merrimack Street, carefully avoiding the pools of mud that were a vivid reminder of last week's snow. She was thankful the weather had warmed a bit, yet the muddy remains made getting about perilous. Even the carriages were having difficulty navigating the streets.

"Careful. That mud is as slick as the snow preceding it."

Mary Margaret looked up at the warning. "Paddy! What brings ya to town this evenin'?"

"I was attending a meetin'—we were havin' discussions about the St. Patrick's Day festivities," he replied, taking a few steps closer.

"Truly? And were ya able to complete the plans?"

He laughed and shook his head, surprised by Mary Margaret's conviviality. "'Twill take more than one meeting for this group ta make any decisions."

"Bridgett tells me the decisions for the dance have already been made and the ladies have begun work already."

"Aye—but it's the women that have taken charge of the

269

dance. Men are a wee bit slower in making arrangements for parades and such—they want to make sure everything is exactly correct."

She laughed. "Get on with ya, Paddy. We all know it's the women that are slow to make decisions but quick to set their hands ta work once they've a plan, while 'tis the men who are quick to decisions but slow to beginning their task. If ya ask me, the men were likely anxious to get out to the pub and tip an ale or two instead of makin' plans for a parade that's more than a month away."

"Quick to pass judgment, are ya?"

"Just telling the truth about what I figure happened. Are ya tellin' me I'm wrong?"

A faint smile crossed Paddy's lips. "Sure and ya know exactly what happened. But they all agreed that we'd make our final decisions at the meeting next week," he quickly added. "I was thinkin' to walk over and see Bridgett and Cullen before headin' back to the farm. Are ya off to do some shopping?"

"No, just wanted to leave the house for a while and get a breath of air. Another one of the girls in our boarding-house lost her position at the mill today. Rather gloomy at the house, so I thought I'd take a walk."

"Well, then, would ya be wantin' to accompany me? If ya do na mind the walk, that is. The wagon is at the black-smith having a new wheel put on, and I'm to pick it up later. But if ya do na mind traveling by foot, ya could visit Bridgett for a bit before returning home."

There was a slight hesitation in his voice. Mary Margaret was unsure if he truly desired her company or if he was merely being polite. But no matter. Since learning more about Paddy from his sister, she was interested in becoming better acquainted, though she didn't want to appear overly anxious.

"I'm not certain," she tentatively began as she clicked open the small watch attached to her jacket and glanced at the time. "I do suppose I could, so long as I'm back to the boardinghouse by ten o'clock."

"Aye. I'll be sure ya're home on time. So ya say one of the girls lost her job today. I hope you and Bridgett do na have to face such a terrible thing," he said as they began walking.

"Bridgett should be safe unless the economy gets much worse. They're terminatin' by seniority, though they've made a few exceptions and let some girls go who they said didn't turn out as much work," she said. "That's what happened to Helen today. She's been with the Corporation longer than I have, but she's sickly and can na work so fast. I'm hoping she will na be bearing a grudge toward me, for it was na my doing."

"Did ya try discussin' the matter with her?" Paddy asked.

"Aye, but she said she didn't want to talk, so I left her to her thoughts. Mrs. Brighton said she could stay at the house, but there's no tellin' if she will. She's a quiet girl that came to our house because she was ill-treated at the place she had lived before. Mrs. Brighton has been kind to her, though Helen seldom has a word to say. At supper Mrs. Brighton told Helen there might be work for her someplace other than the textile mills."

"Does she have some other skills ta offer at one of the other companies?"

"I do na know, but Mrs. Brighton mentioned the company that's begun manufacturing shuttles and bobbins. She said she'd heard there might be a few positions there. She also suggested Helen talk to the owners of some of the shops in town to see if they might be needin' help, but I do na think there's much of a chance for that. Helen's na the type

TRACIE PETERSON / JUDITH MILLER

to be greeting customers in a dress shop or stationery store—she's too fearful of approachin' strangers."

"Ya never know what hunger will do for a person," Paddy said. "She may find she's able to handle such a position if it's all she can locate."

"It's a fact her family's needin' her money, so I do hope she finds work. Mrs. Brighton's willing ta seek aid for her through the benevolent group at her church. She's a kind woman, that one."

"Aye, so I've been told."

Mary Margaret took a deep breath to bolster her courage before speaking. "Are ya making plans to attend the St. Patrick's Day dance?" she asked as they neared Cullen and Bridgett's home.

Paddy turned to glance at Mary Margaret. "Sure and I always attend the dance. What good Irishman would remain at home on such a festive day?"

He didn't give the answer she had hoped to elicit, but she wasn't deterred. She would ask him again as they walked back to the boardinghouse. However, this time she would phrase her question a bit differently.

Paddy was certain he'd heard Bridgett whisper a remark about the St. Patrick's Day parade to Mary Margaret and then giggle as they were preparing to depart.

"I'm wonderin' why the two of them are discussing the parade when what they need to concern themselves with is the dance," he said to Cullen. "Next thing ya know they'll be tryin' to take over the parade."

"To be sure," Cullen agreed. "Bridgett's quite the organizer. She'll be havin' our work done for us if we leave 'er to it long enough."

"Still, they needn't be doin' our job. Although I'm sure

Bridgett would get the work done."

Cullen gave a hearty laugh. "Aye, to be sure. But women would na be women if they did na put themselves in the center of all of our plans. Besides, if I know Bridgett, they're likely discussing the latest fashions they'd like to be wearin' rather than interfering into yar plans, Paddy. Do na worry—there will be plenty for ya to attend to before the seventeenth of March arrives." The women moved closer to the front door. "Best be fetchin' yar jacket. Looks like the lass is ready to leave."

Mary Margaret had her cape fastened and her reticule in hand. She directed a warm smile in his direction, and for a moment Paddy wondered if there might be someone behind him for whom the smile was intended. After all, this lass had been nothing but agitated with him when they'd encountered each other in the past. He'd been taken aback when she agreed to spend time with him this evening; now she was smiling at him as though she'd missed being in his company. He was not a man given to second-guessing people's motives, but Mary Margaret was indeed cut from a different cloth than were the lasses he'd encountered in the past. Why was she now so affable?

She appeared to listen intently as they walked home and Paddy talked of the farm and the horses that would soon be ready for their new owners at West Point and the Virginia Military Institute. He spoke of several of the animals that had been sick and the fact that he missed Mr. Houston's presence at the farm, and he admitted he was sometimes overwhelmed making the many decisions needed in order to run such a fine operation as the Houston farm.

"I have little doubt but what ya're doin' a wonderful job. Mr. Houston has paid you a fine compliment by placin' you in charge during his absence," Mary Margaret said sweetly as she patted his arm.

"Aye, that he has, and I do na want to disappoint him," he said with his gaze fixed upon her hand as she continued to lightly grasp his arm.

"I do na think that would be possible." Her voice sounded thick and sweet like the honey he used to pour on his pancakes when he was a wee lad living in Ireland.

"Bridgett and I were discussin' the St. Patrick's Day dance. She was tellin' me about the new dress she's makin' for the dance."

"That's nice. I'm thinkin' she'll look lovely whether her dress is old or new."

"But having a new gown to wear to a dance always makes a woman feel special."

He didn't know what she wanted him to say. Surely the lass knew he had no knowledge of dresses and sewing, and there was little more he could add to a discussion of dress for the St. Patrick's Day dance—or any other dance, for that matter.

"Will ya be purchasing new trousers and shirt for the dance?" she finally inquired.

Paddy scratched his head. "I do na think so. I do na give much thought to such things until the time is upon me. Unlike you women, I do na plan to be doin' any sewing."

"Of course, if a lass wanted to make a new gown for the dance, she'd have to know some time in advance that she was going," Mary Margaret said.

"Anyone can go to the dance. Ya do na need a special invite," he said. "Well, here we are—I've gotten ya home well before ten o'clock, and now I must be hurrying off before Jake beds down for the night. He will not look kindly on me if I wake him up needin' my wagon."

He tipped his hat and nodded. "Good night to ya, Mary Margaret. I enjoyed spending the evenin' with ya."

"Good night," she replied, giving him another of her sugary smiles.

The girl was a puzzle—of that there was no doubt!

———

Kiara rounded the table and placed a plate of eggs and sausage in front of Paddy. "Get busy with yar breakfast," she ordered Nevan and Katherine, who were busy annoying one another rather than eating the food their mother had placed in front of them.

"You do na have to tell me more than once," Paddy said, picking up his fork. "Has Rogan already eaten and gone with Liam?"

"Aye, about five minutes ago."

He nodded. "I thought I saw him go by when I was mucking out some of the stalls. And how's that fine babe doin' this mornin'? Seems little Aidan is always sleepin' when I come in."

"That's what babies do. They sleep. And thankful we are that they do. He's nearly six weeks old now, Paddy. He'll soon begin to stay awake a wee bit more. Were ya able to get the wagon repaired?" she asked.

"Aye, it's back in the shed if Rogan's needin' it for anything."

"And did ya stop by and see Cullen and Bridgett?"

"Aye, along with Mary Margaret O'Flannery."

"Is that a fact, now? Do tell me how ya happened to be keeping company with Miss O'Flannery," Kiara said as she wiped the apron that covered her green chambray skirt.

Paddy related the entire episode in between bites of breakfast. "If ya do na begin eating that food, Nevan, I'm going to clean yar plate as well as me own," he said to the boy with a grin. "Now, where was I?" he asked, turning his attention back to his sister.

"Where she's talkin' about the dance," Kiara said impatiently.

"Aye. Well, if I did na know better, I'd think the lass was wantin' *me* to ask her to the dance," he finally said.

"And why would that be so hard ta believe? Ya're a fine young man that any lass would be lucky ta have!"

"Ya saw how she acted when she and Bridgett were over here—her nose up in the air as though she did na think much of me. Yet last night, she was sweet as a peppermint stick. I do na understand the mind of a lass," he said, wiping his mouth. "I best get back out to the barns. There's much ta be done today. And I hope the two of ya are done with yar breakfast by the time I come in for the noonday meal," he added with a wink at his niece and nephew.

———————

Kiara began to clear the table while contemplating the information her brother had imparted. 'Twas true Mary Margaret appeared to think Paddy a wee bit full of himself, but Kiara thought she'd noticed the girl's feelings soften—especially when Bridgett was telling her about their voyage from Ireland. Perhaps what Mary Margaret and Paddy needed was a little more time together. Time to get to know one another a bit better in a friendly environment. Perhaps she'd extend a dinner invitation to Mary Margaret—and the sooner the better, for St. Patrick's Day would soon be arriving.

CHAPTER · 17

THE WOMEN AND children were huddled in a small circle, praying Nolan would return with the news they could board the boat. Jasmine had begged Nolan to go into Grand Gulf the preceding night and rent a room at the hotel, but he had refused, saying they would raise too much suspicion and would be too easily remembered should Rupert or his men come looking for them. She knew he was correct: one man, three children, and three women—one of them colored. There was little doubt they would raise eyebrows, especially in their filthy condition. So now they waited, Jasmine leading them in yet another prayer for safe passage home.

"It's Papa," Spencer whispered as they heard footsteps drawing near.

"Shh. Stay quiet. We can't be certain," Jasmine whispered into his ear.

She captured a glimpse of Nolan's brown wool coat as he edged through the thick brush. "Jasmine, it's me—Nolan," he called. He greeted her with a hand to her shoulder. "I talked with a number of men along the docks and some of the merchants doing business near the wharf. None of them had seen strangers loitering near the docks."

"Did you book passage?" she asked excitedly.

"Yes, though I pray I didn't make a mistake. I continue to wonder if we should wait until we reach Vicksburg to board a vessel."

"You may place the responsibility on my shoulders, Nolan. I truly can go no farther, nor can the children. If any of Rupert's men board the ship looking for Prissy, we'll hide her, but I honestly believe they've given up by now."

Nolan glanced about the weary group. "Do you all agree?"

"Yes," they replied in unison.

"Then we shall board. It's not what you're accustomed to, my dear. In fact, we'll have little space since the boat is already loaded with cotton."

"You'll hear no complaint from me so long as I don't have to walk another mile in these uncomfortable shoes. I have blisters on top of blisters," she said while bending over to rub her tender feet.

"We have no time to tarry, for the captain tells me they're preparing to lift the gangplank within the hour. If we're not on board, they'll sail without us." Nolan lifted Alice Ann to his hip. "Can you manage Clara?"

"Yes, of course. Spencer, please help Prissy and Henrietta gather things together and let's be on our way," Jasmine instructed.

Nolan quickly surveyed their camp to assure himself they'd left nothing behind. If Rupert or his supporters searched these woods, they didn't want any evidence to remain that their family had been there. It would take only a piece of fabric or a small toy of Alice Ann's to alert Rupert's men, convincing them to continue their search. When Nolan had finally completed his appraisal of the campsite, he motioned for them to follow.

"God has heard our prayer," Jasmine told Henrietta and Prissy.

"Don' be too sure—we ain't out of here yet, Missus," Prissy said as she hoisted one of the satchels under her arm.

Jasmine ignored Prissy's gloomy response. She could feel God's hand guiding them, so she would not be deterred by anything Prissy or anyone else might say. In her heart she knew they would arrive home safely—all of them.

The dock bustled with stevedores and roustabouts unloading packet boats heavy with freight destined for Vicksburg, while other dock workers hauled cotton bales and freight onto boats destined for Memphis and St. Louis.

"This way," Nolan directed, hurrying the bedraggled group toward a steamer at the far edge of the riverbank. The boat was laden with cotton bales that filled the lower deck of the boat and were stacked high around the front and sides.

Jasmine hesitated as Nolan headed for the gangplank. "Come along, my dear," he said, motioning her forward.

"The bales are stacked so high we won't be able to see a thing unless we go to the upper deck, which, I might add, looks none too safe." She eyed the vessel from the top of the tall black smokestacks and back down again. "They should have a higher railing up there. I truly wonder if this boat is actually seaworthy—especially with so much cargo on board. It doesn't appear well maintained."

Nolan turned to face her, Alice Ann clinging to his neck, and leveled a look of utter exasperation in her direction. "I didn't ask to review the maintenance log. I thought it more important to locate a boat going to Vicksburg that had space for us. As I recall, you said you couldn't walk another mile," he reminded her.

"That's true, but from all appearances, this boat has picked up all the cargo it can possibly carry."

"I told you there would be little space. I believe the boat is safe, but if you prefer to wait for another, we can go back to the woods."

"No, Mama. Please let's get on the boat," Spencer urged. "It's safe. I just want to go home."

Prissy was wringing her hands as her gaze settled on the murky water. "You think we's gonna end up at the bottom of that river, Miz Jasmine? I sure don' know how to swim. I never did like being 'round no water deep enough to drown in. You remember ol' Elijah what lived in the slave quarters?"

Jasmine shook her head. "No, I don't think I knew him."

"Well, he never did learn to swim neither. And one day when he was fishing in the pond down by the quarter, he done fell in and drowned hisself. I sho' don't want that happening to us," she said, her eyes shining with terror.

"We're not going to drown, Prissy," Nolan assured her. "This boat is perfectly sound. Otherwise, the plantation owners wouldn't use it to transport their cotton. Come along now—we're all going to be fine."

A short time later the boat released a long, shrill whistle. They watched from the upper level but well out of sight of anyone who might be watching from the shore as the gangplank was lifted and the boat began to move slowly away from the levee.

"We're going home, Alice Ann," Spencer said brightly. "You'll soon be able to ride Winnie, and I can ride Larkspur once again. Do you think Larkspur will remember me, Papa?"

Nolan tousled Spencer's disheveled hair. "I'm sure he will."

"When Reggie last wrote to me, she said Moses was exercising Winnie and Larkspur every day. I wonder if Larkspur will want Moses to ride him more than me when I get home."

Nolan gently clasped Spencer's shoulder. "I wouldn't worry. It may take a few days, but Larkspur will soon remember you and be happy to have you back home."

A scruffy-appearing seaman approached as the boat began to gain speed and move farther away from the bank. "Captain says to tell you there's a small cabin of sorts that you can use if ya've a mind to—ain't much, but it'll give you a little privacy. Follow me. It's back this way," he said. "Call out if you think you smell anything burning. Don't want this load going up in smoke. Fire's always a problem when we're carrying a big load of cotton. We have one most every voyage, what with all the wood to fire the boilers and all this cotton—guess it's to be expected."

"Then it's good you's got all dis water around," Prissy said as the group followed the man through the narrow passageways.

The crewman laughed at her remark. "If this cotton gets going, that river ain't gonna help us much, except to swallow up the boat when she sinks. Gotta catch 'em early or there's not much hope. Here's the cabin," he said as they came to a stop in front of an open doorway.

Jasmine surveyed the room and though she thought the captain had taken great leniency in calling the space a cabin, she didn't say so. "Do thank the captain for his thoughtfulness," she said instead.

"I don't want to stay here," Alice Ann said tearfully. "I'm afraid we're going to burn in the fire."

"What are we supposed to do when the fire starts?" Spencer asked, his voice quivering.

"There isn't going to be a fire," Nolan asserted.

"That man said there's a fire almost every time they go

on the river," Spencer said. "Now I wish we hadn't come on this boat."

Nolan attempted to calm the children, but both of them were insistent upon further talk of fires or drowning, continuing their questions until their fear was palpable.

Jasmine pulled her satchel close and rummaged through until her fingers touched upon the leather-bound Bible. She pulled it out and handed it to Nolan. "Perhaps you could read to the children about Jesus calming the storm," she suggested.

"Excellent idea," he said and opened the Bible to the Gospel of Luke. "Come sit close while I read these verses. They are very powerful words about a time when Jesus was out in a fishing boat with His disciples."

"Is this a fishing boat?" Alice inquired.

"No, but I suppose it would be easy enough to fish from this boat," Nolan replied. "Now come sit on my lap while I read to you."

They created a tender picture for Jasmine: Alice Ann on her father's lap, Clara on Henrietta's lap, and Spencer between the two—all of them focused upon God's Word. Nolan quietly began reading, the children's eyes growing wide as Nolan read about the storm that suddenly arose at sea and how the disciples hastened to awaken Jesus, who was sleeping in the boat.

"What did Jesus do?" Alice Ann asked, her dimpled chin turned upward as she looked into her father's eyes.

"I'm going to tell you in this next verse—listen closely. 'He got up and rebuked the wind and the raging waters; the storm subsided, and all was calm. "Where is your faith?" he asked his disciples. In fear and amazement they asked one another, "Who is this? He commands even the winds and the water, and they obey him." ' "

"You must remember that Jesus is in this boat with us

right now," Jasmine said. "He's our protector, just as He was for the disciples."

"But I can't see Him," Alice Ann said.

"Because He's in your heart—and you must not ever forget He is with you," she explained. "It's a beautiful day. The sun is shining and it's not overly cold. Perhaps your father would agree to a short walk around the boat so you can become more comfortable with our new surroundings."

The children agreed, even convincing Henrietta to join them on their brief tour while Jasmine and Prissy set about arranging their belongings.

"You truly believe what you tol' your younguns 'bout Jesus being with us and being our protector?"

"Yes, of course. Don't you believe Jesus is watching over you, Prissy?"

"I ain't so sure. Maybe I jes' don't have enough faith, 'cause I sure has had some mighty bad things happen to me. I called out to Jesus, but them bad things jes' kept on happening. Seems like maybe He jes' don't care much 'bout me."

Jasmine reached out and gently grasped Prissy's hands in her own. "God loves you, Prissy. There was a time in my life when I thought God had forsaken me. I was truly unhappy and suffering more than *I* thought fitting for a person who loved the Lord. Eventually, however, my situation changed and my life significantly improved. Our timing is not always the same as God's timing."

"Maybe that's true, but jes' about the time I think things is getting better, then I get slapped back down again. Like me and Toby getting married—now that was a good thing, and I was mighty happy 'bout that. But now Toby's gone, prob'ly sold at the auction to some new owner, and we'll likely never see each other again. And me gonna have dis baby don't make things no better," she lamented.

"I know that's how it must seem now, but you need to keep believing that God is going to see you through this difficult time. I promise we'll do everything we can to find out where Toby is and have him join you. As soon as we arrive in Lowell, I'll pen a letter to my cousin Levi and ask his assistance. I believe he'll agree to help us, and I know we can trust him. Why don't we agree to earnestly pray about this every day? What do you think?" Jasmine asked.

They sat face-to-face, Prissy staring deep into Jasmine's eyes. "I guess we can try, but I jes' don' know if it'll do any good," Prissy replied in a soulful voice.

"We'll both pray, and I'll believe for *both* of us until you gain enough strength to believe for yourself."

Prissy nodded her head up and down, her tawny skin shining like pulled taffy in the warm afternoon sun. "You's a mighty fine woman, Miz Jasmine. You is one of the *good* things God done give me."

"Thank you, Prissy. And I'm going to trust God to send you more good things too."

———

Kiara wiped her hands on her apron, wrapped an old shawl around her shoulders, and walked out the back door toward the stables. Both Aidan and Katherine were napping, and Nevan was off to school. She hoped to make good use of the free time to begin supper preparations, but first she wanted to find Paddy. Simon came out of the stables leading one of the fine Arabians, the horse stomping and snorting in the cold afternoon air. She could not help but admire the horse's beauty. *A fine animal,* she thought as she waved her arm to gain Simon's attention.

When he finally looked in her direction, Kiara cupped her hands to her mouth. "Ask Paddy to come and see me when he has a minute."

Simon waved his hat. "I'll do that, Missus," he called.

"Thank you!" She rubbed her arms under the woolen shawl. "It's cold out here," she muttered while hurrying back indoors.

She was pleased she had decided upon mutton stew for supper. Upon entering the warm kitchen, Kiara checked the dried apples she had earlier placed in a bowl of warm water. The apples were ready to be used in her apple cinnamon cake, one of Rogan's favorites.

"I hear ya're wanting to see me," Paddy said as he burst through the kitchen door.

"Close that door—ya're bringing all the cold air in with ya," Kiara scolded.

He gave the door a shove. "It's closed," he said with a grin. "Now what is it ya're calling me away from my work to discuss?"

"I was wondering if ya would like to join us for supper tonight."

Paddy pulled off his cap and ran his fingers through the dark curls that fell across his forehead. "It's an inviting offer, but I do na think so. I've a lot of work to finish today, and I'll likely work until late."

Kiara glanced over her shoulder and gave him a haughty look. "Since ya have yar own house, ya never seem to have any time for yar sister and her family. Poor Nevan's soon goin' to forget he has an uncle."

"Go on with ya, lass. Ya know I spend far too much time at yar house, and Nevan's out to the stables every day after school, so I do na think he's going to be forgetting me."

"That does na change the fact that I would enjoy havin' ya join us for supper tonight. I'm fixing a fine mutton stew—ya won't want to be missing that, will ya?"

"Ya do know how to win yar own way. I will na promise ta be here, but if I finish all my chores and paper work, then

I'll join ya," he said as he helped himself to a piece of her soda bread.

"Ya should have more than enough time, for I do na plan ta serve supper until seven-thirty."

"Rogan working late, is he? I'll do my best." He pulled his cap back onto his head and opened the door.

He didn't wait for an answer before hurrying off, and for that she was thankful. After all, she did not want to tell her brother an untruth. Nor did she want to reveal her plot to have him spend the evening with Mary Margaret.

The children were cooperative, and Kiara's supper preparations moved forward according to plan. "Go and wash up—we're having company for supper," she told Nevan when he came in from the stables with a piece of straw tucked between his lips. "And take that straw out of your mouth," she said in a stern tone.

"Uncle Paddy does na care if I wash up," he muttered.

"Uncle Paddy's not the only one comin' for supper. Did he say he was comin' for sure?"

"No, he said he was going to try, but he was runnin' behind. Mrs. Houston's brother came to see 'im this afternoon, so he's even further behind with his work. Who else is comin' to supper?"

"Mary Margaret O'Flannery. The lady who works with Bridgett—she's been here to visit several times. Do ya remember her?"

Nevan's brow creased for a moment. "Is she the one that watched ya showing Bridgett how ta make the lace?"

"Aye, she's the one."

"Has Da come home yet?"

"He has, and he's already washed up and tendin' to Katherine."

"Can we be expectin' ta see Bridgett and Cullen at supper too?"

"No. Just Mary Margaret. Now stop with yar questions and get yarself presentable."

He gave her a quizzical look. "Sure and supper is smelling fine," he hollered over his shoulder as he hurried off.

She smiled at her son's remark. Nevan was like his da— he enjoyed a satisfying plate of food and a hearty laugh when he sat down to supper each night. Kiara pulled off her apron and peeked out the kitchen window, checking to see if she could see Paddy, but there was no sign he'd yet left the barns. She sighed, hoping her plan wouldn't run afoul. The good Lord knew Paddy had reached the age at which he needed to wed a fine Irish lass. But, like most men, Paddy was not yet aware of his need. She hoped this evening would be just the thing to heighten his awareness.

"I may just have to go out and yank him in here by the ear if he does na soon show up," she muttered. She glanced at the mantel clock as she passed through the parlor on her way up the stairs. She had only a few minutes to make herself presentable before Mary Margaret's arrival.

"Would ya take Katherine downstairs and keep a listen for Aidan? He should na be waking up, but ya never know," she remarked as she stood in the doorway of the children's room, where Rogan was reading to Katherine. "Mary Margaret should be arriving, so can ya keep a listen for the carriage also? I'll only be a few minutes."

"Aye. Sure and ya seem to be making this supper into an important evening. It's only one young lass coming to have a meal. I do na understand why ya're rushing about like ya're fixing supper for nobility."

"I'm na acting any different than any time when I invite company for supper," she defended.

Rogan swooped Katherine up onto his shoulder. "Say what ya will, lass, but I know different," he said with a wide grin. "Duck yar head, Katherine," he instructed before walking through the doorway.

———————

Mary Margaret turned in front of the mirror. However, the small oval looking glass prevented her from seeing much more than a limited portion of her body at one time. Exasperated, she ran down the stairs and into the dining room, where Mrs. Brighton was clearing off the supper dishes.

"Do I look presentable?" she asked, doing a brief twirl in front of the older woman.

"You look quite lovely. You can be sure Mr. and Mrs. Sheehan will think so too. Have they invited you for supper to celebrate some special occasion?"

"I do na think so. I received a note asking me to come to supper, and that's as much as I know. I must hurry or I'll be late. Kiara said she would delay supper to accommodate my workin' hours, but I do na want her children to become overly hungry because of me. She's even sent a buggy for me."

"Then you had best be on your way. Have a nice time," Mrs. Brighton said.

"Sure and I'm hopin' to enjoy some Irish food and stories," Mary Margaret replied as she scurried down the hallway. She slipped into her woolen cape and then stopped to give Mrs. Brighton a quick wave before departing.

She couldn't imagine why Kiara had invited her to supper, but she intended to use the matter to her advantage. She couldn't be sure that Paddy would join them for the meal, but if he proved to be absent, Mary Margaret might very well ask to see the horses. Surely that wouldn't seem odd to anyone; after all, she had proven herself to be interested in the beasts. And their trainer.

Kiara moved swiftly to tidy her appearance. Within minutes, she looked as though she'd been doing nothing but sitting in the parlor and reading or sewing all afternoon. She walked down the steps and hurried to his side as Rogan started to answer the door.

"Mary Margaret, we are so pleased to have you join us this evening," Kiara greeted. "Do come in."

"I'm delighted. It's most kind of ya to invite me. I hope I haven't caused yar family too long a wait for their supper," she said as Kiara took her cloak.

Rogan laughed. "I do na think it would hurt any of us ta go without a meal or two," he said, patting his stomach.

While Rogan and the children entertained Mary Margaret in the parlor, Kiara took her leave and hurried to the kitchen. After ladling the stew into a large crock, she again checked to see if Paddy was on his way. Simon appeared to be headed for home, but there was no sign of Paddy. If she sent Nevan to fetch his uncle, he would surely reveal that Mary Margaret was joining them for supper. Best to wait a wee bit longer, she decided.

The back door opened just as she was slicing a round of warm caraway rye bread. "I believe I'm smelling rye bread," Paddy said as he walked into the kitchen.

Kiara stopped, knife in midair. "Look at ya! Did ya na think to wash up before comin' from the barns? Ya smell as bad as those stables ya've been mucking. I'll fetch one of Rogan's shirts for ya."

Mouth agape, Paddy stared at her for a moment before regaining his wits. "Ya told me to come for supper. Ya did na say to clean up before I came. I hurried down here hoping I'd na be causing yar supper to be late. There's no pleasing ya, Kiara."

She stomped her foot and pointed to the other room. "And hurry!" she ordered before stepping to the parlor door and motioning to her son.

"Run upstairs and fetch one of your father's shirts. Bring it to me in the kitchen—and don't ask any questions. Just do as ya're told."

As Nevan scurried off, Kiara told the others that supper would be ready in just a wee bit.

"I'd be happy to give ya a hand with the preparations," Mary Margaret offered.

"I won't hear of it. Ya sit there and enjoy yarself," she said, hurrying off before Mary Margaret could argue the point.

After placing the food on the dining room table, she surveyed the kitchen to make certain she'd not forgotten anything.

"Do I pass yar inspection?" Paddy asked as he returned to the kitchen.

"I suppose ya'll have to do, but ya could have dried yar hair a wee bit. Supper's waiting—put on this shirt and come along with ya."

Paddy shrugged into the shirt and fastened the final button as he followed Kiara into the dining room. "Ya're acting strange. I do na see what all the fuss—"

When her brother stopped midsentence, Kiara knew he'd spied Mary Margaret sitting in the adjacent parlor. Stepping to one side, she pulled Paddy forward. "I'm sure ya'll be remembering me brother, Paddy," she said to Mary Margaret.

"Aye, that I do. Good evening, Paddy," she said.

"Good evening. I did na know Kiara was entertaining this evening or I would have dressed for the occasion," he said, giving Kiara a frown.

"Sure and I think ya look quite presentable," Mary Margaret said.

Kiara was pleased to see the sparkle in Mary Margaret's eyes as she spoke to Paddy. And though Paddy might have been reluctant to admit such a thing, there was an undeniable attraction between Mary Margaret and her brother. With a feeling of smug satisfaction, she directed the family into the dining room, being careful to seat Paddy and Mary Margaret side-by-side.

Once the children were settled around the table and Rogan had said grace, Kiara passed the stew to her husband. "Would ya be so kind as ta serve?"

"Aye," he replied, taking the bowls as she handed them to him. "So ya had a busy day did ya?" he asked Paddy while ladling stew into one of the white stoneware bowls.

"That we did. I knew 'twould be busy, but Mr. Wainwright unexpectedly came by to visit and completely ruined my schedule. Na that I wasn't pleased ta see him, mind ya," he quickly added.

"And what brought McKinley Wainwright to the horse farm?" Rogan inquired as he finished serving the stew.

"He had a telegram from Mr. Houston and wanted to tell me that they're on their way home."

Kiara handed the plate of bread to her husband. "That's wonderful news ta be hearin'. I've missed my visits with Jasmine. When will they be arrivin'?"

"They didn't say exactly. Mr. Houston told me the telegram seemed somewhat strange—as though they were afraid to give details."

"Why would they be afraid ta say when they're comin' home?" Kiara asked.

Paddy shrugged. "The telegram said they'd met with some kind of difficulty. They didn't say what and they didn't

291

say when they'd be here—just that they were on the way and anxious to be home."

"Those people down South probably give them a hard time for not believing in slavery or some such thing," Rogan said.

"I'm hoping they'll be back before there's further negotiating to be done with the customers," Paddy said.

"Kiara tells me that ya've done an excellent job taking over for Mr. Houston during his absence," Mary Margaret said, "and ya've shown a deep kindness toward the customers ya've been dealing with."

"Has she now?" Paddy asked as he gave his sister a suspicious look.

Kiara jumped to her feet before her brother could say anything further. "I'm guessing ya all would like a piece of apple cake. I'll be off ta the kitchen for only a wee bit."

"Let me help," Mary Margaret offered.

Paddy pushed back his chair. "Ya should na be helping, Mary Margaret. Ya're a guest. I'll be pleased ta lend a hand."

Kiara wilted. She knew she'd catch an earful as soon as they were in the other room unless she immediately took the offensive. "I was telling Bridgett of your accomplishments with the gentlemen from West Point," she started as soon as they were out of earshot, "and Mary Margaret merely overheard the conversation. Do na think I spend my time telling of my brother's accomplishments to all who will listen."

"Ya do na fool me even a wee bit, Kiara. It's matchmaking ya're trying yar hand at, and I do na need help finding a lass—*if* I've a mind to."

"I see little evidence of that! Ya keep ta yarself like a hermit. Mary Margaret is a fine lass, and ya could do no better even if ya tried on yar own."

"She's nice enough," he admitted.

"Then go out there and talk to her," Kiara said. "I'm

capable of servin' cake on me own, ya know."

"I do na need yar meddling. Nor do I like it."

"Off with ya and take the cake platter with ya. And *talk* to her," she hissed as they walked through the doorway.

"Mary Margaret tells me she's on the committee to help with the St. Patrick's Day dance," Rogan said before taking a bite of the cake.

"From the sounds of things, 'tis going to be a fine celebration," Kiara said. "Paddy's helping with some of the festivities also. Aren't ya, Paddy?" she urged.

"Aye."

"And how are the plans coming?" Kiara asked, wishing she could kick him under the table.

"Fine."

She sighed. Obviously Paddy was going to do his best to prove that he didn't want her assistance. By the time they'd finished supper and visited for a short time, she knew her assessment was correct. Paddy hadn't entered into the conversation except when absolutely required.

"It has been a lovely evening, but I must be getting back to the boardinghouse," Mary Margaret finally announced.

"I'm supposin' Paddy would be willing to drive ya back," Rogan said without waiting for Paddy to comment. "The buggy's out front."

Paddy nodded his agreement, clearly unwilling to cause Mary Margaret any embarrassment by refusing Rogan's request.

———

Mary Margaret settled into the leather buggy seat and attempted to hide her delight. From the moment he had entered the dining room with his damp black curls clinging to his forehead, she had longed to spend at least a few moments alone with Paddy. He'd been particularly quiet during the evening, but now she would have the entire ride back to the boardinghouse to visit with him.

"I do hope ya do na find this too much of an inconvenience," she said as he sat down beside her.

He unwound the reins and flicked them with a practiced ease. "I do na mind—my day has been filled by one unexpected event after another—the evening should be no different."

"I do na know if I should consider that good or bad," she said quietly.

He glanced in her direction and then gave her a lopsided grin. " 'Tis na a bad thing, just unexpected."

" 'Twas nice to spend the evening with your sister's family—she's very kind."

"Aye. A wee bit meddlesome from time ta time, but there's no denying she's got a good heart." A moment passed, quiet but for the creaking leather and horses' hooves. "Do ya still like livin' in the boardinghouse?"

" 'Tis fine, though things are becomin' difficult in the mills. Many of the girls have lost their jobs, and it does na look as though things are going ta get much better in the near future."

"Aye, so I've been told. The men are suffering as well. This downturn in the economy has many facin' difficult situations."

"At least my mind is na on the economy when I'm helpin' to plan the dance," she said. "We all have fun while we're at the meetings and do na discuss our work and such. Is it the same with the men? When ya're planning the parade?"

"Aye—'tis a good place ta forget yar worries," he agreed. Paddy gave her a sidelong glance. "So what kind of plans do ya lasses have? Are ya plannin' something more than in the past?"

"For the dance? The plans seem no different than for most parties. Most of the ladies only say that they're looking forward to an evening of dancing and hoping that there are enough men to dance with. They hope, too, that the downturn does na spoil the festivities."

"I think it would take more than the economy to ruin St. Patrick's Day."

Mary Margaret nodded. "Some of the girls I work with who live in the Acre have already bought fabric to make their dresses. They said they'd do without other things before they'd go without a new dress for the dance."

The dance. It seemed as if every conversation with Mary Margaret turned into talk of the dance. He didn't know why he hadn't yet asked her—after all, she was a pretty lass with a sweet smile, and she would likely say yes. And it wasn't as though he had anyone else whom he wished to escort. After all, if he waited much longer, someone else might ask her. Quite obviously, there was no reason to delay.

He pulled back on the reins as they neared the boarding-house. When the buggy came to a halt, he turned to face her. "I was wondering . . . if ya might . . ." he haltingly began. "That is ta say, if ya do na already have plans . . ." He hesitated once again.

"Yes?" she asked encouragingly.

"Do ya think ya might . . . like ta—" he swallowed hard—"go ta the dance with m-me?" he finally stammered.

"Aye, that I would!"

She replied so quickly it nearly took his breath away. "Ya *would*?"

"Of course I would. I was hoping for an invitation—from you," she hastily added.

"Then I suppose it's settled," he said as he walked her to the door.

"Aye, that it is," she replied sweetly before disappearing behind the door of the boardinghouse.

Paddy hoisted himself onto the buggy seat and flicked the reins. For a brief moment he was proud of himself—pleased he'd had the courage to ask Mary Margaret to the dance and that she had so readily accepted. Yet his thoughts quickly returned to previous conversations with the lass. There was no denying her beauty and the fact that she could be pleasant. On the other hand, she had a stubborn streak a mile wide and a large portion of unbridled determination. She reminded him of his sister! And unlike Rogan, he wasn't certain he could tame Miss Mary Margaret O'Flannery!

"I hope I've na made a mistake this evenin'," he muttered.

CHAPTER · 18

March 1858

FEELING SOMEWHAT uncomfortable, Elinor rapped on the front door of the parsonage. Somehow it seemed improper to be calling on the pastor. Yet when she'd mentioned the need to discuss issues regarding the benevolence fund as she exited church earlier in the day, Pastor Chamberlain had suggested she stop by the parsonage so they could discuss the matter in private. Of course, Reggie would be present, yet if any of the church ladies discovered Elinor was making a personal call upon the pastor, there was little doubt she'd be the topic of discussion for weeks to come—or at least until some other matter captured their interest.

"Mrs. Brighton! Come in, please," Reggie said with an infectious smile.

"Thank you, Reggie. And may I say that your manners are quite lovely today."

She giggled. "Father didn't tell me you were coming to visit."

"Perhaps he wanted to surprise you."

"Exactly!" Justin said as he entered the hallway. "Good

to see you, Elinor. Why don't we go into the parlor. I do hope it wasn't an inconvenience asking you to come here. I had several matters that needed my attention," he added as he led her into the sitting room.

"Of course not. I enjoy a change of scenery, and it's always nice to spend time with Reggie."

Reggie plopped down beside their guest and scooted close.

"Reggie, I need to speak privately with Mrs. Brighton. Could you leave us for a short time?" her father asked.

The girl frowned momentarily, then brightened. "I'll fix us tea. Would that be good?"

"That would be wonderful," her father replied. "By the time you serve tea, we should be through with our discussion."

Elinor stared after Reggie as the girl hurried off to the kitchen. "She's turning into quite the little lady, don't you think?"

"Absolutely, and I have you to thank for the dramatic changes in her. I truly don't know how you've worked such wonders. I knew Reggie needed a woman's influence in her life, yet I was perplexed as to how to find someone willing to take on the challenge. The moment you entered her life and began tutoring her in proper manners and etiquette, she was receptive. Tell me, how have you done it?"

"I've not attempted to change Reggie. I've merely included her in my life. The transformation that has taken place is of Reggie's own doing. Change usually occurs when a person is truly desirous of doing so, not when one is forced by others. Don't you think?"

Justin nodded. "The old adage of leading a horse to water?"

"I believe so. In any event, Reggie seems receptive to having a woman in her life, and I'm confident she will accept your new wife with enthusiasm. At least I've encouraged her to do so. I might add that I'm looking forward to meeting your fiancée as well."

"As am I," Justin said with a startled look on his face. "Wherever did you get the notion that I plan to wed?"

Elinor hesitated. She didn't want to say anything that would cause Reggie a problem, yet she needed to reply. "Well, I-I . . ."

"No need to say any more. The church ladies must have been gossiping again," he concluded. "You can disregard anything you've heard. I have not made any plans to marry. I'm truly astonished at some of the stories that have circulated since our arrival."

"No doubt," she said as a surprising sense of pleasure flooded over her. She was actually *delighted* to hear Justin Chamberlain had no wedding plans. Yet the thought frightened her. Never again did she want to have feelings of love for another man. Long ago she had vowed she would not go through the pain of losing one more husband. Yet her heart had quickened at his words, and she enjoyed his company far too much. Was she becoming like some of those church ladies who were secretly hoping to find themselves a husband? At the thought, she felt the heat rush to her cheeks.

"Is it overly warm in here? You suddenly appear flushed—I do hope you're not becoming ill. I shouldn't have requested that you walk over here in this cold weather," he said.

"No, I'm fine, thank you. Don't concern yourself. Now then, I believe we were going to discuss the benevolence fund."

"Ah, yes. You mentioned you've had additional applicants."

"Indeed. I have three girls who have come to me—two from other boardinghouses and one from my own. I believe their requests are valid. They've all shown me their separation papers from the mill. I had hoped to refrain from using the benevolence fund until it had grown larger; in fact, I had been using my own savings to help some of the girls. However, I fear I used the last of my funds this week."

"By all means, we'll see that they receive assistance. If you'll give me the information, I'll withdraw the funds. But it would likely be less embarrassing for the girls if *you* delivered the money."

"I'd be happy to do so," Elinor replied. "I also received word this week that my boardinghouse may close. Since I've used all of my resources, I'll likely be required to leave Lowell."

"Leave Lowell? Where would you go?"

"My brother Taylor and his family are in Maine. They would welcome me," she said. "I surely find that God sometimes has a strange sense of humor. I had hoped to help others not lose their homes, yet in the process it appears as if I'll lose my own."

"We must put this matter to prayer," Justin said. "I can't believe that you are meant to leave Lowell."

"*Leave?*" Reggie screeched. "Where are you going?" she asked, dropping the tea tray onto the table.

Elinor quickly leaned forward and placed a hand on the teetering china. "It's not definite yet, Reggie. That's why I hadn't told you. I received word this week that my boardinghouse may be closed—I don't know when it may occur. I'm praying it won't happen at all."

"Absolutely. We must all pray for intervention," Justin stated.

Reggie ignored her father's remark. "Would you go to Maine and live with your brother?"

"Yes, if the boardinghouse closes. But I don't—"

"You said you didn't want to go there," Reggie said

without waiting for Elinor's full reply.

"That's true; I don't. But if the boardinghouse—"

"You could come and live with us. Couldn't she, Father?" Her eyes were filled with a mixture of fear and anticipation.

"I couldn't possibly do that, Reggie," Elinor said. "My family would expect me to come to Maine."

"It doesn't matter *what* they expect. You should be able to stay here if you want. Shouldn't she, Father?"

"Well, yes," Justin replied. "And we are going to pray about the situation, Reggie," he promised.

"I'm sorry to upset you, Reggie. I hadn't planned for you to hear me. There's no need to upset yourself, for it's still uncertain whether I'll have to move. Why don't we have our tea? Did you bake those fine-looking cookies all by yourself?"

Reggie nodded, but there was no smile. "It's your recipe for lemon cookies."

"Then I must have one." Elinor took a bite of the cookie, chewing slowly and nodding approvingly while Reggie watched. "I believe they're even better than the ones I bake."

"Truly?" Reggie asked with a grin.

"Truly! They are excellent. You should be most proud of yourself, young lady."

When they had finished their tea, Elinor patted Reggie's hand. "I would be quite pleased if you'd walk me home and stay for supper."

"May I, Father?"

"Yes, of course. Though I must say I'm a bit envious."

Elinor tilted her head and gave him a thoughtful look, unsure what his remark truly meant. "Would you like to join us for supper? I know you mentioned you have several matters needing your attention. Perhaps you could attend to them and then join us at seven o'clock," she suggested.

Justin gave a hearty laugh. "Well, since you insist."

"Absolutely! Reggie and I will expect you at seven," she said as they stood to retrieve their coats.

"I promise to be on time," he said. "Behave yourself, Reggie," he reminded as they walked onto the porch.

"I *know*," she said, giving her father a look of exasperation.

Reggie reached for Elinor's hand and grasped it tightly as they set off down the street.

"Your father tells me he has no plans to marry and was shocked that I had any such idea," Elinor casually remarked.

Reggie's face turned ashen and her shoulders slumped. "You told him I said he was to be married?"

"No, not exactly."

"What did you tell him?" she asked, her eyes glistening with fear.

"I told him I thought you would be most accepting of his new wife. He said he was not planning to wed and then asked how I had conceived such a notion."

"Did you tell him it was me?"

"Before I could answer, he assumed I'd heard some of the church ladies gossiping. I didn't agree with or deny his assumption."

"Thank you!" Reggie sighed and straightened her shoulders. A wide smile curved her lips as though she believed the entire incident now totally resolved.

"Why *did* you lie to me, Reggie?"

A startled look returned to the child's face. "I didn't lie. I said my father met a woman and I *thought* he wanted to marry her. I guess he doesn't."

"Reggie Chamberlain! I do not for one minute believe what you're telling me. Now out with the truth!"

"It was a test."

"A test? What on earth are you talking about?"

Reggie gave her a sheepish look. "I wanted to see if you were truly my friend or if you were like all the others—just being nice to me so my father would like you."

"Is that truly what you believed all the time we were together?"

"No, but I had to be positive. Don't you understand that I had to know for sure that somebody liked me just for me and not because they wanted to marry my father?"

"I suppose I do understand, Reggie, but I can't say I'm not disappointed."

"Because I lied?"

"Because you lied and because you didn't realize my feelings had everything to do with you and nothing to do with your father."

"I'm sorry," she said. "Will you forgive me?"

"On one condition. In the future if you have concerns, I want you to talk to me truthfully. I promise I will give you honest answers in return."

Reggie grinned and squeezed Elinor's hand. "I promise."

———

The parade had proceeded on schedule. Although there were those who said the previous parades had been larger, Mary Margaret was impressed with the entries and those who had lined the streets cheering them on. Two marchers carrying enormous green banners had set off the procession. One of the banners was inscribed with an Irish harp and the words *Erin go Bragh,* and the other sported an American eagle. The members of the Irish Benevolent Society had followed the banners, each member adorned with a long green silk scarf surrounded by a rosette of green and white.

Even the weather had cooperated, the day dawning sunny and warm. The remainder of the afternoon was spent listening to the numerous speeches that both attacked Britain and argued for the repeal of the union or spoke of gratitude for the blessings and advantages enjoyed in this adopted country. And, of course, there were the goodly number of men who happily downed quarts of ale as they cheered their agreement or shouted their disapproval to the speechmakers.

The day had been exhilarating, especially since Paddy had come to sit with Mary Margaret during the speech-making. Afterward, he had even walked her home with a promise to return at seven o'clock and escort her to the dance.

"Did you have a nice afternoon?" Mrs. Brighton asked as she walked into the house.

"Aye. 'Tis a surprise that the Irish were given the day off from work in order ta celebrate. I wish that all the girls had been able to enjoy the parade." She followed Mrs. Brighton into the kitchen. "Were you able to attend?"

"No, I had the noonday meal to prepare, but I'm pleased you had a good time."

"I'm feeling a bit guilty going off to a dance when things seem so bleak for some of the girls."

"Nonsense. Whether you attend the dance or remain at home does not change anyone's circumstances," Mrs. Brighton said as she started peeling some potatoes. "You had best take a few minutes to rest. I'm guessing you'll be tired after an evening of dancing."

Mary Margaret waited until the other girls were eating supper before donning her dress for the dance. Bridgett had loaned her a green plaid silk gown with black piping that edged the bodice and waistline. She tied a wide black ribbon around her throat and another around her red curls before looking in the mirror.

"It will do just fine," she told herself before rushing downstairs.

She remained in the hallway until Paddy arrived and then called her good-nights to the girls.

"I can wait while ya go and bid them a proper good-night," he said.

She shook her head and hurried him out the door. "I feel a wee bit of discomfort going out ta have fun when some of the girls have fallen upon such hard times. I do na want ta go prancing in front of them all dressed for the dance. It does na seem proper."

"Ya have a kind heart, Mary Margaret."

"Thank you," she said as a faint blush colored her cheeks.

When they arrived at the hall, many of the Irish celebrants were already shouting for the music to begin. The music of fiddles and accordions soon filled the air and couples took to the floor, some dancing jigs while other enjoyed a polka or hornpipe.

"Would ya care ta dance?"

"Aye," Mary Margaret replied.

They twirled around the floor with Paddy holding a firm grip around her waist as they performed the intricate steps in time to the music.

"Ya're looking a wee bit warm, Paddy," Timothy Rourke said as he drew near. "Perhaps I should take Mary Margaret as my dancing partner." He attempted to take hold of her hand.

"I do na think so," she told him. "I've been escorted to the dance by Paddy, and I do na wish ta be dancing with another."

"I canna believe ya'd turn down the likes of me for Padraig O'Neill," Timothy said mockingly.

"Ya best believe it, Timothy Rourke. I'll na be having any dances with ya this night," she replied haughtily before turning her attention to Paddy. "I'm a wee bit thirsty. Shall we get something cool ta drink?"

"Aye. That sounds fine," he said, grasping her elbow and leading her to a table where a group of women were serving punch and cookies directly across from a counter where several men were serving ale.

Paddy ordered two cups of punch and picked up several cookies. "We can sit down over there," he said, nodding toward a row of wooden chairs.

"Thank ya for turning down Timothy Rourke," he said. "Though I do na expect ya to turn down every lad asking for a dance, I canna deny I was pleased ta have ya turn him down."

"Ya're welcome. I have no interest in dancing with anyone else, Paddy." She took a sip of her punch. "Have ya been busy at the farm?"

He nodded. "'Tis always busy, but as spring begins to arrive there's always more ta tend to. We've a lot of horses ready to foal, and it's always a worry—ya do na want to lose the mare or the colt."

"And what of Mr. and Mrs. Houston? Have they returned home?"

"We expected them at least two weeks ago, and I was beginning to get a wee bit worried thinking something might've happened to them—what with them saying in their last telegram they'd met with troubles. But I stopped to see Mr. Wainwright when I was in town a few days ago, and he said he'd received another telegram that morning. He said the Houstons will be arriving in the next couple of days."

"That's good news for ya then," Mary Margaret said.

"Aye. It's been a load of responsibility for me while they've been gone. I'm na complainin', mind ya, but still I'll be glad to have them home."

"Mr. Houston is lucky to have someone like ya to depend upon."

"Thank ya," he replied. "The band's warming up ta

begin. Shall we try another dance?"

"Aye," she said, taking his hand.

Above the music, the sound of laughter and chattering voices could be heard throughout the hall. They danced and talked and then danced even more as the hours quickly passed. They were stepping onto the dance floor when they turned at the sound of an angry shout. A mug of ale came flying through the air and crashed to the dance floor, and the rest was a haze—men shouting and throwing punches, glass breaking and women screaming.

"Take hold of my hand and don't turn loose," Paddy shouted above the din.

She grasped his hand and followed close on his heels—down the stairway and out the front door into the cool, star-lit evening. They stopped and looked at the upper windows of the building, where flying fists could be easily detected.

"I hope no one comes crashing through one of those windows," Mary Margaret said.

"We best move from here; I would na want to be the one to break a lad's fall should such a thing happen."

They walked a short distance down the street as other couples began to exit the building, likely afraid they, too, would become injured in the donnybrook.

"If ya had not escorted me to the dance, ya could have remained upstairs instead of waiting down here and wondering what's happening up there," Mary Margaret said.

Paddy grinned and gently pulled her into a warm embrace. "I think I'm more interested in the one who's standing right beside me. We can have our own good time down here."

Before she could reply, he drew her closer. She gazed into his eyes and felt the blood course through her veins as he lowered his head and caressed her lips with a tender kiss.

She leaned heavily against his broad chest and knew she was both safe and protected. How she could have ever thought this sweet man anything but gentle and kind was now beyond logic.

CHAPTER · 19

"JASMINE! NOLAN! Over here," McKinley shouted while waving a hand above the crowd gathered on the train platform.

Jasmine spotted her brother and waved in return before leaning down and whispering to Spencer. "Do you see Uncle McKinley? Run over—he's brought a surprise along with him."

She watched her son run fleetingly through the crowd, knowing she was presenting him with the greatest of pleasures upon his return home—seeing his very best friend. Above the train's whistle and commotion of passengers, she could hear her son's shouts as he called out Moses' name. This one thing had gone as planned, and her heart was filled with abundant joy.

They worked their way through the throng, finally reaching McKinley's side several moments later. "McKinley! I can't tell you how wonderful it is to see you," she said while pulling her brother into a warm embrace.

"It has been far too long," he agreed. "Nolan!" he

greeted, grasping his brother-in-law's hand warmly and then swinging Alice Ann up into his arms before planting a giant kiss upon her cheek. "How is Clara?" he asked, noting the sleeping child in Henrietta's arms.

"She's fine. We all are—especially now that we're back in Lowell," Jasmine replied.

"And who is this?" he asked, nodding toward Prissy.

"Prissy; she was one of Father's house slaves. She is married to Toby," Jasmine explained.

"Truly? It doesn't seem possible Toby is old enough to take a wife. Did you not bring him also?"

"No. We were unable to do so. Once we get home to the farm, Nolan and I will explain the difficulties we encountered. I do hope you have ample time—it's quite an adventure and one that is not yet over, I'm afraid."

"I've been intrigued ever since I received your first telegram, but I must say you all appear in good health and certainly in the height of fashion," he said while appraising Jasmine's traveling suit.

Jasmine gave a harsh laugh. "Your opinion would have differed greatly had you met us in Boston. I fear even the hotel clerk had not seen such a beggarly-appearing group in a long time. Nolan thought it best we telegraph you and then spend a few days in Boston recuperating from the journey. We purchased our clothing while we were there."

"I see. The carriage is out in front of the depot. I had one of your men bring a wagon for your trunks."

"There are no trunks, McKinley. We have only what we're carrying," Jasmine told him.

McKinley's confusion was evident, but he didn't question them. "I'll send the driver back home then and join you in the carriage."

The ride home seemed endless. When the carriage finally rolled to a stop in front of their house, Jasmine felt as though they had been away for years. The house appeared unchanged yet strangely foreign as she walked through the doorway. She smiled broadly at the group awaiting their arrival. Kiara and Rogan, along with Paddy, Maisie, Simon, and a host of servants, cheered their arrival.

As Jasmine circled the group, hugging each one, she stopped several times to silently thank God for their safe arrival home. The journey had been treacherous, and both she and Nolan knew that without the hand of God upon them, they would never have safely returned to Lowell.

"We've prepared a feast ta celebrate yar homecoming," Kiara said. "We did na want to overwhelm ya, so we thought to wait a few hours before the celebration," she added.

"Thank you all so much," Jasmine replied. "Mr. Houston and I do need to spend some time alone with my brother, but before we go into the library, I want to introduce you to Prissy. She was a house slave at The Willows, but now she is free. I would be appreciative if you'd show her the house and make her feel welcome."

Maisie stepped forward and embraced Prissy. "D'you 'member me, Prissy? Me and Simon was at da big house for a little while right after you come dere to work."

Prissy stared hard at Maisie and then looked at Simon. "You was in the kitchen," she said.

Maisie nodded. "Dat's right. I'm right glad to see you, chile. You gonna be mighty happy here. Come along and I'll show you around, and den we'll go out to our house and have us some coffee. Moses, you and Spencer go on over to da house with your pappy. I be along soon."

Jasmine smiled at the boys as they hurried toward Simon. "Can we go see Larkspur before we go to the house?" Spencer asked.

Simon gave them a toothy grin and nodded. "We's gonna go there right now."

McKinley and the Houstons went into the library. Once the doors were closed, the three adults settled into the leather chairs.

Jasmine hesitated a moment before addressing her brother. "I'm trying to think of where I should begin," she said.

It took nearly an hour to relate all that had occurred throughout their time at The Willows and during their journey home. McKinley listened intently as the story unfolded, never interrupting. When Jasmine finally leaned back in her chair, emotionally exhausted from the telling, her brother hunched forward and gazed into her eyes.

"Am I to understand that both The Willows and the entire crop were completely destroyed in these fires? That you've returned with *nothing*? No money from the sale of the crop, no money from the sale of the plantation—*nothing*?" he asked, his voice frantic.

"We've returned with our lives," Nolan replied. "I count that alone a miracle and worth more than any amount of money!"

"Yes, yes, of course. I didn't mean to imply your safety was worth nothing, but I was relying upon those funds."

"I'm sorry, McKinley," Jasmine said. "Though the plantation was in the hands of a broker, Rupert forged my name on documents to suggest that we had given him the property. Cousin Levi promises to help, but I do not expect we'll see anything for some time—if ever. There is grave hostility toward us. Surely you understand that by now."

"Yes, but it is difficult for me to believe Rupert would be in the midst of this. Surely you've misunderstood. He would never forge documents or threaten our family. I'm convinced you were both distraught with the circumstances and misunderstood his intentions. We were, after all, boyhood friends as well as cousins. Rupert and I enjoyed a closer kinship than I had with either of our brothers when we were growing up. I'm certain if I go to Mississippi, I can reason with him. We need to take back what is lawfully ours," McKinley insisted.

Jasmine looked at her brother in great frustration. "Believe what you will, McKinley, although I would have expected you to believe your own sister over a cousin who's had nothing to do with you since you've come north. Both Rupert and Lydia have changed. They are not the same people we knew as children—no more than you and I remain the same. And what is it you hope to gain by going to Mississippi? You can't regain a mansion and crop that have been burned into nonexistence. Do you think you can convince these men to pay you for their dishonorable actions? Surely you don't believe men who have acted in such a manner will now step forward and offer you money for their unjust deeds."

"Then what is it you referred to when you said you feared this matter was not yet finished?" he asked.

Nolan stood up and walked to the doors leading to the garden. He looked outside for a moment before turning toward McKinley. "The slaves. We signed over the papers granting all of them their freedom. In addition, we promised to divide the funds from the cotton crop among them in order to assist them with their new beginning in the North. But as your sister told you, except for Prissy, they were all taken away in shackles and have been either enslaved by the men who committed these crimes or turned over for sale in the New Orleans market. Either way, we are determined to regain their freedom."

"If we can find a way to reason with Rupert, perhaps we can do so," McKinley said, rising to address Nolan face-to-face. "If we agree that we will not bring charges against the men who committed these crimes, assuming they are willing

313

to return the slaves and compensate us for the damages, this matter can be brought to a suitable resolution for all concerned."

Nolan gave a sorrowful laugh. "Do you not understand that these men do not fear the law? In fact, the men who mete out law and justice are among the number who committed these crimes against our family. Like us, you'll find no assistance by placing your hope in the lawmen."

"This issue of slavery goes far deeper than you realize, McKinley. Matters are worsening by the day," Jasmine said. "Soon slavery will divide more than families; it will divide this nation so deeply we will find ourselves entrenched in war."

McKinley shook his head. "I understand you've had a harrowing experience, but I believe you're overdramatizing the entire issue."

"Think what you will," Jasmine said, "but you were not there to see the ugliness that is being called honorable and patriotic by many Southerners. Mark my words, McKinley: you are naïve if you believe the issue of slavery will pass away or be resolved without a real fight."

CHAPTER · 20

September 1, 1858

McKINLEY EAGERLY opened the thick envelope and sat down in his office to read the missive he'd picked up at the post office a short time ago. Though Jasmine remained unaware of his contact with Rupert, McKinley had been communicating with his cousin since shortly after his sister's return to Lowell. And though he'd had a recent telegram from Rupert, McKinley was anxious for a detailed reply to his latest letter, for he wanted to receive both explanations *and* remuneration. To date, it appeared Rupert was the only answer to his needs. After all, McKinley had never believed Jasmine's story about forged documents, even though Nolan had stood in agreement that this was exactly what had happened. He figured them both to be simply victims of the moment. Rupert's correspondence had proven that thought to be correct. Even Jasmine admitted, after receiving a missive from Cousin Levi earlier in the summer, that the property remained in their care. So whatever misunderstanding there had been about forged documents and property being stolen was behind them now.

Still, McKinley had been careful to keep his correspondence a secret from everyone, including his wife. After all, Violet would wonder at his fierce determination to recover the funds, and he could not bear to tell her of their financial losses. Then too she might say something to Jasmine, and McKinley definitely didn't want his sister to know the truth. At least not until much later—after everything was settled. Jasmine might again misinterpret the matter, and she absolutely wouldn't understand McKinley writing to Rupert.

Thus far Rupert's correspondence revealed what McKinley had believed from the time his sister returned home: she had exaggerated the entire incident at The Willows. With great kindness, Rupert had sent several lengthy missives answering McKinley's myriad of questions and advising him that the entire ordeal had been a complete misunderstanding on Jasmine's and Nolan's part. Rupert had eloquently explained that because both of them had become so completely indoctrinated by Northern dogma, they had hastened to recount inaccuracies.

Rupert's initial letter of explanation had gone on to state that he was confident McKinley knew him to be a true Southern gentleman and that his visit to The Willows after the devastating fire was never meant as a threat to Nolan and Jasmine. His sole purpose in going to them had been based upon his deep love and concern for Jasmine and her family. He had simply wanted to warn them of the possible impending danger.

McKinley's excitement increased as he read the most recent letter. Rupert wanted to purchase The Willows, and he would soon be arriving in Lowell to finalize their agreement!

He reread the final sentence: *"Do not tell anyone of my plan to purchase The Willows or my visit to Lowell. As you know, your sister tends to think the worst of any Southerner, and I do not want anything to destroy this final opportunity for both of us."*

"Nor do I, cousin; nor do I," McKinley murmured as he carefully refolded the letter.

———————

Jasmine reached into an old trunk that had been stored in the attic and pulled out a stack of Clara's outgrown dresses and gowns. One by one, she scrutinized each tiny article of clothing, knowing it would likely fit little Emily now that she was more than a month old. Prissy had experienced an easy birth but now seemed to be languishing in a form of melancholy. She nursed the baby with little enthusiasm and appeared hopelessly uninterested in the child.

Upon her arrival in Lowell, Prissy had eagerly embraced the idea of becoming the head seamstress for the Houston farm, and Jasmine had been delighted by the young woman's abilities. Prissy, along with several other women, had been hired to operate the sewing shop. With the many workers employed by the farm, it had proven economical to make and furnish clothing to their employees rather than to increase wages. So talented was Prissy at fashioning clothing that the women of the community were soon seeking her services. Jasmine had watched Prissy flourish throughout her pregnancy, though she never did appear enthusiastic about the impending birth.

"Perhaps these clothes will boost her spirits," Jasmine muttered as she closed the trunk and descended the narrow stairs leading down from the dusty attic.

"Whatever were you doing up there?" Nolan asked as he walked out of their bedroom.

She held up the stack of baby clothes.

"Are you . . ."

Jasmine giggled. "No, my dear. You may breathe easy for a while longer—there's no baby in our future just yet. I'm taking these to Prissy. I thought she might enjoy dressing Emily in something other than the few plain gowns she made for her. I'm hoping it will cheer her a bit."

"That's kind of you, Jasmine. She still doesn't appear to enjoy being a mother, I take it?"

"No, and I do not understand her behavior. Emily is a beautiful child, though she doesn't resemble Toby or Prissy in the least—she's so *white*. I believe she's as white as Moses. In any event, Prissy's behavior surprises me. Although I knew she missed Toby, she appeared to adjust so well. I suppose I assumed she would do the same with her baby."

Nolan placed his arm around his wife. "Do remember, my dear, that having the child has likely caused her to dwell even more upon Toby's circumstances. To be without the man you love when your child is born would be difficult. Poor Prissy doesn't know if she will ever see her husband again or if Emily will ever know her father. And now that she's not busy with her work, she has more time to dwell upon those thoughts."

"You are a very wise man, Nolan Houston. No wonder I love you so much."

He leaned down and kissed her. "I believe I had best be off to the stables. We're to have visitors from West Point today."

She walked down the wide staircase beside him, their arms entwined. "Paddy should be pleased to see them once again," she remarked.

"Yes. He's looking forward to their visit. I can't tell you how proud I am of that young man. He has exceeded my greatest expectations with both the horses and the customers."

"And I think it only fitting that you rewarded him with an interest in the farm. He's added much to the business."

The couple walked together until they reached Simon

and Maisie's house. "I'll leave you to your meetings," she said.

Nolan arched his eyebrows. "Prissy is still living with Simon and Maisie?"

She nodded. "She doesn't want to go back to her little house, and Maisie doesn't believe she should just yet."

"I see," he said. "Well, let's hope those clothes cheer her."

He leaned down to kiss her cheek, then Jasmine watched as he strode off toward the barn before she knocked on the front door of Maisie's house.

"Come on in," Maisie said with a broad smile. "I was jes' fixing me and Prissy a cup of tea. Sit down."

"I brought some clothes for Emily," Jasmine whispered. "I'm hoping they'll bring a bit of pleasure to Prissy."

Maisie shook her head. "I tell you it's a battle getting dat gal to show interest in anything, Miz Jasmine. I can hardly force her out of bed all day long. I told Simon I'm beginnin' to git worried 'bout whether she's ever gonna come around. I has to force her to put that baby to her breast. It's a shame—sech a sweet little thing too. Don' hardly never cry. I keep her out here in da cradle near me. I tried leaving her in da bedroom wit Prissy, but she jes' ignored her cries."

Jasmine crouched down by the cradle and stroked the sleeping baby's soft hair. "Such a beautiful baby. I told Nolan she's as white as Moses—don't you think?"

"Oh yessum—sho' enough."

The baby wriggled and her eyelids fluttered open. "May I hold her?" Jasmine asked.

"'Course you can. Dat chile can use all the loving she can get."

Jasmine lifted the baby into her arms and smiled as Emily began to suck on her own fist. Jasmine stared at the child, her mind beginning to turn cartwheels as she concentrated on the child's coloring. Suddenly she felt the blood drain from her face.

"Maisie, do you think there's any possibility this child could have been fathered by a white man rather than Toby?" She swallowed hard as she watched Maisie's reaction.

With a tilt of her head she met Jasmine's questioning eyes with a steady gaze. "Ain't no doubt in my mind at all. That ain't Toby's baby, an' I figure that's why Prissy rejected the child." Maisie paused and stared at Jasmine. "What's wrong with you, Miz Jasmine? You feeling poorly? You done lost all the pink out of yo' cheeks."

Jasmine didn't want to ask, yet she could not stop herself. "Maisie, tell me the truth. Do you think my father or my brother Samuel could be the father of this child?" she whispered.

"Oh, mercy me! No, ma'am, I ain't even given that a passing thought. Neither one of dem would have ever done such a thing—and dere's nobody could convince me no different. This baby ain't no Wainwright, Miz Jasmine."

"Has Prissy told you that? Has she even told you Toby's not the father?"

"No, she ain't told me nothing 'bout the father, but I know sure as I'm standin' here afore you that the father of dat baby is white. After she was here at the farm for a week or so, I 'member her watching Moses when he was out in the yard playing with Spencer. She ast me how I come to have such a white chile. I told her about Moses' real mama and papa. She kept staring at him, and finally she rubbed her belly and said, 'So dat's what I got to look forward to.' I didn' know what she was talking 'bout den—but I surely do know now."

Jasmine placed the baby back in the cradle. "May I go and talk to her?"

"'Course you can. I'm gonna take this tea in there and

see if I can get her to drink it. You come on along."

"Why don't *I* take it to her?"

"Dat would be mighty kind of you. You want me to put two cups on da tray so you can have some tea with her?"

"Yes, thank you. In fact, let me take care of that. I'm certain you have other matters that need your attention. The least I can do is prepare the tea."

Maisie didn't argue, having learned long ago that Jasmine was quick to help herself and slow to expect others to wait upon her. "Will you keep a listen for the baby while you's visiting with Prissy? I can go ahead with my washing if I know somebody's in here with the two of dem."

"Of course. I'll leave the door to Prissy's room open so I can hear. You need not worry about a thing while you're outdoors."

Jasmine was pleased she could relieve Maisie in some small way. Moreover, knowing she was alone in the house would permit her to speak openly with Prissy. She stopped in the kitchen to get a second cup and then, carefully balancing the tray upon the stack of baby clothes, Jasmine went to Prissy's room. After tapping lightly on the door, she paused a moment and then entered.

"Good morning, Prissy! It's a beautiful day outside. I've brought you some tea and thought we might visit for a spell. In fact, it would be nice to go outdoors with you after a bit—the sunshine is glorious. I think it's warm enough we could take Emily with us if she's wrapped in her blanket."

Prissy scooted up in the bed and rested her back and shoulders against the wall.

"Shall I pour?"

"I'll drink me a cup of tea, but I don' think I'll be gettin' out of dis bed."

Jasmine poured the tea and added cream and sugar before she offered the cup to Prissy. "I do hope you like cream and sugar," she said with a bright smile.

"Um, hum, that's fine. I'm sure you got better things to do than come over here an' serve me tea," she said, slowly lifting the cup to her lips.

"There are certainly other things I *could* be doing, but nothing I'd *rather* do," she replied. "I went up to the attic this morning and found some of Clara's clothing. She outgrew these things long ago, and I thought they would be perfect for our little Emily."

Prissy glanced at the clothes but showed little interest even as Jasmine began to unfold the items for her inspection. "Them's real nice. Thank you. You can give 'em to Maisie. She sees to washing and dressing the baby," she said in a monotone voice.

"Yes, I know, but I think it's time you began to care for Emily yourself, Prissy. And you need to get out of this bed," she said as she walked to the windows and pulled open the curtains.

Prissy blinked against the sunlight and quickly covered her eyes with one arm. "I like dem curtains closed. Don' like it bright in here."

Jasmine shook her head back and forth. "Darkness breeds depression and sadness."

"What *you* know 'bout depression and sadness?" she rebutted bitterly.

"I've had my share of heartache, Prissy, and I also had a mother who suffered from severe headaches and phobias that sent her into the depths of depression. Don't make the mistake of imprisoning yourself with a desire to withdraw from the world, Prissy. There is nothing so great that God won't see you through. You do believe that, don't you?"

"I ain't so sure 'bout God helping me. I been calling on the name of Jesus ever since I was a youngun, but it ain't done me much good."

Jasmine pulled a chair close to the bed and sat down. "I would guess you've had a very difficult life, Prissy, but if you will take your mind off the bad for a moment, you will see that you have been blessed with good things too. You fell in love with and married Toby, and although he's not with you now, we're still praying he'll join you one day. You are freed from slavery and you enjoy earning wages as a seamstress . . . at least you told me that was true."

"That's true; I do like sewing in dat little shop Massa Nolan fixed up for us. I feel more at home there than any-place."

"And you have a beautiful, healthy little girl."

"That child ain't no blessing—she's a *curse*," she hissed through clenched teeth.

Jasmine recoiled at the venomous response. "She is *not* a curse. She's an innocent baby who had no say in her birth."

"Well, neither did I, 'cause if I'd had any say, she wouldn't be here, an' you can believe dat for sho'."

"Toby isn't Emily's father, is he?"

Prissy shook her head. "That's easy enough to see. Just look at her—she's as white as dem clouds floatin' out dere in the sky. She's too white to be my chile."

"Prissy, that's not true. Emily *is* your child. Will you tell me who fathered her?"

"No, ma'am, I'll not be telling that, but we best all hope da child don' turn out nothin' like the man who be her true pappy."

"Do I know him?"

"I ain't sayin' no more, Miz Jasmine. Toby knew the baby wasn't his 'cause he never touched me afore we was married. He asked if I was forced against my will, an' I told him I was. He didn't ask me if it was one of da other slaves or if it was a white man. He jest nodded, and we never talked 'bout it again."

"I've known Toby since he was very young, Prissy, and I believe that since he willingly married you, he was also willing to accept your baby no matter who had fathered her. I don't understand your reluctance to even feed her."

Prissy's face contorted in pain. "I hate that man and what he done to me. I can't love no baby that comes from his seed."

Jasmine poured a cup of tea for herself, then settled back in the chair. "Do you believe Jesus saved you?"

There was a look of surprise on Prissy's young face. "'Course I do. I took Jesus into my heart when I was thirteen years old. Ol' Samuel took me to the big pond and baptized me—I thought I was gonna drown he held me under there so long. Never liked the water much after that. You know I didn't like traveling on those river boats coming back here," she added.

"Yes, I remember," Jasmine replied with a smile. "When Samuel talked to you about taking Jesus into your heart, did he explain that Jesus' death wiped the slate clean and our sins were forgiven?"

"Um-hmm. He told me dat. I told all them folks standing 'round the pond that I was asking Jesus into my heart and wanted Him to forgive me of my sins. After that, Ol' Samuel dunked me in da water."

Jasmine hesitated a moment. "You know, Prissy, when we accept Jesus as our Savior, He adopts us into His family and we become one of His children."

"Um-hmm, I know dat."

"And even though we're soiled and stained from our sins, He wipes us all clean and pulls us close and loves us because we're part of His family. He treats us as though we were spotless and perfect all of our lives."

Prissy eyed her warily, obviously wondering where this

conversation was leading. "I s'pose dat's true enough," she agreed slowly.

Jasmine grasped Prissy's hand in her own. "You and I were sinners, yet Jesus died so we could be adopted into His family. And now here you are with this purely innocent little baby who has done nothing to deserve your disdain," she said as the baby started whimpering in the other room. "I believe it would be most pleasing to God if you accepted this blameless child and adopted her into your heart. There is no doubt He loves little Emily as much as He loves you and me."

A single tear rolled down Prissy's cheek, and Jasmine reached to wipe it away. "Think about what I've said, Prissy. I can't make you love Emily, but she *is* your child. Reject her and you'll dwell in self-pity and despair; love her and you'll reap untold blessings."

The baby's whimpers soon gave way to a lusty cry, and Jasmine rose from the chair. "Shall I bring her to you?"

Prissy nodded. "Guess so. She be hungry—I can tell her cry when she wants to nurse." She turned her sad eyes to Jasmine. "Don' know that I can be a good mama to her, Miz Jasmine."

"But you will try, won't you? At least think about what I've said? After all, Emily didn't choose to come into the world this way. She's as innocent of this mess as you are. Per-haps thinking of it that way will help you to love her."

"Guess that's so." Emily's cries increased and Prissy drew a deep breath. "I's ready for her now."

Jasmine left the room uttering a silent prayer that God would continue to melt the ice that had formed around Prissy's heart.

———

McKinley removed his pocket watch and clicked open the gold case. He'd best leave for the depot in the unlikely event the train arrived early. He didn't want to chance Rupert's being seen in Lowell. Not many folks in town would know him, yet there was always the possibility that Henrietta or Prissy might be in town on errands. And the thought that Jasmine or Nolan could be in Lowell conducting business was worrisome indeed.

"I must remember to be particularly careful. I can't afford for anything to go wrong," he muttered as he drove the buggy through town.

He heard the train whistle in the distance as he pulled back on the reins and jumped down from the buggy. The train would be arriving on schedule. With what he hoped was a casual gait, he walked into the station and mingled with the crowd, some of them awaiting arrivals and some of them departing. He surveyed the depot and sighed with relief when he didn't spot anyone who might know Jasmine or Nolan.

McKinley relaxed and walked to the platform as the train screeched and panted to a halt. He was straining to see above the crowd, hoping to catch sight of Rupert's familiar face when he felt a friendly slap on his shoulder. He turned and was face-to-face with Paddy.

"A fine day, is it not?" Paddy asked as he gazed toward the blue sky lined with filmy threads of pristine white.

"In-indeed . . . yes, yes it is," McKinley stammered, the words sticking in his throat.

"Are ya na working today?" Paddy inquired.

McKinley struggled to organize his thoughts. "Yes, yes I am. I came to escort a gentleman to the Appleton—he's interested in conducting business with the Associates and is meeting with Mr. Cheever."

"I'm doin' the same. The gentlemen from the Virginia

Military Institute are arriving on this train, and I've the privilege of escorting them back to the farm."

McKinley nodded and then moved a few steps away, hoping to distance himself from the young man.

"And there they are, looking distinguished in their military garb." Paddy grinned at McKinley before waving to the uniformed men. "I best be off."

"Yes, you don't want to keep them waiting," he said as he caught sight of Rupert walking toward him. Relief washed over McKinley as Paddy hurried off to meet his guests. He was still watching after the young man as Rupert approached.

The two men quickly exchanged greetings. "I think it best we leave for my home as soon as possible. It wouldn't be wise for Jasmine or Nolan to learn you've come here. I still do not understand why you wouldn't agree to meet elsewhere. This is dangerous," he said as the two men neared the buggy.

"What's life without a bit of danger, McKinley? I don't remember your being so anxious—you need to relax."

"Appears our buggies are side-by-side," Paddy said as he and the three uniformed men drew near. Paddy looked directly at Rupert before turning his gaze to McKinley. "I hope yar business dealings go well."

"Thank you. Give my regards to Jasmine and Nolan," McKinley replied.

"Aye, I'll be sure ta tell them."

"Irish?" Rupert asked.

"How could you possibly guess?" McKinley asked sarcastically. "Nolan has placed him in a position of authority at the horse farm. In fact, Paddy capably operated the business during the months Jasmine and Nolan were in Mississippi."

Rupert laughed as he settled himself in the buggy. "Then

it appears we have come face-to-face with the danger you anticipated."

McKinley stared at him in utter disbelief. "Do you *want* them to know you're here?"

"Not particularly. However, I'm not going to tremble in fear. Besides, the boy has no idea who I am. What harm is done? None!"

McKinley shook his head. "Quite frankly, I have too much at stake in this matter. I've told you in my letters that I must secure funds in order to repay loans. I've taken a beating during this economic downturn. My wife is beginning to question me, and before long, her father will also be inquiring into our affairs. Therefore, it is my sincere hope you came here to conduct business."

"Rest easy, good man. We do, after all, have *nearly* the same goals."

CHAPTER · 21

ELINOR READ the precisely penned notice one final time, then tucked it into her skirt pocket. She should have known this would come. After all, it was the way of things with her. God had granted her a brief respite—time to believe she might enjoy an ordinary life. But now her normal life would be snatched away.

Though deep in the recesses of her mind she had known this would happen, Elinor hadn't remained alert enough to protect herself. She had let down her guard and permitted Reggie and Justin Chamberlain into her heart. Throughout the summer, she had taken delight in their company, enjoying the picnics and fishing, long walks, enlightening conversation, and laughter—joyful laughter. Brick by brick, her inner protective wall had crumbled and had slowly been replaced by an abiding fondness for both Justin Chamberlain and his daughter.

"Fondness? What I feel is not fondness. It's love," she angrily admitted as she began to knead the bread dough with a vengeance. "This is what I receive in return for opening my heart to a little girl and her father," she railed while punching her fists into the soft dough.

"And now what? I must leave Justin and Reggie, this house, these girls, this town—everything and everyone I've come to love. Where is your kindness and mercy, God? Is it reserved for all but me?" she questioned. Defeated, she dropped to one of the wooden chairs and gave herself over to the pent-up tears and pain—the loss and desperation that filled her soul.

She didn't know how long she had been sobbing when she felt the touch of a hand on her shoulder. Elinor lifted her swollen, tearstained face. She hadn't heard the child come in the door. She looked up into Reggie's frightened eyes.

"What's wrong? Why are you crying?" Reggie asked in a trembling voice.

"It's nothing," Elinor replied. "I'm feeling a bit melancholy . . . nothing more."

Reggie shook her head vigorously. "I don't believe you. You told me a long time ago that if I came to you with questions, you would tell me the truth."

Elinor gave her a feeble smile. "You're right. I did promise you I would be honest with you, but I'm not certain this is the proper time."

Reggie folded her arms across her chest like a commanding schoolmarm. "If it's bad news, there is *never* a good time."

"I suppose that's true. You've grown very wise in your old age," she teased.

"Does that mean you're going to tell me what has made you cry?"

Elinor reached into her pocket and removed the notice that had been delivered earlier that day. "I've received notice that my boardinghouse will close at the end of this month."

Reggie fell to the empty chair alongside Elinor. "You

can't go. I won't let you," she said, tears trickling down her cheeks.

Elinor drew her into an embrace. "Dear, sweet Reggie. Please don't cry—I've shed more than enough tears for both of us. It will change nothing."

Reggie sniffed loudly, then wiped her nose on a ragged hanky she pulled from her pocket. "We must go and talk to Father. He'll know what to do."

"There is nothing anyone can do, Reggie. And I can't leave right now—the girls will be home for supper soon, and I've been sitting here feeling sorry for myself rather than preparing their meal."

Reggie grasped Elinor's hand in a death grip. "Promise you'll come and talk to Papa this evening after supper."

"I'll see," Elinor replied vaguely. She avoided making a promise, for she sincerely doubted she would go anywhere but to her rooms after the evening meal.

Reggie gave her a suspicious glance. "If you don't appear by eight o'clock, I promise Father and I will come here to see you."

From the determined look in Reggie's eyes, Elinor knew the girl would carry out her promise. "You might consider giving me until eight-thirty. I'll need to wash and dry the dishes and complete some preparations for tomorrow's breakfast."

Reggie gave a quick nod. "Eight-thirty," she said with authority.

They walked to the door, and before turning to leave, Reggie wrapped her arms around the older woman's waist. She hugged her with a fervor that surprised even Elinor. "We'll find an answer—I just know it," Reggie insisted.

Elinor returned the hug but remained silent. She didn't want to build Reggie's hope, for she already knew the answer. Come the end of September, she would be packed and on her way to Maine. In fact, she decided, she must pen a letter to Taylor and Bella first thing in the morning.

———

Reggie ran home at breakneck speed and rushed into her father's cluttered library. She came to a skidding halt in front of his desk and deposited her lunch pail atop one of the many stacks of papers covering his writing desk.

"We must do something about Mrs. Brighton," she panted, doubling forward to catch her breath.

Her father jumped to his feet and rounded the desk. "Is she ill? What's happened?" he asked while grabbing his felt hat from a hook at the doorway.

"She's not ill—she's leaving."

The hat slipped from his fingers and dropped to the floor. "*What?* Who told you such a thing?"

Reggie sat down in one of the uncomfortable wooden chairs. "Mrs. Brighton—just now. I stopped after school and she was crying. She received a notice from the Corporation this morning that her boardinghouse will close at the end of the month. She says there's nothing left for her to do but move to Maine."

Her father picked up the hat and dropped it back over the hook before sitting down. He rested his face in his hands and said nothing.

"Are you praying?" she whispered.

"I'm thinking . . . though I *should* be praying," he replied, lifting his face and meeting her intent gaze.

"We've prayed every night that Mrs. Brighton's boardinghouse wouldn't close, but God isn't listening."

"He's listening, Reggie. Remember what I've told you over and over? We don't always receive the answers we want—and perhaps this isn't even God's answer. Mrs. Brighton's outcome isn't determined just yet."

Reggie looked straight into her father's eyes. "I don't want her to leave—I love her. Besides you, she's the only one who has ever really cared about me since Mama died. We need to think of some way to keep her in Lowell. I told her you would find an answer and that she must come here this evening."

Her father startled to attention. "You believe I'll have a resolution for this dilemma by seven or eight o'clock tonight?"

"Eight-thirty," she said with a broad smile. "That gives you even more time than you expected."

"I certainly feel much better with that extra half hour," he replied as he glanced toward the ticking clock on his desk.

Reggie stood up and grasped her lunch pail in one hand. "I'll go begin supper and you can begin thinking—and praying," she added quickly.

"If you expect an answer by eight-thirty, *you* had best pray also," he called after her.

She giggled. "I'll pray while I peel the potatoes, but I'll keep my eyes open."

"I'm sure God will not object to your safety measures."

————

The girls had completed their evening meal when Elinor sat down at the head of the table. "Before any of you rush off, I want to share some news with you."

Mary Margaret looked up from her plate of half-eaten food. "Sure and I'm hopin' it's something good. I do na think I can bear more bad news today."

"Did you have problems at work today?" Elinor inquired.

Mary Margaret nodded as she toyed with the food on her plate. "Aye. Mr. Dempsey gave me my termination papers as I was leaving today. He said I'm na to come back after I pick up my pay on Saturday. He had other papers in his hand, so I know I'm na the only one, though I was pleased ta know Bridgett did na lose her position."

"I'm so sorry, Mary Margaret. I fear when you need assistance the very most, I'll not be able to lend a helping hand. My boardinghouse will be closed at the end of this month. For those of you still holding positions at the mills, you'll need to find another house—and that should prove easy enough with so many girls losing their jobs. And for those of you who have remained here since your termination, I fear you must seek other accommodations here in Lowell or depart for home."

There was a collective hum of disapproval toward the Corporation and sympathetic encouragement for both Elinor and Mary Margaret.

"If the Corporation closes a boardinghouse and we're required to move, I think they should send someone to move our trunks for us," Janet said while clicking open the jeweled watch fastened to her bodice.

Elinor stared at the girl. Although she and Reggie had been steadfastly praying for Janet, there appeared to be little change in the girl's heart. Obviously much more prayer was needed! Elinor gathered a stack of dishes and strode off to the kitchen, silently uttering a prayer for Janet. She was about to return when she heard Mary Margaret confront Janet.

"Ya're worried about someone ta lift yar trunks while the rest of us are concerned about losin' our livelihood?"

"Moving heavy trunks up and down all these steps is difficult," Janet whined.

"Have ya considered asking yar friend Mr. Dempsey ta help ya?" Mary Margaret asked. "I'm thinking he oughta be pleased to lend ya a hand."

"What does *that* mean? Are you insinuating Mr. Dempsey shows me favoritism?"

"I'm thinking ya both perform too many favors for one another—especially with him being a married man as well as your supervisor," Mary Margaret replied hastily.

Elinor heard the scraping of a chair against the floor. Janet's angry voice followed. "The Corporation should never have begun hiring *your* kind in the mills."

"Ya do na like me because I speak the truth. But since I no longer have a position at the mills, I can speak without fear of retribution. So if ya're embarrassed to have the truth spoken aloud, Janet, then ya ought change yar ways," Mary Margaret stated, her voice rising in volume.

Elinor entered the room to find three of the girls applauding while another giggled as Janet trounced off. There was little doubt they were pleased someone had finally confronted Janet about her inappropriate behavior. But an air of gloom quickly replaced their giggles. Although Janet had received her comeuppance, they still faced troubling circumstances.

Elinor began to gather another stack of dishes. "Have you any plans, Mary Margaret?"

Her red curls swayed back and forth as she shook her head. "I have na told anyone else. Paddy is ta call on me later tonight. I'm hoping he can give me some advice."

"I'm sure he can." Elinor glanced around the table. "Has Janet already left for town?" she asked, hoping no one would realize she'd eavesdropped on the group earlier.

"I'm na certain if she's left or still upstairs primping," Mary Margaret replied.

Elinor ignored Mary Margaret's curt remark as she surveyed the group of worried boarders gathered around the dining room table. "I want all of you girls to know you will be in my prayers. I trust you will pray for each other and for me as well. I have an appointment later this evening, and I must finish washing these dishes before I depart."

An hour later, Elinor removed her stained apron, patted her hair into place, and removed her cape from the wooden hook inside the doorway. Confusion jumbled her thoughts as she made the short walk to the parsonage. The front door swung open as she reached the top step. Before her stood Justin and Reggie sporting their coats and hats.

Reggie smiled broadly as she caught sight of Elinor. "I thought you weren't coming."

"You were leaving to come to the boardinghouse?"

"I told you if you weren't here by eight-thirty, we would come."

"But it's just now eight-thirty."

"I knew we'd see you along the way if you had already left the house," she said with a shrug.

Elinor laughed at the child's determination as she followed the two into the house. Reggie took Elinor's cloak and carefully hung it alongside her father's coat and her own blue cape.

"All of our coats hanging in a row look very nice together," the child commented. "Why don't you and Father go into the parlor, and I'll bring our tea. I had begun to prepare it earlier, but then when I thought you weren't coming . . ."

"Tea would be lovely, thank you," Elinor said.

Elinor and Justin sat down in the parlor as Reggie scurried to the kitchen.

"Reggie tells me you received notice the boardinghouse will close this month," Justin started. "I'm sure you haven't come to a decision, and I think it would be wise if you would take these final days to consider all of your options before immediately hurrying off to Maine."

"*All* of my options? I can't possibly remain in Lowell

now. With the decline of the mills and so many women out of work, there are no positions available for anyone with my skills in the immediate area." Elinor could see Reggie's arm as the girl stood just on the other side of the doorway.

"There must be something. You've said in the past that you truly do not want to move and that you're not anxious to move into your brother's household."

"All of that is true, yet I see no alternative."

Reggie stepped through the doorway and announced, "I prayed while I was fixing supper, and God gave me the answer." She plopped down beside Elinor.

Justin appeared as surprised as Elinor was. "Why didn't you tell me?" he asked.

"Because it's better to tell you when we're all together."

They both stared at her, waiting.

"Well?" Justin finally inquired.

"We're going to get married." Her eyes shone with delight as she looked back and forth between them. "I love both of you and you both love me and you love each other, so we should get married," she said in a rush.

Elinor looked at Justin, wondering what he must be thinking at this moment—yet unsure if she truly wanted to know.

Reggie held up her hand. "Nobody can say anything yet. First I have to tell you *all* the reasons. Besides all of us loving one another, if you two marry, I will have a mother right here at home to help me with my schoolwork and teach me all the things you want me to learn about being a proper lady," she said while looking at her father.

Then she turned toward Elinor. "And if you marry my father, you will have a house of your very own, and we won't have to share you with the girls at the boardinghouse. *And* you will have me and Father right here so you can still bake and cook and go on picnics and fishing—and take care of us," she added softly.

Reggie glanced back and forth between the two people she loved most in the world. "Well, didn't God come up with a wonderful answer?"

"Indeed He did," Justin replied. "At least I think so. What about you, Elinor? Would you consider becoming Mrs. Justin Chamberlain? As Reggie so adeptly pointed out, I do love you," he said softly. "And I would be proud to have you as my wife if you'll have us."

Reggie giggled and applauded as Elinor clasped her bodice, deciding whether to laugh or cry. Surely this wasn't happening. Justin Chamberlain had just declared his love for her—love she surely returned. A nudging doubt crept into her heart. *If he loves me so much, why didn't he say so before?* She pushed the thought aside. *I love him. Despite my fears, I cannot deny that one thing.* "I would be honored to become your wife *and* Reggie's mother," she whispered.

"And a little child shall lead them," he said, grinning at his daughter. "Now why don't you fetch that tea you promised us so that we may have a few moments alone."

"I'll be in the kitchen for at least fifteen minutes, and I promise not to peek if you want to kiss her," Reggie sang gleefully as she skipped out of the room.

A moment of awkward silence filled the room after Reggie had departed. "Elinor, I want you to know that although it required my daughter's prompting, I have been in love with you for some time. However, I was afraid to express my love because I knew you had vowed never to marry again. I feared if I hinted about my feelings, you might withdraw from my life—and I knew I couldn't bear to lose you. Unlike Reggie, I didn't have the courage to speak of my love."

A faint smile crossed Elinor's lips. "How could you have known that you had broken down the barricade that

surrounded my heart? Like you, I was afraid to hope for anything more than friendship. Until today, I had not even
acknowledged my love."

He clasped her hands and brushed each palm with a
featherlike kiss. "I don't want you to change your answer,
but I do want you to be certain this is what you want and
not a marriage forced upon you by circumstances—or my
daughter," he said. "I want you to come to me because it is
your heart's desire."

"There could be no other way," she whispered as he ten-
derly gathered her into his arms and kissed her with an
ardent longing that spoke of his love.

Slowly he pulled back, and she gazed into the depths of
his greenish-blue eyes, her heart pounding with the force of
a blacksmith's hammer striking his anvil. Suddenly Elinor
knew she had underestimated God's plan for her future.

"With the boardinghouse closing in less than two
weeks," he said, "I see little reason that we should wait to
wed—unless you want time to plan an elaborate wedding."

She laughed softly. "No. I believe all we need is a min-
ister, Reggie, and the two of us."

"Good," Reggie said as she reentered the room and
placed the tea tray on a small walnut table. "Spencer and I
rode Larkspur over to Billerica earlier this evening. Reverend Foster said he would be pleased to marry you on the last
Saturday of the month at seven o'clock in the evening," she
proudly announced. "I told him we'd be sure to arrive on
time."

It was impossible not to laugh. In a matter of only three
hours, Reggie had arranged their marriage. "Have you also
decided what I should wear for the wedding?" Elinor
inquired.

"I think your peach-colored gown with the ivory lace

would be very nice," she replied without hesitating for even a moment.

"In that case, it appears as if the arrangements have been decided, and we need only relax until then," her father remarked.

"Oh, Father!" Reggie said in an exasperated tone. "We must have a reception after the wedding, but you need not worry about that either. Spencer's mother said she would be delighted to host the reception at their house. She said not to worry about a thing."

"You asked Mrs. Houston to host a reception before you knew whether we were actually going to wed?" her father asked.

"Spencer told his mother about the wedding before we went to Billerica; he needed permission to take Larkspur," she explained nonchalantly. "And I didn't ask—she offered."

"I couldn't possibly put Jasmine to such an inconvenience," Elinor protested. "That is far too much to expect of anyone, Reggie. Besides, your father and I don't need a reception."

"Mrs. Houston said you would fuss and argue, but to tell you that once the church ladies got wind of the marriage, they'd plan their own reception for you. She thought you might find her party more enjoyable."

Elinor bit the inside of her bottom lip to keep from smiling. Jasmine was correct; she didn't want Martha Emory and Nancy Sanders planning a party for her. They'd be angry enough when they discovered the pastor was no longer an eligible candidate for either of their daughters!

"Mrs. Houston is right," Elinor said. "I'll go and visit with her tomorrow."

Reggie beamed. "We're going to have a grand wedding, aren't we?"

Mary Margaret was waiting inside the front door, and at the sound of Paddy's voice commanding the horses to a halt, she ran down the front step to greet him.

"It looks like ya're a mite anxious ta see me," he said with a grin.

"Aye, that I am. Do ya think we could take a walk? I have something to tell you."

"Just let me tie the horse and we'll walk down toward the river. Ya're looking a wee bit worried, lass. Is something wrong?"

She nodded her head. "I've troubles more than I'm able ta solve on my own, Paddy. I'm needing some sound advice."

"Then I'll do my best," he said while offering her his arm.

She rested her hand inside the crook of his arm and immediately felt less frightened about her circumstances. "The day I've been fearing for quite some time arrived today. I went into work, and all was fine until we shut down the looms for the evening. I was one of the first to pass by Mr. Dempsey, and he handed me my notice. I've lost my job, Paddy. I do na know what I'm ta do. I was na so terrified at first, for I knew Mrs. Brighton would let me stay on at the boardinghouse." Her words were bursting forth like floodwaters. "But then I get myself home, and she sits herself down to the supper table and tells us she was served with a notice to close the boardinghouse at the end of the month."

"Take a breath, lass," Paddy said as he stroked her hand. "'Tis na such a bad thing that's happened. I did na want my wife ta be working anyway."

"There ya go again with telling me what I can and can na do. I'm the one ta be deciding if I want ta be . . . Did ya say *wife*?" she asked, jerking on his arm and pulling him to a halt.

341

"Aye. I said *wife*. Ya're gaping at me as though ya're surprised, when I know ya've been wondering if I was ever going ta ask ya," he said with a lopsided grin.

Her eyes sparkled with anticipation. "Are ya really asking me ta marry ya, Paddy?"

"I do na know what it's gonna take ta convince ya, lass! Let me try this: Mary Margaret O'Flannery, will ya marry me and be me lovin' wife?"

She wrapped her arms around his neck and kissed him soundly on the lips. "Aye," she whispered. "There's nothing I'd rather do than become Mrs. Padraig O'Neill."

"Ya see? There's no problem at all. I'll talk to Kiara—she and Rogan have plenty of room in their house. Ya can stay with them until the wedding, providing the two of ya won't start making elaborate wedding plans that will delay our marriage. I do na want ta be waiting much longer for ya ta become my bride," he said with a wink.

CHAPTER · 22

"JASMINE! WHAT A pleasant surprise," Violet greeted. "I was just preparing to have tea in the garden. Won't you and Alice Ann join me?"

"I imagine Alice Ann would much prefer a visit with her cousin Zachary. Is he outdoors?"

"Indeed he is. I cannot keep that child in the house until the dead of winter sets in—and even then it remains a difficult task. I'm disappointed you didn't bring Clara along."

"I had a number of errands to accomplish and promised Alice this could be our special day together, but I'm anxious to see the baby. I'm sure little Mattie Rose has grown inches since last I saw her."

"Unfortunately, she's hardly a baby any longer. Children seem to grow up in the blink of an eye, don't you think? Why, she's already pulling up to a stand and toddling about while we hold on to her fingers," Violet proudly announced. "It has been far too long since we've seen you," she continued while looping arms with Jasmine as they walked outside. "Have you and McKinley argued? He denies there are any ill feelings between the two of you, yet since your return from Mississippi, I feel he hasn't made any attempt to socialize with you and your family."

Jasmine hesitated for a moment and watched as little Zachary and Alice Ann embraced each other before hurrying off to inspect the late fall blooms in Violet's garden.

"We haven't argued. His days are likely filled with problems relating to the mills. After all, this is a difficult time," Jasmine said. "However, you might mention that there is a matter I need to discuss with him in the near future."

Violet brightened. "As a matter of fact, he's in the library. Why don't I look after Alice Ann and Zachary while you visit with McKinley? We'll have tea when you return."

"Are you certain he won't mind the interruption?"

"Of course not. He was working on his ledgers when I went outdoors and said he wouldn't be going to the mill until after the noonday meal. Do go and see him," she urged.

After quickly telling Alice Ann to behave during her absence, Jasmine entered the house, crossing through the parlor and turning down the hallway toward her brother's library. The sound of men's voices floated from the library. Jasmine hesitated outside the partially open door. She didn't want to interrupt if McKinley was conducting business, yet Violet hadn't said he was entertaining any visitors.

Her brother was discussing the finalization of a sale as expeditiously as possible. She listened intently to the voice of the man now responding. The deep southern drawl sounded strangely familiar. Her brows furrowed as the man continued to speak. *Cousin Rupert!*

What was *he* doing in Lowell? In McKinley's home? Without her knowledge? And they were discussing the sale of something. . . . *The Willows!* McKinley had gone behind her back and was making arrangements to sell the plantation to that dreadful excuse of a man. How dare he!

"How will you ever get your sister to agree to this sale?" Rupert questioned. "After all, she is part owner, and the sale will hardly be legal without her signature. And," he chuckled, "we don't want any more misunderstandings about my trying to forge her name on papers."

"I'll deal with Jasmine," McKinley declared.

"Well, you also need to deal with a couple of other things. I have some concerns about the contract to purchase."

With every fiber of her being, Jasmine wanted to burst through the door and condemn their appalling behavior. Instead, she forced herself to remain calm and keep her wits.

"I thought we had reached a satisfactory agreement," McKinley said.

"After further consideration, I believe there are a few conditions that I can't possibly agree to."

"And what would those be?"

Rupert's voice lowered and Jasmine strained to hear. She heard him mention buying the slaves and then McKinley replied, yet she couldn't hear his comment. Oh, why wouldn't they speak up—especially now when she wanted to hear what they were saying about the slaves?

Jasmine remained outside the door as they continued to speak in muffled tones. She had no choice but to go inside the room and make her presence known. After all, Violet would certainly ask questions when she returned to the garden. She inhaled deeply and knocked on the door.

"Come in," McKinley called.

She opened the door, prepared to give the acting performance of a lifetime. Neither of them would know she'd heard a thing!

McKinley's eyes opened wide as she walked into the room. "Jasmine! I wasn't expecting you," he blurted.

She smiled sweetly and turned her attention to Rupert.

"Why, Cousin Rupert! Violet didn't tell me you were visiting. She said McKinley was working on his ledgers. When did you arrive?"

"Yesterday. And I'll be in town only briefly. I assumed you'd have little time available, what with your *social* involvement," Rupert said eyeing her cautiously.

Jasmine only offered her most pleasant Southern belle face. She watched her brother begin to fidget as she sat down opposite Rupert. "I'm so surprised you would come north." She held her tongue, not saying the things she really wanted to say. So many times McKinley had told her he thought her reaction and feelings toward Rupert were based solely upon a misunderstanding. Especially after Cousin Levi wrote to say that he had managed to clear up Rupert's supposed takeover of The Willows. She steadied her nerves and looked her cousin in the eye. "So what brings you to Lowell, Rupert?"

"Ah . . . well . . . I'm interested in the possibility of investing in the mills. McKinley extended an invitation so that I might gain firsthand knowledge about the operation. I don't like going into any investment without have a thorough knowledge of the business venture."

His smugness and deceit annoyed her. "I'm surprised you'd be looking to invest in the mills at this time. The outlook is rather bleak right now for investment purposes, wouldn't you think?"

"Not at all. Investing during a downturn can yield huge returns when the economy stabilizes."

"So long as one invests properly," she added.

He smiled at her as though she were a young child to be tolerated for a short time. "I believe my assets show I've had no difficulty in that regard. Speaking of assets, how is my little Prissy faring these days?"

Jasmine grasped the chair arms, her knuckles turning white as she forced herself to remain civil. "Prissy was never *yours,* Rupert. However, she is doing quite well as a free woman. And how is Toby?"

"I really wouldn't have any idea," he said caustically.

McKinley rose from his chair. "I'd like to continue this reunion. However, Rupert and I are expected at the mills within the next half hour."

"Feel free to take your leave. After all, I wouldn't want to keep my dear cousin from investing his money in our *Northern* mills."

Rupert cast an irate look at Jasmine as he departed the room. She waited until the front door closed and then sank back into the chair, her mind reeling. She didn't know if Rupert had actually come to discuss investing in the mills, but there was little doubt he and McKinley were negotiating the sale of The Willows—and possibly even the slaves. And why had Rupert shown such interest in Prissy? She had noted a contemptible glint in his eyes as he had spoken of the girl. Remembering his attempts to take possession of her when they were in Mississippi, coupled with his question this morning turned her thoughts to baby Emily.

She covered her mouth to stifle the scream threatening to escape her lips. *Rupert Hesston* had fathered Prissy's baby!

Jasmine kissed the children good-night, then hurried back downstairs to the parlor. Before supper, she had spoken with Nolan and related the details of her morning visit to McKinley's home. When she had completed the distasteful tale, she had asked for his advice. But instead of taking her side and condemning McKinley, he had requested additional time to think on the matter. After pressing him further, Nolan had agreed they would talk after the children had gone to bed for the night.

"Have you come to any conclusions?" she asked as she

sat down in her rocker and picked up her stitching.

"I think the only answer to this entire dilemma is truth-fulness. You need to tell McKinley you overheard a portion of his conversation with Rupert. Tell him of your suspicions. Explain that you abhor thinking he could turn against the abolitionist movement and that you have a deep concern that he is planning to sell The Willows without consulting you and perhaps even deal in the sale of the slaves. If you approach him honestly, I believe he will feel obligated to answer you in kind. Your brother is a devout Christian man who has renounced slavery, Jasmine. I can't believe he would so easily turn against his beliefs."

Jasmine shrugged, not sure she agreed. "I hope you're correct. I'll go to him tomorrow."

"I'd wait until you're certain Rupert has departed."

She nodded. "When we spoke earlier, I failed to mention that Rupert asked about Prissy. From his behavior regarding her, I've grown to believe he is Emily's father."

Nolan sighed. "It's true his obsession with her was odd. When we were in Mississippi, I truly feared his interest in her went beyond proper boundaries, and I don't doubt your assumption. However, with your capable intervention, Prissy has made great strides in accepting the baby, and we don't want to do anything that would disrupt their bond. No one need know of our suspicions."

She carefully knotted her thread before meeting Nolan's gaze. "I agree. I want to honor Prissy's wishes. It was clear she did not want to name the father, and I now understand why."

It was midafternoon on Thursday when Jasmine approached the offices that fronted a row of brick textile mills. Nolan had suggested she visit McKinley at his office, thinking it best to keep Violet unaware of any possible problem. And Jasmine knew he was correct. This was a matter that was best resolved on neutral ground, away from friends and family.

Her brother's name had been printed upon the glass pane in his open office door—bold black letters surrounded with gold, proclaiming that the office belonged to McKinley Wainwright. He glanced up as she approached, and she noted his look of surprise as he motioned her in.

"I hope you don't mind my calling on you unannounced," she said.

"No, this is fine. Is there some problem?" he inquired cautiously.

"Actually, there are several. May I?" she asked while pointing at one of the wooden chairs.

He jumped to his feet. "Yes, of course. Please be seated."

"Let me begin by saying that I have an admission to make."

He stared at her intently and waited. "Go on," he urged.

"When I visited you at your home the other day, I had been standing outside the library for a short period of time before I entered."

"Eavesdropping?"

"Not intentionally—at least not at first. But as I stepped to the door, I heard you discussing a sale and then I recognized Rupert's voice. The two of you were discussing The Willows—and the slaves," she added.

"If you remained by the door once you knew we were in private conversation, you *were* eavesdropping. Not an admirable quality. I'm surprised you would conduct yourself in such a manner," he said heatedly.

Her eyebrows arched and her jaw went slack. "*You're* surprised by *my* conduct? You've entered into the business of selling our inheritance to a man who tried to steal it and then deal in the buying and selling of human flesh, and *you're* surprised by *my* conduct? Come now, McKinley! You can't believe you're in good standing to take the offensive in this argument."

"I believe that I am, dear sister. You know I have been in dire straits, what with my financial losses and the . . ."

"There is no explanation you can provide that will excuse your behavior, McKinley!"

"Will you let me finish at least a sentence before you interrupt?"

Jasmine fastened an unyielding gaze upon him. "I'm listening."

"As you know, I have been desperate for The Willows to be sold, and that land agent you hired has been of no assistance whatsoever. Even you must admit he's useless."

"I will *not* agree Mr. Turner is useless. I believe he's made every attempt to sell the plantation, and I've notified you each time I've received word from him," Jasmine countered.

"And each time his report is the same. That man will never find a buyer for The Willows. In any event, shortly after you received Mr. Turner's first letter, Rupert and I began exchanging correspondence. I asked for an explanation of all that had occurred while you and Nolan were in Mississippi."

She opened her mouth to speak, but he motioned for her to remain silent.

"As we corresponded, Rupert explained that there had been misunderstandings on both sides. He never meant to threaten you or cause you to believe he was taking The Willows by force."

"He's a liar."

McKinley shook his head. "Perhaps, but it doesn't matter now. Other things have happened. Rupert expressed a desire to purchase the property and said he would also be willing to pay me a tidy sum for the slaves—provided I would return Prissy to him. His offer was extremely generous. My share would be more than enough to free me of any financial woes for many years. The offer was tempting, and I admit I wrestled with accepting his offer. However, after much prayer, I knew it was far more important to free our people than secure my finances. I told him I could not accept his offer. So you see, this wasn't exactly as you thought."

Jasmine's features had softened as he spoke. "I am so very proud of you, McKinley, and I'm sorry I ever doubted you. Can you ever forgive me?"

"Yes, of course I forgive you."

"How do matters now stand between you and Rupert?"

"We've reached another agreement. I have agreed to sell the plantation at a reduced cost in exchange for the slaves."

"And he agreed?"

"Yes, he agreed. He says there may be one or two he cannot locate, but the remainder will be turned over."

"What can I do to assist? While I dislike the idea of Rupert owning the land, if it means freeing our people, I must relent. Do you want Nolan and me to travel south and escort them back here? Or perhaps I can write to Rupert and express my thanks and offer to send clothing and supplies for the journey north," she suggested.

"No, Jasmine. What you must do is remain completely uninvolved in this process. Rupert and I have a history that goes back to our childhood days. I can deal with him much more easily on my own. You will only complicate matters. There is far too much animosity between you and Rupert."

"But I want to help!" she proclaimed insistently.

"What is more important, sister? That you be involved or that our people regain their freedom?"

"You're right. I'll stay out so long as you promise to advise me if there is any way I can lend assistance."

"I promise."

"One other thing: since your inheritance will be greatly diminished by the bargain you've made with Rupert, I'm going to insist you retain all of the money from the sale. Nolan and I have been most fortunate in our business dealings, and I can well afford to give up my portion of the inheritance. It is the very least I can do."

McKinley shook his head. "No, I won't consider such charity. Father intended for you to have a portion of the inheritance."

"I admire the sacrifice you are making by selling the plantation at a reduced price, McKinley, and I *want* to help you. Remember that the Bible tells us we are to bear one another's burdens. You don't want to defy *any* of God's directives, do you?" she asked.

He leaned back in his chair and laughed. "You have always been good to me, Jasmine."

"We have been good to each other—that's why God created families: to love and support one another in the good times as well as the bad."

"And I'm very thankful for you," he said.

———

Elinor took one last look in the mirror. The pale peach cashmere dress was truly lovely, and she was genuinely pleased Reggie had suggested it.

She turned toward the door leading to the hallway and clasped a hand to her chest. "Helen! You startled me. I didn't hear you come down the stairs."

"I'm sorry. I truly didn't mean to alarm you."

"It's all right, Helen. Are you finished packing?"

The girl gave a sad nod. "Your dress is lovely, Mrs. Brighton. I came down to see if you needed any assistance preparing for the wedding."

There was such expectancy in her face that Elinor motioned Helen into the small sitting room. "If you could fasten this around my neck, I'd be most appreciative." Elinor handed her a wide velvet ribbon she'd embroidered with peach and green flowers to match the dress. Helen carefully fastened the ribbon with a small gold brooch that had belonged to Elinor's grandmother.

"Will your brother and his wife be attending the wedding?" Helen inquired.

"No, though I know they wish they could be here. I sent a telegram advising them of my plans. I received their regrets—their children are in school and there was insufficient time to make proper plans. However, they invited us to come visit at our earliest opportunity. I believe we'll wait until school is out next summer," Elinor explained. "I think Reggie would enjoy meeting all of my nieces and nephews."

"That will be nice. I wanted to tell you that I appreciate your kindness since I've been in your house, and I'm sorry to leave here. However, I'm very happy for you. I do hope Reggie knows how fortunate she is to gain you as a mother."

"Why, thank you, Helen. I've enjoyed having you as a part of my boardinghouse family. You *are* planning to attend the reception, aren't you?"

The girl's face glowed. "Oh yes! I wouldn't miss it. Mary Margaret said Paddy is coming to fetch all of your former boarders who live here in town and want to attend." At the sound of an approaching buggy, Helen hurried to the window in Elinor's room. "It's Pastor Chamberlain," she announced excitedly.

"Thank you, Helen. I'll look forward to seeing you at the reception later this evening," Elinor said as she lightly kissed Helen's cheek. The young woman scampered toward the stairs as Elinor checked her appearance once more before going to the front door.

She opened the door to Justin, who was holding his tall silk hat in one hand and a nosegay in the other. "Reggie insisted that you have flowers," he said, handing her the cluster of ivory mums mixed with an assortment of greenery.

Elinor was mesmerized as he stood before her in his black double-breasted wool morning suit. The points of his heavily starched white collar perfectly accented the wide gray-and-blue striped cravat he had chosen to wear.

"May I come in?" he finally asked.

"Yes, yes, of course," she said, regaining her voice.

"You look lovely, Elinor. That color becomes you."

She felt a blush rise to her cheeks. "Thank you. And may I say you look most handsome yourself."

He grinned at the compliment. "Reggie says we must hurry or we'll not arrive in Billerica by seven o'clock. I couldn't even convince her to come in—she said there was no time."

Elinor picked up her cape and reticule. "Then we had best be on our way. We ought not keep the preacher waiting—or Reggie."

"Absolutely not!"

Glancing over her shoulder, Elinor caught sight of Helen standing on the stairway. "We'll see you after the wedding, Helen."

The young woman brightened and waved as they walked toward the carriage.

Reggie giggled as Elinor settled beside her in the buggy. "In only a short time I can call you Mama instead of Mrs. Brighton, can't I?"

"If that's what you'd like to call me, I would be honored." Elinor was thrilled by the child's desire to immediately use the endearing term.

Reggie glanced up at her father. "The dress is very pretty, don't you think?"

Justin nodded his agreement. "The dress is lovely, but not nearly so lovely as the lady wearing it."

Reggie covered her mouth and giggled, and Elinor pulled the child close, almost afraid to believe the goodness God had showered upon her. She would have not only a wonderful husband with whom to share her life, but also this delightful child whom she had already grown to love and cherish. She released Reggie and leaned back into the cushion, offering a prayer of gratitude and thanksgiving that God had sent them both into her life.

The wedding ceremony was simple, but much to Elinor's liking. And to her great delight, after Justin vowed to take her as his wife, Reggie also stated her desire to have Elinor as her mother.

When Reverend Foster asked if she would take Justin as her husband, Elinor promptly replied, "I do, and I take Reggie for my daughter as well."

A short time later they arrived at the Houston farm, where buggies lined the driveway. Two servants stood waiting to greet them. "Go tell Miss Jasmine they've arrived," the man ordered as the other servant immediately raced into the house.

The trio followed the servant up the steps and into the foyer, where a maid quickly took their wraps. "Please follow me," the woman said, motioning them forward.

They moved to the doorway of the large sitting room, where the guests awaited their arrival. "Reverend and Mrs. Justin Chamberlain and daughter, Reggie Chamberlain," he announced in a resounding voice.

The applause was deafening as they stepped into the room. "Thank you all for attending," Justin called out loudly as he motioned the crowd to stop clapping.

Nolan signaled for the music to begin and then he and his wife turned their attention to the new family. "Can we assume all went well with the marriage ceremony?" Nolan asked Justin.

"Absolutely. Reverend Foster did a fine job, though his part in all of this was much less difficult than the lovely party you have arranged," he said, taking in the elaborate decorations about the room. "You shouldn't have gone to all this trouble."

"It was our pleasure," Jasmine replied. "We would have it no other way. Spencer and Moses are upstairs if you care to join them, Reggie. In fact, you may tell them they can come downstairs with you if they promise to be on their best behavior."

"I'll tell them," she said before hurrying out of the room.

"You'll be pleased to see many of your church members as well as girls from the boardinghouse among the crowd," Jasmine told them. "Now, do come fix a plate of food so that the others can begin to eat."

Elinor and Justin followed her to the dining table. Alice Ann was holding a stack of perfectly folded white linen napkins while three maids hovered nearby, prepared to refill the trays with an array of wondrous treats.

"It's abundantly obvious you have outdone yourself," Justin commented as he began to fill his plate with several sweet delicacies. "It's going to be difficult making my choices."

"Then you must come back until you've tried some of everything," Jasmine suggested before turning her attention to the bride. "Do have one of my raspberry tarts, Elinor. I prepared them especially for you. As I was planning what to serve, I suddenly remembered they're one of your favorites."

Elinor placed two of the small tarts on her plate. "Seems the church ladies have gathered for a private conclave," she whispered to Justin.

He winked at her and when he had filled his plate, he

strode to the cluster of women. "We're pleased to see so many of our church members in attendance. Do help yourselves to some of this fine food, ladies. There are many selections to please your palate."

Reggie, Spencer, and Moses positioned themselves in a small nook where the heavy parlor drapes hid them from view yet provided them with an excellent vantage point. They had come down the stairs and circled through the dining room in order to secure the perfect spot. It wasn't until the church ladies gathered in front of the draperies that their view of the guests became somewhat obscured.

"I wish they would move. Now I can't see my mama." Reggie said the last word tentatively, as though she were trying it on to see how it fit.

Martha Emory poked Nancy Sanders in the arm. "Just look at her smiling like the cat that caught the canary. I told you from the beginning that she was out to snag him. *Didn't* I, Caroline?" she asked, now looking at her daughter.

"Yes, Mama," Caroline answered meekly.

"And didn't I tell you that if you'd just assert yourself, you'd have yourself a husband?"

Caroline bobbed her head up and down. "Yes, Mama."

"I believe he was interested in my Sarah until Elinor set her cap for him," Nancy told Martha. "Of course, my Sarah is too much of a lady to throw herself at a man. Unlike Elinor, she could never behave in an unladylike fashion in order to gain a man's attention. Surely you all remember how Elinor marched into that parsonage and took charge— ordering everyone around, just like she owned the place."

Cecile Turnvall was focusing on Jasmine Houston. "For the life of me, I cannot understand why this reception is being hosted by the Houstons. It's as though they didn't think the ladies of the Congregational church could provide them with a reception that would meet their standards. The Houstons are *Episcopalians!*"

"Episcopalian or not, any reception we would have hosted would pale in comparison to this," Winifred Mason remarked. "I imagine it's Elinor who wanted this fancy party—Pastor Chamberlain isn't one to put on airs." She leaned closer to the other women. "Of course, unlike the rest of us, the Houstons appear to lead a charmed life. Even the economic problems don't seem to have affected them."

"I think it's a wonderful party," Caroline offered. "The food is excellent, and I particularly like the music."

A slap of her mother's fan caused Caroline to flinch. "You see! That's exactly why you're going to spend your life as a spinster! Instead of evaluating why you aren't on the arm of Pastor Chamberlain, you're enjoying his wedding reception."

"Sorry, Mama," Caroline said, casting her eyes downward.

"See what they're like?" Reggie whispered to Spencer and Moses. "I told you, but you didn't believe me."

"I feel sorry for dat Caroline lady," Moses whispered. "Her mama is mean."

The young trio sat listening for a short time longer before Reggie decided to take matters into her own hands. She poked Martha Emory lightly in the back and waited until the older woman turned before stepping from behind the burgundy-fringed draperies.

"Good evening, Mrs. Emory, Mrs. Sanders, ladies," she said as though she were a politician preparing to address a group of prospective voters. The women were visibly startled. "The three of us have been sitting here listening to your very cruel remarks. I'm going to kindly request that you immediately cease your disparaging remarks regarding my mother, or I'll be forced to tell my parents everything you've said here tonight," she said in a firm but gentle voice. "I truly don't think you'd want me to do such a thing."

"No, no, of course not," Nancy Sanders sputtered. "We're very pleased for both you and your father."

"That's nice to know, because if you are pleased for me and for my father, I know you'll also be pleased for my mother. After all, she is the one who has brought joy to us."

"Yes, yes, of course," Mrs. Emory stammered as she grabbed Caroline by the arm. "Come along, ladies, we must try some of that punch. It looks delightful."

Giggles emanated from behind the draperies as the women hurried across the room toward the punch bowl.

CHAPTER · 23

Late October 1858

JASMINE OPENED the door as her brother bounded up the front steps.

"You must have been watching for me. Am I late?"

"No. You're exactly on time," she replied. "I have tea prepared and waiting in the parlor."

"Good! It's turned colder since I left home this morning, and I noticed the skies have taken on a somewhat ominous appearance. We could be in for a snowstorm later today."

She shivered. "I know a deep layer of snow would delight the children, but I don't look forward to the biting chill created by these Massachusetts winter storms."

McKinley laughed. "It's our Southern blood. I don't think it's ever going to thicken enough to guard us against this cold weather."

"Perhaps you're correct," she said as she hung his hat on a peg.

"I do hope you've developed a plan. I fear I've had little time to concentrate on the problem of housing the former slaves."

"I told you I would take responsibility for those issues. You're the one who insisted upon remaining involved."

"I know, I know. However, if Rupert questions me, I want to be prepared with accurate answers. I don't want him to suspect you've been involved in our business dealings."

Jasmine sighed. "That's just it, McKinley. I haven't been involved in the business dealings, and Rupert isn't going to care in the least whether we've made adequate arrangements for the former slaves once he gives them over to your care."

"I'm certain you're right on that account. But I'll be more comfortable in my dealings with him if I'm aware of all aspects."

"As you wish," she replied.

McKinley poured a dollop of cream into his tea and then took a sip. "Now, tell me of your idea."

"Actually, it's more than an idea. I've already set to work, so at this point there's no room for objection on your part."

"Why am I not surprised?" he asked.

She shrugged and flashed a sheepish grin. "After reviewing the number of people we could adequately care for here on the farm, I began making inquiries among our abolitionist friends and the colored people already settled in this area. All have agreed to take in at least three and some many more. From the ledger Nolan and I maintained when we freed the slaves, it appears Rupert should deliver nearly one hundred. I've made up a list of where they will be housed until they make final decisions regarding their future."

McKinley shook his head. "There is no stopping you once you've been presented with a challenge."

"It wasn't a difficult assignment. Even in this time of economic depression, the good people of Lowell have opened their hearts and their homes. Nolan and I have agreed to give financial aid to those families who so willingly offered space in their homes but do not possess the adequate financial resources to feed additional mouths. When the former slaves finally arrive here at the farm, we will know exactly where each one will be housed and cared for."

McKinley downed the remainder of his tea. "How could I possibly find fault with such a plan? It seems you've thought of everything."

"We're ready to receive them if Rupert will merely agree upon an exact date for the transfer to take place. That, dear brother, is the task you must complete—and quickly," she added.

He placed his cup and saucer on the tray and rose to his feet. "Let's pray I'll be as successful as you have been."

The servants buzzed about the house, cleaning and polishing while Jasmine and Kiara once again reviewed the list of wedding guests.

"Ya've become quite the hostess these last couple of months," Kiara commented. "First the party for Pastor and Mrs. Chamberlain, and now this lovely reception ya've been planning for Paddy and Mary Margaret. Do ya truly think ya want all this work—not to mention the expense?"

Jasmine laughed. "Nolan and I would have it no other way, Kiara. I don't know what we would have done had Paddy not been here to take care of the farm while we were away. He's grown into such a fine young man, and I know you're very proud of him."

"Aye, that I am, and had it na been for the famine, we'd still be struggling in Ireland. 'Tis strange the twists and turns life takes. I'm still amazed how God takes the tragedy in our lives and turns it into something good. Ya know, when our ma and da died, I thought for sure God had deserted me, but then He saved me and Paddy and we came to this wonderful country. And then when things was so bad between me and your first husband, again I thought God had turned His back on me. Them was hard times for all of us, but God took those terrible things and brought good from them. We have truly been blessed to have the good Lord lift us out of such tragedy and restore our joy."

Jasmine's eyes clouded as she remembered those days when Kiara and Paddy had first arrived in Lowell and the heartbreak that soon followed. She, too, had suffered at Bradley Houston's hands; she, too, had wondered if God had deserted her. Yet God had victoriously delivered them through their circumstances. Now she prayed their former slaves would taste that same victory and be delivered from Rupert's evil hold.

The touch of Kiara's hand caused Jasmine to startle. "Ya look so far away suddenly, Jasmine. Are ya na feeling well?"

"I'm fine. I was merely lost in my own thoughts for a moment. Now what were you saying about the food preparations?"

"Mary Margaret has enlisted Bridgett to take charge of preparin' some special Irish fare, and Maisie and Prissy asked if they could help. Henrietta 'as agreed to keep the younger children in the nursery. I completed Mary Margaret's gown last evening—stitched on the final lace and had her try it on. She looked lovely with that gorgeous red hair and creamy complexion. Paddy's going ta be speechless when he sees her in that gown."

"They're coming! They're coming!" Spencer shouted as he rode Larkspur to the front of the house. He delivered his message to Alice Ann, who immediately raced into the house, nearly tumbling into one of the servants carrying a beautiful cut glass punch bowl.

"Mama, Spencer says Paddy and his bride are here," she

shouted as she rushed into the parlor.

"Thank you for the message, but please cease running through the house. If you don't, there's bound to be an accident," Jasmine warned.

Alice danced from foot to foot. "Can I help, Mama, can I?"

Jasmine smiled at her daughter. "I don't think there's anything you can do."

The child's lips began to quiver as Prissy walked into the parlor.

"It would be a mighty big hep if someone could hand folks their napkins," Prissy said. "I jes' can't seem to make enough room for dem on the table, Miz Jasmine. Can you think of someone who could do dat for me?"

"I could, I could!" Alice Ann squealed in delight.

Prissy grinned at Jasmine and then gave the child an appraising look. "I don' know . . . you sho' you'd be careful to make sure *each* guest gets a napkin?" she asked.

Alice Ann's chestnut brown curls danced up and down as she bobbed her head. "I promise," she said. "I did that for Mrs. Brighton . . . I mean Mrs. Chamberlain's party."

"All right, then. Come along with me and git into place afore them people get in here," she said, taking Alice Ann by the hand. "They's bound to be hungry, so you best be having dem napkins ready."

"Thank you, Prissy," Jasmine said gratefully.

Prissy nodded. "When she gits tired of handin' out napkins, I'll send her upstairs to Henrietta."

The rooms soon filled with an array of guests, and the small group of Irish musicians began to play their fiddles while the guests filled their plates with a variety of tasty treats. Paddy and Mary Margaret briefly visited with their guests before Paddy took her in his arms and they circled the room in a wedding dance. Moments later, the fiddlers scratched their bows in rapid motion, plucking out an Irish jig while the guests clapped in time to the music.

The music went on for hours and everyone seemed to have a wonderful time. Jasmine watched the Irish celebration and found it all to her liking. She knew there had been a time in her life when her path would have never crossed with these people, but she was glad changes had come.

"A bit weary?" McKinley asked when he found Jasmine resting in the parlor.

"One dance too many, I fear," she told him. "These Irish dances take more physical exertion than I had imagined."

He laughed. "I tried one of the jigs, but I don't believe my feet will move that quickly. I think unless you've grown up performing those dances, you'll not learn as an adult."

She unfolded her silk fan and began to stir the air as she flipped it back and forth in rapid motion. "I must admit I had fun trying. Where is Violet?"

"She went upstairs to check on the children. She'd rather be in the nursery than dancing." He nodded toward her hand. "I was thinking that your fan reminds me of Toby and how he used to swing that big feather fan over the dining room table at The Willows."

"That seems a lifetime ago, doesn't it?"

"Yes, so it does. Strange how some things seem to have happened only yesterday while at the same time so far in the past."

A faint smile curved her lips as she nodded. "And speaking of Toby, what do you hear from Rupert? It seems he's done nothing but make excuses. Do you believe he intends to keep his word?"

"He continues to change the date when he's going to send the slaves, but I remain optimistic. His last missive stated there were another five that he had located and he was in the process of making proper arrangements. It seems that each time we agree upon a date, he locates another slave or two. I want to believe the delay is because he's taking pains to locate as many as possible rather than merely prolonging the entire process."

"I truly do not trust him," Jasmine expressed.

"I know he doesn't share our beliefs, but I want to give him the benefit of the doubt and believe he's doing the proper thing. He's agreed they should arrive before year's end."

"Year's end? That's two months away. Surely he can do better. Perhaps if I telegraphed him and—"

"Jasmine! You agreed I would handle the negotiations without interference. Rather than helping matters, a telegram from you could possibly ruin the progress I've made."

She folded her fan and placed it on the side table with a purposeful thwack. "I grow weary of tiptoeing around Rupert and his detestable behavior. However, I will keep my word. Has he mentioned Toby? You tell him that I expect to see Toby leading the group when they arrive!"

"Your demanding tone is exactly why I don't want you dealing with Rupert. But in answer to your question, I asked for the names of those currently in his possession, and Toby is listed among the group. Now, enough of this talk. The musicians are finally playing something I can actually dance to, so let's not miss the opportunity," he said as he offered his sister his hand.

Waving a telegram, Nolan strode into the parlor. "Telegram from your cousin Levi," he said, handing the message to his wife.

Jasmine looked up from her sewing. "This is quite unexpected; I hope he hasn't taken ill. But perhaps he's planning a visit. Wouldn't it be wonderful if he'd come to Lowell and spend the Christmas season with us? In my last letter, I asked him to consider the possibility. Perhaps he's decided to accept my offer," she eagerly speculated.

"Perhaps you should read it and find out," Nolan said with a grin.

She waved the telegram back and forth. "Part of the enjoyment is guessing what's in a letter or package—or, in this case, a telegram." With an air of anticipation, she placed the telegram on the table beside her.

Nolan shook his head and then turned to leave the room.

"Wait! Where are you going?"

"Please feel free to enjoy this period of expectation. However, I have work that needs my attention. I'll look forward to hearing what Levi has to say at supper this evening."

"Oh, all right, I'll open it! I wasn't going to wait but a few minutes, anyway," she admitted.

Nolan sat down beside her as she ripped open the telegram and began to read.

Her eyes narrowed, and the color drained from her already pale complexion. "He's done it again!" she seethed. "He's a lying, despicable excuse of a man."

"Cousin Levi?"

Her husband's shocked appearance nearly made her laugh—nearly. In fact, under normal circumstances, Nolan's reaction would have caused her to burst into laughter. But not now—when she knew Rupert was again attempting to deceive them.

"It's Rupert! Levi discovered Rupert has devised a convoluted plan to actually send our former slaves but then have them recaptured by men posing as bounty hunters. Likely the same group that placed them in shackles when they burned The Willows! He'll not get away with this—I'll see *him* in shackles first!"

"Becoming overwrought will serve no purpose, Jasmine.

The first thing we must do is go to McKinley and learn whether Rupert has sent him any details about when we may expect the arrival of our former slaves. If so, we can then begin to devise our own plan."

"I'll fetch my coat and hat," she said.

"I didn't mean we need to go this very minute."

"But of *course* we must. We don't know when Levi received this information. By now, Rupert may have departed with the slaves."

"As you wish. It's true they may be on their way as we speak."

When Jasmine settled into the buggy beside Nolan, she hoped she'd not be forced to argue with her brother about the necessity of taking immediate action. She would no longer listen to McKinley's concerns—she cared not at all if her interference offended Rupert. If their former slaves were going to reach freedom, McKinley could no longer believe Rupert Hesston.

"Shall I go directly to his office, or do you think we should go by the house first?" Nolan inquired as they approached town.

"I don't think he would be home at this time of day. In any event, I'd rather speak with him at his office. Poor Violet becomes overly upset whenever she thinks there are difficulties on the horizon. While she attended the antislavery meetings and was marginally involved in the movement, she never was completely devoted to the cause. And though I've long ago forgiven her, I've not forgotten her behavior when I proposed to rear Moses. You'll recall she drove a wedge between McKinley and me with her failure to support my position."

"Then we'll hope that he is here," Nolan said as he assisted her down from the buggy. "In fact, there he is coming out of the counting house." He waved to his brother-in-law.

McKinley hastened toward them, bowing his head against the cold north wind. He rubbed his hands together as he grew closer. "To what do I owe this visit?" he asked in a tentative voice.

"Not good news, I fear," Jasmine replied. "We must speak privately. May we go to your office?"

"Of course," he said, leading the way. "Nothing wrong at the farm, I hope?"

"No, it concerns the transfer of the slaves," she said. They entered the building and walked directly to McKinley's office.

"I thought you had agreed to remain detached from the negotiations," he said while removing his coat.

"This is not of her doing, McKinley. Jasmine has received a disturbing telegram from Cousin Levi," Nolan defended.

"More than disturbing," Jasmine interjected. "Rupert is planning to have the slaves recaptured. Have you received any word about arrangements for delivery of the slaves?"

"One moment, Jasmine. You say he's made plans, and I assume you've received this information from Levi."

"Yes, of course. Rupert has hired men to disguise themselves as bounty hunters," she explained.

McKinley looked at her as though she'd taken leave of her senses. "This sounds a bit preposterous. Why would he go to such elaborate measures?"

Jasmine crossed her arms and leaned forward to look directly into her brother's eyes. "*Because he is a cunning man.* Unless he makes a genuine attempt to deliver the slaves—an attempt that can be substantiated by disinterested individuals, he knows we won't believe him. At least he knows *I* won't believe him. If he can prove he's traveled a portion of the way north—with the slaves in tow—he will maintain he's upheld his part of the bargain and insist you uphold your bargain to sell The Willows for the reduced price."

"I believe she's correct, McKinley, and we truly must have more details regarding the transfer. Has Rupert forwarded additional details to you?"

"Yes. I had planned to surprise you by having them arrive shortly before Christmas—as a special gift to you. Obviously, that isn't going to be possible now. Rupert sent me a missive outlining their travel plans, though there's no way of determining if he was truthful."

"Where were you to take possession?" Jasmine asked.

McKinley pulled the letter from his desk drawer and handed it to his sister. "He agreed to bring them up the Mississippi on a riverboat. They'll disembark at St. Louis and travel by foot the short distance to Alton, Illinois. I want the exchange to take place in a free state. And I know he's made the arrangements. I received verification only yesterday of their paid passage from the riverboat company. I doubt even Rupert would expend such a large sum if he didn't intend to bring them."

Jasmine nodded. "He also knows you will expect corroboration from those who would see them traveling that particular route, so he'll surely choose someplace that is heavily populated. Obviously, he won't wait until he crosses the border into Illinois, for he'll want his reprehensible deed to occur in a slave state. However, I fear it's a guessing game as to exactly where he's decided upon."

McKinley rubbed his forehead and glanced toward Nolan. "Any suggestions?"

"I believe we should telegraph Levi and request his assistance. He may be able to discover more details that will aid us." Nolan shifted to the edge of his chair. "I'll specifically ask if he can learn the location where Rupert plans to have this spurious attack take place. If they haven't yet departed

Mississippi, we may still have a little time to develop a strategy."

"Very little," McKinley commented.

"Jasmine and I will go directly to the telegraph office. Why don't you come out to the farm tomorrow and we'll talk further. In the meantime, we can all attempt to formulate some plan of attack."

McKinley agreed and escorted them to the street. "I'm sorry. I shouldn't have been so trusting," he apologized as Jasmine stepped up into the buggy. "I suppose everything you told me about him was true."

"There is no need for an apology," Jasmine said. "Had he been dealing with me, he would have done the same thing."

"Yet you would have questioned him and been more cautious."

"It matters little what I would have done. At this juncture, our energies need to be directed toward dismantling his plans." Jasmine leaned from the buggy and kissed her brother's cheek. "Don't be so hard on yourself, McKinley. If we remain steadfast in our prayers, I'm going to trust that God will see us through to victory. After all, He has overcome circumstances much greater than these."

"I suppose you're right," he said tentatively. "If God could deliver the Hebrew children from the pharaoh, He can certainly deliver our former slaves from Rupert Hesston."

———

Jasmine turned slowly while Prissy marked the edge of her ocean blue merino dress. "Dis black velvet is gonna look mighty fine along da hemline. I should have it done afore Christmas. You can wear it for Christmas Eve church services."

"I believe I'd enjoy that very much," Jasmine said as she turned a few more inches.

"Jes' can't believe Massa Nolan having to leave on business at dis time of year. He shoulda sent Paddy or one of them other men what works for him. The chillens gonna be disappointed if he don' make it home afore Christmas."

"I'm trusting that he'll return soon. If not, we'll celebrate upon his return. The children and I can still attend services at the church. Christ's birth is what we're celebrating, after all, and Nolan knows we'll be thinking of him no matter where he might be."

"I sho' know how that be. I spend lots of my time still thinking 'bout Toby. Sometimes I wonder if he still thinks about me."

"I'm confident he does. And I believe the two of you will be together again," she said as she patted Prissy's shoulder. How she longed to tell Prissy of Nolan's whereabouts. But if he should meet with failure and return home without Toby, Prissy would be devastated. Better to remain silent and pray for the safe return of Toby and the rest of the slaves.

"I done give up on that idea a long time ago," Prissy said dryly.

"Mama! Mama! Come quick!" Spencer yelled as he tore through the house. "Papa's arrived and there's lots of people with him!"

Jasmine grabbed Prissy's hand. "Come on! Let's go see."

Prissy yanked on Jasmine's hand. "You cain't go outside in dat dress. I ain't finished taking up the seams an' marking the hem."

"This is more important, Prissy. Come along and don't worry over the dress."

Jasmine pulled Prissy along, hope filling her heart, as they followed Spencer out onto the porch. An irresistible joy besieged Jasmine as she gazed into the sea of dark faces. Men with their feet wrapped in rags to help ward off the cold walked alongside the wagon; others followed behind and formed a snaking procession that continued to inch its way toward the house. The women and children were piled in the wagon behind Nolan, most of them wearing the coats she'd forced Nolan and McKinley to take with them. They were a cold and bedraggled appearing lot, yet even from the porch she could see the hope that shown in their eyes.

Jasmine spotted Toby sitting directly beside Nolan atop the wagon seat as the wagon moved slowly down the driveway. She grasped Prissy by the shoulders and pulled her forward. "Look, Prissy! Look who's in that wagon!"

Prissy's face registered disbelief as Toby waved and called out her name. She looked at Jasmine and then back at Toby. "Am I dreaming, Miz Jasmine?"

"No, Prissy. Your husband has finally come home. Go and greet him," she said as Nolan pulled back on the reins and the wagon came to a stop in front of the porch.

The young couple ran toward each other with sheer abandon and united in a warm embrace. The onlookers all began to applaud as Toby leaned down to kiss his wife.

"Where's your coat? You're going to catch your death of cold," Nolan said as he hurried up the steps and pulled Jasmine close, rubbing her arms.

"How could I possibly be cold with such a sight before me?" she asked, her face aglow.

"And with your husband to keep you warm," he said, pulling her close and kissing her soundly. "It is so good to be home!"

"And it is so good to have you back again. I can see you were victorious is reclaiming freedom for the slaves, but I must admit I'm anxious to hear all of what occurred during your journey."

"McKinley is following with another wagonload of folks. Let's wait until he arrives, and then I'll give you all the details. But first you go back in the house while I fetch

Simon and Paddy. They have the list of families who agreed to provide temporary homes when we arrived."

Prissy turned to Jasmine. "Did everyone know 'bout this 'cept me?"

"There may have been a few others. Please don't be angry with me. We didn't know if our plans would succeed, and I didn't want you to be disappointed if Toby wasn't rescued."

A lopsided grin curved Prissy's lips. "You done the right thing," she said and gave her husband another squeeze. "You best get out of that dress, Miz Jasmine, 'cause I don' think I'm gonna be doing any more alterations this evening. I's gonna be introducing Toby to our little Emily and showing him his new house."

"I believe the dress can wait as long as necessary!" she assured her.

Nolan leaned down and placed a kiss on Jasmine's cheek. "Go inside. I'll soon be back and give you my full report. It is better than even *you* could have hoped for."

Jasmine fidgeted with the fine lace that edged her handkerchief as she awaited Nolan and McKinley's arrival. Eager to hear Nolan's report, Jasmine patted the settee cushion the moment the two men entered the room.

"Do sit down and tell me everything," she said, giving the men her complete attention.

Nolan rubbed his hands together. "The entire process could not have gone any better. We could truly feel your prayers throughout the journey, and we knew God was in control. How else could we possibly have found lawmen in a pro-slavery state willing to assist us?"

McKinley nodded and laughed. "In fact, when Nolan

and I located those lawmen, we told them they were an answer to prayer."

"I *told* you that prayer was the solution!" Jasmine exclaimed.

"Of course we had no choice but to rely on Levi's information that the subterfuge would occur in St. Louis," Nolan said. "Upon our arrival, I found a lawman who, after listening to our story and reviewing the ledger listing the names of our freed slaves, agreed to help us. He recruited a number of men, and we stationed ourselves on the wharf and then waited for the boat to dock."

"I truly believed Levi was incorrect about St. Louis," Jasmine said. "In fact, I'm still surprised Rupert decided the incursion should occur in such a busy place. I thought he would choose some outlying town along the river."

"I think he worried something might go amiss in a small town," McKinley said. "Perhaps he feared passersby might overhear or actually see what was occurring or possibly even believe the slaves if they spoke out. However, the docks in St. Louis are teeming with people and activity. He brought the slaves off the boat in shackles in order to contain them for his men and also give the appearance that he was delivering slaves. Fortunately for us, he had only three men appear to claim the slaves. You should have seen his face when he spotted us."

"Did he attempt to fabricate a lie in order to cover up his deeds?" she asked as she moved to the edge of her seat.

Nolan nodded. "He said he knew the men, but he had no idea they had plans to capture the slaves. However, his story soon crumbled. The other men were unwilling to take the blame for the part Rupert played in the scheme. We showed our proof that the slaves were ours, and because of Rupert's deception, it was decided that the entire arrangement was null and void."

"What does that mean?" Jasmine questioned.

"It means that Rupert gets nothing," her husband replied. "He's lucky he wasn't arrested. Had we been willing to press charges, it could have gone very bad for him. But he denied everything right up until we left for home. In fact, he was still blaming the others."

"You mean he actually denied knowledge of his own nefarious plot and pointed a finger at his fellow cohorts in crime?" Jasmine asked indignantly.

"Absolutely!" McKinley said. "I fear I completely misjudged Rupert and his intentions from the very beginning."

"Did you not bring any charges against the men?" she inquired.

"No. I didn't want to remain and attempt to bring legal action against them," McKinley explained, "and the sheriff said since they had not yet committed a crime, it would be a difficult battle—especially in Missouri. The court would not look favorably upon our claim."

Jasmine smiled at her husband. "It's better this way. The men he so quickly accused will likely spread word of his cowardly actions throughout the region. His neighbors will have little use for a man who is unwilling to take the blame for his own deeds. I have little doubt that Rupert will be treated with disdain."

"As well he should be," McKinley said. "How can I possibly thank the two of you for all you have done—for the slaves and for me? I pray that one day I'll be able to repay you."

"I think that may soon be possible," Nolan replied with a quirk of his eyebrow.

McKinley's gaze was filled with puzzlement. "How so?"

"The Willows still belongs to you and Jasmine. And Cousin Levi's telegram stated he knows someone who may be interested in purchasing the land. He said he would send the information to the land agent, depending upon the final outcome in St. Louis."

McKinley shook his head back and forth, his eyes growing moist. "This is wonderful news."

"You see? God has blessed us beyond our highest expectations. His grace makes it difficult to question the abiding love He has for each of his children, don't you agree?"

"I do agree," McKinley said. "However, during difficult times, I fear I, too, quickly forget God's faithfulness."

Jasmine moved close and embraced her brother. "Then in the future, I shall take full responsibility for reminding you."

CHAPTER · 24

December 25, 1858

JASMINE LOOKED out the bedroom window and smiled. Nolan had predicted the children would enjoy a sleigh ride on Christmas morning, and now a heavy blanket of snow covered the ground. She squinted against the blinding intensity of the sun's rays as they reflected off the pristine layer of white.

"Did you see? Did you see?" Alice Ann squealed delightedly as she ran into her parents' bedroom. She dove onto the bed and landed on her father with a vigor that caused him to groan. "It's snowing, Poppa, just like you promised. How soon can we go on our sleigh ride?"

He struggled to a sitting position as he lifted Alice Ann off of his chest. "Not until after breakfast, remember? I believe I hear Henrietta calling your name. You had best hurry to your room and get dressed."

The child slipped off the bed and gave Jasmine a fleeting hug before scurrying out of the room and down the hall.

"Oh, for a portion of that youthful energy first thing in the morning," Nolan said as he grinned at his wife. "Did we have a good snow?" He threw back the covers and stretched.

"More than I want to see," she replied with a shiver.

He laughed. "*Any* snow is more than you want to see, my dear, but it doesn't seem like Christmas unless there's at least a smattering."

"This is much more than a smattering." She peered out the window again. "I hope it won't ruin our Christmas celebration. I'll be disappointed if McKinley's family is unable to join us."

Nolan walked to the window and looked for himself. "From the way you talked, I thought we'd had a blizzard." He rubbed his hands together. "This is perfect. Your party will go on as planned, my dear. McKinley will have no difficulty maneuvering a sleigh through these few inches of snow."

Jasmine took up her brush and began to style her hair in front of the mirror. "The party is not as important as having our family together. There are so few of us that it suddenly seems almost critical to me. I suppose it's the reality of losing so many family members in such a short period of time. I had always taken family for granted, but now I realize how precious those ties become as we grow older."

"In some respects, Rupert did you and McKinley a service," Nolan commented.

Jasmine swung around to face her husband. "Rupert? How is that?"

"You and McKinley have drawn much closer to one another. I don't know if that would have occurred without the problems the two of you faced and resolved during this past year."

Jasmine nodded thoughtfully. "I suppose I hadn't thought of it in such a manner, but you're correct. And I'm certain such a thought would cause Rupert severe displeasure."

He laughed. "Indeed! Cousin Levi's last missive is testimony to that fact. Rupert continues to blame everyone but himself for his current situation. I presume he isn't enjoying his life as an outcast from Southern society. It seems a man so incapable of keeping his word is much scorned." He pulled his shirt on and started securing the buttons. "As I understand it, many promises were made by Rupert to his neighbors, and when those promises proved false, well, most folks wanted nothing to do with him."

"In time his friends will forget his misdeeds, but for now he is reminded daily of his despicable behavior. To my own astonishment, I've begun to pray for him—and Lydia also," Jasmine said. "Lydia is surely suffering along with her husband, and it's hardly her fault that Rupert's deception and conniving have put them in this fix."

"I'm proud of you. I shall attempt to follow your example, for there's little else that will cause a change in Rupert." He pulled on his trousers and tucked his shirt in.

"I'm also praying for the strength to forgive him, but I've not yet reached that lofty goal. Sadly, I don't think Rupert feels a need for change, but perhaps in time he will come to that realization. And, perhaps in time, I will be able to forgive him for the wrongs he committed against so many," she said, her voice trailing off as she stared into the mirror.

Nolan stepped behind his wife and wrapped her in a warm embrace. "This has been a monumental year. . . . Much sadness, yet much happiness also," he said, gazing at their reflections.

She smiled warmly at her husband. "Yes, *much* happiness. For we have been able to share in giving a wondrous gift to many—the gift of freedom."

THE DOOR HAD BEEN closed on the past, but opening it was the ONLY WAY FORWARD...

God's forgiveness and true healing are at the heart of this moving family saga. When Jana returns home from a mission trip to find her husband and bank account gone, she reluctantly turns to her mother, Eleanor. But Jana's presence is a daily reminder of her mother's secrets from the past. Eleanor is haunted by the pain and guilt of the memories she keeps hidden away. Can an eccentric aunt bring together these women and remind them they have a future filled with love?

What She Left for Me by Tracie Peterson

◆ BETHANYHOUSE

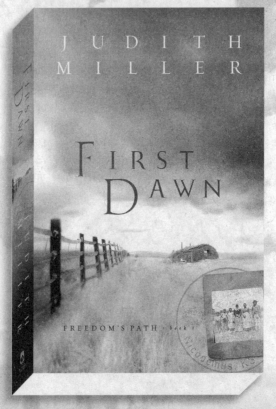